Between HEAVEN *and* EARTH

Between HEAVEN *and* EARTH

Michele Paige Holmes

Mirror Press

Copyright © 2016 Michele Paige Holmes
Print edition
All rights reserved

No part of this book may be reproduced in any form whatsoever without prior written permission of the publisher, except in the case of brief passages embodied in critical reviews and articles. This novel is a work of fiction. The characters, names, incidents, places, and dialog are products of the author's imagination and are not to be construed as real.

Interior Design by Rachael Anderson
Edited by Rachel Bird and Lisa Shepherd
Cover design by Rachael Anderson

Cover Image: Shutterstock #159278246
Cover Image Copyright: Gergely Zsolnai

Published by Mirror Press, LLC

ISBN-10: 1-941145-85-X
ISBN-13: 978-1-941145-85-2

To Bill and Mylene
whose love story inspired this one.

OTHER BOOKS BY MICHELE PAIGE HOLMES

Counting Stars
All the Stars in Heaven
My Lucky Stars
Captive Heart

A Timeless Romance Anthology: European Collection
Timeless Regency Collection: A Midwinter Ball

Hearthfire Romance Series:
Saving Grace
Loving Helen
Marrying Christopher
Twelve Days in December

Forever After Series:
First Light

One

"And . . . now." Cassandra Webb reached forward over layers of white chiffon to crank the volume on the car stereo.

The first notes of "We Built this City" blared from the speakers as Devon, her husband of exactly three hours, stepped on the gas pedal and the Audi gave a lurch of speed as they drove onto the Golden Gate Bridge. A passing car honked, and the passengers waved. Cassie peered through the decorated window to wave back enthusiastically.

"I really hope that paint washes off," Devon said for at least the tenth time since they'd left the reception and discovered that his sister's kids had taken car decorating to a new level.

"It will," Cassie said, unconcerned either way. Would it be so terrible to drive around sporting *Just Married* on the back windshield for more than a day or two? All these friendly greetings from total strangers was kind of fun.

"Wait for it." Devon held his hands poised over the

steering wheel, then played a mock drum intro along with the '80s band Starship as was tradition every time they visited the city. *Our city.* Someday, in the not too distant future, they would live here. Or a bit closer at least.

"Wait for it is right," Cassie said. "Look at that traffic." Her mouth turned down at the cars braking in front of them.

Devon shrugged as he slowed the car. "Rush hour. Told you we should have had a morning ceremony."

"And risked cool temperatures and limp hair from the fog? No thank you." Cassie leaned over the gearshift to give him a quick kiss on the cheek. "Besides. There's no one I'd rather be stuck in city traffic with, Mr. Webb."

"Well, now, *Mrs.* Webb, since you put it that way . . ." Devon's hand left the wheel and found Cassie's amidst the ruffles of her wedding gown. He brought her hand to his lips and let them linger there. "Anything in particular you wanted to do while we're stuck in traffic?"

Cassie sighed dreamily as she leaned her head back and spied the sunroof. "Yes, actually." She reached up to open it. "I've always wanted to do this." She unfastened her seatbelt, then pulled her hand from Devon's to bunch the layers of her gown.

"Cass, what're you doing?" Devon pulled his eyes from the car in front of him to glance at her.

In answer, she climbed up on her seat and pulled herself up through the sunroof so she was standing with her torso outside the car. The driver on their right honked and waved.

"It's beautiful out here," she shouted as she waved back. The afternoon sun reflected off the bay, bathing San Francisco in golden light. The ocean breeze sent her hair streaming behind her, and she brought a hand to her head before remembering she'd taken her veil off already, and it lay safely in the back seat.

"Are you nuts, woman? Get down here." Devon tugged on her dress. "I'd like to have a wife for more than one day."

"I'm perfectly safe. We're hardly moving," Cassie shouted. Hardly moving, but it was enough that she felt so alive. The whole day had passed too quickly; everything had felt surreal. But this, *this* felt real. She ran her fingers over the diamond sparkling on her left hand. She'd really married Devon, and they were on their way to starting a wonderful life together.

"Cass," Devon pled. "Do you want us to get a ticket on our honeymoon?"

She peered down at him. "No one's going to give us a ticket. What cop would want to spoil a couple's wedding day?"

"A few I can think of," Devon muttered. "Just get back in your seat—*please.*"

"Oh, all right." She dropped back down in a whoosh of fabric. "Couldn't you flash your shiny new Sacramento PD badge at anyone who pulled us over?"

"No. I could not." Devon beat away the layers of her dress covering the steering wheel. He looked over long enough that she caught his eye roll. "Seat belt?"

Cassie pulled it across her and snapped it into place. "Spoilsport," she grumped good-naturedly. "Happy now?"

"With you at my side? Always." Devon's grin was back. He held up a finger, signaling silence, then jumped into the song. "Looking out over that Golden Gate Bridge on my gorgeous, sunny wedding day. I'm stuck in bumper to bumper traffic with the most beautiful woman in the world in a black Audi about two-thirds of the way across."

Cassie laughed at his parody. "Don't seem to remember *those* lyrics."

"She's with her favorite guy, in her favorite city. The city by the bay, the city we're gonna rock, the city that never sleeps." He winked. "Especially tonight."

As if they'd heard and approved of his alteration to the song, the driver of the car inching past them blared the horn several times as the passengers waved.

Cassie stretched her arms high through the sunroof and waved back.

"Careful," Devon advised. "That rock on your finger is worth a few grand. Wouldn't want to lose it."

"It's not going anywhere," Cassie assured him. "Just like me. I'm not going anywhere. You're stuck with me now."

"Oh, we're going places, baby. Don't let that tiny apartment in Auburn worry you. We are *going* places."

They drove through the toll plaza and headed toward Marina Boulevard and the presidio.

"When are you going to tell me where those places are?" Cassie closed the sunroof to block out the noise of the city. "Like the one we're going to stay at tonight?" He hadn't told her a thing about their honeymoon, though the budget had been slim, so she knew they couldn't be going too far or staying any place too fancy. For all she knew they could be camping at the beach the next two nights.

"Why tell you when I can show you in just a few minutes?" Devon asked. "Our suite is around the corner."

"Oh, so we're staying in South San Francisco?" Though he'd gone the wrong way if that was the case. "Did you get one of those deals at the hotels near the airport?" Cassie had found at least two that were affordable and had hinted more than a few times that a weekend in San Francisco strolling the pier, eating chowder from hollowed out sourdough bread bowls, and taking the cable car to explore the neighborhoods she dreamed of living in some day was her idea of a perfect honeymoon. Sure, she and Devon had spent dozens of dates here already. It was their city. So what better way to start out their life together than in it?

"A hotel near the airport didn't seem particularly romantic," Devon said. "I don't know about you, but jets flying overhead isn't what I want keeping me awake tonight."

"Not south San Fran, then. Hmm," Cassie mused. She'd hoped for Sausalito, so they could've taken the ferry across to the city tomorrow morning. Now it appeared they'd be farther south and would have to drive in for sure, not to mention parking in San Francisco could easily double the cost of their hotel if they weren't careful. "Burlingame? San Mateo?"

Devon shook his head. He pressed his lips together, his look smug, apparently enjoying himself. "I said we'd be there in a *few* minutes. The definition of a few is typically three to five—not thirty."

"We're staying *in* San Francisco?" *No way.* He'd had to save for months to buy her ring, and they'd barely been able to scrape together enough for first and last month's rent and the security deposit on their apartment. They couldn't begin to afford even one night downtown.

"Can't tell you."

Cassie leaned close. "Don't make me touch your ears while we're driving." She ran her index finger slowly along the side of his ear, down to the lobe.

He swatted her hand away, but she persisted, knowing this kind of pleasant torture could get her what she wanted almost every time.

"Okay, probably." Devon tried to duck out of her reach, but she leaned farther over to his side, her fingers still working their magic, playing with the hair above his ear.

"Geez, Cass. I'm trying to drive—in San Francisco, no less. Yes, we're staying here. You are the worst to try and keep secrets from, you know that?" He shook his head as if disgusted with himself—or her.

"You kept it this long." Cassie ceased tormenting him and moved back to her side of the car. "I'm surprised, shocked really. What'd you do, rob the bank you were a night watchman for?"

"Not quite. Though that probably would have been easier than what we have to do to pay for this place."

"What do you mean?" Cassie turned in her seat to better look at his profile. "We're staying somewhere that isn't paid for yet?" Somewhere in *San Francisco*. She felt herself starting to panic. Their finances were already on the bubble. Devon's new job paid more, but she was planning to quit hers to start graduate school in the fall, so they'd actually be making less than they had been when pooling their previous incomes.

Devon turned right onto Washington Street. He slowed the car and began searching the house numbers.

"Dev, this is the Pacific Heights neighborhood. Poor newlyweds who have just graduated from college and barely landed their first career jobs do not stay in a place like this."

"These poor newlyweds do." He turned the Audi sharply into a narrow, sloped driveway. Cassie leaned forward, peering through the windshield at the three story Edwardian town home.

"Oh my." She brought a hand to her heart.

"Yeah, that's how I felt when I saw the price tag on these places." He turned off the car and set the brake, then turned to look at her. "But I said to myself, Devon, you are marrying the most wonderful woman in the world. If she wants to stay on the moon someday, you'd better figure out how to make that happen, because she. Is. Worth. It."

Cassie forgot about worrying over money as she leaned

toward him and threw her arms around his neck. "I can't believe this. I can't believe you found this place and did this for me."

"Weeks," he mumbled into her hair. "It took me weeks to find it. Though I did have a little help," he admitted. "And there is still the matter of payment."

Cassie leaned back, but kept her arms loosely around his neck—in case she needed to use her hands to strangle him. "This really isn't paid for yet?" She whispered the question, afraid that the house before her was a mirage and would disappear at any second, or even worse, come tumbling down on her head as a few of Devon's other financial decisions had in the recent past, the car they were sitting in being one of those. It had necessitated her delaying grad school until the fall, when she'd been ready to start last spring.

"It is and it isn't. But don't panic." He pressed a finger to her lips before she could protest again. "Annie paid for two nights here. In exchange, we're watching her kids while she and Doug go to Hawaii for a week."

"Annie." Cassie felt a wave of relief followed almost immediately by panic. "A *whole week* with your sister's kids. Seven nights in exchange for two?"

"Eight, actually. If you knew what this place cost, you'd realize it's a fair trade. And hey, you didn't want me to use a credit card for our honeymoon, and I didn't." He tilted his head, stuck his lower lip out, and softened his eyes in a pitiful expression of hope.

Cassie's heart melted, as it did every time he looked at her that way. She was as helpless against the puppy dog look as Devon was when she caressed his ears. "I think it's brilliant. You're brilliant," she amended. Grad school was still on track, *and* they had two glorious days and nights in a dream house.

Devon got out of the car and came around to her side. He opened the door, then held his hand out to her. Cassie gathered her gown in one hand and placed her other in Devon's. He helped her from the car, then swept her off of her feet and into his arms.

Cassie linked her hands behind his neck as he exaggerated staggering up the steps. "Funny. From the guy who lifts five days a week."

"Just trying to add some lighthearted humor—you know, in case my bride has wedding night jitters." Devon stopped at the front door and attempted to reach into his pocket for something—presumably the key.

"The only thing I'm jittery about is watching your nieces and nephews for a week." She leaned back and reached down to Devon's pocket, attempting to help locate the key.

"*Our* nieces and nephews," he corrected with a wicked grin. "All part of this fine package you see before you."

Cassie pulled a silver key from his pocket and held it up to him. She sighed. "I suppose watching them will be good practice for when we have our own kids someday."

"Yep. Our own boisterous boys. All two of them." He snatched the key from her, leaned forward, and fitted it into the lock, tipping Cassie precariously in the process.

"And two girls. Don't forget," she reminded him.

"If you insist." He straightened, then pushed the door open.

"We'll have a child every three years, starting in three years, so fifteen years from now we'll have the perfect family." Cassie knew it was silly, but she didn't care. It was fun to think she had it all planned out. So maybe they'd get three boys and one girl, or some of their kids would be closer or farther apart than the three years. None of that mattered much, just that she and Devon were starting their life together, and someday they'd make a few other lives to join them.

Devon crossed the threshold, and Cassie reached out and pushed the front door closed behind them. He set her gently on the floor, faced her and took her hands in his. Their eyes met, and she felt herself falling in love with his baby blues for the millionth time.

"We are the perfect family *now.*" He held her hands up and kissed the back of each.

Cassie felt a little swoony as she looked at her new husband, more handsome than ever, still in his white shirt and suit pants, his collar loosened, his tie draped casually around his neck. Behind him she could see into the house he'd rented for them, and if Devon hadn't been taking her breath away this very second, she was certain the living room would have, with its period pieces and décor. But there would be time for exploring that later.

"We are perfect," she agreed as she stepped toward him, closing the distance between them. "I love you, Devon." She tilted her head back and leaned up for a kiss. He gave her one, taking her face in his hands and whispering his own endearments against her lips. Slow, delicious minutes passed before they broke apart, breathless and with Devon's fingers tangled in her hair.

"Ouch." Cassie giggled and tried to stand still so he could free himself.

"You've got too much hair, woman." He pulled her face to his chest while he worked at the knot, and Cassie felt a rush of new desire as she breathed in his cologne.

"I thought you liked my hair." She pouted.

"I love it," he said. "Except when it's attacking me." He succeeded in freeing himself and took a step back.

"Wait until you sleep with it," she predicted, a sly and slightly nervous smile on her face. Her hair tended to take on a life of its own during the night. What would Devon think when he discovered himself in bed with Medusa tomorrow morning?

"Do I have to wait?" he asked, his eyes glinting with their usual hint of humor plus a hefty dose of desire.

She shook her head as anticipation rushed from her rapidly beating heart to every nerve ending from head to toe. "You're tired already?"

"Hardly." He swept Cassie up in his arms again and carried her farther into the house amidst her giggles.

They walked through the living room, and Cassie drank in as much of it as she could—the polished wood floors, bay windows, and antiques. Devon seemed to know where he was going and carried her swiftly up the stairs—no exaggerated stagger this time—to the third floor, one enormous suite.

"Oh my," Cassie breathed as he set her on a cushioned bench tucked between bookcases and in front of a large, curved picture window, this one overlooking the bay and the Golden Gate. "Oh, Devon, this is beautiful. I could sit here all night and look at this view."

"Really?" He sank into a Queen Anne chair at the foot of the four-poster bed. "I was hoping another view in here might interest you more."

Cassie turned to look at him, then rose and crossed the room. "I said I could look at that view all night. But *this* view . . ." She walked a slow circle around him, one finger on his shoulder as she made a show of checking him out. "I could look at every night. Forever."

"Forever, huh?" Devon stood and snagged her around the waist, then took a step back and sent them both tumbling onto the large bed. "Isn't that kind of a long time?"

Cassie's laughter turned suddenly serious as love for the man holding her in his arms overwhelmed her. "It will never be long enough." She kissed him with a fierce possessiveness that surprised her, then lay her head on his chest over his heart. Its beat had quickened like her own but was also steady and reassuring, the rhythm of the hundreds of possibilities and years of happiness ahead of them.

The moon reflected off the bay on a rare, cloudless night in San Francisco. Sometime during the night, the fog would roll in, and Cassie anticipated that morning view just as much, when the towers of the Golden Gate would peak through the low clouds. But right now, she wished this view, and this night, would never end.

Devon stood behind her at the window, his arms wrapped around her waist, hovering over the satin ties of her new robe, his chin resting near her shoulder.

"Cass, that was—"

"Don't," she stopped him. "Don't try to put words to it. There aren't any."

"Sacred," he finished.

Maybe that word. She hadn't expected their union to bring her to tears, but when you loved someone so much— She turned in his arms and tilted her face up to his. "I love you, Devon. We're going to have such a wonderful life together."

"I love you, too, Cass. Always. No matter what."

"No matter what," she agreed. "Forever."

Two

Nine Years Later

"Go, Noah, go!" Cassie jogged alongside the soccer field, following her five-year-old's progress toward the goal line at the end. Finally. The first three games of the season he'd shown little promise of having any of her or Devon's athletic abilities. Noah had seemed almost afraid of the ball—and especially of the other players. In spite of all the times she'd practiced with him on her mom's back lawn, Noah hung back when it came to playing with his team, seemingly reluctant to have anything to do with the game. But not now. She could see it in his eyes, had known the instant the thrill of the sport clicked for him.

"All the way Noah!" she yelled, loving this moment, the way his top teeth were fastened over his lower lip as he concentrated, and the unskilled gait of his short legs.

Another movement came into her line of vision. A set of hands reaching out, moving closer and closer—not outstretched to break an awkward fall as so often happened with these little kids, but to purposely push. The foreign hands made contact with Noah's back, and Cassie's moment of parental joy vanished, replaced by fear as she watched her son vault forward over the ball and land face first on the hard field.

She raced toward him, blowing her whistle. "Foul. Foul. Foul." She thought it, but it was the other coach's voice she heard. She skidded to a halt on the still-dewy Saturday morning grass and dropped to the ground beside Noah.

"Are you all right?" Gently she reached for him and turned him over, barely holding back a gasp at the sight of his bloody face. He was too shocked to even cry yet, but she could see the tears building, so after a hasty assessment that nothing appeared broken, she gathered him in her arms and carried him off the field.

"You're going to be okay, bud," she spoke in her calm, mothering voice—a tone which most likely assured every kid with half a brain that things were definitely not okay. Her stomach lurched. Had he landed on his forehead? Did he have a concussion? *Please, not his brain.* She sent the urgent prayer heavenward.

"Where does it hurt?" Cassie asked as the first tears began spilling over his rosy cheeks.

"My m-mouth," he sobbed.

Cassie sat Noah down on the grass beside her mesh bag of cones and extra balls. She never bothered bringing a chair or a blanket, since she was the coach and never got to sit during the games. "Let me see."

She brushed the sweaty hair back from his forehead and was relieved to see only dirt and a few scratches instead of bumps or cuts. His nose appeared to be bleeding, though not badly. But his mouth—

"Open up, bud." He complied, and she glanced inside and felt instantly ill. Noah's top front right tooth hung at an odd angle, and his bottom lip—swelling already—had a tooth-sized cut straight through it. *Stitches?*

Noah caught her worried gaze and began crying harder.

"It's going to be fine," she reassured him, knowing that *fine* would now entail some dental work. "Game's over for you today, though." Cassie leaned forward to lift him again. "Let's go home and get you cleaned up and see what we need to do."

"I'm so very sorry. Is he going to be all right?"

Cassie glanced over her shoulder. A man she didn't know stood behind her, his hand clamped firmly on the shoulder of a boy wearing one of the other team's jerseys. Her gaze lowered to the boy, though he wouldn't look at her and stared at the ground instead. The perpetrator. She hadn't had a second to think about the kid who'd done this to her son, but now that she did, a surge of anger surfaced. Lifting a still-sobbing Noah, she stood and faced the boy's father.

"Does he look okay to you?"

The man studied Noah's lip, then quickly looked away. He reached in his back pocket and pulled out his wallet. "I really am terribly sorry. I'm not sure what came over Austin." He took a card from his wallet and held it out to her. "I'll pay for any medical expenses. Please call me when you know what they are."

"Thanks." Cassie met his sorrowful gaze briefly as she accepted the card. Her initial anger ebbed in the face of his kindness. *His kid is only five, too.* How malicious could he really be? Maybe she'd seen it wrong. Maybe the boy really had been about to fall. Wanting to believe the best of the child, she attempted to soften her expression as her eyes scanned the card. The Sacramento Kings logo was emblazoned across the top, followed by a phone number, below which were the words:

Matthew Kramer
Media Relations

Noah buried his face in her shoulder and continued to cry. She needed to get him home and cleaned up and call the dentist.

"Thank you, Mr. Kramer. I appreciate your offer and especially the example of taking responsibility that you're setting for your son." Thus far that son had remained silent. Cassie wondered at this, wondered why Mr. Kramer didn't get his kid to apologize. She supposed she ought to be grateful he'd come over to speak to her at all. Too often these days, people simply didn't seem to care. She shoved the card in her pocket and bent to retrieve her bag.

Mr. Kramer beat her to it, quickly gathering her things and handing them to her.

"Oh, the game," she said, feeling suddenly foolish as she stared at the empty field. "It's not even half over."

"Our coach called an early half-time," he said. "I don't think any of the parents minded."

"I'd better talk to him." Cassie shifted Noah's weight and tried not to think about the blood and snot mixture he was no doubt leaving on her shirt. What did a shirt matter when he was going to lose a tooth?

Mr. Kramer looked past her. "Here comes the other coach now."

Cassie turned to him.

He faltered as he took in Noah's bloody mouth. "Is your boy okay?"

"He will be," Cassie said. "I've got to go get his lip and tooth looked at, though. Can you finish the game for me? I'm sure one of the other parents can step in and coach our team the last half."

"I can do it," Mr. Kramer volunteered.

"That's very kind," Cassie said, half-wondering why he was still hanging around, "but it's probably better if I ask one of the parents from our team."

"She's right," the other coach said. He removed the baseball cap from his head and rubbed his temple as if he had a headache. "In fact, I was coming over to talk to you, Mr. Kramer. Austin's behavior these past couple of games has forced me to a tough decision. I'm sorry, but for the safety of the other players, I'm going to have to ask him to leave the team." The coach's lips pursed in an expression of regret. "Maybe his counseling sessions will help, and he'll be able to play next year."

"I understand." Mr. Kramer sounded suddenly weary. "Let's get that jersey off, Austin."

Feeling as if she were intruding on private family drama, Cassie turned to go but not before glimpsing the forlorn expression on the boy's face as he raised his arms and the jersey was removed. He still hadn't told Noah that he was sorry for hurting him, but Cassie could see the sorrow in his eyes—the kind of sadness that involved something far deeper than an incident of pushing at Saturday morning soccer.

Not my business or my problem, she told herself as she left the field. She had enough worries of her own, the most immediate of which was Noah's mouth.

"Can I have your frieth?"

Cassie grinned as she leaned across the kitchen table and passed Noah what was left of her French fries. S sounds were going to be a bit of a problem for him for a while, with a hugely swollen lower lip and his top *two* teeth missing. An x-ray at the dentist's office had shown root damage to Noah's front left tooth as well, so she'd had to make the quick, painful decision to have both teeth pulled. It had not been a fun afternoon. The only consolation was that the pediatrician hadn't recommended stitches in Noah's lip, and Noah would have lost those two teeth anyway in a year or so. He'd just be without them a little longer now.

She watched as he carefully navigated a fry over his swollen lip and between the gap where his teeth had been. She'd tried to talk him into skipping the salty treat and going out for ice cream instead, but Noah had a thing for fries, and she had promised him whatever treat he wanted when they were at the doctor's facing the possibility of stitches. A mom had to keep her word, no matter how ill-advised this particular choice seemed to her.

"Do you have thome more ketchup?" he asked.

That lisp is pretty cute. "Right here." She handed him her last packet.

"Thankth." He brought the packet to his mouth and went to rip it open with teeth that were no longer there. He stopped, frowning at her.

"Can't do that anymore, can you?" Cassie stood and began gathering their wrappers. "Guess you're finally going to have to stop using your teeth to open stuff." *Another positive.*

"How am I going to play Legoth?" Noah whined.

Cassie shrugged. "You'll have to find that orange tool that pries them apart. And I suppose to find it, you'll have to clean your room."

Noah leaned his head forward on the table with a sigh of dramatics that Cassie was sure used to be reserved for teenagers.

She dropped the wrappers in the trash and came back to the table. "Here." She took the ketchup packet from his fingers and ripped it open. "There's always Mom if you're stuck. Life won't be that bad." She ruffled the top of his hair.

Noah dumped her remaining fries onto a napkin and arranged them side-by-side. Then he took the ketchup and slathered it across them in an *s* pattern. *Just like Devon.* A queer little pang—part happy, part sad—throbbed in her heart. It seemed to be happening more and more lately, the older Noah grew. When he'd been a baby, the similarities weren't so noticeable. Sure, he had Devon's blue eyes and that funny little cow lick on the front of his forehead, but there hadn't been much else to compare. But now, somehow—even though Noah had never seen his dad eat fries or do any of the dozens of other things that were similarities she'd noticed—Noah was doing them the same as Devon always had.

And will again someday, she told herself firmly. It was just a matter of time.

Noah glanced up at her. "Do I thill get my dollar?"

She arched an eyebrow. "Did you score a goal?"

He shook his head. "But I would have. If that kid hadn't puthed me."

Silently she agreed, but out loud she chose to see what had surely been a bad parenting tactic to begin with through to its conclusion. "Sorry, bud. No goal, no dollar." Exactly what Devon would have said if he were there. She always tried to think of that. *Don't turn our son into a wuss,* she imagined him telling her, but at times like this, she wanted to go easy on Noah. It had been a traumatic day for both of them, and he *was* only five.

She eased herself into the chair beside him once more. "You can try again next week. We'll practice at Grandma's, and you'll be ready."

He shook his head. "I don't want to play thoccer anymore."

She'd been afraid of that, had silently predicted it even but hoped she'd been wrong. "Just because you fall down once doesn't mean you should quit."

"I didn't fall. I was puthed."

"Okay. Just because you got pushed once doesn't mean you should quit." She reached over and stole back one of the fries. "We aren't quitters in this family."

He looked down. "I don't want to play."

"Well, think about it for a couple of days, and then we'll talk again. I'm still the coach, so you'll have to come with me to all the games. And I bet you'd have a lot more fun playing than sitting on the sidelines for an hour."

Noah didn't say anything to this, and Cassie knew enough that it was time for a change of subject.

"In the meantime, there might be another way to get a dollar or two so you're that much closer to being able to buy that new Lego set you want."

He looked up, the hope in his eyes restored just that fast. "How?"

Oh, to be five again. "Those teeth you lost today might be worth something." She mentioned this casually, as if she hadn't been waiting all day for the subject of the tooth fairy to come up. For the first few weeks of kindergarten, that was practically all she'd heard about from him—who'd lost what tooth in class and got to have a prize at school and put a tooth sticker on the bulletin board, and what the tooth fairy had brought those kids, of course.

Just now, Cassie felt grateful for those conversations and all the advance notice they'd provided her. She was ready for this and had a stack of crisp new one dollar bills, all painted with a thin coat of fairy dust—glitter—just waiting in the back of her nightstand drawer.

"The tooth fairy!" Noah jumped up from his chair and practically ran from the room.

"In here," Cassie called to him as he raced toward the hall. "Your tooth treasure box is on the counter."

He raced back to collect it. At the end of his appointment and extractions, he'd been too groggy to appreciate such an item, but now he clutched the little plastic box in his fist as if it were made of gold. "Do you think the tooth fairy will let me keep thith?"

"I'm pretty sure," Cassie said. "But we'll write her a note just to be safe."

"Thanth, Mom." Noah grinned at her and another one of those part happy, part sad pangs struck her heart. The gap left in the place of his baby teeth made him look somehow older. He *was* getting older. Sending him to kindergarten had just about killed her, but she had to face it. Noah was growing up.

And Devon was missing it.

Three

Cassie put her phone on the counter but continued to stare at it long after she'd ended her regular evening call to the care center. Instead of feeling guilty that she wasn't with Devon—as she usually felt six nights a week—her mind was wandering. Silently she scolded herself but still couldn't rein her thoughts onto their usual path. Instead they kept returning to an idea that she couldn't seem to dismiss. A really crazy, possibly stupid idea that she couldn't stop thinking about.

It had come to her while eating ice cream and snuggling on the couch with Noah while they watched the movie her mom had brought over Sunday—*Air Bud World Pup*. Grandma's attempt to get Noah excited about soccer again had been a good one, but it wasn't enough. He was scared to play, scared of getting hurt. It was a pretty normal reaction for a five-year-old and not the end of the world, but lacking the courage to face something after a traumatic experience could have repercussions in the future. Noah had enough things stacked against him already, growing up without a dad as he was. Cassie really didn't want the soccer/teeth incident to grow into something more and lasting.

She racked her brain, thought back to the child psychology classes she'd taken in grad school, and mostly put all her mothering instincts and intuition to work. There had to be a way to help Noah get over his fear, to get him back on that field. Though what she'd come up with was an iffy proposition at best, it might work.

Her phone rang, vibrating against the counter, jarring her from her thoughts. She glanced at the screen and did a double take, then felt her own throb of nerves as she recognized the number—the same one she'd been staring at on the business card for the past several minutes.

Why would he be calling me?

She picked up the phone and answered on the fourth ring before it could go to voicemail.

"Hello." Her voice sounded strange and wobbly. She grabbed her glass from the counter and took a quick gulp of water.

"Hello, Mrs. Webb?"

"Yes. This is Cassie." Hardly anyone outside of the kids at the school called her Mrs. Webb. That had been her mother-in-law.

"This is Matt Kramer. My, uh, son hurt yours at the game last Saturday."

"Yes. I remember." She tried not to sound unkind but wasn't sure she was entirely successful. Remembering the look on his son's face, she knew Mr. Kramer had his parental hands full, too. It was part of the reason she'd come up with such a scheme. Instead of feeling angry at his son, as motherly instinct deemed she ought to, Cassie couldn't seem to forget the forlorn expression she'd seen in the boy's eyes. Maybe this could help him, too.

"I was wondering how your son is, if you were able to get his mouth all fixed up," Mr. Kramer asked.

All fixed up was debatable at this point. Noah would probably always have a scar on his lower lip where his tooth had cut through, and who knew how long it would be before he had front teeth again.

"He had to get his two front teeth pulled," Cassie said.

"I am so sorry." Mr. Kramer's voice rang with such sincerity that she rushed to assure him that the teeth would have come out in the next year or so anyway. His relief was a nearly palpable thing through the phone.

"I meant what I said about paying any medical expenses. Whatever your insurance or your husband's insurance won't pay, I'd like to cover."

Cassie glanced at her wedding ring. Of course Mr. Kramer would assume that she had a husband—in the normal sense, that is.

"I appreciate that. I'll let you know when the bill comes." On her limited income, she was more than grateful for the help.

"If there's anything else I can do, please let me know," Mr. Kramer said, unknowingly providing the perfect segue into her wild hair idea.

"Actually, there might be." She took a deep breath. "Noah—my son—is afraid to play soccer now. He wasn't particularly bold before this happened. Saturday was the first game in which he actually tried to get the ball and participate." Only because she'd promised him a dollar a goal. She wasn't ready to admit that to anyone yet, especially not the father of the child she was hoping to borrow. "Now Noah doesn't want to play anymore. He's afraid of getting hurt again."

"That's understandable," Mr. Kramer said.

Cassie nodded, though he couldn't see her, then continued on with her mad idea. "I have a proposal that might help both of our boys. I was thinking they might be able to play soccer together during the week. I practice with Noah, but it isn't the same for him as playing with other kids. I was thinking that if your son were the one to play with him, that might really help Noah overcome his fear."

"You want Austin to practice soccer with your son, even after what happened?" Mr. Kramer's voice held a definite note of incredulity, causing Cassie to wonder if she'd just made a mistake. Maybe there was something about the boy she didn't know.

"Crazy, right?" She gave an awkward little laugh. "But if Noah can play with the boy who hurt him, then it would seem he might have the courage to play with his team again." What remained unsaid was that Mr. Kramer's son would have a chance to practice being kind to another child, something it sounded like he needed pretty badly. How to suggest that without being too pushy?

"And maybe it might be a good way for your son to—I don't know—make a new friend and sort of—make up for pushing another player."

Mr. Kramer chuckled. "Let the punishment fit the crime. I like it."

"I wouldn't say punishment exactly." There wasn't anything wrong with Noah that Austin shouldn't want to play with him.

"I didn't mean it that way," Mr. Kramer said. "I actually think it's a great idea. I'll spend some time talking with Austin beforehand."

Cassie let out a silent sigh of relief and found herself smiling into the phone. Maybe she wasn't crazy. Maybe this was simple parental instinct and not her inner obsession to fix children coming through.

"All right?" Mr. Kramer asked, sounding uncertain when she hadn't spoken for a few seconds. "I'm game if you are. Where and when would you like the boys to meet?"

"How about a park?" Cassie didn't have a yard of her own, and she didn't want to bring virtual strangers to her mother's house, but a park after school ought to be safe enough. "We could meet at Sugar Pine Ridge Wednesday afternoon. There's a great soccer field there." It was Monday night now, so that gave him a day or so to talk with his wife and make arrangements.

"I'm sorry. Wednesday afternoons won't work for me. I don't usually get home until around seven.

Could your wife bring your son? Cassie was on the verge of asking, but didn't, not wanting to poke her nose into Mr. Kramer's business. *Just into his son's,* her conscience noted. Everyone was dealing with something, and maybe Mr. Kramer and his wife were having problems. Maybe he was even divorced. That could explain the depth of sorrow she'd glimpsed in Austin's eyes. Cassie suddenly wanted this to work out more than ever—for both boys.

"Is there another afternoon that's better?" she asked. "I'm good most days after four."

"Tuesdays and Thursdays I work from home. We could meet tomorrow."

Cassie hesitated. She wanted to try this, but Tuesday was too soon. Noah's mouth needed a couple more days to heal, and even more important than that, she needed a day or so to prepare him.

"Or this Friday I could get Austin there around 4:30," Mr. Kramer said.

Date night. She couldn't let even this situation disrupt that. "Thursday afternoon will be fine. Is four o'clock okay?"

"Yep. We'll be there."

"Great," Cassie said. "I'll bring a ball and cones. Thank you for being willing to try this."

"I hope it works," Mr. Kramer said. "I hope your son can feel confident again."

Yours, too.

◎◎◎

Matt pocketed his phone and refolded the paper with Cassandra Webb's number on it that he'd pulled from his jeans. The phone call had gone a whole lot differently—and better—than he'd anticipated, and he felt suddenly grateful to the stranger who'd given him Coach Webb's number at the game.

She'd already left by then, and he'd been folding up his chairs, wanting to get out of there as fast as possible, what with the parents on both teams staring him down, or so it seemed. He'd been imagining the things they were thinking, and feeling he deserved every one of them. He *was* a bad parent, unable to get Austin's moods and behaviors under control. Completely inept—

At everything. Matt pulled a pair of superhero underwear, tinted pink, from the washing machine. What was it this time? He supposed he should have looked a little more carefully before just dropping everything into the washer, but after a long day, sorting laundry wasn't top on his list.

He continued pulling pink-tinted clothing, including his new white dress shirts, from the barrel. At the bottom he found the culprit—a red permanent marker with the lid off. *Told you,* he imagined Austin taunting him.

"Yeah, yeah," Matt muttered as he tossed the pen in the trash. Like everything else, this was his fault. Yesterday Asher had wanted to color, and Matt had given him the red marker.

"Mom didn't let us use those," Austin had piped up, ever too pleased to make life miserable for his little brother.

Mom's not here. Matt had barely held his tongue. "I don't know where the crayons are, so Asher can use the marker instead."

And now I can buy new dress shirts again. This time he'd be sure to figure out where a dry cleaners was between home and work.

With a disgruntled sigh, Matt tossed the whole load into the dryer, hoping that somehow the heat would miraculously return at least the Incredible Hulk briefs back to their original green and white. If not . . . well, Asher would still wear them. He'd do just about anything for Matt these days, whereas Austin did all in his power to disobey him.

So how was he supposed to get Austin to play soccer, to play nice, with Mrs. Webb's kid? For a second, Matt regretted calling her. Why had that lady at the soccer game given him the number anyway? The well-dressed Asian woman had looked as out of place at the soccer game as he felt, but her words and tone had been kind when she'd handed him the team roster with Coach Webb's phone number and suggested that Mrs. Webb might appreciate a call from him, to check on her son. That call just might have gotten him, what? More trouble? Or maybe this *could* work for Austin. Maybe this was the miracle he'd been praying for. Maybe.

Something about Cassie Webb's voice had reassured him. There'd been no censure in it, he was certain. If nothing else, he was grateful for that. It was one positive he could note for the day. Better than most of the days he'd had recently.

Four

Cassie parked the car, took her soccer bag from the trunk, and coaxed a reluctant Noah from the back seat. "Remember, you play with Austin, and then we go get ice cream afterward." It seemed she was becoming all about bribery lately. She'd always felt like she was on top of the parenting thing, but this was twice in one week—first she'd promised a dollar for a goal, and now she was offering an ice cream for playing with another kid. *What's happening here?*

It really wasn't about soccer. She didn't feel any particular affinity for the sport. It was just the first one Noah had tried, and she wanted him to have fun with it—and some measure of success, if she were being honest with herself. *And if he doesn't?* Not all kids were good at sports, but she wanted him to be. Cassie frowned, displeased with this self-assessment. She told herself she would do better this summer when it was time for swim lessons again. Then it would be Noah who was willing to do anything for a trip to the pool.

He shuffled his feet across the parking lot to the field. "What if he pushes me again?"

"He won't," Cassie said.

"But what if he does?" Noah's eyes were large and frightened as he looked up at her.

Cassie stopped at the edge of the field and knelt down in front of him. "Austin's dad promised me that Austin would be nice." *Sort of.* "So, if for some reason he isn't—" She shrugged. "I guess I'll just have to take down his dad." She punched her fist into her other palm.

Noah rewarded her with that goofy, toothless grin she'd come to love the past few days. His lip wasn't nearly as swollen as it had been, and the cut was scabbing over. Even his speech seemed to be adapting to a couple less teeth. Kids were resilient. Or at least her kid had to be, going through life without a dad around to show him the ropes of boyhood.

"All right then. Let's have fun." She ruffled the top of his hair, then went to set up the cones sideways on the field, since little legs weren't ready to run the full length yet.

She'd just finished marking the goals when a newer model Chevy truck pulled into the parking lot. Next to the shiny silver truck, her 2000 Nissan looked particularly pathetic.

No worries about having Mr. Kramer pay the dental bill. She pulled a couple of balls from the bag and stood beside Noah as they watched Mr. Kramer and two boys climb out of the truck. One she recognized as the pusher from Saturday's game. The other resembled him enough that he had to be a younger brother. *Even better.*

"Look, Noah," she said. "Austin's brought his brother to play, too." Playing with someone smaller than he was would surely increase Noah's confidence.

"Two of them to beat up on me." Noah tilted his head back to look up at her, worry lines furrowing his brow once more.

Again Cassie asked herself how this had happened. How was she raising a child who was suddenly less than confident? She hoped her mom was right and it was just a phase he was going through.

"I hope you don't mind that I brought my other son," Mr. Kramer said as he walked up to them.

"Not at all." Cassie smiled at the younger boy. "What's your name?"

"Asher." From beneath the hair covering his eyes, he looked up at her and returned her smile in a bashful way that melted her heart. She quickly took in both boys' appearances and felt her heart soften even more. Hair badly in need of a cut, jeans too short and with holes in the knees, shirts that looked like they'd seen better days. For someone who drove such a nice truck, and looked pretty good himself in jeans that looked new and an untucked, collared shirt, Mr. Kramer didn't pay a whole lot of attention to his kids' attire.

"Pleased to meet you, Asher." She stuck out her hand, and he shook it without hesitation. "This is Noah. He's five."

Mr. Kramer's gaze swept over Noah's face, and Cassie caught his wince. She wondered if it was because of the yellowish purple bruise still making its appearance on Noah's chin, or if it was the thought of what those missing teeth were going to cost.

"I'm almost five," Asher said. "Austin is six."

"How lucky you are to have a brother," Cassie said, feeling one of her many familiar regrets—that Noah had no siblings. "It just happens that I have three balls, so you can all play. Should we do some warm ups?" Asher nodded enthusiastically, Noah continued to look at the ground, and Austin glared at his father.

Off to a great start.

"First, Austin has something he'd like to say." Mr.

Kramer placed his hand in the small of Austin's back and nudged him forward. A long, awkward moment of silence passed during which Austin said absolutely nothing. Mr. Kramer cleared his throat and narrowed his eyes at his son.

"Sorry I pushed you," Austin mumbled at last while staring at Noah's feet.

Noah glanced up at Cassie, and she read the question in his gaze. *How do I respond?*

"Thank you, Austin. It takes a really great person to be able to apologize like that."

Following her lead, Noah mumbled something that might have been thanks. Cassie exchanged a look with Mr. Kramer in which they each acknowledged this was likely as good as it was going to get.

"All right then." Cassie passed out the balls and instructed the boys to run across the field weaving in and out of the cones she'd set up. "It's not a race," she admonished as Austin pushed his little brother aside to get out in front.

Behind her, Mr. Kramer sighed loudly. She took her eyes from the field long enough to glance back at him and note the discouragement in his eyes. Something was definitely going on between father and son, but Asher seemed like a happy little boy, so maybe it wasn't as all-encompassing as the divorce she'd imagined.

Mr. Kramer walked forward to stand beside her, and from the corner of her eye Cassie noted the absence of a ring on his left hand.

"I'm sorry Austin's not more cooperative," he said.

"We've only just started." Cassie wasn't about to lose hope in her experiment yet. "Give them some time to warm up to each other."

"If you say so."

She didn't care for the skepticism in his voice and

became more determined than ever that this would work. The boys finished going around the cones once, and she blew her whistle and beckoned them.

"All right. We're going to have a scrimmage now. That means a mini game because we don't have a full team. Austin, Noah, Asher, you're going to be on one team. You'll have to work together passing the ball back and forth if you're going to make any goals and win. Not just one person can do all the work. Do you understand?"

All three boys nodded, and Austin actually raised his hand to ask a question.

"Who are we playing against?"

"Me." Cassie planted her hands on her hips and tried to look tough. "Your dad is going to be the ref. Three boys against one girl—think you can do it?"

"Yeah," Austin and Asher said together, but Noah shook his head.

"She's good," he whispered loud enough that everyone could hear.

Cassie tossed a ball to Mr. Kramer and caught him actually smiling.

"Center circle, everyone." She picked up the extra cones as they walked to the middle of the half field she'd created. "Ladies first, so I kickoff."

"That's not fair. We didn't flip a coin like they do at the game. Dad?" Austin grabbed his father's arm as they stopped at midfield.

"If the ref would like it changed, I will concede," Cassie said. "Mr. Kramer?"

"Matt." A corner of his mouth quirked as he set the ball down. "Ladies first is a good rule. Let's see what you boys can do against her."

Cassie removed the lanyard from around her neck and

handed him her whistle. He stepped back, blew it, and the scrimmage began. She kicked the ball hard, straight between Austin and Noah. "You should have worked together to block that," she called as she squeezed into the gap between them and ran downfield.

In a matter of seconds, she'd reached the ball and kicked it between the cones. "One for me." She raised her fists above her head.

"Our turn." Austin snatched the ball and marched back to center field. Matt blew the whistle again, and Austin gave the ball a pretty good kick. Cassie turned and ran toward it, reaching it before any of the boys did. She faced them, dribbling the ball in a sideways pattern. Austin came near, stuck his foot out and kicked it behind her.

"Good move," Cassie praised, "Now what are you going to do? Noah, Asher, you should be on the other side of me, ready to get his pass."

"I got it," Noah shouted a second later and raced toward the goal. Cassie beat him to it. "I'm ready for you, so you'd better have another plan."

Noah kicked it to Asher, and Asher kicked it straight at her. She blocked it and sent the ball downfield. Austin got to it first and started it back her direction. Cassie advanced on him, moving back and forth in front, so he had nowhere to go.

His hands clenched into fists at his sides, and she could see his frustration mounting and knew she was on thin ice, but for this to work—to get the boys to actually play *together*—she had to make this hard for them.

"Can't get it past me, can you?" She jumped side to side, her face in his.

"No fair. You're bigger and can run faster."

"Yes, fair," Cassie said. "There are three of you, but you're playing like there's only one."

He scowled and let out a grunt of frustration just as Cassie moved forward and stole the ball. She started running it downfield when the whistle blew. She stopped then looked back.

Matt still held the whistle between his teeth as he marched toward Austin. "Unsportsmanlike conduct from the boy's team. Penalty kick for Noah's mom." He took a rock from Austin's hand and tossed it off to the side of the field. "No using your hands to pick up the ball *or* rocks, especially not to throw them at people. If I see you do that again, you will spend the rest of this week and the next with no iPad privileges. Got it?"

Austin's scowl deepened, but he nodded.

Cassie picked up the ball and moved it into place. Technically in the K-1 soccer leagues there were no penalty kicks, but throwing rocks was a serious offense, and since part of today's exercise was to help Austin behave and play more appropriately, she took the kick. The ball rolled easily between the cones, and Matt shouted out the score.

"Two zip. You boys better get it together with your teamwork."

"Told you she was good," Noah muttered, his head still hung low.

"Noah's turn to kick off," Matt said, and this seemed to perk him up a bit.

When everyone was in place, Cassie with her legs spread wide and arms stretched, doing her best to look comically dangerous, Noah gave the ball a good kick and sent it sailing straight between her legs. Austin ran past her to get it, while Asher trailed behind. Noah just stood there.

"Come on," Cassie urged. "That was a great kick. Now follow through." She hurried toward Austin, who was already commandeering the ball somewhat skillfully toward the goal.

"Oh no, you don't." Cassie got in front of him and stuck her foot out, trying to get the ball. He tried to go around her, but she was too fast. She blocked him and nearly stole the ball. He took it back, kicking in a way that she suspected was meant to hurt her shins rather than move the ball. Good thing she was fast. Austin continued trying to get it past her, but she refused to let him.

"Kick it to me," Asher called behind him.

Austin looked up. Cassie subtly followed his gaze to Noah, standing several feet away near the goal line.

"Can't get it past me," she said and moved in closer for the steal. Austin hesitated a moment as they made eye contact.

"Get it, Noah," Austin yelled, kicking the ball sideways.

Yes! Cassie felt like skipping down the field.

"Oh no, you don't," she said with mock frustration and turned toward Noah, who was awkwardly scuttling toward the goal, with the ball protected between his legs. She allowed him to get really close before jumping around him, sticking her foot out every time he looked like he might kick it in.

"Pass it to me," Austin said from a few feet away. Noah glanced up, and Cassie held her breath to see what he would do. He hesitated a second, then kicked the ball Austin's direction instead of trying to get it past her into the goal. Austin kicked, and the ball rolled between the cones.

"Argh! You got one past me." Cassie slapped her hands to her head as if she couldn't believe it. Actually, she couldn't. A quick glance at her watch showed her that they'd been playing only fifteen minutes. A quarter of an hour, and a small miracle already.

Matt blew the whistle. "One point for the boys. Nice teamwork." Asher jumped up and down with glee, though he'd had nothing to do with the goal. He ran to get the ball while Austin and Noah stared at one another for a long second.

"Thanks," Austin said.

"Nice goal," Noah said back.

"You can kick the next one," Austin offered.

They continued to play another hour until the sun was setting and Cassie was genuinely tired. She let them beat her but felt a lot more tired than she did when just playing with Noah. It had also been a lot more fun. The kid needed a brother or at least some friends to hang out with, but until Devon got better or she moved, neither of those were going to happen.

Matt and the boys picked up the remaining cones while Cassie collected the balls.

"Thanks for this," Matt said, taking the bag from her when everything was in it. They walked to her car together, the boys trailing behind. "This was a great idea. I owe you a lot more than the cost of Noah's dental work."

"You don't owe me anything for today. I'm glad it went so well." She popped the trunk of her car open, and Matt set the cones and balls inside. Cassie turned to face the boys. "Noah, Austin, Asher. Great game. You guys were tough."

Three smiling, sweaty faces looked up at her, filling her with a sense of accomplishment and hope. "Do you think we could do this again next week?" She hadn't asked Matt, but given that he'd just thanked her, she hoped it would be okay.

"Yeah," the boys chorused.

"That would be great," Matt said. "Same time, same place?"

Cassie nodded, thinking that this could be good, *really* good, for Noah. She reached in the trunk to pull her car keys from the mesh bag and accidentally snagged the extra jersey from the bottom. As she untangled the loose thread from the keys, inspiration struck once more.

"Hey, Austin?"

"Yeah?" He looked up at her with what she could only describe as longing, and it inspired her to keep going with the spur-of-the-moment thought.

"You're a really great soccer player—when you're not pushing people or throwing rocks," she added as a reminder of her expectations.

"Thanks." He shifted his eyes down, and Cassie worried she'd used the wrong approach.

"We had a player on our team break his arm before the season even started, so we've been down one player at every game. Makes it hard to keep the rotations even." She met Matt's gaze and saw only curiosity, so she continued. "We could really use a player like you, if you could play as part of a team like you did today. Would that interest you?"

Austin said nothing for a minute then looked to his dad for direction.

A good sign. Their relationship couldn't be that broken if he sought his dad's guidance so readily. Then again, he was only six.

"What do you think of that idea, Noah?" Matt asked.

Cassie felt the sting of self-recrimination. Noah was the one she should have asked first. He was the real reason for this excursion today.

Noah shrugged, then looked directly at Austin. "Okay, if you're not mean."

Leave it to kids to be direct. There were times, like this, when lacking the adult filter was really great.

"Okay," Austin agreed. "I won't be."

"To Noah or anyone else," Matt said. "On our team *or* the other teams." He looked from Austin to Cassie. "Are you sure that would be all right?"

"I don't see why it wouldn't be," Cassie said. "This isn't

league play but community soccer we're talking about—you know, low-key, parent-volunteer coaches and all." She tossed the jersey to Austin.

"Can I play, too?" Asher asked, his chin raised hopefully.

Thinking quickly, Cassie reached into her bag once more and pulled out the cones and her stopwatch. "I'm sorry, Asher, but the rules do say that players had to be five by September first. However, I could really use an assistant coach, someone to help set out the cones and keep track of my stopwatch so I know when to rotate players in and out. Do you think you could do that?" She held the cones and watch out to him.

His head bobbed as he reached for the offered treasures.

"Now don't lose those or we can't have a game very easily. It will be your job to bring them each time."

Asher's head still hadn't stopped bobbing, and a smile stretched wide across his face.

"That's great then." Cassie closed the trunk. "We'll see you guys on Saturday." She held her hand out to Noah. "Let's go, kiddo." Right about now, a half hour, just the two of them, sitting in a booth eating hot fudge sundaes sounded really great. Keeping these three boys in balance for over an hour had been more challenging than the regular soccer games with eight kids. Plus, she'd run a lot more. *One double scoop with extra caramel coming up.*

"Can they come with us to get ice cream?"

Noah's question caught her off guard. Going out to ice cream, just the two of them, was his favorite thing. And just like that, he was inviting someone else to barge in on their special time?

Cassie knew she was taking too long to answer. Being careful to look only at Noah, she finally said. "That's up to

Matt. He may not let his boys eat ice cream just before dinnertime." Or *for* dinner, as she'd planned.

"That works for us," Matt said, dashing her hopes. "Dairy is one of the main food groups, right?"

"Yay, yay, yay!" Asher jumped up and down, his little fists pumped in the air. "Ice cream, ice cream, ice cream!"

"Great," Cassie said, hoping she sounded more positive than she felt. "We're going to Samantha's. Meet you there."

"Would you like to come with us in the truck?" Matt offered.

"Can we, Mom?" Noah asked, already tugging her that direction.

"No thanks," Cassie answered quickly this time. No way they were going anywhere in a car with another man, even if he did have kids with him. "Noah's booster seat is in the back. We'll just follow you."

"Actually." Matt raised a hand to rub the back of his neck. "How about if we follow you? We've lived in Auburn a whole three weeks and haven't been out to ice cream yet. I don't know where Samantha's is."

"Oh, of course." Cassie felt the tiniest bit better. Maybe he wasn't being too forward. Maybe he'd just wanted them to come along so he'd know where to go. She helped Noah into the backseat, then turned to give Matt a more genuine smile. "Three whole weeks without ice cream, huh? You probably need this more than I do."

Five

She had no idea how much he needed this, how much the boys did, too, which was why Matt had decided to take Noah up on his invite even though Noah's mom wasn't onboard. Under normal circumstances, Matt would've taken the hint that her slow answer more than implied that, for whatever reason, she didn't want him and the boys tagging along. But then, when was the last time they'd had anything close to normal circumstances? Too long.

Until this afternoon which had felt blissfully ordinary.

Though Jenna hadn't been much for running around with the boys outside, Matt had almost imagined that it was her out on that field instead of Cassie Webb, and they were all back in Oregon at the park near their house. Asher was happy, not because he was trying to be for his dad, but because he was having fun. Austin had seemed close to his old self as well, to the funny, tenderhearted boy he used to be. For a few minutes, Matt had forgotten about all of it. He'd let his cares slip away, unnoticed, and just had fun with his boys. Then he'd jumped at the opportunity to extend that fun just a little longer. Soon enough they'd return to their apartment and another lonely night.

"There it is." Austin pointed from the back seat. "Sam-an-tha's ice cream par—parl—"

"Parlor," Matt helped him read the last. "It's an old-fashioned word and fancy way to say shop." He pulled into the parking stall beside Cassie.

"Can I get chocolate?" Asher asked.

"You can get whatever you want," Matt said. He didn't particularly care if the boys spoiled their dinner. He didn't know what he was going to fix for dinner anyway, so if they skipped the meal altogether tonight, so much the better for him.

He put the truck in park and turned off the engine, then hopped out to help the boys. They were still getting used to the tall truck, and Asher had fallen more than a time or two. In retrospect, Matt realized he probably should have bought something smaller and more economical. At the time, he'd simply needed a car to replace the minivan, and he'd wanted something that would pull the trailer with their stuff from Oregon to California. The truck had seemed like the obvious answer.

The boys clamored out, and Matt hurried ahead of them to hold the door open for Cassie and Noah.

"Thanks," she said, then ducked her head in obvious discomfort.

Matt wished he knew what was bothering her. Everything had been fine at the ball field, but now she was definitely uncomfortable. Asher and Austin squeezed their way past to stand on either side of Noah. Matt was last through the door and felt his mood lift again at the smell of chocolate. Bright yellow walls, blue checkered tables, and a mural of the Sierra welcomed them. On the far side of an arched divider, the other half of the shop boasted glass cases full of chocolates and other candy.

Another point for Cassie Webb. Another thing he owed her for. He would be bringing the boys here often. The first bright spot in Auburn.

The boys crowded around the counter, trying to decide what they each wanted.

"Can I get a sundae with mint chocolate chip?" Noah asked.

"Of course." Cassie's look turned tender. "A great soccer player like yourself needs extra whipped cream, too."

He flashed the toothless smile that Matt still felt terrible about. At least lacking front teeth shouldn't keep him from being able to enjoy ice cream.

Cassie ordered for Noah and herself while Matt tried to help the boys decide.

"Just the two of you, or is this altogether?" the girl behind the counter asked.

"Just the two of us," Cassie said.

"Altogether." Matt reached over her arm and handed his Visa to the clerk. He glanced at Cassie and wasn't surprised at her pursed lips and general look of dismay. "I owe you for today." For a lot more than that if her soccer team worked out for Austin.

"Thanks." Still looking uncomfortable, arms folded across her chest, she stepped aside while he ordered for the boys. Noah's sundae came first, and Matt handed it to him. Asher's and Austin's came next, then Cassie's salted caramel.

"Aren't you getting anything?" she asked as she took it from him.

"Yeah. I'm just a bit overwhelmed. I mean, eight flavors of whipped cream—wow."

"You know us Californians," she said. "Over the top with everything."

"I guess so." He returned the brief smile she'd given him and felt glad that she didn't seem too upset that he'd tagged along and paid. "I think I'll try a Nutella crepe."

Cassie followed the boys to the table, leaving him to casually observe them from across the room while he waited for his order. She sat next to Noah but quickly engaged all three boys in conversation. He watched and found himself mesmerized as she blew on her metal spoon then carefully balanced it on her nose, a feat which impressed his boys at least. Noah had apparently seen this trick before and was busy attempting to balance his own spoon. He nearly had success until it fell abruptly and hit the table and his sundae just right so that a blob of whipped cream vaulted onto his chin. They all laughed, Asher bursting into a full fit of giggles. It was sweet music to Matt's ears, and he felt a surge of more than gratitude for Cassie Webb as he observed her hand come up to cover her mouth and her ponytail bob up and down.

Thank you. He was grateful to God or fate, whoever or whatever had brought this Good Samaritan into their lives. Who knew, a few months earlier, that something as normal as a soccer scrimmage and watching his boys laugh while they ate ice cream would mean so much to him?

He continued watching as they moved on from the spoon trick and became invested in their sundaes. Cassie propped her elbows on the table and appeared to be savoring each bite. Matt watched as her mouth closed over her spoon, then seemed to linger there. He imagined her pretty brown eyes closing in a moment of bliss.

"Your order, sir."

Matt jerked his own eyes and thoughts around to the

counter and to the woman holding the most delicious-looking crepe he'd ever seen in his life.

"Thank you." He took the plate in his hands but felt very much like he deserved it in his face with the direction his thoughts had been going. Sure, Cassie was an attractive woman, but she had a ring on her finger. Even if she hadn't been married, it wasn't like he was ready to even think about women in that regard yet.

Matt crossed the room, took the empty chair beside Asher, and noticed that half of his face was already covered in chocolate. Noah didn't seem to be doing much better. Austin was quiet as he ate, but he wasn't scowling at anyone, and that was about as good as it had been at any mealtime that Matt could remember in recent months.

"So, do you come here often?" Matt asked.

"Every Saturday," Noah said.

Matt was seated directly across from Cassie and once again caught her obvious dismay at the release of this information.

"It's our date night once a week," she explained. "My husband and I have our date night on Fridays, but Saturday night is reserved for Noah and me."

Points taken. She is married, and she liked her alone time with her son. If he brought the boys here, Matt would be sure it wasn't on a Friday or a Saturday night, so he didn't barge in again.

"Today was sort of an extra ice cream date because Noah tried playing soccer again even after he'd been hurt."

Matt nodded. "I'm sorry if we cut in on your mother-son time."

"That's okay," Noah said, speaking around an extra-large bite.

"It is," Cassie hurried to assure him. "It's fine. Noah

doesn't have many friends—there aren't any other kids close to where we live—so this is good for him."

But not for me, she might have added. Her body language said as much. She wouldn't look at Matt directly and sat almost stiffly in her seat, glancing around frequently, as if she were afraid someone she knew might see her here.

Of course. Matt felt like a selfish jerk. She was worried about what her husband would think. He felt like smacking himself in the head. Jenna would never have gone out to ice cream with another guy, and if she was still alive, he certainly wouldn't be sitting here with another woman and her child. Man, he was clueless sometimes.

The boys chattered away about Lego sets while he and Cassie—Mrs. Webb—ate in silence.

"I'm sorry if I'm making you uncomfortable," Matt finally said, hoping that acknowledging it would help. "Would you like us to go sit at another table?" He looked around for an empty one nearby.

"No. Of course not." She bit her lip, appearing chagrined that he'd noticed her discomfort. "It's not you. It's just that—"

"You're married, and this is weird?" He finished the last of the delicious crepe and leaned back in his chair.

"Yes." She let out a sigh that sounded both sad and tired.

Matt wondered what her story was. It didn't appear that her husband had been at the game last Saturday, but that didn't necessarily mean anything. People had to work on weekends sometimes.

"We shouldn't be here. With you. Not that we're with you, but—"

He held up a hand. "I understand."

She nodded and swallowed back whatever else she'd

been about to say. Sticky fingers touched Matt's arm and he looked over to see Asher's chocolate-covered face alarmingly near his own.

"Can we get some candy?" Asher stood on his chair and leaned close.

"Not tonight," Matt said. "Besides. You've still got half a sundae left on your face. When are you planning to eat that?"

Austin snickered at this, and Noah giggled. Asher didn't seem to mind either. "Please, can we see what they have at least?"

Matt considered for a minute. "If you promise that you won't ask me to buy anything, then you may look."

"Can we get something next time?" Asher asked.

"Fair enough," Matt said, having no idea if that was really fair at all or if he was the biggest pushover ever. Basically he'd just promised them that there would be a next time, and he would buy them candy then. Austin and Asher scampered off to look in the glass cases.

"Can I look, too?" Noah asked his mom.

"Same rule," Cassie said. "We're not buying anything today."

He nodded and hurried off.

"Don't put your sticky hands or face against the glass." She stood and quickly began gathering the empty cups. Matt helped her, collecting the used napkins and doing his best to wipe up the table.

"Are all kids this messy?" he asked as he bent to wipe down Asher's chair as well.

"I'm not really sure," Cassie said. "Probably, but I only have Noah, so I can't say."

They both finished their tasks at the same time and stood, facing each other awkwardly across the table.

"You're really good with kids," Matt said. "Noah's a lucky boy."

"Thanks." Cassie fiddled with her keys and looked over at the candy counter. "He's pretty great. I'm the lucky one."

"I really appreciate your help today," Matt said, though he'd already thanked her a time or two. He wanted her to know how much her invitation to play soccer had meant. "Austin's been having a rough time, and I haven't been able to help him, but I think that today did."

"I'm glad to hear that." Her gaze drifted back to Matt. "It helped Noah, too. I really didn't want him to be afraid of the game, and I think Austin deserves another chance to play. I'm happy to make sure he gets it."

Matt nodded. "He didn't used to be aggressive, but lately, since . . ." Matt shoved his hands in his pockets in an attempt at being casual when inside he felt anything but. His heart raced, and words pounded through his head as he fought the unexplainable desire to tell Cassie Webb more about his life and circumstances.

"Since?" she prodded, her gentle tone suggesting that she really wanted to know. He had the feeling she'd be a good listener.

Matt breathed in deeply then exhaled. He hadn't even shared this with his coworkers at his new job yet. "My wife passed away about eight months ago. Since then, Austin hasn't been himself." He shrugged, uncertain why the first person he'd chosen to tell this to in California was Cassie Webb. He barely even knew her, yet he wanted her to understand or at least partially excuse Austin's earlier, poor behavior.

I'm not a completely awful parent. Just a struggling one.

Her expression softened from one of forced aloofness to genuine compassion. She met Matt's gaze directly for the first time since they'd left the soccer field. "I'm so sorry."

"Me, too." His eyes lingered on hers a few seconds

longer than necessary or probably appropriate, but thankfully she didn't seem to go back to feeling awkward. Instead she surprised him with another offer.

"If there is anything else I can do to help you get situated here, or with your boys—" She hugged her arms to herself. "Being a single parent is really hard and—I mean I imagine it's hard. I work at a school and see a lot of kids and parents . . ." Her voice trailed off, and she pursed her lips, as if regretful she'd said as much as she had.

"I appreciate that," Matt said, purposely ignoring all the clues about herself that she'd inadvertently given him. He could think about those later tonight. It would be a good change of pace from what he usually thought about at night after the boys had gone to bed. "Allowing Austin on your soccer team is plenty, though."

She nodded. "Well then, I'd better get going. I have to work early tomorrow, and Noah definitely needs a bath tonight."

"Me, too," Matt said. "Work I mean." He brought a hand to his forehead, embarrassed. "Though a bath—shower would be good as well. Being a ref was a workout."

She grinned. "Try being the other team."

"Maybe next time I will."

She called Noah over, and he beckoned to Austin and Asher, not trusting himself to go any nearer to the candy where it would be that much easier for them to talk him into getting something. Nope. He was sticking to his guns this time. Furthermore, he was going to make both boys take a bath when they got home even though it wasn't Saturday night. Kids their age probably ought to bathe more than once a week, anyway.

They left the ice cream parlor together, Matt grateful that Cassie didn't seem to mind his holding the door for her this time. After a quick wave, she and Noah were in their car and gone.

"Did you boys have a good time?" he asked once he was on the right road headed home.

Austin nodded.

"I like Noah," Asher said. "And his mom."

"Me, too," Austin said.

Silently Matt agreed.

Six

Matt reached up to the top bunk and pulled the quilt over Austin. He paused a moment to look at his son and felt a deep regret for all the harsh words that had been exchanged between them the past few months. Even in sleep, Austin's expression appeared serious, as if the days of carefree boyhood dreams were gone. Matt hated that, hated the heartbreak his boys had suffered almost more than he hated his own loss. At least he'd had a childhood. It felt like Austin's and Asher's had been stolen right away from them. Matt wasn't at all certain how to get it back, or if that was even possible.

He bent down, picking Asher's favorite stuffed dog off the floor and tucking it in beside him. How wonderful it had been to hear Asher laugh today, to see both boys smiling and playing, having fun like five- and six-year-olds were supposed to. He mulled this over as he stepped over piles of clothes and toys strewn across the room and into the hall. Maybe that was part of the solution to their problems. Until today, they hadn't had any fun in a long time. It had seemed wrong, somehow, with Jenna gone, but little boys still needed fun. They probably needed it more than ever when they'd lost their mom.

Matt ran his fingers through his hair and sighed wearily as he took in the colossal mess that was the hall and their front room. Little boys needed fun, but they also needed some rules and order in their lives. Matt doubted that Cassie Webb's living room looked like this. It bothered him to imagine what she might think if she saw his. Not that she ever would.

He needed to quit thinking about her, about what she'd almost said about being a single parent. Because she was married, wasn't she? And he definitely didn't want to be the kind of man who found another guy's wife attractive.

He made his way down the dark hall to the master bedroom and bath. He turned on the shower, unrolled his sleeves, and unbuttoned his shirt. As he pulled it off, Cassie's forgotten lanyard and the whistle attached to it thumped against his chest. He tossed the shirt aside in one of the piles on the floor. He really needed to get a hamper. Little wonder his kids were such slobs when he wasn't much better. He hadn't thought through things very well when packing and didn't even know if the laundry hamper was in storage or what. He'd been going through the motions on autopilot, simply trying to get them here and in an apartment before school started and the first day of his job.

Now that they were here, he needed to get it together, the way Cassie Webb seemed to have it together with her kid. Matt removed the lanyard and whistle. *Her mouth has been on this.* Just thinking about it, about her, gave him an undeniable rush, and for a few seconds, he allowed himself to enjoy the memory of her running up and down the field, laughing and playing with his boys.

Of course fate would lead him to a married woman. Matt tossed the whistle on the counter. On top of everything else, he didn't need to turn into a pervert.

He finished undressing and stepped into the shower before it could get any warmer. A cold shower would serve him right, and a cold shoulder from Cassie Webb would be best from now on, but of course he couldn't warn her.

Instead he spent the rest of the night warning himself and fell asleep laying on his side, facing Jenna's picture on his nightstand.

Cassie tugged at the tie on her robe as she left the tiny bathroom. Three steps later, she stood in the doorway of the room she shared with Noah. She hoped he'd picked up his Legos like she'd asked him to but supposed she'd find out in a minute. With necessitated bravery, she started into the room lit only by the glow of the *Cars* night light on the far wall.

She'd almost made it to her bed when the ball of her left foot encountered the all-too-familiar sharp pain of a small plastic brick. Clenching her teeth, Cassie bent to retrieve it.

"Two by three," she muttered. Small, but not so small that Noah shouldn't have seen it and put it away.

Tossing the offending Lego aside, she continued into the room, stopping to pull her bed from its upright position on the far wall. It creaked slightly as she lowered it, and Cassie glanced over her shoulder, worried that Noah would wake. Instead he turned over in his loft bed and mumbled something that sounded happy.

"Pleasant dreams, sweet boy," she whispered, the foot-stabbing Lego already forgotten as she sat cross-legged on her bed to comb out her wet hair. Tonight she felt certain Noah's dreams would be pleasant instead of worried as he had been in the days leading up to this afternoon.

The soccer plan had been even more successful than she'd hoped. Not only had Noah conquered his fear, but he'd made two new friends—an even-more-important feat. Austin and Asher seemed to have benefited from the interaction as well. Now that Cassie knew their story, she felt certain she'd done the right thing in inviting Austin to play soccer with them. Losing their mother must have been devastating for the boys—and their father. Noah had never known Devon, so he didn't fully understand what he was missing, didn't know what it was like to have two whole, functioning parents, a real house, siblings . . .

Cassie glanced around the crowded room and wondered if he would ever know those things. At the least, she needed to provide him with a better apartment with a room of his own. Turning her bed into a Murphy bed and getting him the loft had helped, but it wasn't the same as private space. Heaven knew she could have used a bit of that herself. Though that would mean sleeping alone, truly alone, and she didn't look forward to that. Hearing Noah's deep, even breathing at night was soothing.

Her pregnancy had been the comfort she needed after Devon was shot. Noah's arrival had given her something to look forward to, and when he was born, someone to live for. She'd thrown herself into being the best, most attentive mother she could be, but now, already, she could tell that she needed to start pulling back a bit. Noah wanted his own room. Soon he would need it. She would have to move.

Cassie worked through a tangle in her hair and promised herself that if Devon's situation didn't change by next summer, she *would* move. She'd find a place closer to school, an apartment complex where other children lived. She'd start putting Noah's needs first before what she believed would be best for Devon when he came home. Until then, they'd muddle along as they had been. She supposed there were worse things for a five-year-old boy than having to share a room with his mother.

Things like not having a dad. Cassie set her brush on the nightstand next to Devon's picture. She scooted back against the wall, stuffed her pillow behind her, and pulled her knees up to her chest as she stared at the photo.

"We need you, Dev." She said it often, but tonight she felt that need more keenly than she had in recent months.

Unbidden, the image of Matt, hopping around the field and doing a victory dance after Asher's lone score, came to mind. Noah needed a dad to cheer for him like that, a dad to teach him to open doors, a dad to swing him high in the air when he scored a goal, a dad to set limits on how much chocolate would or would not be purchased at Samantha's.

Because she was definitely no good at that. It had taken some serious willpower to walk out of there today without a visit to and purchase from the candy counter.

Cassie took Devon's picture from the nightstand and propped it against her legs. She stared at his handsome face, remembering that weekend they'd spent at Tahoe just two months before he'd been shot. She leaned her head back and closed her eyes, trying to summon the memory of his voice, the smell of his cologne, the feeling of her hand in his.

Tonight she felt the six years that separated the life they'd had together from her life now stretching into a wide chasm that was difficult to cross. She hadn't heard his voice for so long, he only smelled of the antiseptic at the care center now, and though she held his hand each week, he never squeezed hers back.

She'd stayed here, in their tiny, isolated apartment all these years, not to save money so much as to preserve things as they had been when Devon was here last so that when he came home someday, it would be to a place he remembered. But she was fooling herself, thinking that anything would be remotely the same when Devon woke up. Sure, she was in the same apartment, but it was also occupied by a five-year-old boy and a few hundred Legos now—neither of which Devon knew anything about. The fancy glasses that had once filled the cupboard, the ones they used to toast each other with, had been replaced with plastic. His and hers monogrammed towels that used to hang in the bathroom had been exchanged for a hooded dinosaur towel that hung from a low hook. Devon's guns were in storage at a friend's house, and his car was in storage, too. She hadn't started it in two years. Who knew if it even ran anymore? Nothing would be the same when Devon came home, but she didn't care. She just wanted him home. Wanted him back any way she could have him.

"Please." She opened her eyes again to beg his smiling face. "Come back to me. To us." She stared at the picture for several seconds, waiting for some premonition, some hint that soon her plea would be answered. But as with all the other times she'd asked and the hundreds of hours she'd spent at Devon's side since his injury, she received nothing in return. Cassie kissed the glass briefly, then set the photograph aside.

She took off her robe and lay on her bed, thinking through the past, struggling to summon a memory of Devon for her dreams, but they remained on the periphery of her mind, out of reach and blocked by the stronger memory of Matt Kramer and the stoic expression on his face when he'd told her his wife had died.

Seven

"On three," Cassie said to the group of sweaty five- and six-year-old boys huddled around her. "One." Their stacked hands bounced in unison. "Two. Three."

"Teamwork!" they shouted. "Good. Job. Bulldogs." Sixteen little hands flew up into the air, the one closest to her inadvertently smacking her in the face on its ascent.

Cassie straightened and stepped back from the huddle as Asher ran toward them, his arms laden with juice boxes. Matt followed, carrying the rest and stopping to pick up those Asher had dropped.

"Good thing they make these sturdy." Matt held up a partially crushed box as he met Cassie on the field.

"Good thing they make *kids* sturdy." She inclined her head toward the mob attacking Asher. "You'd think he was handing out Halloween candy or something."

"Hey guys, over here." Matt stepped forward, offering the remaining drinks to the swarm of kids. In short order, they were dispersed, and Cassie thanked him then bid him farewell, taking Noah's hand to lead him from the field. She needed to be at the care center in an hour, and she still had to drop Noah off at her mom's and pick up dinner on the way to see Devon.

"You did great today." Prior to the game, she hadn't been at all sure that Noah would. Last Saturday's game had been rained out, and Matt ended up having to go into the office and stay late the following Thursday, so it had been a full week and a day since Noah had played any soccer and since he, Austin, and Asher had been able to interact; however, Noah and Austin had both played with heart this evening, and it seemed the friendship that had started in the most unlikely of ways was apt to take hold.

"I didn't get a goal." Noah's shoulders drooped, and he hung his head.

"But you played great." She gave his hand a squeeze. "The only reason I offered you a dollar a goal was to motivate you to get in the game and play. And now you're doing that."

"So do I get the dollar?" He looked up hopefully.

Inwardly Cassie groaned and cursed her bad parenting. "No, not yet, but there are a lot of games left in the season. Keep playing like you did today, and I'm sure you'll make at least one goal."

The hunched-over look returned, so dramatic that Cassie had to be careful not to laugh. Maybe she ought to enroll Noah in acting class somewhere. He'd certainly been good at exhibiting his moods lately. She jiggled his hand to get his attention. "Why is that dollar so important? What Lego set are you wanting *so* desperately that it can't wait another two-and-a-half months until Christmas?"

"Not a set," he huffed and gave her a look that suggested she knew nothing and never listened to him. "I'm saving for

Lego*land*. For a ticket for you like the one for me that came in my magazine."

"Ohh . . ." She remembered him showing her that ticket, and he *had* been chattering on a lot about Legoland lately. She'd thought it was because of a commercial he'd seen on TV. But this sounded a bit more serious.

They reached the edge of the field, and Cassie began gathering her things. "That is very sweet of you to want to get me a ticket. But it would take a lot of dollars to buy one, and we'd need more than just tickets to go. It would cost money to drive or fly there, and we would have to find a hotel."

"They have one!" Noah said excitedly. "It's built out of Legos and everything."

"Really?" Cassie pictured a bed made out of the hard bricks and couldn't feel enthused. "That sounds interesting, but it would still cost a lot of money—money we don't have while your dad is sick."

"I know." Noah looked at the ground but not before Cassie glimpsed the disappointment on his face. "I just thought that if I scored enough goals . . ."

"Oh, sweetheart." She knelt in from of him and pulled him close. "Legoland is a good dream to have. Don't give up on it, but we have to be patient." *The story of our lives.*

"Everything okay?" Matt paused on his way toward the parking lot. Beside him, Austin and Asher were busy slurping their juice boxes.

"We're good." Cassie stood and grabbed her things. "Noah is just lamenting not having scored a goal this game, but he'll get there."

"Absolutely, he will," Matt said.

Noah looked up at him, and Matt gave him the thumbs up. "You were great today."

"Thanks." Noah visibly perked up at this praise, leaving Cassie feeling slightly disgruntled that her words of encouragement hadn't had the same effect.

"We've got to get going," she said. "Grandma's expecting you."

"I have a grandma, too," Asher said, taking his mouth from his straw just long enough to impart that information.

"Grandmas are the best, aren't they?" Cassie said as they walked together.

Asher nodded.

"Mine plays games with me and gives me ice cream while Mom and Dad have their date," Noah boasted.

This elicited a scowl from Austin.

"Can we get ice cream, too?" Asher asked.

"Maybe," Matt said vaguely, "but hamburgers are more what I had in mind."

"Well, see you at the game tomorrow," Cassie called as she reached her car. She purposely had not said anything to him about the boys practicing on Thursdays again. When Matt had called the previous day to tell her that he had to work, their phone call had felt stilted and awkward. Whether he'd intended to or not, he'd put off the vibe that he didn't want to be around her—which was probably for the best. Though she had been hopeful about Noah having some friends to play with outside of school. She also thought she understood Matt. She knew how painful it could be to see other couples when you were by yourself. At least she had the possibility of being with Devon again, but Matt's loss was permanent. She could only imagine how he must feel and how difficult that must be.

Cassie got into her car, and with a last wave exchanged between them, she drove off, telling herself the same thing she had when leaving the last game—it wasn't her problem.

The world was full of sad situations, hers included. Becoming wrapped up in other people's heartaches wasn't any way to heal her own. She'd done what she could for Austin and Asher, what was appropriate, by inviting them to join her team. She didn't have a team for Matt; the best she could do there was to remember him in her prayers and hope that time really did heal.

Fifteen minutes later, she pulled into her mom's driveway. Noah slumped against the door in the backseat, his eyes closed almost convincingly. She sighed out loud as she unbuckled her seatbelt. "Poor Noah fell asleep. Now Grandma will have to eat all of the ice cream herself."

"Nuh uh!" Noah jumped up and sprang at her.

Cassie twisted in her seat. "You tricked me."

He burst into giggles, as if this were the funniest scenario ever to occur even though it had played out dozens of times before. She dreaded the day he realized she wasn't really fooled and stopped playing.

"All right little trickster, out you go." She got out of the car and opened his door for him. Noah skipped ahead of her up the walk to her mom's front door. Before he could ring the bell, the door opened.

"How's my date for tonight?" Janet Jensen asked as she bent to scoop Noah into a hug. To Cassie she said, "Running late, aren't you?"

Cassie nodded. "We had a make-up game from last week's rainout, remember?"

"That's right," Mom said. "How did you do, young man?" she asked Noah.

"No goals," he said, "but Matt said I played good."

"Who's Matt?" her mom asked.

"Gotta go." Cassie jumped in her car before her mom could ask any more questions. When Noah and her mom had gone into the house, Cassie backed out of the driveway and tried to back everything out of her mind except Devon. Friday nights were his and his alone. She knew, if she tried hard enough, someday he would wake up and realize that, too.

Cassie glanced at her watch for the third time. Ikeda's was busy tonight. No surprise, for the best burger place to be found for miles around, though it seemed to be taking longer than usual to get her order. And she was already late.

"Number ninety-three," a girl at the front counter called, and Cassie gratefully hurried forward to take her bags.

"Thanks."

On the way to her car she used her teeth to pull the paper off the top of her straw so she could start on her milkshake. The thick, cool, strawberry concoction slid down her throat and brought a smile to her face. She'd made it to another Friday.

Maybe this will be the last one I have to come alone. Maybe next week she'd be bringing Noah with her, and they would be on their way to do more than just see Devon because he would be awake. Then a few months after that, Devon might actually be home, and she wouldn't be going to the care center at all. Eventually he'd be well enough to come with her, and they could sit and eat together at one of those little tables inside. Then afterward, they would wander up and down the aisles of the farm produce half of the store, picking out the last of the season's fruits and vegetables, like they used to do on date night.

Maybe.

For some reason she felt more hopeful than usual as she

walked to her car. Something about the evening seemed full of promise, and Cassie felt her spirits lift. She was forever looking for a sign that her life was about to improve, that Devon was going to get better. Perhaps this feeling, this subtle change, was what she'd been waiting for.

She put the bags and cups on the hood of her car while she opened the door then balanced everything in the box lid on the front passenger seat. She'd kept that box lid in her car for six years now. It would be great if it was gone, too, if she never needed it to transport their dinner to the care center again.

The key turned in the ignition, but her Nissan refused to start. It wouldn't even turn over, so Cassie let it rest a minute, hoping against hope that the engine would spring to life when she tried again.

"Nine hundred dollars in the last year to keep you going," she muttered. The dumb thing had better start. *At least tonight,* she silently pled. She could deal with a broken down car tomorrow, but not now, not tonight with dark falling quickly, Devon to visit, and dinner cooling on the seat beside her. *Please.*

She knew better than to ask or think, *Why me? Why not me?* was a lot more applicable question. Devon's partner hadn't survived the shooting. His wife was a widow, raising three teenagers on her own. At Sierra Long-Term Care, Cassie had witnessed more heartbreaking situations than she would have ever stopped to consider in her life before. Children were born with crippling disabilities. Young people had strokes. Alzheimer's robbed husbands and wives of their relationships. Often she left the care center simply grateful for the lot that was hers. Noah was healthy. She was healthy. Devon would be healthy again, but she had to help him get there. And to do that, she needed these visits with him.

Please start. Cassie tried the car again with the same results, then leaned her head forward against the steering wheel and groaned as she considered her limited options. *Call Mom. Call a tow truck.* She wasn't positive but was fairly certain she'd already used her max towing benefit for the year. A quick call to her insurance carrier would clarify what, if any, benefit she had left and tell her what she'd be paying for tow service. *Probably a better option than calling Mom, no matter what it costs.* Cassie wasn't up for another lecture on why she should get Devon's car out of storage and drive it. Of course she should. On a common sense level, she knew that.

But on another level . . . She didn't think she could drive the Audi without inflicting some serious emotional pain on herself. It was too full of memories, everything from the fight they'd had when he bought it, to driving on their honeymoon in San Francisco, to Devon holding her close in the privacy of the car after the doctor appointment in which they'd learned that having children of their own, on their own without serious medical intervention, was improbable at best.

Cassie leaned her head back against the seat and closed her eyes, remembering that day as if it were yesterday. She'd held it together in the OB's office, and Devon's supporting arm had gotten her out the door and across the parking lot, but once in the car, she'd fallen apart and into his arms, where they'd cried together over their shattered dream.

That hadn't been so shattered after all, not in that regard, at least. She'd had Noah a mere fifteen months later, without any heroic interventions, though she still wondered at the timing and what God was trying to tell her. She'd learned of Noah's impending arrival just weeks after Devon was shot. It almost felt as if it was God's way of telling her that she couldn't have it all. She'd had Devon for a while and wanted Noah. Now she had Noah, but she still wanted Devon, and that was simply too much to hope for. Other women had both a husband and children, but not her. Tonight, she didn't even have a car that would start. Cassie tried the engine one last time. Nothing. She'd have to call the insurance company, and she'd have to put whatever repair she needed on her credit card, but she couldn't drive the Audi. She wouldn't drive it until the day she brought Devon home.

Cassie flipped through the cards in her wallet, searching for her insurance information. She ought to have the number memorized by now; she'd called it so many times this past year.

"Coach!"

Cassie jumped in her seat and barely stifled a scream at the face pressed against the driver's side window.

Faces. Two of them. Two sets of eyes above two smashed noses stared at her from the other side of the glass. A third joined them a second later as Matt bent down to peer at her.

"Sorry," he mouthed, pulling his boys back from the car a little.

"No worries." Cassie opened the door to talk to them since her window wouldn't roll down.

"Having a boys' night out?" she asked Austin and Asher.

"That was the plan. So is this place as good as it's rumored to be?" Matt asked.

"Better." Cassie leaned behind her to grab a few fries. "Try these." She handed one each to Austin and Asher then reached the last one up to Matt.

He popped it in his mouth, then smiled. "Just what the doctor ordered after a long week."

"I'd like to meet the doctor who recommends French fries," Cassie joked, "and one who prescribes strawberry shakes as well." She picked up her shake and took another drink, noting that it already wasn't as thick as it had been a few minutes ago. Dinner was going to be ruined by the time she made it to see Devon.

"Where's Noah?" Austin asked, looking past her to the back seat.

"He's at his grandma's," Cassie said. "Friday night is the night I spend with his father, though just now my car won't start, so we might not get a date this week after all."

"Do you need a jump?" Matt braced his hand on the roof of the Nissan and leaned in.

"I'm not sure," Cassie said. "It won't even turn over. I was just getting ready to call my insurance to have it towed."

Matt didn't respond right away but seemed to be considering something. His eyes flickered to the bags on the seat beside her, then to Austin and Asher, and finally to the line of people coming out the front door of Ikeda's. "How about if we give you a ride instead? The boys and I can drop you off and eat somewhere else tonight. It doesn't look like we'll be getting a seat soon anyway."

"That's very kind of you," Cassie said, feeling both grateful and uncomfortable at the same time. If Matt were to give her a ride now, she'd still have a little over an hour to spend with Devon, but she wasn't sure how she felt about getting a ride from another man. And she really didn't want to explain her situation to Matt.

But it seemed he had taken her response for a yes. "Let's go, boys. There are other fries to be had in this town, and we can always have ice cream for dinner again if we can't find anyplace else to eat." He pulled the door of Cassie's car all the way open.

Trying to dismiss her unease, she hurried to collect the bags of food and her shake. These in hand and her purse over her shoulder, she stepped from the car. Matt closed the door behind her and she clicked the remote to lock it, though she wasn't sure who in his right mind would want to steal her car.

Matt opened the front passenger door of his truck for her. "Want me to hold those while you climb in?"

Cassie handed him her bags and shake, uncertain how else she would have managed to get into the high truck without the use of her hands. Once she was seated, she took her dinner from him, then waited while he helped Austin and Asher get buckled in the back seat.

The inside of the truck was as nice as the outside and had that new car smell to it. She glanced behind her at the boys and noted how clean the back seats were as well. The truck had to be new—no one with kids could keep a vehicle this immaculate for very long.

"Did you just buy this?" she asked Matt when he was seated.

"A little over a month ago." He avoided her gaze, paying particular attention as he backed out and causing Cassie to wonder if he felt embarrassed to be driving such a nice vehicle when hers was anything but.

"I like it," she said sincerely, hoping to put him at ease. "I haven't ridden in many trucks; this one is very comfortable."

"Thanks," he said, almost curtly. "Which way?"

"Right." She pointed toward Lincoln. "Do you know where the hospital is?"

Matt shook his head. "Haven't been there—yet," he added, inclining his head toward the back seat, "but with those two, it may be just a matter of time."

The two in the back were busy poking and pinching each other and appearing rather glum about having had their dinner postponed. Cassie opened one of the bags and took her fries from it.

"Here," she said, holding them out to the boys. "I think you need these more than me."

"Thanks!" Asher and Austin chimed, eagerly claiming the fries.

"You didn't have to do that," Matt said.

"You didn't have to give me a ride." Cassie smiled at him. "But I really appreciate it." She felt an unexplainable urgency to see Devon and guessed that it had to do with the feeling she'd had earlier, the buoyancy of hope. "You'll want to turn here to catch Bowman. We'll stay on that about a mile, then turn left onto Bell."

"Bowman to Bell. Got it," Matt said. "So does your husband work at the hospital?" "No," Cassie said. Here came the questions she'd dreaded. "He's at a care center right next to it. So what kind of gas mileage does this thing get?" It was a lame attempt at avoiding the truth and changing the subject, and she was pretty sure Matt saw right through it, but he played along.

"About sixteen around town. A little better on the highway."

"Not much worse than my car then," Cassie said, attempting levity, though the atmosphere in the car felt suddenly heavy and serious. "What made you decide to get a truck?"

"Mommy wrecked our car when she died, so we had to get a new one." Asher's voice carried from the back seat.

"I'm so sorry." Cassie turned and gave both boys a look conveying deepest sympathy. "I was all grown up when my father died, but it was still very hard, and I miss him so much. You must miss her a lot."

Austin stared at his lap, but Asher nodded and reached his hand forward, as if to touch her. Cassie reacted instinctively and placed her free hand on the back of the seat, over his little one. "It hurts losing someone you love, especially a mother." Her gaze drifted to Austin, her heart breaking for his that was surely tender. *What would Noah do without me?* It didn't bear thinking of.

Beside her, Matt cleared his throat uncomfortably. "Jenna had a brain aneurysm. We didn't know. She was driving when it burst."

"Oh, Matt." Cassie kept her hand on Asher's but felt a desire to reach out to Matt, too, and offer some gesture of comfort, miniscule though it might be. "What a lot you've all been through."

"Yeah." Matt let out a slow, weary breath. "But we're getting through it, right boys?"

Asher nodded, but Austin didn't respond. He'd stopped eating the fries and still sat with his head down.

Cassie wished she had some sage wisdom or words of genuine comfort but felt at a loss for either of those. There wasn't anything she *could* say that would make their situation or their lives better, just like there wasn't anything that anyone could tell her that would make her own lot easier or less painful. She'd spent the last six years learning that sometimes you simply had to get through hard things. You had to go on living even when you didn't want to. And sometimes you hurt. A lot. Her heart ached for this kind man and his children and the loss they'd suffered.

They drove the remaining distance in silence, which Cassie broke the last minute, directing Matt to the right driveway. He stopped in the pull thru of Sierra, and Cassie thanked him and said goodbye to the boys. She let herself out of the truck, holding tight to her bags and shake as she jumped down.

"Thanks again." She closed the door and held a hand up as he drove away.

Only then did she turn and enter the sliding double glass doors, leaving all else behind and returning to her world which revolved around Devon.

Eight

Cassie strode down the extra-wide hallway that smelled perpetually of ammonia. She'd become accustomed to the strong scent of cleaning supplies over the years, though it never ceased to cause her nose to tickle and burn every time she entered the building.

"Someday soon," she said to herself. Devon would smell of something else, like his favorite cologne when they were going out, or of fresh cut grass when he'd been out working in the yard they were going to have. She'd even take him sweaty after the gym over the antiseptic aroma she'd come to associate with him.

She'd take a lot of things over this place if given the choice, but for now, it was the best she could get, so she tried to make the most of every Friday night. Cassie thumbed through her iTunes and pulled up her playlist of Devon's favorite songs as she walked toward room sixty-seven. She'd planned to introduce him to a new song tonight, partly because she was sick of his playlist and partly because she hoped that somehow, subconsciously, his brain was absorbing all of his interactions and would remember them when he awoke.

Playing new songs for him, or telling him about books she'd read or movies she'd watched was also a good way to fill up the time. Because two hours of one-sided conversation—week after week, year after year—got a little stilted at times. She remembered when they were dating, how they'd talk for hours about everything and nothing, and the feeling she'd had that she would never grow bored of talking with him. And she wouldn't, it was just that talking *to* him had taken some getting used to. Some nights she was better at it than others. She'd learned to plan ahead, to think through the things she wanted to tell him. There was less silence that way, and she felt like she was doing something that might help.

Cassie reached Devon's room and was surprised to find the door ajar. Her heart. Devon rarely had other visitors. His parents had both passed away, his sister lived back east, and the doctors on staff should have all gone home for the evening.

Cassie paused, anxious to find out what was going on, though her mind was already racing with expectation. Something must have happened. It had to be good. She'd have had a call if it wasn't. No medical team consulted in the hall. There wasn't a crash cart, though she wouldn't have seen one of those anyway, even if something had gone wrong. Last year, after he'd had a particularly bad infection that sent him to the ICU, she'd made the difficult decision to sign a "do not resuscitate" order.

She had vowed to do everything she could to bring Devon back from where he was, but if he took a turn for the worse, if his physical condition declined rapidly again, she wasn't going to subject him to more painful intervention.

But that's not going to happen. Something good was. Maybe it already had. Cassie stepped through the doorway to find a lone woman wearing pale pink scrubs standing at the foot of the bed, a slim laptop in her arms, which she looked at periodically when taking her eyes from Devon.

A neurologist at last? It seemed an unusual hour for a visit from a doctor, but Cassie couldn't think of who else the woman might be. Was it possible? Cassie was afraid to even hope that her repeated petition to the state had at last been granted. She'd been requesting a neurological evaluation yearly, near the anniversary of Devon's accident, since he'd been at Sierra. Each time, her request had been denied. Maybe this time someone with a heart had happened upon her request, someone who felt as she did, that the $145,000 to have Devon's brain evaluated and a course of therapy prescribed was worth it, that all hope was not lost.

Devon had served the people of Sacramento and California well during his three years on the police force. Couldn't they serve him now in return, and give him a better chance than they had, sending him off to Sierra for little more than custodial care? He didn't need a custodian. He needed a doctor, a specialist, who knew how to help patients with severe brain trauma. Maybe at last that doctor was here.

"Hello." Cassie walked farther into the room and looked closely at Devon, eyes closed—not uncommon for this time of night—limbs unmoving, breathing even. Her gaze shifted to the machine on the other side of the bed. The steady bleep of the monitor always comforted her, though she longed for the day when he wouldn't need one anymore.

"Hello, Cassandra. It's so nice to finally meet you."

Cassie returned the greeting with a tentative smile as she crossed the room.

"Have we met?" she asked, thinking it odd that the

woman had addressed her so informally, given that they were strangers. *Maybe she's the doctor who read my letter.* She always poured her heart out in those petitions, hoping that sharing their story and reminding the recipient of the person Devon was and could be again might prompt the decision maker to act on his behalf. If this woman had read the letter, she might certainly feel they weren't strangers.

Cassie set the Ikeda's bags beside the pictures of her and Devon and her and Noah on the otherwise empty nightstand, then turned to face the woman as she closed her laptop and set it on the foot of the bed. Her dark eyes appeared somber as she walked forward, her hand extended.

Cassie accepted it warily. On closer inspection, the woman did not look anything like Cassie imagined a neurologist might. She'd always imagined someone young, who hadn't been practicing too long, but had gone through residency recently enough to know of all the cutting-edge research and therapies for brain injury patients. This woman, if she was a doctor, had probably gone to school decades earlier.

Not that she couldn't be just as good, just as up to date, as someone half her age, Cassie told herself. But something about the woman didn't seem to match with the scrubs she wore. She didn't even look like a nurse, or at least the ones who worked at Sierra. Cassie couldn't guess her age, but the soft, delicate skin of the woman's hands and the creases on her face dictated that she was too old to be working in a facility where life and death walked a fine line and emergencies were a constant.

She wasn't exactly frail but neither did she look like the type who could lift many of the patients, as nurses here often did to perform basic care routines. Her mostly dark hair was swept back into a stylish bun with an antique, pearl-embedded comb helping to hold it in place. Crow's feet lined the corners of almond eyes that seemed to be taking Cassie in as well, and the woman's perfectly manicured brows rose, as if assessing her.

"Are you new here?" Cassie had thought she was at least acquainted with all of the employees.

"Oh no. I've been in this area for quite some time." The woman's gaze grew almost tender. "Though I was away for a while recently, visiting Sisters, Oregon. Lovely little town."

"Were you a doctor there as well?" Cassie asked, wishing the woman, whoever she was, would either explain her presence or leave her alone so she could spend what was left of visiting hours with Devon.

"Not exactly, though you could say that I've helped mend a heart or two."

"You're a cardiologist?" Cassie's eyes flickered to the laptop on Devon's bed, then up to his monitors again. There was nothing wrong with Devon's heart, was there?

"I'm not a cardiologist." The woman shook her head. "But I do like to help people. Please, call me Pearl." High cheekbones lifted with her kind smile.

"You're here because you think you can help my husband?" Cassie pressed her lips together to hold back the barrage of hopeful questions she wanted to ask. *This is it, the premonition I felt earlier.*

Pearl hesitated a moment before responding. "I *can* help him, though not in the way that you desire me to."

"What do you mean?" Cassie asked, not at all liking the sound of that. She wanted Devon to wake up and begin to be himself again. What other way *was* there to help him?

"He is trapped." Pearl swept her arm gently over the bed. "Your husband is not dead, yet he is not among the living either."

Cassie felt her throat thicken as she nodded. "I know. He needs to wake up. Can you help him?" Her hope of a moment ago was fading fast, and in its place a new trepidation moved in. Something about this doctor, or nurse or whatever she was, seemed off.

"I am only a human being," Pearl said, "and a healer of hearts, not minds. Devon wants to be released from the prison his body has become. He wishes to be free."

"Can he be?" Cassie stepped closer to Devon's bed, near enough to touch his arm and feel that his skin was warm. Perhaps Pearl meant that he would be different when he awoke, that he would not be the same man he had been. Cassie knew this was a very real possibility, but just as she refused to believe he would never wake up, she refused to believe that Devon couldn't find himself again once he did wake up.

"Can he be free?" Cassie asked once more. *I am ready and willing to meet the new Devon and to help him remember the old.*

Pearl's eyes sought Cassie's and held them, searching in a way that discomfited. It was as if the woman had access to her very thoughts.

"The power to free him lies within you, and only you. Devon lingers on Earth because your heart calls to him to stay. If you would release him, he would go and find peace at last."

"You mean he would *die?*" Cassie's voice rose as she took a step backward. "What are you? Some kind of advocate for euthanasia? You don't even work here, do you? How did you get in?"

"I am at work right now," Pearl said firmly, though empathy still tinged her words. "And no, I am not and have never been in favor of so-called mercy killing under any circumstances. To do so would be to dishonor our ancestors and God." She retrieved her laptop from the end of the bed but did not open it again. "I am not discussing any procedure, medical or otherwise, that would end your husband's life."

Cassie sank onto the edge of Devon's bed, wanting to find relief in this statement but not quite believing it. She took Devon's hand in her own and lifted it to her, pressing their joined hands close to her heart.

"When a love is strong, as yours and Devon's, there is an almost tangible connectivity between hearts." Pearl's voice had softened, and when Cassie dared to look at her again, she saw only sympathy in the older woman's eyes. "No doubt you've heard of elderly couples who pass away within days of one another. Their hearts literally cannot survive without each other. Such beauty in a love that deep." Pearl's gaze turned inward, her lips half curving in a melancholic smile. "Your love and Devon's love is strong, as evidenced by his lingering this long, but it is not *that* strong. You haven't had fifty years together, and for the last five years, your heart has been divided, split between your love for Devon and love for Noah."

"How do you know about my son?" Still clasping Devon's hand, Cassie pushed off the bed and stood.

"I know that you love him dearly and that you would never leave him." Pearl searched Cassie's eyes once more. " I know that the two of you can have every happiness in the future."

"We're happy now," Cassie said, growing more agitated by the minute. It was obvious this woman wasn't a neurologist or a visiting specialist offering a miracle. She had no business being here, intruding into her, Devon's, and Noah's lives. "If you'll excuse me, I have only an hour to visit with my husband tonight, and I'd like to do that in private."

"Visiting schedules have changed for today," Pearl said. "It was on the notice at the nurses' station in the hallway."

"No one said anything." Cassie placed Devon's hand carefully back on the bed and moved toward the doorway, intending to check out this notice. Hours never changed, and even if they had, immediate family were always allowed in to be with their loved ones, day or night. She only needed to check in and get a bracelet, showing she'd been cleared to stay. The few times she'd done that, they'd given her the paper bracelet but never made her put it on. It wasn't as if they didn't know her well after all this time.

"The staff did not know I was coming," Pearl said. "I find it better to get a true assessment of a situation if I arrive unannounced."

An auditor or inspector? Cassie knew that both insurance companies and health providers sent representatives several times a year to make sure patients were being properly cared for. Was Pearl one of those? "Do you work for Kaiser or Sutter?"

Pearl smiled and answered vaguely. "Yes. I work for those higher up."

She can't or won't tell me.

"If you would like to return tomorrow, you will find visiting hours as they were previously."

"I would like to stay *tonight*." Cassie inclined her head toward the bags on the nightstand. "Friday evenings are my time with my husband. I have to arrange a babysitter, and I always bring dinner."

"Yes, I know." Pearl's mouth compressed in a straight line, and she folded her arms in front of her. "Cassandra, you and I both know that Devon is not going to eat one bite of that sandwich you brought him."

"He might smell it," Cassie said defensively. "Sensory

stimuli is important for brain injury patients. You never know what might trigger a reaction, signaling the mind to wake up." Doctors had told her as much, shortly after the shooting. They'd also told her chances of that happening were slim, especially after Devon moved from a coma to a vegetative state, but a chance was a chance. As long as there was any possibility for Devon, she wasn't going to give up on him.

"He's had the opportunity to smell those sandwiches for six years," Pearl said, her voice quiet. "And you've played his favorite songs so many times you almost can't stand them anymore." Her gaze drifted to Cassie's phone sticking out of her pocket. "It's time for you to try something else, to allow what should have happened six years ago to happen now. It's time to let go."

"I'm getting security." Cassie strode toward the door. "I don't care who you work for. You don't have any right to talk to me like that, to imply—" She didn't bother to finish her sentence but marched out to the hall to the nearest nurse's station. Veronica and Lynn should be working. They knew how much she loved Devon, that she'd do anything for him. They would help her get rid of the crazy woman in his room.

The nurses' station was vacant, and just as Pearl had said, a plastic-encased notice stood front and center, proclaiming that visiting hours, for this evening only, had been altered.

In all Devon's years here, this had never happened, nor could Cassie recall when at least one nurse hadn't been at the desk. She walked farther down the hall, peeking into partially opened doors, listening for familiar voices, but none came. She circled the floor, found the front desk unattended as well, and returned to Devon's room. A security guard she'd never seen before stood in the hall, his arms crossed over his uniformed shirt, the gun at his hip reminding Cassie painfully of Devon dressed in his PD uniform. Pearl waited for her in the doorway.

"Your dinner is getting cold." She held out the bags and shake cup. Cassie snatched them from her and tried to step past Pearl into the room.

"Search your heart, Cassandra." Pearl moved surprisingly fast and efficiently for someone her age. Though her frame was tiny, she managed to block the entire wide doorway. "Open yourself to other possibilities, and I promise that both you and Noah will be blessed with much happiness, joy, and love."

"I have love," Cassie insisted as she blinked rapidly, furious that this woman had brought her to tears.

"Then use it," Pearl advised, "and free your husband from his prison. You can keep him trapped in that bed another six years or longer, or you can tell him he is free to move on, and then *you* can move on." She stepped backward into Devon's room, her hand on the door handle to pull it closed.

"Wait," Cassie pled. "Please let me sit with him. I won't make a sound. I won't interrupt your work."

Pearl shook her head. "I'm sorry. I can't do that." Her lips pursed, then seemed to soften as she studied Cassie's face. "The hospital cafeteria next door is a nice place to eat. They have a microwave you could use to heat your dinner. Why don't you wait there for an hour and come back after that. You can visit with Devon then."

"I—"

"Or Mike can escort you to the lobby." Pearl inclined her head toward the guard. "I'm sure he wouldn't mind."

"No." Cassie managed to turn from the door. Leaving wasn't what she wanted, but at least she would be able to see

Devon in an hour, after Pearl left, and to reassure herself he was okay. She didn't like the woman or the cryptic way she spoke. Cassie wiped tears from the corners of her eyes as she walked down the hall, promising herself that she would find out who Pearl worked for, and at the least she would report the woman for her inappropriate and curt bedside manner.

The front desk was still deserted, so Cassie left Sierra, assuming that other inspectors must be overseeing patient care in other rooms. Perhaps the regular nurses were accompanying them, or maybe they'd been asked to leave, too. Maybe something had gone wrong with one of the patients, and the care center was under investigation. She'd always felt that Devon was treated well there. No one was doing anything to help him get better, but at least she'd known he was adequately being watched over. But what if there was cause for concern? She wished she knew what was going on.

If only I'd arrived earlier.

If I'd just come straight from Mom's.

If only—Cassie stopped herself mid-thought. This was a game she knew better than to play, because every single "if only" always circled back to a single one.

If only Devon had never been hurt.

Nine

Asher's hand hovered over a bowl. "Can I get Jello?"

"Go ahead," Matt said, grateful that at least one of the boys was happy with the dinner selection. Cassie's fries hadn't satisfied them for long. They'd begun whining about two seconds after he'd dropped her off, so he'd decided to feed them at the first available place. He'd spotted it as he did a U-turn in the Sierra Long-Term Care Center parking lot, and the hospital cafeteria sign came into view.

"Two Jellos?" Asher asked, his hand already reaching again.

"One." Matt slid the tray forward before Asher could take a second bowl. A few feet behind them, Austin was dragging his feet, scowling at all of the salads on the other side of the glass. How Jenna had ever gotten that kid to eat any vegetables or fruit was beyond Matt. He really wished he'd paid more attention to what and how she'd cooked that the boys liked. He wished he'd paid more attention to a lot of things.

Live and learn, his mother had said to him on more than a few occasions in his life. Living with the regret that he hadn't been as good a husband and father as he could have or should have been was particularly painful. The lessons were difficult, made more so because Matt knew he deserved every single frustrating moment that came his way, but maybe tonight he'd get away with minimal frustration and would only have to pay the usual daily price of self-recrimination late into the night while in bed alone.

Matt moved past the boys to the soda fountain near the checkout. He filled a large cup with coke, knowing, but not really caring, that the caffeine wouldn't exactly help his sleep issues.

"Fried chicken and mashed potatoes!" Asher's happy voice carried over to the cash registers. Matt turned around to see him eagerly pulling the entrée toward his already crowded tray. "Just like Mom's."

"No, they're not, stupid!" Austin stomped on Asher's foot. Asher yelled, and his knee jerked up and caught the edge of the tray, flipping it toward his brother.

Matt's three strides weren't fast enough to stop the Jello, fruit, and mashed potatoes from plastering the front of Austin's shirt. "Boys!" He set his coke on Austin's tray, then separated them, holding each by an arm.

"They're not like Mom's. Nothing is like Mom's," Austin shouted. Asher was howling, his mouth open so wide Matt could see his tonsils.

"That's enough," he said sternly, wishing, not for the first time, that he could simply disappear from that moment, from life. Austin seemed hell bent on humiliating him in public, and Asher cried about everything. Matt supposed he ought to be used to these scenes by now, but the awkward silences and judging glares from those around them got to him every time.

Still holding onto the boys, he steered them toward the closest booth, one near the door, for a quick getaway if things got worse. At the very least, he had to go back to pay for the food they'd just wasted, and if they left, he'd still have to take them somewhere else for dinner. With the extra soccer game this evening, he hadn't had time to go grocery shopping, and there wasn't much at the apartment besides overripe bananas.

With more force than was probably necessary, he sat the boys on opposite sides of the table. "Don't move. Don't talk." He made eye contact with each and felt a swell of guilt for being stern with Asher when this was clearly not his fault. The tear-filled eyes of his youngest demanded that he do something to fix the situation, so Matt crouched at Asher's height and gave him a quick hug. "I'm not mad." *At you.* "I'll get you some more Jello."

He hardly trusted himself to look at Austin again but tried to focus on the pain he'd heard in Austin's words. *Nothing is like Mom's.* Of course it wasn't. This wasn't even close, but it was the best he could do right now, and he wished Austin could accept it.

Matt stood and took a step to the other side of the table. He perched on the edge of the seat beside Austin. "Hurting your brother isn't going to bring Mom back. Asher was just being grateful that there was something here he liked to eat."

"There's nothing here I like to eat." Austin folded his arms in front of him on the table and buried his head.

"Then I won't get you anything," Matt said, striving to keep his voice calm. "You can have a peanut butter sandwich at home." He was pretty sure that, along with the black bananas, there were a couple of bread heels left. He walked away from the table before Austin could come up with anything else nasty to say.

So much for $500 a month for counseling. Matt couldn't see that they'd had any benefit from that yet. Unless the therapist was telling Austin to express his anger with his dad in the most public places he could, that is.

Matt apologized to the cafeteria worker who'd already come around the counter to clean up what food hadn't made it onto Austin's shirt and had fallen to the floor. He grabbed a fistful of napkins near the register and bent to help the woman wipe up the red Jello, strawberries, grapes, and mashed potato concoction. *My wife died,* he wanted to explain to her. *My boys are hurting, and I'm not so great at this dad gig.* Instead he remained silent, imagining the things she was likely thinking about him.

When the mess was as cleaned up as it could be without an actual mop, he retrieved Austin's tray—still empty except for the Coke—then added everything Asher had selected to it, including two little bowls of red Jello. Because the kid deserved what happiness and pleasure he could derive from their miserable existence.

He paid for everything—twice—then returned to the booth and the forlorn figures hunched over the table on each side. "Your dinner, Sir Asher." They'd read a book about castles and knights a few days ago and had been pretending like that ever since.

After a second's hesitation, Asher's face brightened. "Thank you, oh page." He giggled. Matt gave an internal sigh of gratitude. The kid was like a light switch. Laughter turned on as easily as tears.

"Want one of my Jellos?" Asher held out a bowl toward his brother in what Matt thought was a gallant gesture of an olive branch, considering Asher wasn't the one who'd committed the offense. Austin shook his head. Asher shrugged and dug into his own red squares.

If only we were all as quick to forgive and move on. Matt learned a lot from his kids every day. He wished he'd taken the time to observe and learn sooner. He leaned back against the booth seat and watched Asher move on from the Jello to his mashed potatoes. They didn't look half bad. He should have bought some for himself. Matt wondered vaguely if there were enough bread heels at home for two peanut butter sandwiches. With Austin in such a volatile mood, he didn't dare leave the boys at the table again to grab something.

As he leaned forward to take a drink of his soda the cafeteria door opened. *Cassie.* He sat up in surprise. *Mrs. Webb,* he silently corrected himself. He'd tried not to think of her all week, and when that was unsuccessful, he'd tried to at least focus on her married status. Driving her to meet her husband for their date—during his break at work or something, Matt assumed—had helped remind him of Cassie's unavailable status. At the moment, that didn't matter. The woman he'd dropped off less than twenty minutes ago was standing inside the cafeteria doorway looking lost. This was a different Cassie, one who appeared almost disoriented and was definitely not her usual, confident self. She still held the Ikeda's bag clutched to her chest, the paper cup she'd had earlier in her other hand.

Matt's heart gave a little lurch of distress and an awful hope at the same time. Had her husband done something? Sent her away for some reason? *I'm such a louse.* He shouldn't even think it, yet wasn't the fact that Cassie stood there *alone* a few feet away, evidence that something about her date had gone horribly wrong?

Her gaze traveled the room slowly, starting on the side opposite their booth. Matt wondered what she was searching for, and by the time her tear-filled eyes landed on him, he'd already made the decision to help her find it, whatever it was.

He was halfway out of his seat before she opened her mouth to speak and at her side, hands shoved in his pockets, when she managed to choke out an awkward, "Hello."

"We need to stop meeting like this," Matt quipped, attempting to lighten a bit of her burden, whatever that might be. "You with your car broken down, me with my kids covered in potatoes." He inclined his head toward the booth, where Austin still sat sullenly and with a healthy portion of Asher's meal choices smeared across his shirt. Asher turned to grin at them, showing off the leftover strawberries and potatoes clinging to either side of his mouth.

"There's supposed to be a microwave here," Cassie said, hardly looking at Matt or the boys but continuing to search the room. "Our food is cold."

Of course she could only be referring to the meal belonging to her and her husband. Matt felt his ire rise on her behalf as he wondered if the guy was some kind of jerk who'd sent her over to warm up his dinner—a prima donna, workaholic doctor who ignored his wife and thought he was better than he was. *Like I used to. Takes one to know one.* Why was it always so easy to see the shortcomings in others before his own? Regardless of her husband's issues, it wasn't Cassie's fault their car had broken down and she'd been delayed.

"I think the microwave is over by the drinks." Matt nodded that direction. He was pretty sure he'd seen one tucked in the corner when he was getting his Coke.

"Thanks." Cassie walked across the room, leaving him standing there alone, feeling once more as if everyone was staring at him. He returned to the booth and slid back into the seat beside Asher and tried not to watch or think about Mrs. Webb. So she'd helped him with Austin last week. He'd just given her a ride tonight. They were even, right?

Except he didn't want to be even. He wanted to know more about her, like what had upset her between the time he'd dropped her off and a minute ago when she'd walked through the cafeteria door. Worse, he not only wanted to know, he wanted to fix whatever it was.

Matt pulled a napkin from the dispenser and dipped it in Asher's water glass. "Are you sure you're my son?" he joked as he turned to Asher and began wiping the leftovers from his face.

"Is this seat taken?" Cassie stood next to their booth, looking down at Austin, who merely shrugged in answer to her question.

"Do you mind if I join you?" This time it was Matt she addressed. Their eyes met briefly, and he saw that she was struggling to push past whatever had upset her. He was only too happy to help.

"Please do."

She slid in beside Austin. "So, how's the food? I've never eaten here."

"There's nothing I like," Austin grumbled. "Dad promised us burgers."

"Ah." Cassie's eyes widened in understanding as she glanced between the boys and Matt. "Because of me you didn't get your hamburger."

"That's not it at all," Matt hurried to reassure her. The last thing he wanted was to make her feel worse.

"Sure it is." She attempted a lopsided smile, then bent her head toward Austin. "How about if you share half of mine?"

"You don't have to do that," Matt insisted even as Austin perked up at the suggestion. "The boys already ate your fries," Matt reminded them both.

"I'm not very hungry tonight." She opened the bag,

removed a burger, and unwrapped it. Matt's stomach reacted to the aroma, reminding him he'd hoped for one, too.

"Seeing as Austin doesn't have dinner, but I do"—Cassie split the burger in half—"and I need someone to eat with, I think it's a fair trade. What do you say, Austin?"

"Yes." He nodded and eagerly accepted his half. Cassie bit into hers, and they shared a smile. "Food is always better when shared."

"I tried to share my Jello," Asher said.

"I can tell." A genuine smile lit Cassie's face as her gaze shifted to the front of Austin's shirt.

Matt felt almost grateful for his earlier humiliation if it was taking her mind from her troubles now. He rolled his eyes and gave her what he hoped was an, "I'll explain later," look.

"What did *you* eat?" she asked suddenly as she stared at the empty table space in front of him.

"I'm going to grab something at home." Those bread heels were really calling him. "The boys were hungry, so we stopped here before it could get any later. I wasn't sure if all the other places in Auburn were going to be as slammed as Ikeda's or what."

"Depends." Cassie said. "Weekends do tend to be worse. Auburn could use more restaurants."

"Maybe," Matt said, "but it already seems about as big as it can get while maintaining its small-town feel."

Cassie didn't reply but instead seemed to be considering something as her gaze shifted from Matt to the bag in front of her. Her top teeth rested on her bottom lip, as if she was weighing a heavy decision. Matt worried he'd said something that circled back to whatever was troubling her.

"Here." She thrust the bag at him suddenly. "Have this. It's the best Philly Cheesesteak you'll ever eat." Her cheeks were flushed while the rest of her alternately appeared to be draining of color, starting at her forehead and moving down.

"No thanks." Matt pushed the bag back across the table. "I'm not going to eat your husband's food." *Even if he deserves something like that.*

"It will just be wasted then," Cassie said, "because Devon can't eat it."

Can't or won't? I was right. Matt's thoughts alternated between feeling angry at this unknown husband to feeling secretly grateful to be the lucky one who happened to be in the right place at the right time to play the hero.

"Maybe Noah's dad just wants a hamburger, too," Asher said.

Noah's dad. Asher's words had an immediate effect, like a bucket of ice water dumped over Matt, cooling the part of his brain that had leapt into action at her distress. So what if Cassie and her husband had fought? Married couples did sometimes. He and Jenna had. But it never meant anything. He supposed that for most couples it usually didn't. And in Cassie's situation, it *couldn't.* She and Devon were parents. There was a child involved. Matt recognized quickly that the very best thing he could do for her was to take his boys and get out of there as fast as possible. He had no right to be interested in her. It wouldn't help her at all, but could potentially only hurt them both.

"Noah's dad would probably love a hamburger," Cassie said. Matt caught the tears welling in her eyes once more before she looked down at the table. "But he can't eat those either. He doesn't eat anything anymore. His feeding tube provides what he needs."

What? Matt heard his own, sharp intake of breath. The care center. Of course. She'd never said what her husband did. He wasn't at work at all.

"What's a feeding tube?" Austin asked, interested enough that he'd refrained from taking another bite before speaking.

"It's one of the things that keeps a person alive when he is very sick." Cassie had composed herself enough to look up at all of them.

"What kind of sick?" Austin asked, his face turned to Cassie. "Is it chickenpox? My friend had that, and he got them on his tongue, and he couldn't eat either, except for ice cream."

"It's not chickenpox." Cassie shook her head sadly. "Noah's dad's condition is called PVS."

"I know what that is," Asher said, surprising Matt, and Cassie as well, he could see from her confused frown.

"I watch that channel on TV," Asher continued. "But how can someone be in it? And why does it make him sick?"

A sad smile lifted the corners of Cassie's mouth, but just barely. "You mean P*B*S—Public Broadcasting Service. We watch that channel at our house, too. But P*V*S is something different. It means that someone's brain is asleep and has been for a very long time."

"Oh," Asher said while Austin's brow furrowed as he seemed to grasp the severity of this explanation. "It isn't exploded like our Mom's brain?"

Matt winced and wished for the hundredth time that his teenage nephew had used a little more care when speaking about Jenna's aneurysm. "No. It just means that the person is asleep. Noah's dad is still alive, but he can't eat hamburgers or talk to Noah or play soccer with him right now."

Cassie nodded without looking up. Matt noted her half burger on the wrapper, mostly untouched.

Asher leaned his head against Matt's arm. "That's not fair," he said, his voice solemn, then almost instantly he perked up. "Noah could borrow you sometimes. Like when we played soccer."

"Yeah," Austin said, completely surprising Matt. "We don't mind sharing our dad."

Cassie's hand covered her mouth when she looked up at them again. "That is so kind of you boys. So generous—" A tear slid down her cheek, and she hastily wiped it away as Matt averted his gaze.

"I don't usually cry," she said. "I've been doing this so long now. Six years—"

"*Six.*" *Years?* He'd barely made it six months on his own. His admiration for her grew as the realities of what she'd said sunk in. Noah couldn't even know his father. They'd never played ball together or read a bedtime story or done any of the things he took for granted each day with his boys. Matt reached an arm around Asher and hugged him close while gazing tenderly at Austin. After Jenna died, he'd promised himself that he wouldn't take those he loved for granted anymore. Yet it seemed he was doing it again, in spite of his good intentions.

"It's just that there was this woman there tonight, and she said some things . . ." Cassie shook her head as if to shake off whatever those things were. "I am completely ruining your dinner. I am so very sorry." She passed the bag across to Matt once more. "Please, I really would like you to have this. It's the least I can do for keeping you from eating out."

"It wasn't for you?" Matt asked, wanting the sandwich less and less.

Cassie pressed her lips together and glanced away again. "It wasn't for me. It was silly. Cheesesteak is Devon's favorite. It's what he always used to order, so I bring one every Friday—you know, just in case." She shrugged. "I told you it was—"

"It's not." Matt reached his hand across the table to cover hers, realizing after the fact what he was doing. *Too late now.* Besides he was only offering comfort. He'd touch his sister or his mother the same way. Only Cassie's hand didn't feel like his mother's or sister's. It was small and soft and warm beneath his, and when his fingers curved sideways over her palm, she didn't pull back but returned his gesture with a slight movement of her own.

That simple act, the pressure of her hand against his, stirred up a pool of emotion he'd not expected. *Nearly nine months since I've held Jenna's hand.* He'd missed that, had missed the affection between them as much as he missed their physical intimacy. Sure, the boys hugged him and climbed all over him each day, but this was different. Holding Cassie's hand was more than pleasant. It soothed yet made him yearn for something more at the same time.

Who's supposed to be comforting who? he reminded himself sharply as those yearnings began to surface.

"It's not silly at all," Matt said. "Hope never is."

Cassie gave a shaky sigh. "That's what I've always thought, but this woman tonight—she pretty much told me I need to stop hoping."

"Did she tell you how you're supposed to go on without that? Because I can tell you from experience it's rough."

"I'm sure you can." Their eyes met, her brown ones still swimming with unshed tears, his trying to convey the dozen thoughts running through his mind. *I had no idea. I'm so sorry. You hold it together amazingly well. It must be so hard.*

"What happened to your husband?" he heard himself asking, then wanted to kick himself the second the words left his mouth.

Cassie's gaze shifted to the boys, then back to Matt. "There was an—incident. Devon worked for the Sacramento

PD." She didn't say more, but Matt could guess the rest, and he didn't want her to restate or relive the details. He imagined she did enough of that on her own already. She pulled back, and Matt moved his hand so she could withdraw hers to her side of the table. He felt her emotional withdrawal with the movement, too. She hugged her arms to herself as if cold. He felt like doing the same after losing the warmth of her hand.

"Don't let that what happened tonight upset you," he advised. "If your husband has hung around this long, there must be a reason. Bringing him his favorite sandwiches and keeping your date night like you do isn't doing any harm. I think it's pretty great." He liked to think he would have done the same for Jenna if given the chance.

Matt opened the Ikeda's bag, ready to move on to a lighter subject and sensing that Cassie wished to as well. "Let's see if it this cheesesteak has anything on the one I had *in* Philly a couple years back."

"What were you in Philadelphia for?" Cassie asked, likely expressing more interest than she really felt. He imagined her grasping onto any normal or mundane topic right now like a life raft. He'd done the same himself a number of times in the past months. Anything to get the mind off of reality for even a few minutes and avoid being emotional in front of others.

"My job. Before coming here, I worked for the Portland Trail Blazers. We had a game against the 76ers at the Wells Fargo Arena in Philadelphia."

"What did you do for the Trail Blazers?"

Too much. "Sportscasts, interviews. Things like that." A year ago he would have happily bragged about his position. He'd been proud of it. Traveling with the team and being in the booth at the games was a big deal. *He* was a big deal. Or so he'd thought, when really he'd been missing the real deal right at home. Matt peeled back the wrapper and took a bite of the lukewarm sandwich. "Mmm."

"Mmm as good as in Philly, or mmm better?" Cassie propped her elbows on the table and leaned forward expectantly, seeming more like her usual self. He felt glad to be distracting her.

He held his hand out, palm wavering. "Pretty close. I think this sauce may be better." He took a drink of his Coke. "What about you? Have you traveled much?"

"Nope." Cassie shook her head. "Elementary school secretaries don't really need to leave the county, let alone the state."

"You're going to Legoland," Asher said. "Noah told me."

"Did he?" Cassie said as she looked at the boys. "I think Noah would *like* to go to Legoland, but elementary school secretaries also don't make a lot of money for travel either."

"He said when he loses more teeth and scores some goals you can go," Asher said. "Can we do that, too, Dad?"

"We'll see," Matt said noncommittally.

"That means no." Austin had finished his burger and seemed to be returning to his former, bad mood.

Now would be a good time to leave before something else happened, but Matt found himself not wanting to go just yet. He wanted to make sure Cassie was going to be all right. He wondered how she'd get home, since her car was broken down miles away and her husband couldn't exactly drive her.

"We'll see means just that," Matt said to Austin. "It means we have to see how much it would cost and then save our money, and I would have to get vacation days off. When we've figured those things out, then we would be able to go." It wasn't a half-bad idea actually. Maybe he'd take the boys for Christmas. It would be better than staying at home and missing all of the things Jenna used to do during the holidays.

"Thanks, Dad," Asher said, ever appreciative.

How did I merit such a great kid? Matt glanced across the table at Austin. *And such a stubborn one?* The answer was obvious, and he needed to quit thinking in those terms. Asher was more like Jenna, whereas Austin . . . *is more like me.*

"I should go now." Cassie rewrapped her uneaten food and picked up her cup. "They'd changed visiting hours on me, but in a few minutes I should be able to get in to see Devon."

"How will you get home after that?" Matt asked. There weren't exactly dozens of taxis to be found in Auburn.

"I'll call my mom," Cassie said. "Noah is at her house, and she can take us home."

"Or," Matt suggested. "I could wait for you, and the boys and I could drive you both home." If he found out where she lived, he could get her car there tomorrow.

She bit her lip, clearly hesitating. "You've already gone to so much trouble."

"No trouble," he said. "Friday nights are a little lonely at our place. It's actually good for the boys and me to be out doing something. We need to run to the store tonight anyway." Bread heels and mushy bananas weren't going to cut it for breakfast tomorrow morning. "We'll go shopping, then come back to get you. Would that be okay?"

"If you're sure—"

"Positive." He stood and started gathering the remnants of their dinner onto the tray as Cassie slid from the booth. "When would you like us to be back?"

She pulled her phone out of her purse and glanced at it. "Would forty-five minutes be too long?"

"Not at all." That was more time than he'd spent at a grocery store thus far, but maybe a longer trip would save him having to go every other day. Jenna had managed to go only every other week, and he had no idea how she'd pulled that off. No matter what he bought, the boys seemed to devour it within a few hours.

"Thank you. I really appreciate it." She gave him a sad smile that didn't reach her eyes or come close to conveying anything near to happiness.

"You're welcome." Matt leaned forward, helping Asher from the booth. *My pleasure.* Or something like that anyway. Helping Cassie was taking his mind off his own problems, and while he certainly didn't delight in having met someone with a worse situation than his own, he also felt filled with purpose for the first time in a while. He could help her—do little things like fixing her car—and in turn that might help him and the boys see past their own misery.

Ironic. On a night her hope was waning, his felt stronger than it had for quite some time.

Ten

Cassie left Matt and his boys and headed back to Sierra. It hadn't been quite the hour Pearl had told her to wait, but Cassie planned to be there a few minutes before, waiting outside Devon's door for the second it opened and Pearl left.

With purpose, she strode through the double glass doors and into the lobby, then down Devon's hall. Lynn was at her usual post at the nurses' station and looked up as Cassie approached.

"Hey, Cassie." Lynn smiled warmly. "You're late tonight. Everything all right?"

Was anything *ever* all right for people visiting loved ones here? "I had car trouble." Cassie held back her sarcasm and her simmering temper. Now that a bit of time had passed since her confrontation with Pearl, Cassie felt her initial hurt turning to anger, but Lynn had been here since that first painful day Devon was transferred from the hospital—the day the doctors gave up on him—and had been nothing but compassionate and competent. She didn't deserve the tirade Cassie intended for Pearl.

"You really need to get a new car," Lynn said. "Don't worry about an after-hours bracelet. Go on down." She waved her hand in the direction of Devon's room.

"Thanks," Cassie said but didn't move. Maybe Lynn could tell her who Pearl was and what she was doing here. "I did have car trouble earlier tonight, but I still managed to get here before visiting hours were over—or were supposed to be. Why were they changed tonight?"

"They weren't." Lynn pushed some papers into a file. She looked up at Cassie again. "Hours never change. Something like that would require notifying all the family and friends who visit, and that would be next to impossible, given the number of patients we have, their contacts, and our constantly changing residents."

"I was here an hour ago, and there was a sign right here on the counter." Cassie pointed to the spot. "It said that visiting hours had been changed, and neither you nor Veronica or any other nurse was to be found at this station or the front one. I know. I walked the halls looking for you, hoping for an explanation or an exception of the changed hours, because she wouldn't let me into Devon's room."

"She?" A pen dangled from Lynn's unmoving fingertips. "Who wouldn't let you in? Are you certain you're all right?" Her face grew concerned. "What kind of car trouble did you have? You're not acting like yourself, Cassie."

"I'm fine, but I'm not all right." Cassie blew out a frustrated breath. "I came to see Devon like I do every Friday night, and none of the staff I knew was around, the posted visiting hours had been changed, and there was a strange woman with Devon in his room. And she told me—"

"What strange woman?" Looking alarmed, Lynn rose

from her seat and came around to the other side of the counter.

"She said her name was Pearl. I thought maybe she was a nurse." Cassie left off the explanation she'd originally believed, that Pearl was the neurologist she'd prayed for. "She was wearing scrubs and sort of implied that she worked for Kaiser or one of the other health insurance companies or providers. There was a new security guard stationed in the hall, too."

"We haven't hired anyone new." Lynn started walking toward Devon's room, and Cassie followed.

"What else did she say? Go on," Lynn urged.

"She made it sound like it was my fault that Devon was still here. That he wanted to be free—to die."

Lynn hastened her steps. "How long ago was this?"

"Almost an hour," Cassie said, feeling panicked. If Lynn didn't know about the strange woman either, then who was she, and what had she been doing in Devon's room? "You don't think—"

"I don't know what to think." Lynn reached Devon's door first and pushed it open. Cassie entered and crossed to his bed.

"He's fine." Lynn let out an audible sigh of relief as she double-checked all of Devon's connections and monitors. "Are you sure about all this, Cassie? A stranger was in here?"

"Positive." Cassie sank into the chair next to the bed. "I tried to find you, or any other nurse to tell you, but no one was around."

"We must have all been with Arnold," Lynn said, flashing an apologetic look at Cassie. "There were a lot of us in his room. Probably none of us realized that no one was manning the station."

"Arnold?" Cassie asked, her heart quickening as she

pictured one of her favorite patients at Sierra. "Ivy's husband, Mr. Leifter?"

Lynn nodded. She sat on the edge of Devon's bed and folded her arms across her middle. "It's been a strange night all around." She glanced up at the clock above the door. "About an hour and fifteen minutes ago the alarm for his room went off. I went to see what had happened—if he'd tripped and fallen over a cord or something—and found that he'd unplugged everything in his room and was sitting in the corner in the dark."

"Poor Mr. Leifter," Cassie murmured. He and his wife Ivy had become residents here about a year after Devon had. Arnold's Alzheimer's had progressively worsened since then but never so bad that he couldn't push Ivy, who had suffered a stroke before coming to Sierra, around the courtyard each day. While Ivy's body was failing, her mind had remained sharp. She'd joked with Cassie on more than one occasion that between her and Arnold, they made one whole person. *But you've got to be two whole people all by yourself for your little boy.* Instead of bemoaning her own situation, Ivy had often kindly inquired over Cassie's. Until two weeks ago when Ivy had suffered a second stroke and passed away.

"Is Mr. Leifter okay?" Cassie asked with concern. Did he miss his walks with his wife? Or did he even notice she was gone? He hadn't spoken at all the past couple of years, something Cassie and Ivy had discussed at length and the common bond that had made them friends. She was the only one who ever really understood what it was like to talk to your husband and know he won't answer, to have him living, but not alive. Cassie had missed Ivy the past couple of weeks, even if her husband hadn't.

Lynn didn't answer directly. "Arnold was sitting in the corner, holding her picture and crying." When we tried to help him back to bed, he kept telling us, "No. Get Ivy. My Ivy."

"He said her name?" Cassie brought a hand to her mouth. "He does remember." Her other hand covered her heart as it hurt for him.

"We got him sedated, then ten minutes later, his alarm went off again." Lynn faced Cassie. "I went down there again, but this time—"

"What?" Cassie leaned closer.

"He'd stopped breathing," Lynn said quietly. "He was still in his bed, still clutching Ivy's picture, but he was gone."

You've heard of elderly couples who pass away within days of one another. Their hearts literally cannot survive . . .

Goosebumps sprang up on Cassie's arms as she recalled Pearl's words. Had she visited Mr. Leifter's room as well? Could she have anything to do with his sudden death?

"I'm sorry, Cassie. I know you were his friend." Lynn stood. "And I'm so sorry about earlier. I have no idea who Devon's visitor might have been. We can file a report if you'd like."

"Please," Cassie said. "In case we can find out who she is. If she does work for Kaiser or someone else, she needs to be reprimanded for the things she said, at the least."

"I'll see what I can find out," Lynn promised. "Auditors and inspectors are supposed to tell us when they're coming, but that isn't always the case. And where Ivy's death is so recent, it is possible they've sent someone. It's not unusual after a patient passes away."

"Thanks for looking into it," Cassie said as Lynn exited the room and closed the door behind her, leaving Cassie alone with Devon and with a feeling of eeriness she didn't usually have here.

She pulled her phone from her pocket and saw that

she'd used twelve of her precious forty-five minutes already. It had been a weird night for sure. It felt like it had gone on forever, yet she hadn't spent any of it with Devon. She remedied that situation at once, getting up and pulling the chair close to his bed, facing him. His eyes were still closed, but she told herself that was a good thing. His body was observing normal sleep patterns, with his eyes opened during daylight hours and closed at night.

"Crazy night around here, Dev." She took his hand in hers and, starting with his index finger, began gently moving it, bending it at the joints. Muscular atrophy was a significant problem for PVS patients, so she did what she could during her visits—little though it was—to help prevent that. Working out had been an important part of Devon's life. When he woke up, he was going to have enough to deal with without the added problem of having to relearn to use his hands. As it was, he'd be devastated when he realized what his once-bulky frame had dwindled to.

Trying not to think about that, Cassie moved each of his fingers purposely as she talked to him. "Noah's lip is almost healed. I'm so glad the doctor didn't recommend stitches. I bet when he gets older we'll hardly be able to see the scar at all." Cassie touched Devon's finger where his wedding band had been. They'd taken it off at the hospital and hadn't wanted her to put it on him since then until he was fully awake and aware again.

"Noah played soccer tonight. He didn't make any goals, but he got in there and played. I was really proud of him. But guess what? He's trying to make goals because I told him I'd pay him a dollar a goal. Lame parenting, I know." Cassie rolled her eyes, as if Devon could see her. "This is why you really need to wake up and help me out. I need someone to consult with before I make these kinds of bad decisions.

Anyway, Noah wants to make goals to earn money so we can go to Legoland."

Cassie moved onto massaging Devon's thumb. She always took extra time with his thumbs since they were such a vital part of hand function.

"They've been running a commercial about Legoland. Noah's the perfect age to visit, but I can't afford to fly, and I don't want to drive all the way to San Diego just the two of us, not in my old car. It's barely making it around town. I know I could take yours, and I know I used to drive all over California by myself, but that was before we had Noah. Now that I'm a mom, I really think about stuff like that—about his safety and mine. So if you could wake up soon, I was thinking we could take him for his birthday next April. That's a good six months away, so you'd have plenty of time for rehab, plenty of time to get those muscles up and running again." She placed Devon's hand on top of the covers then moved from the chair to the side of the bed so she could reach his other hand.

"The Nissan broke down again tonight. I have no idea what's wrong this time. It's ridiculous how much I've spent on that thing this year. I might as well have a car payment. Except if I do, then I won't have money for anything else. I'm going to have to move soon, Dev. I want you to come home to our apartment, to how it was when you left, but the truth is, it's not even that way anymore. Noah needs to live somewhere with other kids nearby. He really likes those boys I told you about last week, the ones he played soccer with. I bet he'd love to have them over, but Noah needs a room of his own. I don't know how much longer we can stay in the apartment. I want to, for you, but you've got to help me out and wake up soon. If you don't . . ." Cassie shrugged. "I don't know."

She wasn't issuing a threat or even stating a fact. The truth was she didn't know what she'd do if Devon didn't wake up soon. Then again, she'd felt that way for six years now. *Six.* She hadn't missed the shock on Matt's face when she'd told him that tonight. She could see he'd wanted to ask her how she'd made it this long. She wasn't sure what she would have told him. She'd just kept going, and she supposed she'd keep muddling through as long as she had to. As long as Devon was hanging in there, so would she.

You can keep him trapped in that bed another six years or longer, or you can tell him he is free to move on.

Cassie's head jerked up, and she turned her body toward the doorway, fully expecting to find Pearl standing there, so clearly had she just heard her voice and earlier advice. The door was still closed.

"I'm not the one trapping him. I didn't do this," Cassie said to no one, starting to feel defensive and hurt and angry all over again.

The power to free him lies within you. And only you.

"That's not true." Cassie leaned her head back, as if talking to God instead of some imagined voice. "I don't know how to wake Devon up. If I did, don't you think I would have done that long ago?"

Devon lingers on Earth because your heart calls him to stay.

"Of course my heart calls him to stay. He's my husband." Cassie thought of poor Mr. Leifter, missing Ivy the last couple of weeks. Someday, when she and Devon were old, one of them would have to say goodbye to the other, and it would be a terrible, awful, sad time. But that time wasn't now. They were young, and they had Noah to raise.

If you would release him, he would go and find peace at last.

"No!" Cassie's goosebumps reappeared as she stood, turning a slow circle in the dimly lit room, making sure no one really was here with them. After all, no one had seen Pearl leave. What if she hadn't? The seldom-used door to the adjoining bathroom caught Cassie's eye, and she crossed quickly to it and pulled it open. Empty. She turned to the floor to ceiling closet next to the sink in the room, then grabbed the double doors and pulled those open as well. Nothing. She didn't feel relieved. Great. Now she was imagining things. She hadn't imagined the entire encounter with Pearl, had she?

Cassie returned to the chair next to Devon's bed. "You know what I worry about most? Aside from you, that is." She sighed heavily. "I worry that something will happen to me— that I'll get sick or hurt or I'll become mentally unstable, like I feel like I might be right now—and then where will Noah be? What will happen to him? So I'm asking you, begging you—" Cassie swallowed back a swell of emotion, determined not to cry anymore tonight. She took Devon's hand again and pressed it to her cheek.

"Wake up and be with us. Wake up soon. Please."

Eleven

In the rearview mirror, Matt could see Austin's face screwed up in confusion.

"So it's kind of like Noah's dad is dead, except he's not?"

"That's a pretty good summary," Matt said, surprised that an hour after their initial conversation with Cassie, Austin was still on this same subject. He'd asked questions—most of which Matt didn't know the answers to—throughout their trip to the grocery store and had continued asking them on the drive back to the care center. A kid-sized snore rumbled from Asher's open mouth as he slept beside Austin in the backseat.

"When do you think Noah's dad will wake up?" Austin unbuckled and leaned forward as Matt pulled into a parking stall in front of the care center.

"I don't know," Matt said. "I don't think his doctors even know."

"But he will wake up, right?" Austin asked, unmistakable concern in his voice.

Matt shut off the engine, unbuckled his own belt, and turned around in his seat. "Why don't you come up here with me, buddy?" *How long has it been since he'd used that term? How long it had been since he and Austin had thought of each other as buddies or treated each other that way?* Matt waited for Austin's rejection but was pleasantly surprised when instead, he clambered head first to the front.

Capitalizing on this unexpected moment and Austin's unusual mood, Matt hurried to help Austin right himself, then put his arm around his son and pulled him close. "Noah's father may never wake up. You know that sometimes brain injuries are like that." There was a world of difference between an aneurysm and what Matt suspected had happened to Devon Webb, but that wasn't easily explainable to a six year-old. A quiet moment passed, Matt wondering the whole time what was going through Austin's mind.

"I feel bad." Austin's voice sounded small and quiet.

"So do I," Matt said, silently applauding the return—temporarily, at least—of the tenderhearted son he used to have. "That's how we're supposed to feel when something sad happens to someone we care about." *And I'm starting to care—a lot.* He shouldn't, he knew. Cassie was still as married as she'd ever been, and he'd learned tonight just how very faithful a wife she was. But that didn't mean he couldn't care for her as a friend, did it?

"I don't just feel bad because I like Noah," Austin said. "I feel bad for what I did to him."

"Ahh," Matt said. *Finally.* He pulled Austin a bit closer. "That's good you feel that way. It means you're a nice person. We're supposed to feel bad when we make a mistake and do something wrong. Hurting people isn't who you really are, and I think you can make it up by not hurting anyone else and by being Noah's friend."

Austin's head fell forward, hair hanging over his face, so Matt couldn't make out his expression. "I pushed Noah because I was mad he had a mom and I didn't. And she was there with him all happy, and I was sad. But now that I know he doesn't got a dad, I kind of want him to push me back."

"Because that would make you feel better?" Now they were getting somewhere. Why hadn't the $125-an-hour therapist figured this out?

Austin gave a solemn nod. Matt answered with one of his own, completely understanding. For months now, he'd expected and almost wished for something truly awful to happen to him. He deserved it for being a less than attentive husband. He should have died instead of Jenna. But life didn't work like that. He felt sorry that Austin, too, wished it did. They were so alike it was frightening. *Poor kid.*

"Do you think you could ask Noah to hit me or something?" Austin looked up at Matt.

"No." Matt shook his head. "Because then *Noah* would feel bad. Doing something mean never makes anyone feel happy."

"Oh." Austin's sigh sounded far too heavy for someone so young.

"But if you want you can help me do some nice things for Noah and his mom, and I promise, *that* will make you feel better." Matt was feeling much improved just from this conversation. He felt truly terrible about Cassie's husband and about all she had been and must still be dealing with and going through, but he also felt, strangely, that her situation was somehow going to make his life and Austin's and Asher's better. It was probably as simple as thinking about someone other than themselves, something he thought he'd have figured out before now.

But apparently he hadn't, basking in misery for the last several months as he had been. He was ready for that to change and believed Austin was, too. Asher didn't need to change; he'd stayed kind and loving all along. Sitting in the dark truck, with his arm around Austin for the first time in weeks, felt really good. Something had happened between them tonight, and Matt felt exhilarated by it.

Before he could contemplate his plans too much, Cassie came out the front doors of the care center. She gave him an appreciative smile as she approached, then opened the passenger door and climbed up into the truck.

"Sorry I didn't get your door for you," Matt said, looking down at Austin, asleep against his side. "We were having a conversation a minute ago. I guess I talked him to sleep."

"I'm sorry it's so late," Cassie said. "It was selfish of me to make you wait."

Matt leaned over Austin, closer to her and only just barely resisting the urge to place his hand over Cassie's on the seat. "Nothing about coming to visit your husband is selfish, but I would have been the biggest codfish alive if I'd have left you here without a ride home."

"Codfish?" She tilted her head, and her mouth quirked in amusement.

"Codfish," Matt reaffirmed. "The boys and I watched *Peter Pan* a couple of days ago, after which Austin pronounced me a worse villain than Captain Hook when I wouldn't let him have donuts for dinner." Matt nudged Austin toward the middle of the seat and pulled a seatbelt around him. "I didn't help the situation much by singing, 'Dad is a codfish' as I served his dinner."

"A plate full of fish and vegetables I suppose," Cassie said.

"Um, yeah." Those breaded things he'd bought were fish sticks, right? And prewashed, ready-to-eat mini carrots were the staple of every meal. He started the truck. "Where to? I don't know a lot of streets yet."

"No problem," Cassie said. "We'll go to my mom's first, then my place is out in the country a bit." She directed him to an older neighborhood with mostly kept-up homes, from what Matt could tell in the dark. He waited, getting out to open the back door for Noah, while she went up to her mom's house to get him. When she left the house carrying him in her arms, Matt hurried up the walk and took Noah from her.

"Thanks," Cassie said, not sounding at all irritated, calming Matt's worry that he'd just overstepped his bounds.

"He's getting heavier," Cassie said. "I'd better start working out more or pretty soon I won't be able to lift him at all."

Matt situated Noah in the backseat while Cassie got in front. As Matt walked around the car to the driver's side, he saw a face peering at him from the part in the curtains at the front window. He thought about lifting his hand to wave but decided against it, in case he wasn't supposed to see that he was being observed.

"It's about twelve minutes from here," Cassie said, directing him to the right road once more. "I really appreciate this. My mom's getting older and really doesn't like to drive at night."

"I'm glad to do it," Matt said, happy to spend a few minutes more in Cassie's presence and to find out where she lived.

"Right here," she said a few minutes later as she pointed to an old barn about a hundred yards off the country road they'd been driving on.

"You live in a barn?" Matt peered through the dark but could see no other buildings.

"On top of it, actually," Cassie said. "Devon found this place for us when we first got married. The rent is cheap, and I was going to school then . . ." Her voice trailed off, and Matt wondered where her thoughts had drifted to as well.

"Let me carry Noah up for you." He turned off the truck and jumped out before she could object. Noah slumped easily into his arms when Matt opened the back door, and he followed Cassie across a dirt yard and up a steep staircase tacked to the side of the barn. After the first few steps, he paused and purposely stayed a few stairs below her to space out their weight because the stairs appeared so rickety. He felt it nothing short of a miracle when they'd safely reached the top.

"Who's your landlord?" Matt asked, eyeing the stairs again.

"Some guy in Sacramento," Cassie said. "He's never been up here since we've lived here that I'm aware of."

"Well he should come," Matt said, "and fix your stairs, at the least." He worried what the inside of the apartment would look like as Cassie unlocked the door.

She stepped inside and turned on a light, and Matt found himself pleasantly surprised. The space seemed in good repair though it was small, tiny really, with room for only a loveseat, round kitchen table, and two chairs. A three-foot countertop and smaller-than-normal stove and fridge lined the far wall past the table.

"This way," Cassie said, flipping on another light. Matt followed her past a bathroom to the only other door that he could see, into a bedroom only slightly larger than the master bath at his previous home.

"Noah sleeps in the loft." She reached up to pull the

covers back so Matt could place Noah beneath them. This he did, then took an extra few seconds to take Noah's shoes off and tuck the blanket up around him. As Matt handed the shoes to Cassie, he took in the rest of the room, a strange combination of little boy and grown woman, with bins of Legos on one side and a jewelry hanger on the other.

"Where do you sleep?" Matt asked, then realized how personal and intrusive the question was. "Sorry. None of my business."

"It's all right." Cassie walked the few steps to the opposite wall and pushed on the lower part of it. The top jutted out, and she reached up and pulled down a bed. "Pretty lame that my son has to share a room with his mom, but for now . . ."

Matt got it, or at least he thought he did. She drove an old car and lived in 500 square feet above a barn. Money was an issue. *But not her biggest one.* He thought of the expression on her face again when she'd told him her husband had PBS, or whatever it was—that he was in a coma. Matt couldn't fix that, but he could fix some other things for her, starting with her car tomorrow.

He suddenly couldn't wait to get over to Ikeda's and pick it up first thing in the morning. He'd jump it with the truck, then drive it over to the auto parts store for a diagnostic, but he'd have to have her keys for that.

"About your car—"

"Ugh." Cassie brought a hand to her head and rubbed her temples. "I'll get it towed over to the mechanic tomorrow morning and deal with it then."

"Why don't you let me tow it instead?" Matt suggested. "I'll get a buddy of mine to help me. My truck can pull it no problem."

"I can't ask you to do another thing," Cassie said.

"You didn't." Matt held out his hand. "I offered. That's completely different. Keys?"

She looked at his hand for a few seconds, then finally went into the other room and retrieved the keys from her purse. "I owe you dinner or something."

"You don't owe me a thing," Matt said. "Because of you, I'm getting my boy back. Whenever we're with you, I see glimpses of the old Austin returning."

"That's great." Cassie leaned against the table, looking tired enough that she might collapse.

"I'll call you tomorrow, and you can tell me where to tow it." Matt headed for the door. With a little luck, he wouldn't have to tow it at all. He and his buddies, Austin and Asher, would be able to take care of the problem themselves.

"Good night." Matt lifted a hand in farewell.

"Good night," Cassie returned.

He closed her door behind him and descended the treacherous stairs. Knowing what he did about Cassie now, he wondered how she could ever say that it was a good night at all.

Twelve

Cassie sat on her bed, staring up at Noah, sleeping peacefully, and thinking about how Matt had so easily lifted him into his loft and then tucked him in. Devon had never had that privilege. Noah had never been tucked in by his dad, and tonight, if Matt hadn't been here to help her, Cassie would have had to wake Noah to get him into his bed.

Such a little thing, yet how it had struck her, and how she appreciated it. She flopped back onto her pillow and closed her eyes, thinking back through the day that had felt like about five years.

The school hours had crawled by. Fridays were always the worst, as children and teachers alike were eager for the weekend. The extra soccer game had been fun but tiring. After that, everything else was a blur. Dropping Noah off at her mom's, Ikeda's, the stupid car, the care center, Pearl, and the things she'd said. Cassie refused to allow them into her mind again, or not tonight at least. But she felt Pearl's words nagging at her and knew at some future point, she'd have to contemplate them at least.

She continued her mental review of the evening. Eating dinner with Matt and his boys, finally visiting with Devon, the news about Mr. Leifter, Matt driving her home and carrying Noah inside.

It seemed almost providential that Matt had been at Ikeda's tonight. Though why shouldn't he have been there? It was the best burger place in town, and as a newcomer, of course he'd probably looked something like that up and wanted to try it for himself. That he'd also been at the hospital cafeteria had simply been a blessing. Just at the point she felt she might lose it, Matt and his wonderful boys had been there to rescue her, to help her regain perspective and keep on going. Because in spite of what Pearl had told her tonight, she still had hope. Matt didn't. He would never again have the opportunity to be here with his wife, to talk to her, wake up next to her, have her beside him to watch their boys play soccer. Cassie couldn't imagine what that kind of loss must be like, or how it would feel if someone took away the hope she felt. She wished there was something she could do for Matt, the way he'd done so much for her tonight. Just listening to her had been such a service.

Her phone vibrated on the nightstand.

Oh, Mom. Cassie reached over and picked it up, having already ignored two calls while she was showering. For some reason she didn't feel like explaining who Matt was to her mom. Though it should have been simple.

He's just a really nice guy. With cute kids and crappy circumstances.

"Hi, Mom." Cassie answered on the third ring, figuring she might as well get this over with. It was 11:30 already, and if her mom hadn't given up on getting an answer tonight, then her curiosity really must be driving her crazy. *No sense in both of us being unable to sleep.*

"Hello, dear," a high pitched voice that was definitely not her mom's squeaked back.

"Who is this?" Cassie demanded as she sat up.

"Um, me—" the high voice said. The caller cleared his throat. "Matt."

"Very funny," Cassie said sarcastically, though she smiled into the phone. "What has you calling so late?"

"I was thinking."

"That's always good," Cassie prompted, her smile widening. "About what?"

"You. Me. Us. What Asher and Austin said at dinner tonight." The last words tumbled out of Matt's mouth, as if he'd wanted to hurry and clarify what his first words had meant.

Cassie was glad. Those first words had sent her heart racing and plummeting at the same time. *There can be no us.* But then Matt had to realize that. He knew she was married. He'd driven her home from visiting Devon tonight, hadn't he?

"Asher and Austin said a few things at dinner. What were you referring to?" Cassie asked, her own tone cautious.

"Well, definitely not the part about watching PBS."

"That was sort of funny," she admitted. "Or it would have been under different circumstances."

"Yeah, I know," Matt said. "I'm sorry. I'm not trying to make light of anything with your husband. I've been thinking about him, actually, and about Noah and about what my boys said about sharing their dad, sharing me. Then I was thinking about the way you really helped them both by allowing us to be a part of your soccer team."

"Sounds like a lot of thinking," Cassie said, still unsure

where he was going with all that. She turned sideways on the bed and lay back, allowing her still-damp hair to hang over the side.

"Well—" Matt paused. "The sharing parents thing is a good idea, for both of us, *all* of us," he clarified. "We could help each other with our boys, if you want to, that is." He sounded suddenly unsure, and Cassie felt an emotion she couldn't quite put a name to as she imagined the expression on his face. He was probably trying to look nonchalant about the whole thing, as he'd attempted when he'd told her that his wife had died. Why did guys always think they had to hide their feelings?

"What I'm trying to say," Matt continued. "Is that, if it's all right with you, I'd like to be friends."

A nugget of warmth stole its way into her heart with his suggestion. That he'd felt the need to formally ask her or to get her approval seemed almost chivalrous. Cassie touched a finger to her lips, as if to contain the tiny bubble of happiness his words had called forth.

"You still there?" Matt asked. "Is that asking too much, the being friends thing, I mean?"

"Not too much at all," Cassie hurried to assure him as the warmth that had begun in her heart overflowed to the rest of her. "In fact, we already are."

Matt pushed Asher's feet aside as he settled on the end of the couch next to his sleeping boys. He'd been carrying both at once when he got home, and it had been easier to deposit them on the sofa than to walk all the way to their bedroom. It didn't appear they were losing any sleep over it.

He opened his laptop, propped it on his knees, and

waited for the internet search bar to appear. As soon as it did, he typed "PVS" and hit "enter."

Potomac Valley Swim Club appeared at the top of the screen. *Nope.* PVS Pest Control. Not that either. He continued to scroll down. Passport and Visa services. PVS Specification and Verification. No and no. Matt didn't know what the latter was about, but it didn't sound like a medical condition. About three fourths of the way down the page, he found what he was looking for. Persistent Vegetative State. He clicked on the link and began reading.

An hour and a half and nine websites later, he leaned his head back and closed his eyes, feeling drained and stressed simply from reading about patients like Cassie's husband. He'd learned that they could breathe on their own but received all nourishment—as Cassie had mentioned—through a feeding tube. They had periods when their eyes were opened and others when they were closed, but a PVS patient's eyes never tracked or followed anything.

Cassie's husband never looks at her anymore, yet he's awake, sort of. How freaky that must be. Matt tried but couldn't quite block the image of Jenna's lifeless body—but with her eyes open, staring past him—that came unbidden to his mind. At least that was something he hadn't had to endure. He couldn't imagine how Cassie coped with that and everything else.

He was shocked to read that there were between one and a half and two million TBI, traumatic brain injury, patients in the United States every year. Most of those were from vehicle accidents, but a few— like Cassie's husband, Matt suspected—were from gunshot wounds.

Closing all but the original page he'd referenced, Matt opened a second window and typed "Officer Webb" into the search bar. Images of several different uniformed men appeared at the top. Matt wondered which, if any, of the men was Cassie's husband. She'd mentioned his name a few times tonight, but Matt couldn't remember what it was now.

He started scanning the articles listed below the photos and was further disturbed to find stories about five different officers with the last name Webb who had each been shot in the line of duty. Four had been killed, but the last, Officer Devon Webb of the Sacramento Police Department, had been shot and critically injured a little over six years ago while responding to a domestic violence call. Matt read the entire article and learned that Devon's partner had been killed during that same call. Another link led to the officer down memorial page for the partner, but Matt couldn't find any additional information on Devon, though this article had been written about two months after the shooting.

Matt stared at Devon's picture on the screen. The fallen officer had pages of accolades and memories written about him, while Devon Webb—still living, but not with any kind of quality of life—seemed pretty much forgotten. Matt hoped, for Cassie's sake, and for Noah's, that the city or state was providing her with some kind of benefits or compensation, and that her husband had been honored in some way for his sacrifice.

He thought about her little apartment, way out on that lonely road and above a rickety barn. Whatever help she was getting, if any, didn't appear to be much. Matt reminded himself that he needed to follow through with paying for Noah's dental bill, and he'd figure out whatever it was that was wrong with her car and get it fixed. He'd do some of the things he should have been doing for Jenna, things he'd done the first few years of their marriage before he'd become caught up in the life of an NBA commentator.

Matt closed his laptop and stretched. He felt tired

enough that he might actually be able to sleep tonight. But he was also filled with purpose. Tomorrow wouldn't just be about getting through another Saturday with the boys. It would be about doing something good for someone, and then having some genuine fun with Austin and Asher. After the soccer game, he'd take them back to Ikeda's to get that burger he'd promised, then maybe they'd go to a park, and after that, he'd take them to get ice cream again. This time, they'd buy chocolates, too.

Thirteen

"Dad, can you pour me some milk?" Something cold and wet touched Matt's arm, and he jerked upright a split second before milk sloshed from the open carton onto his arm and the bed.

"Asher!" Matt jumped up, grabbed the carton from Asher's hand and marched into the kitchen. "Who opened this?" he demanded, staring at the only possible culprit; Austin sat at the table, busily slurping down an overflowing bowl of Cheerios.

"Haven't I told you not to open the milk yourself?" Matt stared at the mangled top of the carton. It looked like someone had taken a chainsaw to it, with a quarter of the side ripped off. If most of the milk hadn't already spilled all over his bed, it certainly would have gone bad, sitting in the fridge, unsealed as this one was.

"You said not to wake you up on Saturdays." Austin jammed the spoon into his mouth again.

"Next time wait for me to get up," Matt grumbled. He crossed to the table and poured what was left of the milk into

Asher's bowl. So much for not going to the store for another week.

"We were hungry," Asher said.

"You're always hungry. That doesn't mean you have to eat breakfast at six a.m." As Matt crossed the kitchen to wash the residue milk from his hand and arm, his eyes strayed to the clock propped against the wall on the counter. Nine fifteen? No way.

He pulled up the blinds covering the window over the sink. Sunlight streamed in, over the apartment building next to theirs, confirming how late he'd slept. *Serves me right.* He let the blinds go and brought a hand up to massage the back of his neck. He supposed this was what he got for staying up, searching the internet half the night. What he'd learned had been important. It—along with his new resolve—came rushing back. Cassie's husband. Cassie. Her car. The soccer game.

He ran to his room to pull on jeans and a t-shirt. The game was at eleven. If he hurried, there might still be time for him to figure out what was wrong with her car. He called to the boys to finish eating quickly, then rummaged through the pile of clothes on their floor, searching for the soccer jersey Cassie had given Austin. After a good two minutes of pawing through clothes, some clean and others not so much, he gave up and went to the kitchen.

"We're leaving in two minutes." Matt took a slice of bread from the bag he'd just bought the previous night. As with the cereal and milk, the loaf had already been pilfered by little hands, and several of the slices were smashed together. "Both of you get your shoes on, and find your soccer shirt, Austin."

"I'm wearing it, Dad," Austin threw back at him. "I had a game last night, remember?"

Matt glanced over his shoulder. "Right." He did a double take. Austin was wearing a lot more than the shirt. Asher's dinner was still smeared across the front of the jersey, partially covering the white lettering. Matt braced his hands on either side of the sink, leaned his head down and cursed silently. "Come here."

Austin drug his feet across the linoleum to Matt's side.

"Hands up," Matt commanded. Austin obeyed, and Matt pulled the shirt over his head. "Go find something else to wear while I wash this." Austin slumped off toward his room while Matt turned the shirt right side out and inspected the damage. Both boys had been asleep when they got home last night, so he hadn't bothered with brushing teeth or getting into pajamas. They hadn't even slept in their beds, but on the couch where Matt had deposited them, though he had grabbed a couple of blankets and covered them up.

He wasn't entirely negligent, though he felt a bit hopeless as he stared at the shirt. He took it to the sink and ran it under the water, then squirted some dish soap on it and rubbed it together. Maybe that would do the trick. After a few minutes of brisk scrubbing, he rinsed the whole thing then wrung it out, hoping the stains were gone but not bothering to look. It was what it was at this point, and the jersey would just have to dry on the way.

The clock now said 9:31. An hour and a half until the game. He hoped whatever was wrong with Cassie's car was something easily fixed. If not, he'd have to pick her up instead of returning her car, up and running, as he'd hoped to.

"Let's go, let's go." He marched the boys in front of him. While they buckled into their booster seats in back, Matt started the truck, rolled the passenger side window down a crack, fitted Austin's wet shirt in it, then rolled the window up all the way.

"We forgot drinks," Austin whined.

"Nope. Got that covered," Matt said, feeling pretty good about his parenting skills at the moment. When they'd had the scrimmage with Cassie and Noah, he'd noticed she kept water bottles in her trunk. He'd bought a case of them himself last night and left them in the truck bed. "We've got enough water to last the rest of the season."

As they drove to Ikeda's, Noah's jersey flapping in the breeze, Matt filled the boys in on his plans for the day. He was pleasantly surprised that they both liked the idea of trying to fix Cassie's car for her. Once he'd pulled his truck close to her Nissan and had both hoods up, Matt let the boys get out, and he showed them the jumper cables and how to attach them.

"It's like magic," Asher exclaimed a few minutes later when the Nissan's engine finally sputtered, then gradually grew stronger.

Matt transferred the boys' booster seats, the water bottles, and the nearly-dry-but-still-stained jersey to Cassie's car, then locked his truck before driving the Nissan to the auto parts store. The diagnostic there showed the battery was dead, so Matt purchased another—the top of the line, with the longest life and warranty. He installed it, and by 10:23, they were on their way to Cassie's barn.

"Who wants to beep the horn?" Matt asked as they pulled up.

"Me!" Austin and Asher answered together, already scrambling from their seats. After both boys had hit the horn no less than three times each, Cassie and Noah appeared at the top of the stairs that were even more noticeably dilapidated in daylight.

Matt stood beside her car, his hands jammed in his pockets, with what he was sure was a goofy smile on his face as he looked up at her. He liked this role, the knight in shining armor—or at least the guy who rescued her car. He really wished he'd tried helping a damsel in distress out much earlier—with his wife.

"My car!" Cassie came bounding down the stairs, her ponytail flopping and Noah right behind her. She stopped just short of Matt. "Is it—fixed?"

"Yep. Just needed a battery."

Her face fell. "You didn't buy one, did you?"

Uh oh. Matt hadn't considered that purchasing a battery might be outside the realm of their terms of friendship. "Well, I had the car at the store already, and—"

"Which store? Where?"

"The one between here and my apartment. It's downtown, by—"

"Those cheats," Cassie muttered. She kicked the front tire. "This is the third battery I've had since January. Nothing they sell is any good."

"Wait a minute." Matt held up a hand. "*How* old was your battery?"

Cassie shrugged. "Two, three months, maybe. It was on a really hot day when it died. The guy at the store said heat can do that sometimes."

"But he replaced your last new battery for free, right?" Matt asked.

"It was discounted, but not free." Cassie stood with her hands on her hips as she frowned at her car. Noah had already climbed inside and was talking to Austin and Asher.

"Well, *this* battery is going to be free," Matt said. "We'll take care of that right now. Are you ready to go to the game?"

"Everything is in the trunk," Cassie said. "I realized that last night after you left with my keys. Let me grab my phone and call my mom really quick. She's on her way to pick us up, but I'll tell her just to meet us at the game."

"Great," Matt said, wondering what, if anything, Cassie had told her mom about him. "We'll stop by the store on the way. Do you have the receipt from your last battery?"

"In the glove box. Be right back." Cassie sprinted up the stairs, and Matt forced himself to look away, watching the boys playing in the car instead of admiring the way she ran. He'd done enough of that at their scrimmage game and felt plenty guilty about it afterward. For a lot of reasons.

I'm sorry, Jenna. He hadn't even been on his own a year yet, so what did that say about his character to be noticing and admiring another woman? And one that was married, at that. Cassie had basically been alone for over half a decade, and her faithfulness hadn't wavered. Matt felt like the worst kind of creep for the thoughts that kept stealing through his mind and the undeniable attraction he felt. Helping Cassie wasn't exactly an altruistic act. He liked being around her, plain and simple.

The only comforting and self-redeeming thought was that his eyes had never strayed when Jenna was alive. He might not have been home enough, and he'd definitely neglected her and the boys, but the only affair he'd ever had was with basketball. And in the end, that had fouled him pretty bad.

When Cassie returned, Matt already had all three boys squished into their seats in the back. He sat in the passenger seat but had left the driver's side door open for her.

As they drove back to the auto parts store, Matt briefed Cassie on the possible reasons her car might be eating batteries.

"How much is it to replace an alternator?" She pressed her lips together in a worried expression.

"Depends. Every car is a little different. Let me see if I can find a YouTube video for your model. I might be able to do it."

"Matt." She looked over at him and gave a slight shake of her head. "I can't let you do all this stuff for me. It isn't right."

He thought he read the underlying meaning of her words. *You're not my husband or even my boyfriend.* He was ready with a response.

"What if I came up with a fair trade?"

"Like?"

It seemed a good sign that she hadn't shut him down right away.

"Austin and Asher go to daycare after school a couple days a week when I work late. They hate it."

"We hate it," Austin echoed from the back seat.

Too late, Matt realized this was a discussion he shouldn't have started in front of the boys.

But Cassie's face had brightened. "I could pick them up after work. I'm usually done by four, unless the principal has a late meeting." She glanced in the rearview mirror. "What would you think of that, Noah? Would you like to have Austin and Asher come over a couple times a week to play?"

"Yes. Yes. Yes." Noah's head bobbed up and down.

Matt thought he was starting to sound a lot like Asher, or maybe all five-year-olds answered in triplet. He wouldn't know. He hadn't been around a whole lot when Austin was five last year.

"I'll have to pay you, of course," Matt said. The last thing he wanted to do was to take advantage of her.

Cassie looked over and rolled her eyes. "Friends don't pay each other for helping out. And we are friends, right?"

Mission accomplished. "Right."

Fourteen

"Where'd you learn to fix cars like a pro?" Cassie leaned against the side of hers, while Matt, his torso engulfed beneath the hood, worked on replacing her alternator.

"I wouldn't say this was like a pro. Someone who really knew what he was doing would have been done an hour ago."

"And that someone would have charged me an arm and a leg."

Matt peeked out from behind the hood with a deadpan look. "Who says I'm not?"

She laughed. "Because the evidence of my wealth is all around me." She inclined her head toward her apartment over the barn. "You're working on my biggest collateral right now. So payment will have to come in the form of cookies or something."

"Deal." Matt returned to his position beneath the hood where she couldn't see his face. "Do you do okay, Cassie?"

His concern touched her. "Noah and I do fine. We don't

really stay here just because it's cheap. I've thought about moving to a better apartment—I'm still thinking about it, actually—but when Devon comes home, I want it to be to a place he remembers."

"I see."

She doubted Matt really did, but that was okay. No one who hadn't lived something similar could understand what it was like to be in her situation, and she wouldn't want anyone she cared about to really understand because then they'd have to be going through it, too, and it was lousy.

"Is that why you still drive the Nissan? Is it your husband's car?"

"No. Devon hated this thing, even back then." How she'd worried that one day he was going to show up with a new car for her, whether she wanted it or not. Appearances—at least as far as vehicles were concerned—had been more important to Devon than to her. "I think I'm still driving it because I hate car shopping, and I don't want to have a payment again. We were saving for a house when Devon was injured. Obviously we're not saving for one anymore, but I do want to minimize our expenses, so that when he comes home, we can pick up where we left off with our dreams and our goals."

"I hope this keeps you going a little longer then." Matt stepped back and closed the hood. "All done. Hopefully that's the end of your battery woes."

"I think they ended this morning when you told off the manager at the store." Cassie grinned, recalling the way Matt had stood up for her and accused the manager of taking advantage of female clients. Matt had not only gotten the entire cost of her new battery refunded, but Cassie was pretty sure she'd never have an issue at that store again.

"Well, if your alternator really was on its way out, that

may not have been entirely fair of me." Matt took the rag she offered him and wiped his greasy hands. "However, more often than not, it seems places like that do take advantage of women. So my chat with the manager was probably a good reminder. Not to mention that your battery was under warranty. Two months. Good grief." He shook his head.

"Yeah," Cassie said. "Good thing there aren't a lot of cliffs around here, or I might have pushed this thing off one by now."

"Don't let it come to that," Matt said, his tone more serious than a moment before. "With anything Cassie. I meant what I said last night about being friends. I want to be here for you for whatever you need."

It was the nicest thing anyone had said to her in forever, or at least since Devon was hurt. It seemed the last six years when she most could have used good friends and occasional help, just about everyone but her mom had abandoned her. "Thank you, Matt. I want to be your friend, too, and help you and your boys."

"You already have." Matt finished with the rag and bent to pick up his tools. "More than you know. I think Austin may finally be starting to come around to himself again."

"I'm so glad." They stood staring at one another awkwardly. Cassie had already brought out lemonade a half hour earlier, but maybe Matt was thirsty again. All three boys were upstairs playing Legos in Noah's room, so she supposed it would be all right to invite Matt up. It wasn't like they were going to be alone. They'd just be two parents taking a break for a minute.

"Would you like some more lemonade or some ice water? We could go inside."

"Sounds good." Matt wiped his forehead with his sleeve. "Is it always so hot here in September?"

"It seems like it, the past few years at least. We need rain, and the mountains need a serious snowpack. Maybe this will be the year we get it." Cassie pushed off the car and led the way to the stairs. She ran up them quickly, then turned around to find Matt still near the bottom, bent over examining the framework.

"These aren't exactly safe, you know."

"If you walk closer to the wall of the barn, it's a bit better. I always hold the rail."

"Until that falls off, too," Matt muttered, giving it a good shake and watching as it moved back and forth a couple of inches. "Mmm. Secure. I feel better."

"Rent is cheap," Cassie reminded him and went into the apartment, which smelled strongly of sweaty little boys who'd played hard at soccer. She opened the kitchen window wider and sat at the table beside the glasses and pitcher of lemonade. Matt joined her a second later and quickly downed the glass she poured for him.

"I did some reading last night," he said.

"First thinking and then reading. Unusual habits for you?" A smile played at the corners of her mouth. She couldn't help but tease him, the same way he teased her. It was fun to enjoy that kind of camaraderie again. It had been far too long.

"I'm afraid my library is mostly limited to books like *Go Dog Go.*" His answer was accompanied with a slight shake of his head, which somehow only encouraged her playful mood. Until he swallowed the last drop of lemonade from his cup, and his expression turned serious.

"I did some reading about PVS and TBI's."

"Ahh." So much for lighthearted. For her, those terms were the equivalent of dousing a forest fire. *Not that there is even a flame here.*

"I had no idea it was such a prevalent thing," Matt said, "or of the intricacies of a patient with PVS—that they're awake sometimes, but not really there."

"That's a pretty good summary," Cassie said.

"It sounds disturbing." Matt brought a fist to his chin. "I mean, of course it's disturbing. It's a terrible thing. But it seems like it would be especially difficult to try to communicate with someone who is awake, but doesn't see you, or sees right through you or—"

"It can be," Cassie said, rescuing him from his futile attempts to explain or understand, "but I rarely feel that way. When Devon woke from his coma about three weeks after the accident, I was overjoyed to see his eyes opened. I'd been warned he might not wake up at all, so to get to see his eyes again, even if they weren't looking at me, felt like such a blessing."

"I wouldn't have thought of that," Matt said. "You're a glass-half-full kind of person, Cassie."

"Not always." *Not last night.* "I try, though. It never helps to wallow."

"I think I'm figuring that out," Matt said, "having wallowed for nine months now. Tell me you did some of that yourself, after your husband was hurt."

"Mmm, sort of," Cassie said. Recalling that painful time wasn't something she enjoyed. "At first I think I was just in shock." But that year had also been bittersweet. "Then, just weeks after Devon was shot, I found out we were going to have a baby, and I was over-the-moon about it. We'd been trying for more than a year, and the prognosis wasn't good." She stopped suddenly, realizing how personal their conversation had become. Matt was easy to talk to. Too easy. She hurried to finish explaining so they could move onto a less-serious subject.

"Noah was a miracle, and because of that, I expected a miracle with Devon as well. From the very beginning, I've felt he's going to get better. He's going to come back to us. I just have to be patient."

"Wow." Matt leaned back in his chair, his stance casual, but his gaze was full of intensity and admiration. "I think you're my new hero."

Cassie waved away his praise. "There's nothing heroic about survival and being happy with the people we've been blessed with. Now, if I didn't have Noah, this conversation would probably be very different." If she didn't have Noah, there would be no conversation. Matt and his boys wouldn't be here. She wouldn't be a soccer coach; she wouldn't be a mother. *I'd be a lonely mess.*

"Noah's a lucky boy," Matt said. "He's got a great mom. Poor Austin and Asher are stuck with a clueless dad."

"You're not giving yourself enough credit," Cassie said, wanting to help him as much as she wanted to help his sons. "Your loss is still new, and it is a loss. You have more to be grieving than I do. I can't imagine what that must feel like."

"Don't try," Matt advised. He picked up the pitcher of lemonade and poured himself another drink. "It's been pretty awful, but at least I'm on the other side of it. It's got to get better eventually, or so I've been told. It seems you must feel like you're stuck in the same cycle. In some kind of limbo, waiting for life to go forward again and having to deal with an awful lot during the interim."

It was a perceptive statement from someone she hadn't known that long. That he'd taken the time to learn about her husband and what she was dealing with and going through touched her, but she couldn't allow Matt to think her lot was harder.

"All of that is right, but I still have a chance. You've had to let that go." She shook her head. "So difficult."

"And I imagine that you have to keep digging deep every day to keep your hope alive." Their eyes met above the rim of his glass raised to his lips.

"Are we arguing about whose life sucks worse?" Though it wasn't funny, she grinned.

"Apparently." He returned her smile.

"Well," Cassie proclaimed. "It would seem that neither of us have a right to a pity party. Look at the great kids we have. I'd be ungrateful to say my life is bad when I've got Noah."

"As I said, glass half full." Matt raised his lemonade in a toast. Their glasses clinked then they both drank and listened a moment to the shouts and sounds coming from the bedroom.

"What are they doing in there?" Matt turned in his chair, as if contemplating the need to intervene before someone got hurt.

"I'd bet they're playing superheroes." Cassie didn't even wince when there was a crash against the bedroom door. One nice thing about living in a dumpy apartment was the lack of worry over doing anything to make it worse. "Noah has a set of Lego superheroes. He likes to string dental floss from the top of his bed across to the door. Then he attaches the Lego heroes and has them slide across the room on the lines."

"That's some pretty big noise for Legos to make," Matt said, still looking toward the bedroom.

"Oh, the Legos aren't the only things that are flying," Cassie said, still unconcerned. "Noah likes to jump from his loft onto my bed. Unfortunately, when my bed's down, it's so close to the door that it bangs against it every time a kid—" She paused as three thumps sounded against the bedroom door. "—or three land on the mattress."

"Sounds fun." Matt's gaze swung back to her, appraising. "You're the first mom I've ever met who encourages jumping on the bed."

Cassie shrugged. "The kid needs some perks for having to share a room with his mom."

"And what about you?" Matt leaned forward, elbows propped on the table. "What perk do you get from sharing a room with your son?"

"I sleep better," Cassie said without hesitation. "Noah's a heavy breather. Listening to him, I don't feel quite so alone."

Matt nodded, and Cassie read the understanding in his eyes.

"That would be why I allow Asher to end up in my bed most nights. There are worse things than a wiggly kid." Matt's gaze held hers, and she felt a stirring of compassion and wished she could say something encouraging.

"Lots worse." She wanted to tell him that it would get better, that five or six years out, he'd be able to sleep easier without his wife beside him, but that would have been lying. She still missed curling up beside Devon and waking with his arm around her. Loneliness didn't have an expiration date.

"Do you mind if I go see how the boys are doing?" He turned in his seat toward the bedroom once more, and Cassie took a second to mentally shake herself from melancholy.

"If they invite you to race the superhero Legos, be sure to ask for Hawkeye. He's the one with the bow, right?"

"Yep." Matt stood and pushed his chair in.

Cassie gathered their cups and the near-empty pitcher. "Hawkeye slides better than the others because of his bow, so he always makes it to the door first."

"Thanks for the tip. You're a good mom."

"I try. It's hard doing it all myself. As you know times two." She rose from her chair.

"Two kids or one," Matt said, "it probably doesn't make much difference when you're parenting on your own. Just like grief isn't always about death. It's about attachment and separation."

"Wow." Cassie paused midway to the counter with their glasses. "That's kind of profound. It sounds like something from one of my psychology textbooks." Earlier, while Matt was installing the alternator, they'd discussed their pre-marriage lives, the schools they'd gone to and plans they'd had.

"Actually, I read that on the internet last night. I thought it was a keeper."

Did he just wink at me?

"I'm going to tell Austin and Asher to start cleaning up now. The boys need baths, and I promised them that tonight they'd get their burgers and fries."

"Get to Ikeda's early," Cassie advised, half-wishing he'd invite her and Noah to tag along.

"Want to come with us?" Matt asked. "Or is it ice cream only for you and Noah on Saturday nights?"

A smile she had absolutely no control of spread across her face. She'd just wished for something, and it had happened. The prospect of her and Noah spending a Saturday evening with Matt and his boys sounded delightful.

"Tonight's the last movie in the park for the year as well," she said. "We could eat out and then go to that."

"I'd like that, and I'm sure the boys would, too." Matt's smile seemed to match hers. Meet you at Ikeda's around five?"

"Sounds perfect," Cassie agreed. It wasn't a date. He hadn't offered to pick her up. They were simply two parents joining forces to help their boys have the best time possible during these difficult situations in their lives.

She helped Matt extract Austin and Asher from the intricate web of dental floss stretching across the bedroom, then walked the three of them to the door. She and Noah stood at the top of the stairs, watching until Matt's truck had disappeared.

"Has it been a good day so far?" Cassie asked Noah, ruffling the top of his sweat-dried hair.

"The best," Noah said. "Friends are good."

Cassie couldn't have said it better.

Fifteen

Cassie read over the grant application, checking one last time to make sure all I's were dotted and T's were crossed, figuratively speaking, so the fifth graders had the best chance of getting iPads for next year. This wasn't her favorite part of her job, but she did enjoy it when they had success and the school received the funds or equipment they needed.

"Straight in here, young man." Mrs. Kendall's stern voice echoed in the hall a few seconds before the door to the principal's office banged open, and she thrust a student forward into the room, then marched in behind him.

Austin. Cassie's eyes widened in recognition, but she refrained from saying anything or following her impulse to lean forward and remove Mrs. Kendall's hand from the collar of his shirt.

"What can I help you with, Doris?" Cassie smiled sweetly and forced herself to look away from Austin's red, splotchy face.

"This student, this *boy*—"

Cassie clenched her teeth together and thought, not for

the first time, that Doris Kendall should have retired long ago. She was notorious for disliking boys, or at the least being prejudiced against those in her class. She'd had only daughters, and that had been close to four decades ago, so she had neither patience with nor empathy for the unfortunate males in her classroom. Last year, after numerous complaints from fourth grade parents, she'd been reassigned to the less mouthy, tenderhearted children in first grade. Cassie already had plans to do whatever it took to keep Noah from being in her class next year.

"This boy what?" she prompted, her eyes flickering to Austin. No matter what he'd done, the second Doris left the office, Cassie was going to give him a hug.

"He attacked another student, tackled him right to the ground."

Cassie took a pen and began writing so Doris would think she was taking notes for the principal. Really she was taking notes for Mrs. Kendall's file, full, unfortunately, of incidents just like this. "Was the other student provoking him?"

"Most certainly not," Mrs. Kendall said, staring down her nose at Cassie. "Students do not provoke one another in my class. The incident happened as I was reminding the children about our Moms and Muffins activity coming up."

Oh no. Cassie stole another glance at Austin and caught sight of a tear rolling down his cheek. It frustrated her that the school continued to have events like Dads and Donuts or Moms and Muffins when so many children these days did not come from traditional two-parent families. She could only imagine how Austin must be feeling right now.

"Mrs. Kendall," Cassie began quietly, choosing her words with care. "I believe what may have happened is a simple misunderstanding, a case of hurt feelings, of a child sensing a prejudice against him, his family, and their circumstances. Were you aware that—"

"It is absolutely a case of prejudice," Mrs. Kendall snapped. "The child who was attacked had just asked if he could bring both of his mothers to school for our activity. The very moment he asked, Mr. Kramer here"—She tugged on the collar of Austin's shirt again while Cassie dug her fingernails into her palm to keep from reaching out to attack someone herself—"jumped from his spot on the rug and tackled the student, simply because he'd mentioned his two mothers." Mrs. Kendall glared at Austin. "If that isn't blatant prejudice, then I don't know what is."

Doris Kendall didn't know anything. "Thank you for briefing me." Cassie scribbled a few more words—angry, venomous, spiteful, and she wasn't referring to Austin—before setting her pen down and standing on the other side of her desk. She looked down at Austin first and attempted to make her voice the right mix of kind and authoritative. She couldn't bear the thought of making him feel worse, but she also had to convince Mrs. Kendall that justice would be served.

"You may sit on that bench." Cassie pointed to the long wood bench that backed Principal Garrett's wall. When Austin did not move because he was still fettered by Mrs. Kendall's fist around his collar, Cassie then fixed a stiff expression on her face and stared pointedly at Mrs. Kendall until she released him.

"Principal Garrett is currently in a meeting, but I will pass this information onto him and see that this issue is resolved as soon as possible." It was a good thing he had left his light on again. It shone through the cracks of his closed blinds, giving the impression that someone was in his office. With a little luck, Doris would think his meeting was there, when in reality, he was at the superintendent's office and expected to be there the remainder of the school day.

"I'm sure your other students must need you," Cassie said gently. "You wouldn't want to have valuable time go to waste." Doris was also known for giving children only ninety seconds to use the bathroom, anything more than that being a frivolous waste of time.

"I've left them with an assignment," Mrs. Kendall stated and showed no sign of going anywhere. "They know they must complete it, or else."

No doubt *or else* involved some over-the-top form of punishment. *Terrorized in the first grade.* No wonder kids hated school.

"Very well." Cassie returned to her seat and tried to refocus her attention on the grant application while inside she was seething.

"How long do you suppose Mr. Garrett will be?" Doris asked when a minute or two had passed. She hadn't sat down but remained standing before Cassie's desk, her arms folded, eyes narrowed, and lips puckered like she'd been sucking on one of those sour candies Noah liked.

"His meeting just started." That much was the truth. "It could be quite some time before he is available." *Like tomorrow.*

"Perhaps I'll just take this student back to class and give him consequences there."

Oh no, you won't. Cassie raised her head to meet Mrs. Kendall's gaze, then leaned forward to whisper, as if she didn't want Austin to hear. "Do you really think that wise? In such a clear cut case of prejudice? You wouldn't want something else to happen in your classroom, would you?"

Mrs. Kendall looked from Austin to the door and appeared to be considering her options.

"I assure you, this office believes in justice, and consequences are designed to fit the crime." Cassie prayed she wasn't terrifying Austin any more than he already was. But getting Doris out of the picture was the first step to helping him.

"All right then," Mrs. Kendall said at last. "I'll trust you to do your job and apprise Mr. Garrett of the situation."

"I promise," Cassie said, her face as grim as she felt. Mr. Garrett was absolutely going to hear about this.

As soon as the door closed behind Mrs. Kendall, Cassie jumped up and ran around her desk. She knelt in front of Austin so she was closer to his level—if he would just lift his head to look at her, that is.

Cassie placed her hand gently on his arm. "I didn't realize you go to school here, Austin. I'm so happy to know that, and I'm so sorry you are in Mrs. Kendall's class. We're going to try to change that tomorrow, okay?"

He didn't respond, so Cassie stood, ready to move onto plan B to get him talking. She opened the door connecting to the teacher's lounge.

"Be right back," she said to Austin, then hurried through the lounge to the far door which led to the front office. Cassie poked her head through the doorway and caught her coworker's eye.

"Gloria, can you cover my phone for the next hour or so while I take care of a situation with a student?"

"Sure." Gloria's brows rose. "Are you all right? Need any help?"

"I'm fine." Cassie inhaled, taking a calming breath and pasting a smile on her face. "But Mrs. Kendall may not be after this latest incident."

Gloria mouthed an *O,* then wished Cassie good luck as she returned to the teacher's lounge. She went to the freezer and retrieved two of the popsicles reserved for kids who got hurt or were sad or having an especially bad day. She felt pretty confident Austin met the criteria for all three.

Popsicles in hand, Cassie returned to Austin, still sitting outside of Principal Garrett's office.

"Come on." she held her hand out to him. "I've got some ice cream bars for us, but we'd better eat them in the other room in case anyone else comes in." *In case Doris comes back.*

She opened the door to Principal Garrett's office, then waited until Austin slid from his chair and shuffled after her.

Once he was inside, Cassie closed the door behind them and clicked the lock. "You can leave anytime you want to." She showed Austin how turning the knob released the lock and opened the door. "But I'm locking this so no one can interrupt us. Okay?" The principal's office wasn't exactly what most children would classify as a safe environment, but it was the best she could do for now. If she hoped for any kind of communication from him, he had to feel that no one—particularly Mrs. Kendall—would bother them.

Cassie arranged two chairs facing each other and sat in one. "Orange creamsicle or fudge bar?" She held both out to Austin, hoping she wouldn't have to wait until each started dripping before he gave his answer.

"Chocolate," he said after a few seconds. Cassie picked up his hand, turned it over and placed the fudge bar on his palm. "Good choice. I like those, too. But then, I don't think I've ever had ice cream I didn't like." She leaned back in her chair and tore the top of the wrapper off of the creamsicle. "You can sit if you want."

Austin stood for probably another minute, holding the fudge bar and not moving. Cassie took a bite of hers. "Mmm. This is perfect on a warm afternoon. Would you like me to open yours?"

He nodded, so Cassie took it, tore off the wrapper, and handed it back to him. As Austin's small fingers gripped the stick, she felt a pinch of sadness in her heart for the motherless boy. Dads were great. Heaven knew she wished Noah could be with his. But sometimes men missed children's cues that moms seemed to pick up on intuitively. Did Matt understand why Austin had been acting out? Other than in the vague sense of it relating to his mother's death? Had Matt taken the time, over ice cream, to talk it out with his son? And more importantly, to listen? Silently, Cassie prayed to know the right things to say and do, to help Austin endure this latest hurt.

"First," she began by sounding upbeat instead of dire. What he'd done was wrong, but it also wasn't unforgiveable. "I want you to know that Principal Garrett is not a mean man. He is very kind, and he really likes children." *Unlike your teacher.* "He isn't here right now and won't be back at school today, but tomorrow he will want to talk to you about what happened in Mrs. Kendall's classroom. If you would like, I can be with you when you talk to him."

Austin nodded, then stepped sideways and sidled into the chair across from her. Cassie noticed his fudge bar starting to drip and snagged a couple of tissues from the box on Mr. Garrett's desk. She handed these to Austin.

"Better hurry and eat that—unless you like ice cream soup."

"Ice cream soup?" He lifted his head to look at her.

"Never heard of it?" she asked. "Noah and I have it for dinner sometimes—when the ice cream we buy at the store melts before we can get it home, and we're too impatient to try to freeze it again. But it's not very good." She added the last in a whisper and as an incentive for Austin to take a bite. It worked. Cassie finished her own treat, tossed the stick in the trash and waited silently until Austin had finished the fudge bar.

She took his stick and threw it away as well. At the ice cream parlor, he'd been the neatest eater of the three boys, but today chocolate lingered around the sides of his mouth. It reminded Cassie just how young six really was, especially for all he'd had to deal with. "Feeling a little better now, I hope?"

Austin shrugged again.

"Well, I feel better," Cassie said. "Ice cream has a way of cooling people off, and I'm not just talking about our tongues. I was pretty hot, pretty angry, with Mrs. Kendall when she brought you in my office, holding your collar like that. I wanted to jump up and shout at her and push her away from you, but that would have made me just as mean as she was, and I don't want to be mean." Cassie waited a heartbeat to try to gauge if Austin was listening. "But while I was eating my ice cream, I had time to cool off and think a little more. Now I feel better, and I'm really glad that I didn't lose my temper."

"I did." Austin looked down at his legs, swinging back and forth, not quite touching the floor.

"You're right," Cassie said, "and that wasn't the best thing to do. It's kind of the same thing that happened when you pushed Noah at the soccer game, isn't it?"

Austin nodded. "But it isn't fair that Bradley gets two moms, when I don't have even one anymore."

"I agree. It *isn't* fair, and I can see how you'd feel angry and hurt by what Bradley said." Cassie leaned forward, elbow on her crossed legs, chin in her hand. "But did you ever think that maybe it isn't always easy for Bradley to have two moms?"

"What do you mean?" Austin's forehead bunched as he looked up at her again.

"Well . . ." Cassie tried to think of the best way to explain it. "Having two moms can mean a lot of things. Maybe Bradley's parents are divorced, which means they aren't married and living together anymore. It would be like your mom living in one house, and your dad living in another, and you couldn't be with both of them at once. And then maybe your dad married someone else, so you had a new mom. So when it was Moms and Muffins day, you wouldn't know who to bring, and maybe they both wanted to come."

"I'd bring my first mom," Austin said, clearly missing the point.

"All right," Cassie said. "Or maybe Bradley has two moms and no dad. That's how some families are these days." Trying to explain that to a six-year-old was difficult. At least Austin wasn't old enough to understand the anatomy of being parents and question how that worked without a dad. "Watch and see if Bradley brings his dad for Dads and Donuts. In fact, I want you to notice all of the kids in first grade that day and count how many don't have a dad to bring." Cassie estimated that at least a fourth of the kids at school didn't have a dad in their lives, Noah included.

She had sudden inspiration, remembering what Austin himself had said over their shared hamburger at the hospital cafeteria a couple of weeks ago. "You know, you can bring someone else to Moms and Muffins. It's not the same as having your real mom there, but it might be better than being alone."

"My grandma's in Oregon. She came with me to my other school last year, after my mom died."

"You could borrow Noah's grandma," Cassie suggested. "Remember you met her at the game last week? It could be kind of the same as when you offered to share your dad with Noah."

"Maybe." Austin's legs continued to swing. "Or you could come with me."

"I could," Cassie agreed. "If that's what you would like." The kindergarten usually had their Moms and Muffins on a different morning or time, to accommodate mothers with children in different grades. It could work for her to go with Austin, and it could work for Matt to go with Noah to Dads and Donuts. She wondered what Matt would think of that trade.

"We'll talk to your dad about it," Cassie said. "But there is something even more important I want you to think about first."

"What?" Austin said when she hadn't said any more after a few seconds.

"It's a question." Cassie scooted her chair a few inches closer to Austin's. "Last month when you hurt Noah, and today when you hurt Bradley, did that make you feel better about not having your mom here?"

As she'd expected, Austin shrugged again.

"Or," Cassie continued, "did doing those things and being unkind make you feel worse?"

Austin didn't give an answer out loud, but when he finally looked at her again, she could see that he understood what she was getting at. The misery on his face said it all.

"I know it is hard to be happy when someone you love isn't with you anymore." Cassie reached out and took Austin's hand in her own. "It's hard not to feel jealous when we see other people and they have a whole family when we only have a part."

"Do you ever feel that way?" Austin's wide, watering eyes were all the invitation she needed to gently pull him from his chair and enfold him into the hug she'd wanted to give him from the moment he'd come through the principal's door.

"All the time," she said, bending her head close to his, breathing in that little boy scent that reminded her of Noah. "It *isn't* fair that your mom died. It *isn't* fair that Noah doesn't have a dad like you do. But being mean won't change either of those. It won't ever make anything better. It will only make it worse. I don't want things to be worse for you, Austin."

He sniffled and buried his head in her shoulder. Cassie tightened her embrace and felt her own tears welling. He just needed to be loved, and he needed a teacher who realized that.

"Can you make a promise—for me and Noah because we're your friends and care about you—that you will try really hard not to make things worse for yourself? That you'll hurt people less and eat more ice cream instead?"

Austin nodded his head against her shoulder.

"Good." Cassie hugged him a minute longer, knowing that what she'd asked of him was easier said than done.

Sixteen

Matt fitted the new stair riser between the two old rotting ones beneath the staircase leading to Cassie's apartment.

"Drill," he mumbled through the screws sticking out between his lips. Austin and Asher handed him the tool together, it taking both boys to lift it.

"Thanks." Matt fitted a screw into the bit and connected the riser to the new step he'd already placed above. It would have been a whole lot easier to simply tear the old staircase down and build a new one, but he didn't suppose Cassie would appreciate being stuck in her apartment all day. Not to mention that she and Noah would have missed the soccer game as well. Matt just hoped he'd started early enough to at least get the risers installed before the game. He could finish the actual steps this afternoon.

"Think you boys can unload the rest of the wood from the truck?" Matt could tell they were getting bored and restless, and that always led to trouble. He'd promised to let them help, and he would when it came time to attach the steps, but there wasn't much they could do right now—except start fighting.

"Asher's looking at me funny."

"No, I'm not."

"Are, too."

"Hi, Austin! Hi, Asher!" Noah called from the top of the stairs.

Saved by the friend with the Legos, Matt thought gratefully. He moved out from beneath the stairs and glanced up just as Cassie, wearing an oversized t-shirt and with her hair piled crazily on top of her head, joined Noah outside her front door. She looked down at him as if half asleep and confused.

"It's six-thirty in the morning. What are you doing, Matt?" She covered her mouth as she yawned.

"Saving you and Noah from a broken leg or worse." He held up his drill and inclined his head toward the bed of his truck filled with lumber and supplies. "The boys and I are replacing your stairs today. Thought we'd better get an early start."

"Can I help, too?" Noah didn't wait for an answer but was already bounding down the stairs in bare feet and pajamas.

"Matt, you already fixed my car." Cassie crossed her arms in front, hugging herself and causing the shirt to rise higher on her legs. Matt forced his gaze to her face, a difficult task when he was already looking up at her.

"And all that work on your car will go to waste if they have to take you out of here in an ambulance. I'm fixing these stairs," he insisted. "It's that or tracking down your landlord to give him a piece of my mind. Your call." He could be stubborn, too, especially about something as important as this.

"I have to pay you then. All that stuff must have been expensive." She waved a hand at the back of his truck.

"You can start with breakfast," he suggested. She'd already delivered on the cookies for the car. "But the real trade came last week." Risking life and limb once more, he ran up the stairs to finish their conversation. He didn't want the boys to hear what he was going to tell her. As he approached, Cassie took a step back so she was standing in the doorway of her apartment.

What if her floor joists were in as bad a shape as the stairs outside? The sudden thought worried him. He'd have to find a way to check those as well, though what he really ought to do was find a way for her to move to a better place. But that, he was pretty certain, would definitely be overstepping the bounds of their friendship. By her own admission, Cassie still lived here for Devon, waiting for him to come home.

After reading all that he had about PVS patients, Matt realized that outcome was unlikely, but Cassie's faith in her husband, along with her unfailing loyalty, couldn't be faulted. Matt hoped—for her sake and Noah's—that she'd get the miracle she believed in.

Cassie held one hand to her hair, self-consciously tucking straying curls into the floppy bun piled on top of her head. Her other hand tugged at the large shirt, as if to pull it down past mid-thigh where it fell. Was it Devon's?

The thought should have cooled Matt's attraction. Instead, a corner of his mouth lifted in a roguish smile. He couldn't help himself. She wore the just-stumbled-out-of-bed look very well. He'd never seen her more appealing.

"Good morning, Mrs. Webb." He leaned a hand against the outside wall of her apartment and stared pointedly at her hair. "New style?"

"Yes, actually," she said, not missing a beat even as a blush crept up her face. "What do you think? Will I scare the children at school?"

"No." Her banter only heightened his desire. It was all he could do not to reach out and touch some of that tempting hair. "But the other secretaries and the teachers may be jealous that you can look so completely alluring only a minute after getting out of bed."

"I don't—*Matt,* you shouldn't say things like that." She crossed her arms again and looked down at her bare feet as the charming blush was replaced by obvious discomfort, reminding him of that day at the ice cream parlor. This time he was clearly out of line, and he knew it.

"I'm sorry," he apologized as he turned away. Two steps down, he stopped and looked back up at her. "Actually, I'm not—sorry about complimenting you, that is. What I said is true. You're a beautiful woman, Cassandra Webb, and I imagine it's been a long time since a man has told you that. Be mad at me if you will for noticing, but it's a truth I think you ought to hear once in a while." He resumed his retreat before she could respond.

"Matt, I can't let you fix the stairs," she called down to him.

At least she let my behavior slide.

"I still haven't paid you for the alternator," Cassie continued. "And now all this wood—"

He remembered what he'd come up to tell her before his mind had been completely shut down by the sight of her in that t-shirt. He paused on the stairs. "I told Austin's therapist we're done." Instead of looking up at Cassie again, he stared out at the yard where the boys were playing tag, like any other three boys—with normal lives—might. "You've helped Austin more in a few weeks than either therapist—here or in

Oregon—has been able to do in months. Not only is that going to save me over five hundred bucks a month, but I'm getting my son back. So the way I see it, I'm in your debt. Now, if you'll excuse me, I'd like to get back to work."

Before he reached the bottom, Matt heard the apartment door close. He hoped he hadn't offended her or been too pushy. Cassie was plenty independent, and he didn't want to take that away from her, but it also seemed she could do with someone to look out for her and lend a hand occasionally.

He spent the next twenty minutes helping the boys think they were helping him to unload the lumber from the truck. Even if he didn't finish the entire project today, he figured the supplies would be safer here than driving around town in the back of his truck, where anyone could take them.

By the time the last board had been stacked, the smell of bacon wafted from Cassie's apartment, and Matt was relieved to feel a desire for something other than her stirring in his gut. It had been a while since he and the boys had eaten anything besides cold cereal for breakfast, and he was sure that whatever she was cooking would be better than anything he attempted to make.

He had the second new riser, the one closest to the side of the barn, installed when Cassie called them in for breakfast. The boys bolted upstairs ahead of him. Matt followed at a slower pace, hoping his earlier words wouldn't make things awkward between them.

The door to Cassie's apartment was open, and her table for two had been pulled over in front of the love seat, so it was possible to seat four. *Five,* he amended, as she brought a stool from the bathroom. Matt noted with some regret that she'd changed into jeans and the shirt she usually wore when coaching and had tamed her hair into a braid.

"Noah, you stand on this." Cassie wedged the stool between the two chairs. "And Asher and Austin will sit on either side of you. Matt and I will sit on the sofa."

Apparently he needn't have worried, if she felt comfortable enough to sit that close to him. She returned to the tiny kitchen on the opposite wall and brought over two steaming plates, one piled high with pancakes, and the other with strips of bacon. Matt's mouth watered, and his stomach grumbled. He'd worked up more of an appetite than he realized.

"Can I use your bathroom to wash up?"

"Of course. You know which door." Cassie set out plates and mismatched cups as he left the room.

He flipped the switch in the bathroom and found himself inside a room smaller than his closet. But it wasn't the size, or lack of, that held his attention. Officer Devon Webb stared down at Matt from the upper corner of the mirror, a paper taped below him with the words, REMEMBER ME TODAY handwritten with bold marker.

As if Cassie needs a reminder. But the picture and words made Matt wonder if she ever did. Six years was a really long time, longer than the time she'd had with her husband at her side.

Does she ever wish that you had just died? Matt thought as he stared at the picture. And worse, *Would I have chosen Jenna's death, or would I have waited enough years, like Cassie, with the hope of her returning to me if I was patient enough?* It was an idea he didn't care to examine too closely. Of course had there been any chance at all to save Jenna, he would have wanted it, would have done anything no matter the expense or sacrifice or any of that, but could he have hung on the way Cassie had?

As Matt hurried to wash his hands, he had the

uncomfortable feeling that he couldn't.

"More syrup definitely made it onto the floor than into Asher's mouth," Matt said from his position under the table scrubbing the carpet.

"As long as I don't stick to it when I'm barefoot, it's fine." Cassie worried she should have made more food as she carried the empty plates to the sink. Had Matt gotten enough to eat? It had been a long time since she'd fed a man; she was a little out of practice.

"I'm starting to wonder if something is wrong with him," Matt said. "Asher's far more clumsy than Austin ever was, and he can't seem to get a fork or spoon straight into his mouth to save his life—or mine," he added, then continued muttering as he picked pieces of pancake off the floor.

"Maybe there is something wrong." Cassie crouched down to join Matt beneath the table. "Have you ever had his eyes checked?"

"No." Matt raised his head, his mouth partly open, a definite light-bulb-moment expression on his face. "It *could* be his eyes. Jenna's vision wasn't great. She wore contacts. Asher is so much like her in every other way."

"A lot of young children have poor vision." Cassie used a napkin to blot up a spot of juice. "It even causes behavior problems sometimes. Last school year, we had two cases like that."

"And you were the one who figured that out," Matt guessed.

"I was," Cassie said, remembering the sense of accomplishment she'd felt when both students had been able to get glasses and their behavior had improved dramatically afterward. It was one of those few times she felt she was actually doing something of real value that maybe another school secretary couldn't or wouldn't.

"Just like you figured out why Austin acted out at school last week." Matt's hair brushed the underside of the table as he looked up at her, his face just inches away.

A little thrill of excitement pulsed through her, at their proximity. It was different yet the same as she'd felt that night at the cafeteria when his hand had covered hers. *Traitor*, she silently scolded her racing heart and worked to keep her attention focused on their conversation.

"Most of the time children act out for a reason. A behavior is the symptom, but not the real problem." *This attraction I'm feeling to Matt is a real problem.* "Often just listening and being observant will lead you to what the real issue is. In Austin's case, it was very easy to realize what was going on. As soon as Mrs. Kendall said the incident had occurred while she was talking about Moms and Muffins, I had a pretty good idea what had upset Austin. And," Cassie added, "he was willing to talk about it." *Austin has Matt's eyes,* she realized as his hazel ones locked on hers.

"He was willing to talk because he trusts you," Matt said. "And now you're his hero—and mine, too—because you were able to get him out of Mrs. Kendall's class."

Cassie's sigh was about much more than the week's events. "I wish I could get *all* of the kids out of Mrs. Kendall's class, but clearly Austin had to be moved. I'm glad Principal Garrett was on our side."

"Me, too," Matt said. They picked flecks of pancake out of the carpet for another minute before he spoke again. "Who's on your side, Cassie? Who is going to stand up for you and tell you it's time you switched jobs? Time you start using your degree to help a lot more kids?" Matt picked up the last visible piece of pancake and backed out from under the table.

"Apparently you." Cassie gave up on any more juice coming out of the carpet and stood, then held the napkin out for Matt to drop the crumbs into.

"You're way overqualified for a school secretary." After standing and ridding his hands of the breakfast debris, he wiped his palms on the front of his pants. "Seeing you in action, the way you explained things to Mr. Garrett, the way you understand kids . . . it seems a shame you aren't doing that full time."

"I like my job," she said, feeling more guilty as charged than defensive. How many times had she thought the very same thing Matt was suggesting? "I like being close to Noah."

"Think of the benefits you could give him if you were earning the salary you deserve." Matt took the napkin from her and wadded it up in his hand. "I was paying a therapist $125 an hour for Austin's sessions, and she wasn't even any good. Think about the things Noah is going to need in the coming years. Most kids get braces these days, they play sports or have band instruments, they drive cars and go to college."

"Whoa." Cassie held her hands out. "He's only in kindergarten, and that was hard enough for me. Please don't send him off to college yet. Besides," she said brightly, "long before then, Devon will be part of this equation. He'll be here to help make all those things happen."

Matt took a step closer to her. "Then think of Devon. Think about the things he might need when he comes home. Think about the years you'll have to make up for, and the dreams you'll have to pick up. How long is it going to be before you get that house you were saving for? What about taking Noah to Legoland as a family? What if Devon can't work as he used to for a while? Those are all realities, Cassie." He ran a hand through his hair. "All I'm saying is that you have a gift with children, and using it could not only help more kids, but it could help you and Noah as well."

"Wow." Cassie braced her hands on the back of a chair and leaned forward, not trusting herself to share her expression with Matt. His observations and analysis were spot on. *And he thinks I have a gift.* But it was the fact that he'd cared enough to share his opinion with her, to encourage her to revisit old dreams, that had her feeling emotional. She wasn't used to having someone care so much, and she'd never had a man encourage her like this. Devon had never understood her passion for psychology. He'd never understood her need and desire to delve into other peoples' problems and help them find solutions. Somehow Matt did.

"Those are some good things to think about," she finally said when she trusted herself to both speak and look up at him. "I promise that I will."

"Good." Matt sounded relieved.

"Now will *you* consider allowing me to pay for the wood for *my* stairs that you're fixing?"

"Hmm." Matt's mouth twisted in a pondering expression for all of two seconds. "Nope." He held his hands out, palms up. "Fixing your stairs." He dipped one palm down a few inches like a scale. "You fixing Austin." His other hand dipped almost to the floor. "No comparison."

"You might be exaggerating a bit," Cassie called over her shoulder as she headed for the sink.

"Not in the least. You're helping my son to be himself and happy again. Plus you've probably figured out Asher's problem, too. I'm going to set up an eye appointment for next week." Matt tossed the napkin in the trash, then sidestepped in front of her to reach the sink first. "I'm a lousy cook, but I can wash dishes."

"I don't think so." Cassie joined him at the sink and tried to nudge him aside. "Go play with your power tools. I've got this."

"Can't do that." Matt's wide-legged stance didn't budge. "I'm a modern man—multi-faceted, well-rounded. I can use a drill *and* dish soap." Tipping a plate sideways, he started scraping leftover pancake into the sink.

"Wait—don't." Cassie put her hand over his to stop him.

Matt turned his head sideways and frowned at her. "Are you one of those women who takes issue with someone else in their kitchen?" He sounded amused. "I wouldn't have guessed it of you, Mrs. Webb."

Cassie pulled her hand away, though the damage had already been done. The brief touch and Matt's teasing had sent her insides flip flopping again. She took a huge step back and held out her hands in a gesture of surrender.

"Have at it," she said. "Wash every dish in the place if you'd like, and when you're through"—she smiled sweetly—"you can dig out all of the food you put down the sink and fix the disposal that's been broken for the past three years."

Seventeen

"Your turn." Cassie propped her chin on her hand and watched as Noah drew a card from the pile. A second later, his little nose wrinkled, and a fiendish smile emerged.

"Sor-ry," he crooned, not acting sorry at all as he swiped her player from the board and set him back in home base.

"I'll get you for that," Cassie promised. She drew her own card as Noah suffered another fit of giggles. No other game got him laughing like this one. It was the reason she chose it every time it was her turn to choose. Well, that and the fact that it didn't take forever to play, like Candy Land or Chutes and Ladders.

She moved a dismal three spaces and waited for Noah to go.

Devon was a big game player. Too big at times, though Cassie tried to forget those painful occasions and focus on the fun they used to have playing together and with friends. Their twice yearly trip to Tahoe had always been about more than the skiing or the lake. Some of her fondest memories were the times that six or eight of them gathered around a table in the lodge or on a blanket at the beach, where both the cards and the laughter flew. She and Devon had been nearly unbeatable at spades. They'd known how to read each other so well.

Maybe that was part of the reason she couldn't give up on him now. He might not be able to speak to her, but that didn't mean he wasn't hearing her or that they couldn't communicate, did it?

"Mom, *Mom.*" Noah tugged on her sleeve. "Your turn."

"Sorry." Cassie pulled her attention to the board. "Not that kind of sorry. Though—" She looked at the card she'd just drawn. "Actually, yes. *That* kind of sorry." She slapped the card onto the discard pile and rubbed her hands together with mock glee. "Let's see . . . who wants to go back home?"

"No one." Noah's giggles erupted once more.

After a quick scan of the board, Cassie realized that all of his players were either home already or in the safety zone.

"Noooo," she wailed, then reached over to start tickling him. "You're beating me *again.*"

Amidst their tickle war, during which the entire pile of remaining cards got knocked to the floor, Cassie's phone started ringing. She ceased tickling Noah and got up to answer it as a flicker of hope sprang up in her chest.

I was just thinking about Devon. It was going to happen like this—a phone call one day, telling her he was awake. And this was an odd time of the afternoon for a call. She and Noah had only been home a half hour. She seldom received calls in the afternoon. She seldom received calls at all.

Their Tahoe friends and others had mostly faded into the background and out of the picture the past six years. She couldn't blame them entirely, knowing it had to be uncomfortable at best, trying to figure out what to say and how to act around someone with a husband commonly known as a vegetable.

Cassie dug through her purse for the phone and felt her hope deflate at seeing Matt's name instead of the care center. *Today isn't that day.* She tried to mask her disappointment as she answered.

"Hi, Matt. What's up?"

"Some creepy things. Up, down, all around. I need your help, Cassie."

"I don't kill spiders. You're on your own there." She went for lighthearted, as had become part of their unspoken friendship pact. When one of them was having a difficult day, it was the other's job to raise spirits. So far it had worked pretty well, and she was happy to take her turn. He'd done so much for her lately.

"Asher got sent home from preschool today. He has lice."

"Ohhhhh." *Eeeuuw.* Her own scalp suddenly began to itch.

"They gave me a paper with all these instructions on how to get rid of them. I can't send Asher back to school until they're gone. And I'm pretty sure Austin has them, too."

"Okay. Don't panic," Cassie said to herself as well as Matt. "I'll go to the pharmacy and pick up what they need if you'll send me a text with a picture of the note from school. Can you meet me at my mom's in half an hour?"

"Your mom's?" Matt sounded confused. "Does she have experience with head lice?"

"I don't know, maybe," Cassie said, her hand busily scratching at her hairline on the back of her neck. "But she has the tools for what your boys need to start with—haircuts."

"I can't thank you enough, Mrs. Jensen," Matt said as Austin, sporting a nice, new buzz, hopped down from the stool on Cassie's mom's small back porch.

"Please, call me Janet." Cassie's mom picked up the broom and began sweeping up a lot more hair than Matt would have believed could come from his boys' heads. He hadn't realized just how long their hair had grown, but now that it was cut, and he saw how great they looked, he wouldn't let it get out of control again. He knew where to get it cut now, and he liked Mrs. Jensen.

"How about you, Noah? Do you want a haircut today?" she asked.

Noah shook his head. "You just gave me one last week."

"That may be true," Cassie called from inside the screened door to the kitchen, where she leaned over the sink, scrubbing Asher's head. "But you're getting your hair washed with this stuff just to be safe."

"Mo-om," Noah groaned.

"Don't 'Mom' me," she said. "I don't want to take any chances. I'm going to use this shampoo myself tonight."

"Me, too," Matt said as he threaded the lice comb through Austin's hair in preparation for his turn with the shampoo.

"Can Matt wash my hair then?" Noah asked Cassie. "He doesn't have sharp fingernails like you."

"I'd be glad to wash your hair," Matt said, feeling he was the one who should have been doing that chore all along. Cassie had insisted she preferred the washing over pulling the lice out of the boy's hair with the comb, but Matt didn't imagine her job could be a whole lot of fun either. None of this was fun, yet she and her mom had helped him without hesitation.

He finished combing through Austin's short hair and then, when Janet wasn't looking, Matt pulled a fifty dollar bill from his wallet and slid it between the folds of the cape she'd had the boys wear during their haircuts. When he turned back toward the house, he caught Cassie watching through the kitchen window, her eyes on him, filled with appreciation.

"Thank you," she mouthed.

Matt gave a slight nod and turned away, embarrassed to be caught, yet grateful to have scored a point or two with Cassie. It was apparent that her mom didn't have a lot of money. Everything in her home felt like it was dated in the seventies or eighties. The house was clean but without many luxuries.

Much like Cassie's tiny, over-the-barn apartment, Matt realized. Maybe living frugally as she did wasn't as difficult as it might have been, having grown up as she probably had, without a lot. It was one of the things he liked about Cassie. She was down-to-earth and unpretentious. He and Jenna used to be that way, too, until he'd made enough money that they'd decided to move to Portland's prestigious Healy Heights neighborhood. Thinking back on the past several years now, Matt could see that was when he'd started to change.

"I haven't cut anyone's hair except Noah's and Cassie's for quite a while." Janet swept the last of it into a dustpan and carried it to the garbage. "I must say, this has all been rather exciting. You boys will have to visit me again for haircuts, but without the bugs next time."

"We'll do that." Matt ran a hand through his own hair, thinking he'd come visit her soon as well, but not today. He had a mess at home to deal with. Based on the instructions on the paper, he was going to be busy tonight.

"Next," Cassie called to Austin as she faced Asher toward Matt and gave him a nudge that direction. Matt sat on a stool and towel dried Asher's hair. Then he took a clean comb and started at the top of Asher's head, checking for any lingering wee beasties.

A half hour later when the boys' heads had all been treated and the towels were in the wash and the kitchen clean, Matt stood to thank Cassie's mom again.

"I really appreciate this, Janet. Thank you so much for your help."

She waved off his gratitude. "It was nothing. The real work is still ahead. Why don't you leave the boys here to eat dinner and watch a movie while you and Cassie go tackle cleaning your apartment?"

"Yes. Yes. Yes." Asher jumped up and down, his new glasses askew. "Please, Dad," he begged, as if he'd just been offered something much more exciting than dinner and a movie at his friend's grandma's house.

"Can we, Dad, please?" Austin asked. Matt's eyes narrowed with suspicion at the *please* he'd tacked on at the end. While that was a normal word in Asher's vocabulary, Austin rarely used it. No doubt he'd pulled it out tonight intending manipulation.

Matt shook his head. "I appreciate the offer, Janet, but I can't do that to you or to Cassie." *Especially to Cassie.* His gaze slid to hers, and he caught the surprised, questioning look she was sending her mother.

"Why ever not?" Janet persisted. "You've fixed her car and made those awful stairs of hers safe again. It would seem she could help you with a little laundry."

If it had been just a little laundry they were talking about, Matt might have consented. He couldn't deny that some time alone with Cassie, no matter how unglamorous the circumstances, appealed to him, but the thought of her seeing the apartment—

"And I heard you installed a new disposal in her sink. Such a convenience," Janet mused. Matt recognized the hefty dose of parental guilt laced within her words. He tried that approach frequently with his boys, but mostly they were too young to fall for it. Cassie, however, was not.

"Great. It's settled then." She removed the apron she'd been wearing and draped it over the back of a kitchen chair. "I'll just get my purse."

Matt exchanged an uneasy glance with Janet when Cassie left the room.

"I don't think—" he began.

"Good." She cut him off. "In a situation like this, I believe not overthinking things is for the best. Just enjoy the friendship. I know Cassie is. And you've both been through so much." Janet's smile was sincere as she turned and left the room.

Matt was left to wonder if she was trying to encourage him toward a more serious relationship with her daughter. Perhaps it was simply that she wanted Noah to have a father figure present in his life. With Janet being a widow since before Noah was born, he didn't even have a grandfather to pal around with in place of his dad.

And my boys have both. But no mom, and now their grandmother was far away, too. Matt decided Janet was right. Why dwell on the unique and challenging circumstances he and Cassie faced? Instead, he planned to enjoy the time with her, or what he could of it, for the next few hours while he and Cassie did laundry and cleaned his messy apartment.

Eighteen

Matt inserted the key in the lock but didn't turn it. "Promise me that we'll still be friends after you see this place."

"Of course." Cassie clasped her hands in front of her, feeling not the least bit worried, and ready to tackle stripping bedding and vacuuming floors, though she was still dressed in her brown skirt and cream sweater from work.

"Maybe we should go to your place so you can change first." Matt's hand dropped away from the door as he angled a look at her.

Cassie placed a hand on her hip and rolled her eyes. "I work in an elementary school, Matt. Nothing at your apartment is going to do anything more to my clothing than some of the mishaps it's endured at school. Did you know a kid threw up on me last year? He was so sick he mistook the principal's office for the nurse's and walked right in and projectile vomited all over the top of my desk and me, and that was only Monday morning." She grimaced, remembering the incident all too clearly. Her blazer had never recovered. Matt's apartment couldn't even come close.

She reached out to grasp the key, intending to turn it and unlock the door, but Matt acted a split second later, his hand covering hers.

"Sorry." Cassie slid her hand from beneath his but not before the impact of their brief contact made its way to her head; she felt dizzy, her stomach fluttering and heart beating rapidly. She felt her face heating, too, and silently berated herself for acting like a foolish schoolgirl.

Am I thirteen or thirty-one?

"I'm sorry, too." Matt stared at her hand and his own, a foot apart now. She heard the meaning in his words. No apology for their accidental touch but regret for the feelings it aroused.

In both of us? Cassie dared to meet his eyes, and glimpsed the yearning in them that surely shone in her own. *Oh, Matt.*

"Friends touch each other sometimes," he said, so quiet Cassie found herself leaning closer to hear him. "They shake hands or give hugs. And it's all right. Sometimes a person just needs that, you know."

She did, but she was already playing with fire, being alone with him like this. In fact, she and her mom were going to have a long talk about that later tonight. What in the world was her mom thinking to suggest this?

"I don't think that's a good idea," Cassie said, trying to keep the regret from her own voice. She looked at Matt's strong arms. In the past month, she'd learned how capable his hands were, and at this moment, nothing in the world sounded better than to have those arms around her and his hands at her waist or pressing her close. She closed her eyes, shutting out the image and trying to shut down her desire.

"Agreed," Matt said after several seconds had passed, during which Cassie felt herself precariously close to losing the battle. She heard the key turn in the lock and opened her eyes just as light flooded the stoop when Matt flipped on a switch. She followed him inside to a large living room, made to feel small by the piles of toys and clothes scattered haphazardly around the perimeter.

A big screen TV took up most of the main wall, and stacks of DVD's and game cartridges toppled into one another on the floor in front of it. Controllers were strewn across the carpet, a coffee table, and the large sectional. Glasses and soda cans and rings from previous drinks littered the end tables, alongside wadded up socks, boys' underwear and shorts, other articles of clothing, and stacks of paper.

"Still friends?" Matt asked, hands in his front pockets, his mouth twisted with worry.

"I don't know," Cassie said. "I haven't seen the bedrooms yet." She cracked a smile, then laughed out loud as his expression increased from worry to alarm.

She reached out, placing a hand lightly on his sleeve. "I'm teasing."

He sagged with false relief then placed his hand over hers before she could pull away. "Come on." He tugged at her fingers, then clasped his hand around hers and towed her farther into the apartment while Cassie wondered wildly what had just happened to the no touching agreement she thought they'd come to outside a moment or two earlier.

"I'll show you the bedroom." Still holding her hand, he led her toward a hallway.

Cassie fought the sudden and absurd urge to giggle.

"What?" Matt looked back at her, catching her futile attempt to choke back laughter. "Feeling sorry for how pathetic I am, or are you laughing so you won't cry?"

"Neither." Another giggle escaped. She chalked it up to nerves or misfiring neurons or whatever was happening inside of her because he was still holding her hand. "Do you realize what you just said and how that sounded—as you're pulling me toward your *bedroom,* no less." She attempted a severe expression. "I'm not that kind of woman."

He dropped her hand at once, leaving Cassie both relieved and disappointed.

"I'm not that kind of man, Mrs. Webb."

She wondered if his use of Mrs. Webb was to remind him or her or both that she was married.

Either way it seemed to work. A couple of awkward seconds passed, then he was walking ahead of her, apologizing for the piles of things they had to step over in the hall and the general condition of the place.

"I'm not much of a housekeeper. Jenna would be horrified to see how we live now."

Cassie wondered that the thought wasn't motivation enough for him to change. She was constantly weighing what Devon would think of what she said and did. It was enough to continue to shape her actions, from the place they lived to the fact that she still hadn't become licensed and pursued a job in her field. It had taken a day or so of considering Matt's suggestion that she do just that for her to realize the root of what was holding her back.

And that realization had bothered her ever since.

The difference, she supposed, between her and Matt was that his wife wouldn't ever be coming home; she wasn't going to see his messy apartment. Whereas Cassie expected Devon to return. Someday. Soon. And she wanted him to be happy with her when he did.

With a little difficulty because of something on the floor, Matt pushed the door to the boys' bedroom open.

Cassie peeked inside and winced, really winced, as the enormity of the task ahead of them set in.

"Matt, we're supposed to wash everything—bedding, towels, clothes they've worn recently, stuffed animals they sleep with . . ."

"Yeah. I know. Would you like me to take you back to your mom's now that you've witnessed my shame?"

She took in his forlorn expression and knew she couldn't abandon him. So what if he was a slob? There were worse things. And what did she care? It wasn't like they were getting married. She brushed the thought aside as quickly as it had come and rolled up the sleeves of her sweater. "Where are your garbage bags? Let's get started."

His relief was palpable, and Cassie soon found she didn't mind the work because she knew it was helping him. Fixing her stairs and installing that disposal couldn't have been fun, to say nothing of the new alternator he'd put in her car. What was a little laundry potentially laced with bugs? She owed him. As soon as the first bag was full, she had Matt direct her to the small laundry room—also a mess—and the washing machine. Cassie started a load, then returned to the trenches. Three large garbage bags lined the hall, and Matt was just stripping the sheets off the boys' bunks.

"What's this?" Cassie caught a plastic baggie, midair, as it fell from the top bunk.

"Teeth." Matt shuddered. "Austin's insisted on keeping every one he's lost since Jenna died. He sleeps with them. I have no idea why."

"Maybe you should suggest that the tooth fairy might like them." Cassie counted four teeth inside the plastic bag.

"Tooth fairy?"

Matt's look of confusion was too real to be anything but genuine.

"Oh, Matt. Really?" *Poor Austin.*

"What?" he asked.

"How can you *not* know about the tooth fairy? It's a big deal for little kids."

His blank, clueless look continued.

Cassie patiently explained the tradition, especially the part about bragging rights at school.

"Now that you mention that, I do remember it from when I was a kid." Matt's look of confusion turned to one of distress. "So you mean all these months Austin has been keeping this under his pillow, hoping for some fairy to bring him something in return?"

Cassie nodded. "Yep."

"Man, I suck at this parenting thing." Matt shook his head, and it was all Cassie could do not to reach out and comfort him.

"It's okay," she said instead. "We can fix this. I have some crisp, sparkly ones at my house, and I even have a couple of two dollar bills for molars. We'll stop at my place on the way to pick up the boys, and you can stock up."

"But won't Austin find it suspicious if four dollars suddenly appear in place of this baggie?"

"Not necessarily," Cassie said, a plan forming in her mind. "Not if they appear tomorrow morning, with a note from the tooth fairy about how she's glad the boys finally have a clean room so she could safely enter and find the teeth."

"I like how you think." Matt's smile was back.

"It does look a lot better in here." Cassie noted the size of the room, the plush carpet, and quality furniture. Noah deserved a room this nice.

"If only we could keep it this way," Matt lamented.

"You can," Cassie said brightly. She opened the closet

and noted the shelves and ample rod space. "I can help you get it organized, just not tonight."

For the next three hours, the washer and dryer ran non-stop, churning out more boys' clothing than any two kids needed, their sheets and blankets, and even Asher's favorite stuffed dog. Cassie vacuumed the carpets while Matt used the hose attachment to vacuum the walls and baseboards, window sills, and any other surface he could reach. They remade the boys' beds, folded and put away clothing, and dusted the furniture.

When they'd finally finished what they could in the living room, Cassie leaned wearily against the wall, there being nowhere to sit since the sofa slip covers were still in the washing machine, and the cushions stood at odd angles around the room where Matt had vacuumed them.

"Almost done," she said, noting that it was 9:40. She hoped her mom had made the boys go to bed. If not, tomorrow morning wasn't going to be pleasant for any of them.

"Almost?" Matt questioned. "We are done." He tossed an uncovered cushion onto the couch and collapsed on it.

Cassie shook her head. "Not unless you're intending to sleep on that sofa. We've still got your room to do."

"I don't have lice," Matt said. "My stuff is fine."

"Do your boys ever climb in bed with you?" Cassie already knew the answer.

Matt muttered something unintelligible under his breath, then leaned forward, head in his hands.

She pushed off the wall. "Come on," she urged, taking the lead this time. "Your room can't be any worse than the rest of this place." She marched briskly down the hall and opened the door at the end, revealing a suite larger than her entire apartment.

"Oh my." She stood in the doorway, staring at a room vastly different from the rest of the apartment. It was immaculate for one thing, from the made bed, including decorative throw pillows arranged on top, to the photos carefully arranged on the walls, dresser, and nightstand. The whole room had a sense of opulence, as if it wasn't part of the apartment, but a grand house. She sensed Matt's presence behind her and turned to him, an apology on her lips.

"I'm sorry. I shouldn't have barged in."

"It's all right. I've seen your bedroom, remember?" A corner of his mouth lifted.

"Yeah, and it's just decorated with Legos. This—" She didn't even know how to describe the beautiful room. It reminded her a little of the house she and Devon had stayed at on their honeymoon, years ago when she'd been young and dreamed of having nice things and living in an elegant home someday.

"I wanted to preserve something of our old home, something of Jenna's," Matt said. "I got the idea that the bedroom would be the place to do it. You know." He shrugged then walked past Cassie into the room. "This is the furniture and bedding she picked out. That's the nightstand where she kept her water glass and jewelry at night. The pictures of us—" All traces of lightheartedness fled his expression, replaced by a bleakness so encompassing that Matt dropped to the bed, sitting hunched over as if weary. "The pictures are to remind me of what could have been."

"What do you mean?" Cassie took a step closer, concerned with the change that had come over him. She knew Matt well enough to recognize his tone of self-recrimination. "There's nothing you could have done to stop her aneurysm. It's just one of those things that happened." For all the times she'd heard such lame sentiments herself,

Cassie couldn't quite believe she was feeding them to someone else now.

"I couldn't have stopped it," Matt agreed, "but we could have lived more before it happened. There should be a lot more pictures on these walls." His hand swept the room, over the dozen or so framed photos that made up his wife's shrine. "I wasn't always the best husband."

"I find that very hard to believe." Cassie came farther into the room, then sat on the end of the bed, a few feet from where Matt still sat hunched forward, elbows braced on his legs.

"I was caught up in my career and justified it in the name of providing for my family."

"I imagine that's something a lot of men do," Cassie said, strangely relieved to find that was his definition of not being the best husband.

"I don't want to be like a lot of men," Matt said vehemently. "I shouldn't have been. I should have been an attentive husband who loved and appreciated his wife more."

"But you weren't, or you think you weren't," Cassie clarified. "So you've put up all these pictures as a sort of continued self-flogging?"

He didn't answer, so Cassie stood and walked to the head of the intricately carved four-poster bed and the matching nightstand that held a close up of Matt's wife. She picked up the photo and returned to the foot of the bed, this time sitting slightly closer to Matt.

"She's very beautiful," Cassie said, admiring the picture of the smiling, blonde-haired, blue-eyed woman.

"Jenna was beautiful. Inside and out."

Was. The word struck Cassie's core. Jenna was never coming back. Matt would never hold his wife again. They'd never have another chance to talk or laugh or make love.

There was no hope for recovering the past he'd lost. Cassie's heart physically ached for him as she tried to imagine how awful that must be. She could still have all those opportunities again. Devon would return to her. Life would go on, happier than it was right now. She just had to be patient and try to do her best during this difficult time.

Part of that best can be helping Matt. Maybe that was the reason she had to wait a little longer for Devon to wake up and come back to her. If he were awake now, she certainly wouldn't be here with Matt. The possibility brought a sharp and conflicted pain to her chest. She certainly wasn't wishing for Devon to remain as he was. But since he had . . . well, she could only feel grateful for having Matt in her life, and not just because he could fix things for her.

Maybe I can fix this one big thing for him.

"How old are you, Matt?"

He turned sideways to look at her, question in his eyes. "Thirty-four. Why?"

"The average life span in the United States is somewhere around eighty years now, isn't it?" Cassie mused. "Another forty-six years is a long time to be alone, don't you think?"

"What is it you're suggesting?"

She wasn't quite sure. She was sort of making this up as she went, but she hadn't forgotten everything she learned in school. She relied on that training now, along with the sincere desire to help him.

"Keep all of these pictures up for now, but give yourself a deadline for when they need to come down." Cassie stood and, starting with the pictures on the wall, studied the couple in each. The first two photos showed a younger Matt, dressed as he did now, in jeans and an untucked shirt, but the farther she moved around the room, the more the photos changed. Jenna's hair was perfectly styled, and she wore more jewelry.

Matt's shirts were tucked in and accompanied by ties and jackets. The locations changed from places like the beach to fancier venues.

"Events through my employer," Matt said, as if he'd heard her unspoken question. "NBA stuff."

"Do you miss it?" Cassie asked.

"Not as much as I thought I would."

She heard the revelation in his voice and turned to see that his face mirrored the discovery of his statement.

"It was an exciting life," Matt said, "but I was missing out on the real excitement."

"Like head lice." Cassie grinned.

"Exactly." Matt laughed.

She turned back to the photos and finally placed the one in her hand on the nightstand again.

"As you were saying . . ." Matt prompted.

Good. He wanted to hear this. He wanted to feel better. She'd learned during her internship that there were people who, oddly enough, didn't want to get better but preferred to remain miserable, though Matt had never struck her as that type.

"Keep all of these up for now," Cassie repeated, "but give yourself a deadline for when they need to come down. Maybe by the one year anniversary of Jenna's death. When is that?"

"January." Matt was looking down again.

"All right." Cassie surged forward with her plan. "In January, I will come and help you take these down if you'd like, or you can do it gradually over the next few months. That might be better. You can keep one out, maybe this one." She glanced again at the picture on the nightstand. "And the boys ought to have a photo of their mother in their room or readily available to them, too."

"So I take the pictures down, then what?"

His interest encouraged her. "With each picture you take down, you have to forgive yourself for something with your relationship with Jenna, something from the past. You need to say it out loud and literally pack it up for good, put it in the box with the picture and tell yourself that it's in the past. That part of your life is done. Unfortunately, none of us gets a do-over."

Even Cassie realized she wasn't going to get that. Devon would never be able to live the first five years of Noah's life. They couldn't have those lost years back, but they could at least go forward together, just as Matt needed to move forward.

"What we get is a 'do better.'" *That's pretty good.* Her education was kicking in now, filling her with excitement and ideas. "With each picture you remove, you should put up a new one of a memory with you and Austin and Asher, of the things you'll be doing with them between now and then. These will be your doing better photos." Instead of punishing himself, Matt would see his successes and the happiness he could have with his boys now. "Along with putting the pictures and the past away, you need to make some long term plans for the future."

"I did," Matt said. "I sold our house, bought a new car, got a new job, moved."

What more could you ask? she imagined him thinking. She was going to ask anyway, going to push him a bit.

"What about pursuing a new wife?"

His gaze was sharp as he turned his head to her again. This time he sat up so they met eye-to-eye.

"You think it's that easy?"

"I didn't say anything about it being easy or hard or anything else," Cassie said. "I just asked you to consider it.

You've got two little boys to raise, and you've got your whole life ahead of you." *What is with the trite phrases tonight?* "You could make some woman very happy, and you could be happy, too."

"I'm happy now."

"Liar." The word was out before she realized it. Cassie clapped a hand to her mouth as she uttered an apology. "I didn't mean that. You're not a liar."

"Any more than you are, at any rate." Matt looked at her appraisingly. "I'd say we're both pretty good at pretending, though you've had a few more years than I have to perfect the deception."

"Some things make me very happy," Cassie said defensively. "Like Noah. I love being his mom. We have a lot of fun together."

"And yet . . ." Matt prodded.

Cassie shrugged. "Okay, so the nights are bad. I miss Devon. I'm lonely. And sad. A lot." She released a breath and looked away, not quite believing she'd just told him so much, so easily. How had this conversation been turned toward her problems? This was supposed to be about helping Matt.

"I know you feel all those same things," Cassie said. "The difference is you have the choice to move on. I get that you're still grieving right now, and dating probably sounds terrifying." It did to her. She could only feel grateful that wasn't her problem. "But you don't have to do it all right now. I'm just saying that you need to quit punishing yourself for the past. No one's perfect. Be as good as you can now, for Austin and Asher and for yourself. That probably means figuring out how to not be alone for the rest of your life."

There. She'd said it. Now let him hate her or not.

Matt leaned closer, bracing his hand on the bed, so close to Cassie's that their fingers were nearly touching. "The night

I called you and asked if we could be friends I figured out how to not be alone."

"That's not what I—"

"It's not a perfect situation." Their gazes locked. "Some of the kinks are pretty big, but I think it mostly works. I'm happier. The boys are happier—mine *and* yours—when we're together. I'd like to think that you do a little better, too, that my friendship maybe eases a bit of that loneliness you just admitted to, or that I'm at least worth hanging onto for my repair skills."

"You are. You do." Cassie fumbled for the right words that wouldn't say too much and finally settled on his. "I am. Happier."

"Good."

Neither moved for a long moment. Part of her never wanted to move but wanted to suspend time in this moment, with Matt sitting so close that every nerve in her body was aware of him. His hair was a mess from the many times he'd run his hands through it all evening in various stages of frustration. She longed to reach out and smooth it down for him, the same way she wanted to soothe the hurt in his life.

In his eyes, she read unmistakable desire, which she knew she should have rejected at once, but it felt good to be noticed by a man. Probably without even realizing it, Matt frequently said and did things that made her feel like a desirable woman instead of the frumpy school secretary and soccer mom she worried she'd become.

Her gaze slid down to his arms and hands that were always serving her. How she wanted to feel those arms around her, not in a romantic sense so much as to feel of their comfort. She knew what a hug from Matt would mean because she knew what she'd say with hers if she ever gave him one, which she couldn't. But if she did, it would mean so many things. I'm sorry for all you've been through. You're such a great person. Thank you for being my friend. I need you. I care about you. I—

"I should go." Cassie stood abruptly. "Tomorrow's a school day and—"

Matt pressed a finger to his lips as he stood. "Don't ever feel like you have to hide what you're feeling or really want to say to me. We're not sophomores in high school. We're mature adults with a tricky situation, and a friendship I don't want to mess up."

"Okay." Cassie nodded, then turned to go. Matt caught her arm.

"We'll do better with each other if we're honest. So I'll say it tonight. Being together like this—alone—while awesome, isn't a good idea. So we won't do it again because I find you too attractive; we're both too lonely, and I, at least, am only too human." He raked his hand through his hair again and sighed heavily. "It would be too easy—"

"Good summary," Cassie agreed as she hurried from the room.

This time, Matt let her go.

Nineteen

"Going all the way!" Matt's fists raised over his head as he dribbled the soccer ball downfield.

"Go, Dad, go!" Asher jumped up and down in the same spot mid-field that he'd been at all game.

"This one's ours," Matt shouted.

"I don't think so." Cassie ran in front of him, then turned, jogging backward so they faced one another. A sheen of sweat glistened on her forehead, and her ponytail swung back and forth as she jumped side to side, trying to block him.

Come and get me, he wanted to say, but knew that would only earn him a frown since she'd realize he wasn't just thinking about soccer. How was he supposed to care about that with such a beautiful, vibrant woman just a few feet away?

Cassie's eyes flickered briefly to his side, and just as Matt realized the look was a signal, Noah had stolen the ball from him.

"Hey!" he cried. "Austin, Asher. Where are you guys? You're supposed to be guarding."

"Teamwork," Cassie smirked as she moved past him, putting herself between Matt and Noah. "Plus, you should keep your eye on the ball." She ran off toward the opposite end of the field, giving him a fine view of her legs.

Just her legs. Admiring a woman's calves was not a sin. Cassie's were developed nicely, along with the rest of her.

"Better things to look at than a ball," he muttered.

"I heard that," she called over her shoulder.

"Good," he shouted back, smiling to himself. Thursday had become his favorite day of the week because of their afternoon scrimmage games. Sometimes they played all three boys against him and Cassie. Sometimes it was Webbs vs. Kramers, like today. Once they'd played girl against boys, Matt included, but she'd given them too much of a run for their money for him to risk humiliation with that match up again. She said soccer wasn't her game, but he begged to differ. At any rate, she outran him just about every time.

"Dad, stop them. We're losing," Austin whined.

"You stop them," Matt said, slowing his pace to a walk. Truth was, he didn't mind if Cassie and Noah won and he had to treat them to ice cream. He liked doing that anyway, and losing gave him the excuse he needed.

"Da-ad. You're not even trying."

"All right." Matt started jogging again. "But where were you a minute ago? If I steal the ball, you'd better have my back this time."

"Okay." Austin's face set in a look of grim determination that Matt read easily. Being beaten by a boy younger than him and a girl wasn't acceptable.

"Partners?" Matt held his hand out as they ran, and Austin slapped it. "Get your brother down there, too," Matt said, then sprinted toward the opposite end of the field. Cassie and Noah were close to the goal and would have been there already had she not allowed Noah to control the ball the entire length of the field. Matt felt bad to take a goal away from him, but his boys needed a score, too.

With a war cry and an exaggerated stride he dashed past them and jumped in front of the goal, arms outstretched. "Just try to get one past me. Just try."

"You can do this, Noah." Cassie nodded her encouragement, and Noah kicked, sending the ball straight at Matt's middle. He caught it but tripped in the process and staggered backward, falling fast onto the grass and hard ground beneath.

"Goal!" Noah shouted, jumping around with glee as Asher joined him. Asher always celebrated, regardless of the team that scored.

"Is not," Austin cried. "Dad caught it."

"But he caught it behind the posts, so technically it is a goal." Cassie picked up the ball and tossed it to Austin. "At least it's your turn to kick off. Rally the troops to center field."

"*Technically* I caught the ball in *front* of the posts and then tripped," Matt said after the boys had marched off. This wasn't worth starting a fight over, and he was glad Noah had made the goal. He pulled a decent-sized rock out of the ground between his legs. "Tripped on this." He held the rock up for Cassie to see.

"Sorry. Falling behind the posts counts, too. Any way the ball makes it back there, it's a score." She stepped closer and held a hand out to him. "Are you all right? That was a pretty hard fall."

"I'll say." Matt accepted her outstretched hand and promptly pulled her down beside and nearly on top of him.

"Matt!" she scolded as she scooted away and brushed grass from her shorts. "What was that for?"

"Just wanted you to know what it feels like to fall hard." *Like I have and am.* It was exhilaration and temptation and deprivation all at once in his case. He jumped up, held a hand out then helped Cassie up. Instead of letting her go right away, he held onto her a few seconds more as they stood facing each other.

An afternoon breeze whipped loose strands of hair across her face and stirred up more longing within him. Why did she have to be so beautiful? Worse, why did she have to be that way on the inside, too? A pretty face he could have resisted, but it was becoming harder and harder to resist the whole package that was Cassandra Webb.

"Matt?" She tugged her fingers free and took a step back, alarm in her eyes, as if she suspected he might try to kiss her or something. And he might have—certainly wanted to—but that Jiminy Cricket conscience of his was constantly nagging him to back off, reminding him that Cassie was already taken, and he was fortunate to be her friend.

"You keep saying my name," he teased. "Kind of like the sound of it, don't you?"

She placed her hands on her hips. "Know what? You're sounding like a big shot NBA commentator right now. Maybe it's that head of yours that made you lose balance."

"Ouch." He winced but took the deserved jab. It effectively doused the internal burning he hadn't been very good at controlling this afternoon. The last thing he wanted to act or sound like was the guy he used to think he was. "Sorry." He ducked his head and put his hands in his pockets, where they'd stay out of trouble. Now if only his mind and his mouth would.

"I was just going to ask if you and Noah would like to

come trick or treating with the boys and me next week. I don't imagine the candy selection is too good in your part of town."

"Not unless you count walnuts," Cassie said. "There are a couple of pretty big trees on the next farm over, but that's about it as far as neighborly goodies."

"So you'll come then?" Matt asked, always hungry for more time with her, especially just doing normal family things like playing soccer or going to the school carnival together like they all had last week.

"I can't," Cassie said. "It's one of the few nights of the year when I take Noah to see Devon."

"Halloween?" Matt was sure his expression must be as perplexed as he felt.

"The care center puts on this event, and families are encouraged to come, bring their children, and trick or treat from room to room."

"At a facility where patients are unable to care for themselves?" Matt scratched the side of his head. "I'm sorry, but that just sounds like a really bad idea."

"I thought so, too, at first." Cassie started walking toward the boys, who were poorly attempting to head butt the soccer ball to each other. Matt fell into step beside her.

"You have to realize that all the patients aren't like Devon. There are a lot of sweet old people there, and they get lonely. They love the kids. There are even a few children who are patients at Sierra, too. Their disabilities are such that their parents just couldn't care for them, so they live at the center permanently. It's really sad."

"And people in masks and scary costumes make it better?" Matt was starting to see her point, but it still seemed like an event of this nature had a lot of potential for disaster.

"Masks aren't allowed," Cassie explained. "There's a

dress code, actually. No weapons, real or pretend, no monsters, no blood, etc. Think of it as a kinder, gentler Halloween."

"If you say so." He wondered if seeing some of those patients, and particularly his father, might not be the most frightening thing of all for Noah.

"I can see that you don't believe me, so you should come with us. I'll put you all down on the list." Cassie stopped walking and caught Matt's eye. "You could meet my husband."

"All right." His answer probably wasn't as enthusiastic as she'd hoped, and her invitation certainly wasn't what he'd envisioned for Halloween night. The mirage of him and Cassie, bundled up and walking close together behind the boys as they went from house to house, vanished, as did his other plans for later—sitting on the sofa together, drinking cocoa and talking while the boys divvied up their loot.

Trick-or-treating at a care center wasn't what he wanted, but then, when was the last time Cassie'd had anything *she* wanted? He swallowed, uncomfortably conscience of how selfish his thoughts and motives had been of late, since the evening of the head lice, really, a few weeks earlier.

It was as if some parasite had invaded his brain and siphoned away all logic regarding his relationship with Cassie. Their friendship. That's all it was. All it ever could be. Maybe seeing her husband would be the solid reminder he needed.

Twenty

"All right, where's this surprise?" Matt exaggerated stumbling as he weaved his way around Janet Jensen's front room, a hand outstretched. His other hand reached behind him, to keep Asher from sliding off his back. Asher's sticky little fingers pressed tightly to Matt's eye sockets, not quite blocking his entire vision, but an effective blindfold nevertheless, as fear of being gouged encouraged Matt to keep his eyes securely shut.

"Not that way, Dad." Austin grabbed Matt's hand and pulled him toward the kitchen and the sound of a chair being pulled out.

"Sit," Austin said a minute later when they'd reached their apparent destination. Matt obeyed, only too happy to shrug Asher from his shoulders and to relieve the pressure from his eyes.

"Don't look yet," Noah said.

"Wouldn't dream of it," Matt said, grateful for the extra seconds to recover.

Shuffling and giggles filled the air around him until finally Cassie's voice silenced them.

"You may open your eyes now," she said.

He did to see three small-sized, hat-topped, mustached, caped Musketeers standing before him, each brandishing a foam sword.

"One for all, and all for candy!" they chorused.

"That's not what we practiced," Cassie scolded, her brow arched at Austin, the ringleader, no doubt.

"It's better." His cheeky smile all but admitted guilt.

"I suppose when you're five or six it is." Cassie shifted her gaze from the boys to Matt.

He stood, walking around each of the Musketeers, admiring the feathers sticking out of their wide hats and the emblems on their tunics. "Did you make these?"

"My mom and I did," Cassie said, as Matt noted the two sewing machines at the far end of the table.

"Cassie did most of the work," Janet called from the pantry.

"I thought you were just watching the boys over here after school because there was more space for them to play. It would appear I've been tricked."

Asher giggled and wrapped an arm around Matt's leg.

"More space really is the main reason," Cassie said.

"Do you like us, Dad?" Asher asked.

"Do you know who we are?" Noah's expression mirrored Cassie's when she was concerned.

"Of course I like you. And I know who you are." Matt crouched in front of them. "The Three Musketeers are famous. 'All for one and one for all,' meant they stuck together no matter what, protecting each other and the king. You guys are from a book and at least a few movies."

"See," Cassie said. "Nothing to worry about." To Matt

she said, "Noah is concerned no one will know who they are. He was hoping for a more popular costume, Batman or one of the Avengers. But no masks and no—"

"Weapons?" Matt placed his hand over Asher's and attempted to slice the floppy foam sword through the air.

"Well, I hardly think those count," Cassie said.

Matt didn't think so either, and he could understand Noah's disappointment. What kid wanted a play weapon that resembled a sponge? He decided his contribution to Halloween—post care center, of course—would be some better swords for the boys to play with.

"The costumes are great. Perfect, really." Over the past two months, the three boys had become nearly inseparable. Matt wasn't certain if it was because of the afternoons they spent together when Cassie watched them, or if Noah was so eager for friends that he'd bonded with both brothers and that somehow made Austin and Asher closer as well. Whatever magic was at play, Matt hoped it continued. He guessed that Cassie did, too, as he watched her smiling fondly as the boys chased each other around the table, their capes flying.

"Ready for tomorrow night?" she asked.

"Yeah." Reluctantly Matt pulled his attention from the boys. He'd enjoyed the temporary respite, but Cassie's question brought the imminent visit to the care center front and center. He wasn't ready to see her husband, to see any of the patients at Sierra Long-Term Care, truth be told. It was too close to a hospital, and a hospital represented sickness and death, and that was too close to the memory of losing Jenna and to his own pain. Ready or not, tomorrow night he'd have to face it all.

"Nice." Matt's voice was sarcastic as it carried from the guest bathroom at Cassie's Mom's house. "The boys are heroes. You get to dress like a princess—"

"Seventeenth century French nobility," Cassie called out, correcting him. She lowered the cape and studied her head full of curls in the hall mirror. Not bad. She couldn't remember the last time she'd curled her hair before this and was secretly glad her mother had taken pains to make this costume that warranted an elaborate hairstyle, even if it had taken over an hour to achieve.

Cassie told herself it was important she look especially good tonight because she'd be seeing Devon, and it was a special day, a holiday. If he were awake, she would certainly dress up from her usual Friday night attire. They'd probably be going to a costume party together after they took Noah trick or treating around the neighborhood, of course.

Dreams. No doubt dressing in costume only fed them.

"Really?" More disgruntled sounds came from the bathroom.

Cassie imagined Matt struggling with a ruffled shirt or powdered wig. "Mom?" she called to her mother in the other room. "What costume *did* you make Matt?"

Mom came down the hall, drying her hands on a dishtowel. "Well, you said he couldn't look like he matched you, like you were a *couple*," she added under her breath.

Cassie nodded. That had been her mom's first plan until Cassie nipped it in the bud when she found the patterns for the man's shirt and pantaloons.

"We're not a couple," Cassie whispered fiercely as she pulled her mom away from the bathroom door. "We're going to see Devon tonight. I don't know how you could suggest that Matt and I dress alike."

"Well, you aren't, so you needn't worry about that."

Mom frowned her disapproval. "But you *are* friends, and you have been acting as a family of sorts, so he needs to look like he belongs, too."

"What did you do?" The talk she'd had with her mom after the night she and Matt had spent alone cleaning his apartment had only seemed to fuel her mother's fire that Matt was more than a friend. Cassie couldn't understand her mother's rationale. She loved Devon, too. Cassie had even asked, were the tables turned, and it was her father lying in that care center, would her mom continue to be faithful. Janet had been upset that Cassie had even asked such a question.

"But this is different, dear," her mother had said.

"How?" Cassie demanded.

"It just is," Mom said, as one of those far away smiles graced her lips.

It just isn't, Cassie thought, *especially not tonight.* Sounding like a frustrated teen, she sighed as her mom retreated to the kitchen again.

"Matt," Cassie called. "We're going to be late."

"Go on without me."

"No way." Cassie gathered the heavy skirt in her hands and marched down the hall. She pounded on the bathroom door. "Quit acting like a ninny and come out here."

Unintelligible muttering came from the other side of the door. A few seconds later, it opened to a very disgruntled Three Musketeers candy bar. Cassie burst into laughter. She couldn't help it.

"See." Matt started to push the door closed, but she wedged her way in, no easy feat with the wide skirt of her dress.

"It's awesome," Cassie said, taking in the back of the Three Musketeers costume in the mirror. Beneath the shiny fabric wrapper, complete with appliquéd lettering, Matt's bare hairy legs stuck out. She bit her lip to keep from laughing again.

"I look good enough to eat?" he joked.

"Definitely."

He perked up. "In that case—"

Cassie backed out of the room in a hurry. How was it they kept getting in this situation—flirting, standing too close to one another, becoming too familiar and comfortable. The red danger button flashed and blared in her mind, but down the hall, her mother was looking on and smiling.

"Do you like his costume?" she asked as Cassie marched past.

"It's great," Cassie said. Her mom had honored her request; they didn't match, but somehow it had gotten her into trouble anyway.

The boys were just finishing dinner in the kitchen, and they, too, laughed out loud when Matt appeared.

"Hey," he quipped. "Don't laugh at me. This is all your fault." He placed a hand on Austin's head. "One for all and all for *candy*."

The boys laughed louder but instead of joining in, Cassie felt something melt inside of her. Matt looked ridiculous, yet he was willing to for his sons. *And mine.* Because of Matt, life had been so much better the past couple of months. Fighting a sudden swell of emotion that had her near to tears instead of laughter, Cassie pulled her hood up and started for the door.

"Come on everyone. Let's go."

Twenty-One

The antiseptic smell dredged up painful memories the instant Matt stepped through the doors of Sierra Care. He glanced down at Austin and Asher to see how they were faring and was relieved to see they both appeared to be busy taking in all the bats and ghosts hanging from the ceiling. He'd never taken them to the hospital to see Jenna to say goodbye to her. It hadn't been a choice, really. The accident had transfigured her face in a way that made it almost unrecognizable, and he hadn't wanted the boys to see or remember her that way.

Like I do. He didn't usually; all the pictures in his bedroom helped with that, but just as he'd feared, the care center brought it all back.

Matt shuffled along behind Cassie and the boys, almost looking like a patient here himself. Janet had sewn the cloth candy bar straight, all the way to the bottom of the costume which fell to his knees—*so no one will be able to see up under it,* she'd told him—and the result left him with very little stride.

Cassie led them past a living room-like foyer, straight back, then down one hall and then another. Halloween music piped from the intercom, and, still waddling behind the others, Matt rocked out a bit to the Ghostbusters theme. Anything to get his mind off of where they were.

People come here to die. Maybe it wasn't such an inappropriate place for a Halloween party, though not one five-year-olds attended.

At the nurse's station, Cassie introduced Matt and the boys.

"Lynn, these are our guests tonight, Matt Kramer and his sons, Austin and Asher."

"I love your costumes," Lynn said, her amused gaze lingering on Matt as she distributed plastic bracelets to each of them.

"My mom made them," Cassie said by way of explanation.

"Ah." Lynn nodded. "Tell her I said hello, will you? I haven't seen her for a while."

"She comes to visit during the day now," Cassie explained. "Her eyesight is getting too poor for her to drive at night."

"Well, tell her I miss seeing her then."

"I will." Cassie turned to the boys and Matt. "Okay, here's the deal. We're going to start with the children who live here. We'll visit with each of them for a few minutes. Most can't eat candy, so the treat for them is having visitors tonight."

"They're going to laugh at Daddy," Asher predicted.

"Maybe." Cassie's eyes flickered to him, and Matt gave

her a smile and thumbs up to let her know he was still on board.

Just barely. The costume was the least of his worries now. It was memories from last January that were causing a cold sweat to break out across his forehead.

"Remember what we talked about and the movie we watched," Cassie said.

"Movie?" Matt asked.

"Last week. You were at work," she clarified. "I showed them a documentary about children with severe disabilities. I wanted them to be prepared for what they'd see today."

"Oh. Great idea." He was impressed. Once again, Cassie'd shown how thoughtful a person she was. In this case, it was thinking not only of the children who lived here, but thinking about how Austin, Asher, and Noah would handle this place. He wished there had been a video he could have watched to prepare.

The first room they came to belonged to a nine-year-old girl with cerebral palsy. She was also blind, so Matt felt unable to provide much entertainment value. He was astonished at what Cassie and the boys did, especially Noah. It was clear he'd been here before and felt comfortable around these types of children. Asher was quick to warm up as well. Only Austin hung back, standing near Matt while the others held the girl's hands and talked to her.

"What's wrong with her, Dad?" Austin whispered. "What's that thing Cassie said she has? Can we catch it?"

"We can't catch anything that anyone here has." Matt explained what he'd already heard Cassie say several times. "Cerebral palsy means that her brain didn't develop right."

Austin seemed to think about this for a minute while Matt watched as Cassie helped the girl run her fingers over the feather in Noah's hat.

"Brains sure hurt a lot of people," Austin said.

"They can," Matt agreed, "but they also do amazing things. Your brain is like a computer for your entire body."

"When I grow up I'm going to learn how to fix them," Austin declared with as much passion and intensity as he'd exhibited during the fits he'd thrown the past months. "So people like mom don't have to die and people like Noah's dad will wake up."

"That's a fine idea." Matt pulled Austin up against him. "It would make Mom very happy to hear that."

By the next room—belonging to a fifteen year-old born without legs and with much of his torso deformed—Austin was participating, too. When the patient, Zack, showed extreme interest in Matt's costume, Matt joked with him, saying that the costume would be perfect for Zack, and he wouldn't have to worry about anyone checking out his hairy legs. Cassie promised that Zack could wear it or she'd have her mom make him one of his own next year. Matt would have been only too happy to give it to him now.

After they'd visited all of the children's rooms, he began to see why this activity began at four-thirty and went until nine. At the pace they were going, they'd be here past ten. But the boys were enjoying themselves, and somewhere between the teenage girl recovering from an amputation and the elderly woman with Alzheimer's, Matt realized he'd stopped thinking about his own loss and had started counting his blessings instead.

He caught Cassie's eye over the bed of an elderly man, as they each held one of his hands, and mouthed a thank you. Cassie's answering smile told him she understood. Matt felt like he understood her a little better now, too. The past six years had likely shaped her into the kind, compassionate, observant woman that she was. He could see that being around people like this each week would either change a person for better or worse. It seemed she'd gone for better and found the sweet within her difficult experiences. He guessed that was what held the bitter at bay.

The sweet of his trial has been finding her and Noah. If he could change things, Matt knew he'd still wish Jenna back, but he wouldn't want the life they'd had before. He'd want to be better, to be the man he was becoming. He also realized that if they hadn't lost Jenna, he and the boys wouldn't be here right now. He would never have met Cassie, would maybe never have learned the lessons of the past two months from her. For the first time, he felt grateful he hadn't been given that choice.

She saved her husband's room for last, and Matt could see in her body language—refusing to look directly at him, and the anxious way she kept glancing at the clocks in each room—that she'd become more and more tense as the night progressed. Finally, just before they were to go in, Matt touched her arm and pulled her aside as he called to the boys to wait up a minute.

"Maybe Austin, Asher, and I should go now," he suggested.

"You're our ride home," Cassie said, not disagreeing entirely, telling him he'd been right about her conflicted feelings.

"We won't leave you. We'll go over to the hospital cafeteria again, see what food the boys launch at each other this time." He smiled lopsidedly at the memory of that pivotal night.

She considered a moment. "No. I think this is good. I want you to stay, if you want to, that is." She looked up at him.

"We're still in," Matt said, feeling stressed for her, with her, something.

They approached the room quietly. The candy bowl was outside of Devon's room with the nurse stationed there. "No visitors who aren't family or friends," the sign on the door said. As if understanding the solemnity of the situation far beyond their years, the boys quickly took one candy, without pawing through for their favorites as they'd done at other rooms, and walked single file past Matt as he held the door open.

His first look at Devon surprised him. He pictured the photo of the well-built man on Cassie's bathroom mirror and tried to reconcile it with the man in the bed. His body seemed to have shrunk. He appeared almost small lying there, so very still. Six years was certainly time enough to lose one's muscle tone and probably a lot else, Matt realized, but Devon also looked like he was simply sleeping.

Unlike Jenna. Before the doctors had realized what had caused her car accident, they'd been working frantically, hoping to save her, and when Matt was finally allowed into that ER room, it had been to find her surrounded by machines and wires and medical instruments. Everything had been removed from her by then, the machines turned off, the life-saving apparatus pushed aside, but it didn't matter. He'd been able to imagine well enough all the medical interventions that had been put in place in an attempt to save her.

In contrast, Devon's room held very little medical equipment beyond a single monitor tucked into the corner on the opposite side of the bed. Whatever feeding or other tubes he was hooked up to must have been placed beneath his clothing or the blanket covering him. Devon didn't move other than the slight motion of his chest as he breathed. Matt was relieved to see that his eyes were closed.

"Hi, Dad." Noah walked right up to his father and took his hand.

"Happy Halloween, Devon." Cassie leaned over the bed and placed a kiss on his forehead. "We brought some friends this year. This is Matt, Austin, and Asher."

The boys looked to Matt, as if uncertain what was expected of them. Was there a movie on this protocol, too? He wished he'd thought about that a bit more beforehand.

Following Cassie's and Noah's lead, Matt walked up to the bed, took Devon's free hand and shook it as best he could. "I've heard a lot about you. It's nice to finally meet the man Cassie talks so much about."

"Noah, Austin, and Asher are dressed as the Three Musketeers this year," Cassie said. "Mom helped me sew the costumes, and she made mine, a French aristocrat. I even curled my hair to go with it—I know, you'd be shocked—but the style reminds me a little of how it looked at our wedding. I wish you could see it."

The wobble in her voice helped Matt forget the awkwardness he felt. *Every single week* for over six years she'd gone through this, filled with hope and yearning and then what had to be heartbreaking disappointment. Tonight at least, he could help her.

Cassie pulled up a chair beside Devon, then took the hand Noah had just let go of. She pressed Devon's hand between her own and raised it to her cheek, holding it there, her eyes closed.

It hurt Matt to see this, but not like he would have thought. He hurt for Cassie, not himself. *This is her husband, the man she married and loves. And he* is *still here.* Devon's hand had been surprisingly warm, unlike Jenna's cold one when Matt had said goodbye to her in the hospital.

Cassie was right. There was still a chance.

For a wild second, Matt imagined shaking Devon's shoulders and somehow miraculously waking him. Surely

Cassie had to have had the same crazy thought before. He wondered if she'd ever acted on it, how often she broke down.

Matt came around the side of the bed near Cassie. "You've got quite the wife, Devon, and she does look very beautiful tonight." He squeezed Cassie's shoulder lightly. She glanced up at him, a grateful smile fighting to overcome tears that hadn't fallen. Matt thought he understood. It wasn't the compliment that had her feeling gratitude, it was someone else talking, someone else trying to reach Devon, someone here at her side while she hurt.

Matt decided he would try. He'd do whatever he could because suddenly, more than anything, he wanted to see her be happy again. Just because his ending hadn't been happy didn't mean that hers couldn't be. He'd never known someone more deserving.

He pulled up a chair next to hers and sat as best he could, his costume riding up to mid-thigh and straining at his shoulders.

"Don't cry, Mom," Noah said.

Cassie shook her head. "I'm not. Just remembering for a minute, but it was a happy memory."

Behind Matt, Austin and Asher still stood uncomfortably. Matt beckoned them, and they came to join Noah, all three boys standing side-by-side at the end of the bed.

"Austin, Noah, Asher, you boys are having an experience that most kids your age don't get to have. You know what it's like to not be able to be with one of your parents."

Austin's startled, angry gaze flickered to Matt's, and he could see that Austin had picked up on his choice of words, *get* implying opportunity or something good.

"What you each have to go through is hard, but you can make it into something good, like your mom has, Noah. She loves you so much, and she appreciates every minute she has with you. Austin, Asher, I hope you know I feel the same way about you. Sadly, it took losing your mom for me to learn how important each of those minutes are. You boys can learn that now and can help us grown-ups remember, too. We can all spend our time feeling angry or sad that we don't have what the other person has, or"—Matt reached out and rubbed his hand along Austin's arm—"we can be glad for what we do have, even if it isn't everything. Being here with Noah's dad tonight is helping me to be glad and grateful."

It was quite a speech for such little kids, but somehow Matt felt like they got it. Asher nodded solemnly while Noah put his arm around Austin.

Behind Matt, Cassie sniffled, and he was pretty sure it didn't have anything to do with thinking about her wedding day.

"Why don't you boys wait in the hall for a few minutes?" Matt suggested. "Just sit outside the door, and you can each have two pieces of your candy while Noah's mom and I visit with his dad just a few minutes more. Then if you want to come in again, Noah, you can take as long as you want."

Six feet exited the room, relief almost evident in their hurried steps. Part of Matt wished he could join them even as another part of him realized he'd just taken control over a situation that wasn't his to direct.

He faced Cassie, an apology on his lips. "I'm sorry. I should have asked what you wanted us to do. I can go outside with my boys and send Noah in if—"

"Stay." Cassie's hand covered Matt's for a brief second. "Talk to Devon. He rarely hears anyone's voice but mine, and that's not even every day. The nurses speak to him sometimes, but it isn't much. I worry he must be so lonely. He hasn't heard another man for a really long time. His friends—"

"Didn't turn out to be so great?" Matt guessed.

"Yeah." She gave a little shrug, trying to act like it didn't bother her, but Matt could see how much it did. "People are busy, and doing this is—hard."

Her voice broke again, fueling Matt with more courage and ambition in this situation than he'd have imagined possible. Squaring his shoulders and silently praying for words—lots of them and the right ones—he began a one sided conversation.

"You're a lucky man, Devon. Cassie is an incredible woman. She's more faithful and dedicated to being a wife and a mother than anyone I've ever known. She loves you unfailingly. She loves your son, and she does everything she can for him. You. Are. A. Lucky. Man." Matt leaned forward, elbows propped on the side of Devon's bed.

"I was a lucky man, too, married to a great woman, one I didn't really deserve. I have two boys who are pretty darn awesome when they aren't driving me crazy. I had a nice house; Cassie tells me you were saving for one before your accident. I worked for the Trail Blazers, traveled with them, working the games, wined and dined and had quite the life. Then the floor fell out from under me when I lost my Jenna." *My Jenna.* What he used to call her those first, pre-successful career years of their marriage.

"She died without any warning—no sickness, no indication that anything was wrong at all. I wasn't home when it happened. I wasn't even in the state." Matt swallowed with difficulty. Now it was his voice struggling. These were the very memories he'd hoped to avoid tonight, and here he was spilling his guts to a guy who couldn't respond and maybe didn't even hear him.

"My last chartered jet was my emergency trip home. It was lucky, I told myself the whole way, that I had such connections and could get there so quickly. I only knew that Jenna had been involved in a car accident and it was serious. When I got to Portland a couple of hours later, I realized how little my ability to fly home quickly mattered. What mattered is that I should have been home before then, should have slept in our bed with my arm curled around her the night before, should have kissed her that morning and told her I loved her, should have treasured every single second we had together instead of wasting so many of them chasing the dream of being the big shot who got to tell the world about a *ball* going up and down the court."

Now would have been a really good time for Devon to respond, to concur with Matt's stupidity, or Cassie could have at least chimed in with some well-meaning but futile words of comfort. There was no comfort in his situation. None was deserved when he'd treated what was most precious so lightly.

That was what he was attempting to share with Devon now. Sure, his situation was different, but time was slipping away for him, too. If there was the slightest chance that he had any control over anything with his body, if there was some part of his conscious that heard and understood, then Matt wanted Devon to hear this, to think and to know and then to find the strength to act so he didn't lose what is most precious like Matt did.

"I didn't realize how fortunate and blessed I'd been until I lost Jenna." Matt forced the words to continue, though he didn't want to say or hear them. "I blew it, and I don't get a second chance. What was it you said?" He turned to Cassie.

"There are no do-overs." Her voice was soft, her eyes misty.

Matt nodded. "No do-overs. Just do betters. So that's what I'm trying. Your wife is helping a ton with that. She's gifted at that, helping people. I hope that soon she's able to do that full time for her job. I also hope that you—" Matt's voice rose as a swell of energy and emotion pushed its way to the surface. *Who is this guy* not *to wake up?* It wasn't a logical thought, and it wasn't as if it was Devon's fault he was in this situation.

"It's time for you to do better, Devon. You need to open those eyes, look at your wife—really look at her—and figure out how to get out of this bed. She needs you. Noah needs you. You need them, too, whether you realize it or not. Get up. Be a husband; be a father. Take this beautiful woman in your arms and love her like she should be loved."

Or I will. The selfish thought startled him, so abrupt was its interruption into his previous train of thought. Matt felt more disgust with himself. Apparently, even when face-to-face with Cassie's evident love for her husband, he could only think of others before himself for so long. If that was the case, he had no business being here any longer. Matt pushed back his chair and stood. "I'll get Noah." He headed for the door, eager for fresh air and a better perspective.

"Matt," Cassie called.

"Yes?" He didn't stop or turn to look at her.

"Thank you."

"You're welcome." Though she wouldn't be if she could see into his thoughts at the moment.

Out in the hall, the boys sat in a circle playing Halloween bingo while a different nurse than had been here previously, this one wearing a silk embroidered dress over her scrubs, called out the pictures to cover.

"Bingo." Noah placed a piece of candy over a cartoon of Frankenstein.

"Very good." The nurse leaned forward and dropped a tootsie roll into his bag.

"Perfect timing," Matt said. "I think your mom's ready for you in there."

"Will you watch my candy while I say goodbye to my dad?" Noah held his bag out to Matt.

"Sure." Matt took the bag, then pushed the door open for Noah. When it had closed behind him, he thanked the nurse for playing with Austin and Asher, then told the boys it was time to clean up. Awkwardly, with his costume riding up again, Matt crouched to help them collect the candy and game pieces. When they'd finished, he stood, just as awkwardly, and handed everything back to the nurse.

"For you boys." She dropped the candy markers into their bags. "There are donuts and punch at the nurses' station, if you'd like some."

"Can we, Dad?" Asher asked, but Austin was already on his way.

"Go ahead. Get one for Noah, too." Matt imagined how bedtime was going to go—or not go—tonight with all that sugar coursing through their veins.

"It was difficult in there?" the nurse asked, one perfectly manicured brow raising in question as her eyes shifted to Devon's door.

"Yeah." Matt pulled his gaze from the boys to her and wondered if maybe she was a volunteer instead of a nurse. She seemed a bit on the old side to be working at a place like this, more like a grandmother instead of a medical professional. There was something familiar about her, too, though he couldn't quite place what it was.

"You are a good friend to Mrs. Webb to come with her tonight," the grandmother nurse said.

Matt shrugged. "It's been a pretty cool evening for the most part. Very eye-opening. I think I'll understand Cassie better now."

The woman smiled. "Understanding is good. If anyone needs that, it is Cassandra."

Matt nodded his agreement. "She just has so much hope that her husband is going to get better, and I worry for her if she ever loses that—if he never does. Get better, that is."

"Hope is a beautiful thing when it is channeled properly." The nurse stood and faced him—his chest, anyway. She was petite, easily a head shorter, but that didn't seem to bother her in the least, nor did imparting what Matt could only describe as words of wisdom.

"And if it isn't channeled properly?" he asked.

"Time and patience." The woman's smile was kind, and the lines around her eyes suggested she had experience to back up her advice. "Don't give up on Cassandra, even when all seems impossible. Don't give up on her or the two of you." She glanced toward Devon's door once more, her expression changing.

"My work here is over for now. Time for me to leave." With a last smile at Matt, she began walking down the hall as he pondered her odd choice of words. *The two of you.*

She'd gone but a few steps when she paused and turned back to him, wearing an amused smile.

"You give new meaning to the term—what is it the youth say these days—candy for the eyes?"

"Eye candy?" Matt frowned.

"Yes." Her gaze traveled down Matt's Three Musketeers costume to his bare legs and sneakers. "Eye candy. Very good for Cassandra. As is her eye candy for you." With that, the woman turned away, her laughter floating back to him just as the light overhead caught the sparkle of the pearl comb in her hair.

Twenty-Two

"What kind of pie would you like for Thanksgiving?" Pen in hand, Cassie added whipping cream to her grocery list. No matter what kind of pie her mother chose this year, they'd need whipping cream to go with it and for that silly pie in the face game Noah always liked to play after dinner. Cassie smiled, anticipating a repeat of the fun tradition.

Her mom paused her work at the computer and swiveled in her chair to face Cassie. "About that, there's been a change of plans."

"You want something besides pie this year?" Cassie added mini marshmallows to her list to go over the yams so Noah would eat them. "Would you like cheesecake? Brownies and ice cream? Anything but fruitcake and I'm good. Just tell me what it is so I can add the ingredients to my list. I only want to go shopping once this weekend. Next week I'm not going anywhere near the store."

"What are Matt and his boys doing for Thanksgiving?" Mom asked, more than a hint of suggestion in her tone.

Cassie put down her pen and looked toward the family room and the happy sounds coming from within. Today her mom had allowed the boys to make a fort, using both sets of couch cushions and at least a dozen old blankets. *They'll never want to play at my apartment again.*

"Matt's taking the boys to Oregon to visit his parents." *Nice try, Mom.*

"That's too bad." Janet seemed suddenly worried.

"What's bad about it?" Cassie returned to her list and the store ads that were spread across the table. "It will be good for Austin and Asher to see their grandparents and for Matt to visit his family."

"Yes, but that leaves you all alone."

Cassie rolled her eyes. *Here we go again.* Her mom continued to be bent on matchmaking the two of them, which was so weird. Her mom loved Devon, and she believed in marriage and fidelity. Cassie couldn't figure out what her mom's deal was, but it was really starting to bother her. "I wouldn't call Thanksgiving with you and Noah all alone."

"I won't be here, dear."

What new ploy is this? Cassie took up her pen again, tapping the end of it on the table. "Are you finally going on that Caribbean cruise you've been talking about for the past ten years?"

"Yes, actually." Her mom smiled. "Well, that was easy. And here I'd worried about telling you." She swiveled her chair around to face the computer again.

"You're serious?" The steady thump of Cassie's pen increased its tempo.

"It was a difficult decision, only made because I believed you wouldn't be alone over the holiday, but I can't back out now. My flight is booked, and I got such a fantastic discount through Karen's friend."

"What does Karen have to do with this?" Cassie asked. "Is this a Bunco cruise or something?" About the only social thing her mom ever did was attend Bunco twice a month, so Cassie supposed it made sense that any kind of trip her mom was planning would be with those friends.

"Not exactly." The printer started up, and a few seconds later, her mom picked up the paper it had spit into the tray. "Here's my itinerary." She crossed the room and handed it to Cassie.

"You're going to be gone for ten days?" Cassie couldn't quite believe that her never-go-anywhere-or-do-anything mom was actually going to fly across the country and spend an entire week at sea.

"Ten glorious days." Her mom clasped her hands together and wore an expression akin to that of Noah surrounded by a pile of birthday presents.

"That's—that's crazy," Cassie finally said. "I mean, it's wonderful that you're going, but it's just not you."

"And why not?" Her mom sauntered past the table and into the kitchen. "I'm not so old that I can't have a bit of fun."

"I didn't mean it that way." Cassie tried, but she couldn't imagine her mother swimming with dolphins, snorkeling, or biking around some island. "I just—" She was just confused and a tiny bit hurt. Her mom had been the one constant she could count on, everything from being a shoulder to cry on to watching Noah on Friday nights. With both Mom and Matt out of town, the next week stretched ahead, long and bleak.

"You and Noah will be fine," her mom said, as if she'd read Cassie's thoughts. "Go see a movie on Thanksgiving. Get ice cream at Samantha's."

"My oven isn't even big enough to hold a turkey," Cassie lamented.

"Cook it here," Mom said. "I don't mind."

Cassie did. The thought of being here without her mom was strange and worrisome, yet someday, though hopefully not anytime soon, she'd be faced with that very scenario when her mother died. If she felt alone now, she knew it would be ten times worse then. Her mother was more than a mom; she was her friend and confidant. The thought of being without her was frightening.

Whistling a tune that sounded like "A Pirate's Life for Me," Mom came to stand behind Cassie and leaned close. "Noah will keep you company."

"He will." Cassie tried to sound positive. Three days off with Noah was a gift, and she'd enjoy it, but Lego superheroes could only go so far. The same loneliness she'd grappled with continuously since Devon's accident hit her again. It seemed to be getting worse lately instead of better. She loved Noah, adored him. Being his mom was enough.

Only, what if it wasn't?

Twenty-Three

"There's no school this morning. Go back to bed, Noah. Better yet, come snuggle with me." Half asleep, Cassie patted the bed beside her.

"Get up, Mom. Someone's at the door."

Cassie bolted upright in bed, nearly bumping heads with Noah as he leaned close. "Someone's—"

The knocking came again, and Cassie threw back the covers. "Stay here," she ordered then tiptoed to the front room, though she needn't have bothered. The floor was so squeaky it sounded like there were three of her marching around.

"Cassie, I know you're in there." Matt's voice.

She placed a hand on the arm of the loveseat and leaned on it a second while her pounding heart slowed. What did Matt think he was doing, scaring her half to death, coming over at—she glanced at the clock on the stove—*six* a.m. Cassie slid the chain lock and flung open the door.

"What are you doing here?" she demanded in a voice snarly enough to match the morning tangles in her hair.

A lazy smile spread across Matt's face as he took in her disheveled appearance. "Kidnapping you." He held up a pair of kids' plastic handcuffs and a bandana. "Though with that hair, you're the scary one." He pushed past her into the apartment. "Come on, boys. You know what to do."

Austin and Asher marched in behind Matt.

"Get Noah's toothbrush and pajamas," Austin said.

"Stuffed animal and blanket." Asher hurried to follow his brother. A second later, the sound of the three boys' happy reunion came from the bedroom. Since the soccer season ended and it had become too cold for their scrimmage games, they hadn't been seeing as much of each other. Noah had really missed them.

Cassie closed the door, then leaned against it as she faced Matt, her arms folded. "Kidnapping is a felony with some pretty hefty consequences, you know."

"I'm well aware of that, Mrs. Police-Officer's-Wife." Matt picked up her purse from the table and glanced inside. "Wallet, check. Where's your phone? You'll want your charger, too."

"Planning to use my Visa and reroute my calls as well?" Cassie stifled a yawn. "You've thought this out." She dropped onto the couch and lay back, kicking her legs up over the arm.

Matt set her purse by the door. "You want to pick out your clothes, or should I?"

"I get to bring clothes? Goody." Cassie closed her eyes and tried to hide her smile and her secret joy that Matt and the boys were apparently staying for the holiday. She wondered what he had planned for the day. Maybe they were taking the boys to the zoo and spending the night in the city or—

"Only if you want clothes." Matt picked up her feet and started pulling her. "If you're comfortable wearing that same t-shirt and sweats in front of my mom all weekend, then I'm cool with it, too."

"Your mom!" Cassie kicked him away and jumped up. "What are you talking about?"

"You and Noah, me and the boys, and Oregon. It's about time you left this town. According to your mom, it's been years since you went anywhere."

"My mom put you up to this, didn't she?" Cassie folded her arms and silently berated herself for not catching onto her mother's scheme earlier. "She went on a cruise this week so I'd be alone and go with you."

"I know she likes me," Matt said with jovial arrogance, "but leaving town just so you'd come with me sounds a bit extreme, even for your mom." He pointed a finger down the short hall. "Heading to your room for clothes. Oregon can be a little chilly. We'd better at least get you a sweater or two."

Oregon. Matt's parents. A long weekend with Matt and the boys. Her heart beat a staccato rhythm at the thought alone. She grabbed Matt's sleeve before he was out of reach. "I can't go with you." Disappointment leaked through her words. She *wanted* to go.

"Why not? What's holding you here, Cassie?"

He knew what kept her here, the reason she never left. *If Devon woke up while I was away . . . and with another man, no less.*

"I can't leave because of Devon," she said resolutely. "I'd miss seeing him on Friday night."

"You would." Matt's gaze was even. "But will he even know you're gone?"

"He will if he happens to wake up while I'm away, and even if he doesn't, that was mean and uncalled for." Cassie crossed her arms in front of her and tried to move past Matt to the bedroom. He blocked her way.

"I didn't intend for it to be, but I'm not thinking about Devon right now. I'm thinking about you and Noah and what's best for the two of you this weekend. It seems a little vacation would be both well-deserved and enjoyed."

"I can't just think about myself and Noah," Cassie argued. "I have to consider everyone in our family."

"I respect that." Matt's words were soft and slow, giving her the impression he was choosing them carefully. "What I'm asking is that you think about Noah first this weekend. Put his needs above Devon's. What would Noah enjoy more, the weekend here with you—not that I'm saying that's a bad option—or a big family weekend in a house on the beach with a tableful of conversation and food, kids running around, bonfires and marshmallows, memories and fun?"

Cassie closed her eyes against the vivid, enticing picture. No doubt Noah would love such a weekend. She would, too, but leaving Devon here alone and being with Matt felt wrong. And she was dearly sick of feeling conflicted and wrong all the time. It was a heavy price to pay for her friendship with Matt.

"I'm ready, Mom."

She opened her eyes to Noah, fully dressed and with his bulging Lego backpack slung over his shoulder, standing in front of her.

"Asher said there are donuts in the car and they're still hot. Can you hurry and get dressed so we can go?" The question was more a statement, and Cassie could see in his joy-filled expression that he had no doubt they were on their way to an adventure. She thought briefly of sending Noah with Matt and staying here alone but quickly dismissed the idea; being separated from Noah for a whole weekend might kill her, to say nothing of how truly lonely she'd be then.

Swinging her gaze up to Matt, she fixed him with her worst glare possible. "You don't play fair."

A corner of his mouth lifted in a roguish smile. "Never said that I did. Sometimes you have to play hard ball."

"Don't get all sportscaster on me," she grumbled as she stomped past him to the bedroom. She slammed the door for full effect of her tantrum. *Oregon. Matt's family. This is crazy.* But Noah's happy face crowded out all else in her mind. She grabbed a duffle from the closet and began throwing clothes in it, admitting to herself that the two of them were probably overdue for a little crazy.

Matt gave Cassie what he hoped was an appropriately repentant look. "Still mad at me?" She'd spent the first two and a half hours of the drive curled up with her pillow as far away from him on the bench seat as possible, sleeping with her head against the passenger window.

"Furious," she said, covering a yawn. "What time is it?"

He glanced at the dashboard. "Around nine."

"The time I'd planned to get up today." Cassie pulled her legs out from beneath her and sat up.

"Sorry to have disturbed your beauty sleep."

"No you're not," she shot back at him.

"Actually—" He tried but couldn't hide his grin. "You might need some more. Beauty sleep, that is. Your hair—"

Cassie flipped down the visor and looked in the mirror. "I may just keep it like this all weekend. See what your parents think of me."

"My dad probably wouldn't notice, and Mom would think it's just some California style. She warned me about all kinds of bizarre things that go on there before we moved."

"Like what?" Cassie asked. "Are we all hippies or something?"

"Exactly." Matt nodded. "Liberal hippies with nose and belly button rings and tattoos from head to toe."

"You don't have people like that in Oregon?" Cassie asked.

"Sure," Matt said. "But *everyone* in California fits that description according to my mom. You're all a bunch of extremists."

"Look who's talking," Cassie said. "I've never kidnapped anyone."

"I don't see any handcuffs or blindfold. You came willingly. The boys are my witnesses." Witnesses, who were, at the moment, completely oblivious to anything except the game on the iPad held between them.

"Hmmph. It was still a low trick." She pulled a brush from the bag at her feet and began pulling it through her hair. "Using my son like that," she added in a harsh whisper.

"If you still feel like I've used him at the end of the trip, then I'll do whatever you ask to make it up to both of you, but give this weekend a chance, Cassie." He looked over at her. "Please."

She sighed. "I will. I just feel guilty, you know."

"I'm sorry." Matt concentrated on driving, though all of his senses were on alert with Cassie seated just a foot or so away. He winced when she hit a particularly bad snarl, and then wished he could run his fingers through her hair a few minutes later when it lay soft and sleek against her head.

From the corner of his eye, he watched as she ate a donut and licked her fingers. *Would've taken care of that for you,* he thought, then wrestled to rein in his unruly desire. Nothing would make this weekend a disaster quicker than him overstepping their boundaries. They had both spoken and unspoken rules. No touching. *No wanting to touch.* No being alone. Three smallish chaperones weren't too bad. No getting too close to each other. *Too late for that now.* Matt couldn't imagine his life without Cassie and Noah. He was pretty sure his boys couldn't either. As much as he realized that it was foolish, he couldn't seem to help himself from envisioning a future with the five of them together.

"It's so beautiful here," Cassie said sometime later when the grassland and rolling hills of California had given way to the lush green forests of southern Oregon.

"Have you ever been to Oregon?" Matt asked.

"Never. We didn't travel much when I was a kid, and Devon and I weren't in a financial position to take many trips, aside from Tahoe, that is." She told Matt about yearly trips with their friends, winter skiing, and nights in a hot tub.

He wrestled against the jealousy that picture ignited. He didn't want to think of Cassie in a hot tub with Devon, but it was ridiculous to feel that way. He'd probably been in a hot tub with Jenna sometime during the same years Cassie was talking about.

"We were supposed to take a vacation the week after he was shot." Cassie glanced over her shoulder, checking to see if the boys' attention was still on the game, Matt guessed.

"Devon had booked a houseboat on Shasta." She gave a short, half-hearted laugh. "Our friends went without us. Devon was the one who'd paid the whole deposit."

"They gave it back I hope," Matt said.

Cassie shook her head. "No. It was the least of my worries then. As time went by, I'm sure everyone just forgot."

Some friends. Everyone was a jerk was what it sounded like to Matt.

"Tahoe is beautiful, but this is incredible." Cassie pulled out her phone and started snapping pictures. "Everything is just so green."

"Just wait," Matt predicted. "You're going to love Newport." For the next hour, he told her about his home and his family.

"My sister is bossy, but she means well, a lot like my mom, actually," Matt said, realizing the similarity. "My brother was mostly a pain when I was growing up, and now it's his kids who are mostly a pain, but overall we have a good time."

Matt told her about his father's crabbing and fishing business, about growing up with the beach for a backyard. They told each other about their engagements and when and where they'd married. Matt learned that Cassie loved the California coast, too, and especially San Francisco. He tucked that info away for later, hoping he'd get a chance to take her there. So far he'd just seen the city by the bay from across the bay but hadn't actually made it there. It seemed he had a good reason to go now.

Two bathroom breaks, a stop for lunch, and five hours later, they neared Newport.

"Now Noah and Cassie, I don't want you to be frightened by my mom," Matt said.

"Is she scary?" Noah asked, glancing back and forth between Asher and Austin.

"Grandma's funny," Asher said.

"And loud," Austin added.

"Funny and loud doesn't sound too bad." Cassie had the visor down again, rechecking her hair.

"She's very opinionated in a flamboyant sort of way."

Matt knew his attempts at explaining his mom weren't adequate. There probably wasn't a way to describe her. Some things—people—you just had to experience.

He left the highway and turned down their street a few minutes later, nervous anticipation setting him on edge as well. What would his family think of Cassie and Noah? He prayed they would welcome them both and quickly see Cassie for the wonderful person she was. Matt felt almost certain that was how things would go.

Just as soon as they got over their surprise.

Twenty-Four

Cassie stepped from the truck and stomped her feet on the gravel drive a few times, trying to restore circulation to her legs. The nine-plus-hour drive was a lot more sitting than she'd done in a long time. It was also a lot more time than she'd spent with Matt previously, and she'd been surprised how the hours had flown by as they'd talked. She'd told him more about her life both before and after Devon was shot than she'd told anyone, except maybe her mom.

In return, Matt had told her all about Jenna and the life they'd shared. Standing here now, at Matt's house, Cassie couldn't help but think that a year ago, Matt and the boys would have been pulling up about this same time, in a different car, and with Jenna seated right beside him. What did his parents think about him bringing someone else home, not even a year later?

What would his parents think of me? Will they understand our 'just friends' status? Or would Matt's mom be appalled that he was keeping company with a married woman? Even worse, would his mom be as Cassie's had become, always hinting at the possibility of more between them when such a thing was impossible?

Light flooded the front of the house, and the door opened to a couple of people and a hum of noise behind them. Matt had pointed out the other cars in the driveway belonging to his sister and her family and to his brother's family. That meant four additional adults and six kids in the house that Cassie had to meet on top of his parents.

Twelve people. Cassie almost wished she could grab Matt's hand for reassurance. Instead, she reached for Noah's and held tight when he would have surged ahead with Austin and Asher. *No reluctant adventurer here.*

"Give them a minute to greet their grandmother," Cassie whispered. The noisy background remained, but only two people—Matt's parents, she assumed—stood silhouetted in the porch light.

"Okay." Noah ceased pulling against her hold.

After the boys had been properly smothered with kisses and enfolded in hugs by both their grandmother and grandfather, Matt made his way forward and embraced each of his parents.

Cassie still hung back, taking in the pines surrounding the house and covering much of the weathered paint. The square porch, while not large, held a rocker, some planters, and several signs hanging at lopsided angles along the wall. *Do you want to speak with the man in charge or the woman who knows what is going on?* fit with Matt's description of his mother and gave Cassie a fair idea of what Mrs. Kramer was like.

Absolutely no soliciting unless you are selling Thin Mints, made Cassie smile, but the sign directly over the door gave her pause.

Welcome friends. The rest of you, get the hell off my property.

Cassie wondered what would happen if she didn't qualify as a friend. Over the past few hours, she'd become almost comfortable with her decision to come, but that sign brought every hesitation she'd had and reason not to be here into sharp relief once more. What did Matt's parents think about him bringing a married woman to visit? Could they possibly understand the friendship she and Matt shared? *Probably not.* Cassie wasn't even sure she did half the time.

I don't belong here. Noah and I should have stayed at home, near Devon.

"And who is this handsome young man?" Mrs. Kramer asked loudly as she stared down at Noah. She'd yet to make eye contact with Cassie, furthering her insecurities.

"I'm Noah," he announced proudly, pulling free from Cassie's grasp. "It smells good here."

"Why thank you," Mrs. Kramer said. "I like this young man, Matt."

Noah can stay at least. Maybe being his mom will earn me points.

"Come on, Noah. Come see the toy room." Taking Noah's hand, Asher wiggled around his grandfather, and the boys disappeared into the house. This left only Matt and Cassie, standing awkwardly a few feet apart from each other.

"Mom, Dad, this is Cassie." Matt flashed her an encouraging smile. "Cassie, these are my parents, Maureen and Tom." To his parents, he said, "I've invited Cassie and Noah to be our guests for the weekend."

"Oh, Matt." Mrs. Kramer's hands flew to her rounded

cheeks. "You should have told us. Of course they're welcome," she said, as if Cassie wasn't standing right there.

"You didn't *tell* them?" Cassie gave Matt a look that promised murder at the first opportunity, but before that, she needed to find a bus or something to get her and Noah home. *Welcome, indeed.* She'd never felt more unwelcome or awkward in her life.

"Because it was spur of the moment, and I knew they wouldn't mind." Matt's expression pled forgiveness for the second time today. "You don't mind, do you?" Matt threw at his parents.

"Of course not." His dad stepped forward to stand beside his wife. "Maureen and I are glad to have you." His smile was warm and welcoming, helping Cassie feel the tiniest bit better.

"Cassie and Noah befriended us shortly after we moved to Auburn," Matt hurried to explain. "Cassie coached Austin's soccer team."

"Oh, so you're a coach?" Mrs. Kramer asked, not at all disguising the oddity she found this to be.

"Actually, no," Cassie said. "That was just a volunteer position."

As if sensing she was on shaky ground, Matt stepped in to rescue her. "Cassie works at a—"

"Tattoo parlor," she blurted, just managing to keep a straight face at seeing Matt's shocked one.

"O-oh," Mrs. Webb said, nodding her head, even as her eyes, full of questions, shifted to Matt's.

"Whatever you do, welcome." His dad held a weathered hand out to her. Cassie shook it appreciatively, but she wasn't quite ready to let Matt off so easily. He deserved to squirm, tricking her into coming when he hadn't even asked his parents if it would be all right.

225

"Matt and I met when he came in to get the Sacramento Kings logo tattooed on his calf."

His mother gasped. "Working for the enemy wasn't enough, Matt? You had to go and defile your body like that? You'll never be able to attend a Trail Blazers game again. What will our friends think? What were *you* thinking?"

Cassie bit back laughter. "I did a really great job. Show them Matt." She flipped her foot behind her, kicking him in the back of his leg.

"Sure." His smirk held a challenge as he turned around and lifted first one, then the other pant leg, revealing nothing but bare, unblemished skin.

"Oh, that's right." Cassie smacked her forehead. "Got you confused with one of the team that came in with you. You got your tattoo elsewhere." She rolled her eyes at Matt's mom. "You're probably not gonna want to see it." Cassie patted her backside, suggesting the location of Matt's imagined tattoo.

"Matthew Kramer, I ought to take a spoon to your butt like I used to. I can't believe this. Why would you do such a thing? I just—I swear. God must love stupid people; he made so many, my own son included."

Cassie smiled to herself, thinking Matt deserved every word of that reprimand. Maureen's hands opened and closed at her sides, as if she wished to seal them around her son's neck.

"Now, honey." Mr. Kramer placed a restraining hand on his wife's arm. "Let's go inside, and we can talk this over like nice, normal folks."

"Normal," Maureen huffed. "With a grandson who wears an earring and a son with the traitor's team on his rear? Only thing 'normal' around here is a setting on the dryer."

Cassie pressed her lips together to keep from laughing as she followed Matt's parents into the house.

"Kids are born wet, naked, and hungry, and things just get worse from there." Maureen threw a look over her shoulder at Matt as she led them past what sounded like a room full of kids and into a kitchen papered with floral motif from the nineties. More signs with sayings like the ones on the porch hung from the walls and were propped on various-sized wood signs and tiles around the room. *Be reasonable, do it MY WAY! There will be no crisis this week, my schedule is full,* and *I'm busy now; can I ignore you some other time?* all contributed to the picture Matt had painted of his mom and what Cassie had observed of her so far. She had a feeling that opinionated and loud just scratched the surface.

"Have a seat," Mrs. Kramer ordered. Cassie obeyed, though she really felt like standing after the long drive. Matt, on the other hand, began unbuckling his belt.

"What're you doing son?" his dad asked.

"Showing mom my supposed tattoo."

"I don't care what you have down there. I don't want to see it." She fluttered the back of her hand at him dismissively. "Not even six months in California, and look what's happened. At the drop of a hat you go and do something completely idiotic. Told you we shouldn't have let him go, Tom."

"He's thirty-four years old," Matt's dad reminded her. "A little past the age for grounding." He winked at Cassie, cementing her first impression that he was a good guy.

Like Matt. She ignored the unwelcome thought, feeling he deserved to have her angry with him a little longer.

"Cassie, will you please tell them?" Matt ran his hand through his hair, a telltale sign of frustration.

"Tell them that you came to my apartment at six this

morning, woke us up, and used Noah as a way to get me to come?" Her eyes narrowed as she remembered the way he'd manipulated the situation for his benefit. "Or did you want me to tell your parents that you failed to mention that they didn't know that I was coming? In fact—" Cassie shifted in her chair to better face Matt's parents. "Has Matt even mentioned me before?"

"No," Maureen said, fixing Matt with a look that made Cassie's seem harmless. Growing up with a mom who could shoot daggers like that must have been a bit terrifying. Cassie felt the tiniest bit bad for him and thought she maybe understood why he hadn't told his parents about her. Maybe.

"I imagine he wanted us to meet you ourselves instead of hearing about you." Tom jumped in, trying to salvage the situation once again. Cassie imagined that with a wife like Maureen, he had frequent practice at this sort of thing.

"Isn't that right, son?" he asked.

"Yes." Matt turned to Cassie, his eyes pleading.

Maureen held her head in her hands as she rocked forward and back. "The Kings. The Kings. Forever on his a—"

"Actually, I work at a school," Cassie said. She was such a pushover. She ought to have made Matt suffer a lot longer. "I'm the principal's secretary at the elementary school Austin attends."

"And she has helped Austin tremendously," Matt said. "Cassie has a master's in psychology and is going to be working in the field of child psychology soon. She's going to make a great therapist and help a lot of children and their parents."

"So, there is no tattoo?" Mrs. Kramer looked from Matt to Cassie as both shook their heads.

"I'm sorry," Cassie apologized. "I didn't mean to upset

you. I was a bit put out with Matt for not telling you we were coming, so I'm afraid I saw an opportunity for revenge and took it."

Tom began to chuckle.

"Revenge?" Maureen said. Her lips curled up, and she snorted. "Tattoo of the Kings—that's a good one. Almost had the boy dropping his pants. I should have let him." She slapped her knee and snorted again, then burst into full blown laughter.

"What's up, Mom?" A slightly scruffier version of Matt, sporting the same brand of jeans and an untucked flannel shirt, stepped into the kitchen. "Everything all right in here?"

"Everything's great." Matt sounded a lot less tense than he had a minute earlier. "Cassie, this is my brother Mark. Mark, this is Cassie, Mom's new best friend."

"I'll say." Maureen wiped her eyes as she pushed back from the table. "This girl's the best thing since sliced bread. Anyone who can pull one over on me like that and set a good one on Matt is on my team for sure." She ambled around the table and held a hand out to Cassie. "Come on, dear. I'll show you where you'll be sleeping. You can have Matt's old room. *He* can use an air mattress downstairs."

"I don't mind using an air mattress," Cassie said, as unwilling to put anyone out as she'd been wanting to discomfit Matt just a few minutes earlier.

"Take the bedroom," Matt said, his smile telling her all was forgiven on his part, at least. She reserved the right for additional revenge or payback at some future time. "The boys and I can sleep in the den."

"It was nice to meet you," Cassie said to both Matt's dad and brother, then followed his mother up the stairs, past pictures of Matt and his siblings when they were much younger. His mom still scared her a little, but already Cassie could see that if you got past her gruffness and onto her good side, this was a welcome place to be.

Happy shouts rang from the downstairs play room, and Cassie imagined Noah already enjoying himself with Austin and Asher and their cousins. This place, and this family, had all the makings of what the Thanksgiving holiday should be. When Maureen turned at the top of the stairs, took her hand, and gave her a genuine welcome, Cassie was suddenly very grateful for Matt's nefarious method that had convinced her to come.

Twenty-Five

"He's actually playing with his kids." Matt's sister, Megan, stood at the sliding glass doors, mouth agape as she looked out to the beach, where Matt and the boys were spending Thanksgiving morning flying kites—or attempting to, at least. From what Cassie had glimpsed, so far they hadn't achieved a lot of air time.

"I never would have believed Matt could embrace fatherhood so quickly." Megan's gaze slid to Cassie. "It's obvious you've been a great influence on him."

"I don't know about that." Cassie glanced up from the cutting board and celery she was chopping. "He seemed like a pretty great dad already when we met him." *Cut your brother some slack.* Matt had been right when he'd described his sister as bossy, nosy, too.

"Well he wasn't great before he left Oregon," Megan said.

You try being a single parent, Cassie thought. No one who hadn't done it could ever really understand just how difficult it was in so many ways.

"He wasn't into his kids the way he is now," Megan continued. "Matt was all about the NBA and his career. Has he told you what a big deal he was?"

"He's told me what a big mistake it was to be wrapped up in his job like that." Cassie resumed chopping, wanting to get the task done so she could go out and play with the boys, too. She'd felt the need to offer to help Matt's mom and wished Megan did, too, so they could all be done a lot sooner. *Instead of spying on your brother, we could join him.*

"Matt has grown a lot this past year," Maureen chimed in from the other side of the island where she was rolling out crusts for a couple of pies. She glanced at Cassie. "In a very tragic way, losing Jenna has been a blessing in disguise. It's helped him see what really matters—loving his boys and others. I'm happy for him that he's arrived at this place and found someone else so soon."

Uh oh. Cassie realized she needed to clarify that she wasn't someone else in the sense Maureen was thinking. She slid the rest of the celery from the cutting board into the bowl for the stuffing then wiped her hands on a dishtowel.

"Matt and I are just friends. I tend Austin and Asher on the evenings he works late, and in return Matt has fixed my car and disposal, things like that. We help each other out."

Megan's snort sounded similar to her mother's the night before, but Cassie didn't take it as well.

"That's why you're wearing that diamond?" Megan stared pointedly at Cassie's left hand. "It's okay to tell us. We won't let on that we know before Matt shares the news with everyone at dinner. I mean, if he really wanted to keep it a secret, he'd have waited to propose until after you got here."

"It's not like that between us." Cassie gripped the edge of the counter as her mind scrambled for the best way to handle this situation and the two overbearing women.

"Phew, it's getting warm in here." Maureen fanned a hand in front of her face.

No kidding. The cool ocean air sounded even more appealing. It was all Cassie could do not to run out of the kitchen straight toward the beach.

"Having hot flashes again, Mother?" Megan asked.

"I don't have hot flashes, I have power surges, and I'm having one now. Get that table set." She pointed the rolling pin at Megan. "And leave our guest alone."

It was the perfect exit from the uncomfortable conversation, and Cassie should have been grateful, but all she could think of was that she had to fix this.

"How come Laura isn't helping?" Megan asked, sounding like a petulant twelve-year-old.

"She's nursing her baby. You want to give me another grandchild, you can get out of helping with dinner next Thanksgiving." Maureen's face softened as she looked over at Cassie. "I adore my grandbabies—should've skipped my own kids and gone straight for grandchildren. I really hope I'll get some more, from Matt at least, since Megan here thinks two children are plenty."

"And you think *I'm* harassing our guest," Megan huffed. "Cassie and Matt aren't even married yet, and here you are suggesting they have more kids."

For as flushed as she knew her face must be, Cassie felt as if the rest of her had frozen with a rock lodged firmly in her throat. *I would love to have a baby.* Just not Matt's. For a millisecond, she allowed herself to wonder what a child they created together might be like. Some combination of Noah, Austin, and Asher, only tinier, and maybe a girl. Powerful yearning swept over her, taking her off guard. The fantasy family in her imagination vanished. *Devon.* She needed to think of Devon, the fact that she was his wife, and her faith that he was going to get better.

Matt's mom was watching her closely, almost giving Cassie the impression that Maureen had seen the brief vision that had just completely thrown Cassie off balance.

She hadn't even considered that they might think her wedding ring was an engagement ring from Matt. Her gaze flickered to the foursome on the beach. She had to put a stop to this rumor before the boys or Matt heard of it and anyone got hurt.

Cassie said a silent prayer for the right words as she looked from Megan to Maureen, then held her hand out. "This isn't an engagement ring. It's my wedding ring. I'm married."

The silence in the room was thick enough to slice with the knife she'd just been using. If the kitchen had been warm before, it was positively cooking now. Maureen's hand fanned double time.

"Matt got married without telling us? This isn't another tattoo joke, is it?"

"No," Cassie exclaimed. *No and no and no.* "That's not what I meant. It isn't what you think. I am married, but not to Matt." She plunged on, determined to give them the Reader's Digest version of her story and spare Matt the chore. "My husband is a police officer. He was shot six years ago. He isn't able to care for himself or even respond to others right now. His condition is known as PVS. That stands for Permanent Vegetative State." How she hated that term, as if Devon had left his human form and turned into a zucchini or something. The medical community really ought to come up with something better.

"Oh, my poor dear." Matt's mother left her pies and crossed the kitchen, her arms held out. "What a terrible thing." She wrapped Cassie in a floury hug, which felt awkward at first, then strangely comforting.

"It's hard," Cassie admitted when Maureen had stepped back and the flour dust around them settled, "but Noah and I manage okay, better now that we've met Matt and Austin and Asher. We've all become great friends."

"But Matt and you aren't—" Megan seemed unable to connect the words.

"We aren't dating," Cassie said. "We aren't a couple." *Could I spell it out any clearer?* "He knows all about my husband, Devon. Matt has even been to the care center with me to see him." A night she wasn't soon to forget. Never had she appreciated or cared for Matt more than in those minutes they'd spent together at Devon's bedside when he'd proved himself the best kind of friend, one she didn't want to lose, so she needed to figure out how to make this work with his family.

"Friends. I get it," Megan said, but Cassie could see that she didn't.

"I realize the situation is unusual. It's one of the reasons I was hesitant to come here, but Matt convinced me that Noah would love a true family-filled Thanksgiving, and he is." Cassie glanced out the glass doors again and caught sight of Matt running alongside Noah, the kite string in their joined hands.

"We're so glad you've come," Maureen said, sounding more and more sincere every time she spoke the words. "And you *have* been good for Matt. He's growing into the dad he's meant to be, and for that, we thank you."

"Six years is a long time," Megan said, a half-smile of apology on her lips at the same time her eyes were appraising

Cassie in a clearly speculative way. "I'm sorry I assumed."

She was still assuming, or guessing at least. "It's all right," Cassie said aloud. *Think what you will. I don't care.* Except she did, for Noah's sake, and Matt's and his boys' sakes. "I hope—as I imagine you do as well—that someday Matt is able to meet someone else and remarry." Even as she spoke the words, she couldn't help the spark of jealousy that sprang to life at the thought of Matt with someone else. "Losing Jenna has been very hard on him and the boys. It would be nice for them not to be alone forever."

It would be nice for me, too. Cassie turned away from Megan and the picturesque scene on the beach behind her.

I won't be, just as soon as Devon wakes up.

"Why do I always end up in the middle of the table," Matt complained as he passed yet another dish to the opposite end, this one to his brother-in-law, Ned.

"Youngest child, middle of the table. Life's tough, bro." Mark fished a roll from the basket in front of him. "Pass the butter, will you Matty?"

"Matt*y*?" Cassie looked at him and grinned.

"Childhood torment. Don't go there," Matt warned. Their fingers accidentally brushed as he handed her the butter dish. It was enough to make him forget that his brother was still a pain as a grown up and to feel grateful he and the boys had come home with Cassie and Noah.

He thought the trip was going pretty good so far, though she'd seemed a bit on edge earlier in the day when she'd joined them on the beach for kite flying. He'd tried standing behind her, teaching her how to move the strings to guide the trick kite once it was airborne, but she'd wanted nothing to do with that, insisting that his instructions would suffice. Independent as Cassie was, she'd done all right, catching on quicker than most beginners, but he'd been disappointed at the missed opportunity to give her a lesson and to be close.

Having her sit beside him at dinner was almost as good. A couple of months ago, he'd dreaded the approaching holidays, but Cassie had changed that and so many other things for him.

"Tell us about your job as a tattoo artist." Mark's wife Laura was seated opposite Cassie, and the two seemed to be taking an instant liking to one another.

Solidarity, Matt supposed. It had to be hard for a woman to come into this family, even as a temporary visitor. It had taken Jenna a couple of years after they were married to figure out and feel comfortable around his mom and sister. All things considered, Cassie was holding her own pretty well.

"Wait. You really are a tattoo artist? I thought that was a joke," Megan said.

"You'll never know." Matt winked at Cassie. All these years later, he still loved annoying his sister, and now he was too old for her to do anything about it. Cassie ignored him, or tried to anyway. Matt was pretty sure he'd caught a split second of reaction—an almost smile and slight flush.

"I work at an elementary school," she said.

"Whoa." Mark whistled under his breath. "They start young in your state. In Oregon you've got to be eighteen to get inked."

"Funny," Megan said.

Matt thought it was. Now that the joke wasn't at his expense, he found it amusing. His mother did, too, given her pleasant expression and the lack of idioms spouting from her mouth.

"Well, regardless of California's strange laws," Laura began, "it appears to have been a good move for you, Matt. The boys seem to be doing much better than when they left."

"It's Cassie," Matt said, turning his head to her. Behind her, through the pass through to the kitchen, he could see Austin and Asher at the kids' table, chatting happily with their cousins and Noah.

"It's Matt." Cassie refuted his praise. "You, not me," she said directly to him. "It's you playing and interacting with Austin and Asher. It's really listening to Austin, having conversations with him, allowing him to go through the grieving process and still loving him while he does."

"Austin does seem more like himself again," Megan said, "and Asher doesn't seem to be crying as much or constantly trying to please everyone and make everything better."

Because it is better, Matt acknowledged. It had happened so gradually over the past few months, from that first outing for ice cream to last weekend when he'd driven the boys up to the mountains to play in the first snow of the year, that he hadn't really thought about all the changes that had taken place.

"That's great," Mark cut in. "The boys are great. You're great. I'm great. Some pie would be great." He leaned back in his chair and rubbed his stomach, as if anticipating stuffing it even more.

"How about a round of Pie in Your Face first?" Cassie said.

Matt choked on the bite of stuffing he'd been in the process of swallowing. Half-laughing, half-coughing, he grabbed his glass of water and poured it down his throat. A few long seconds later, when he could finally breathe again, he looked around the silent table to see everyone staring at Cassie.

Seemingly oblivious that she'd said anything surprising or wrong, she took a bite of mashed potatoes, then realized, as the fork left her lips, that everyone's eyes were on her.

Matt leaned close. "Who are you, woman, and where did this wicked sense of humor come from?" Not that he was complaining. Anyone who could stand up to his mom and siblings was someone he wanted on his team.

"What do you mean?" Cassie's eyes darted nervously back and forth from Mark openly frowning at her to Maureen with her mouth screwed up in confusion. Other than the clatter of voices and silverware from the children's table, the room remained silent.

Matt leaned closer yet, brushed some of Cassie's hair aside, and whispered in her ear. "First the tattoo bit and now you tell my brother to have some pie in his face. I'd never have guessed; you're usually so reserved."

Cassie's eyes widened, and her lips parted in an *O* of horror.

"It's a game," she blurted. The stunned looks continued coming from nearly everyone at the table. "A *board* game," she clarified. "It's a tradition in our family. Noah and I play it every Thanksgiving before we eat the real pie. I've seen it advertised quite a bit, so I thought..."

"Must be another California thing." Mom shook her head.

Dad leaned in from the opposite end of the table. "A game where someone gets a pie in his face?"

"Well, not an actual pie, but the whipping cream, yes," Cassie said. "I can get the game if you'd like. I brought it with me in case anyone wanted to play."

"Sign me up." He threw down his napkin. "I want the first turn." He stared down the table. "My pie's headed straight for your face, Maureen."

"Me. What did I ever do to you?" She planted her large hands on either side of her plate and stood.

"Dangerous question, Mom," Matt warned.

"You married me, that's what," Dad said, sounding as uncharacteristic as Cassie had a few moments ago.

"The deadline for complaints was yesterday," Mom said, "so don't bother."

"Oh, it's no bother." Dad rubbed his hands together gleefully. "Where's this game at, Cassie?"

"In Matt's room. I'll get it." She pushed back her chair and stood. "But it doesn't actually involve throwing—"

"If Dad gets to throw one at Mom, then I get to throw one at Matt," Megan said. "For being such a twerp and spying on me whenever I had a date."

"That couldn't have been much spying then." Mark leaned into Megan, bumping shoulders in a sort of high five at his joke. "You had, what, three dates total during high school?"

"Watch it," Ned warned. "You're talking about my wife."

"I know, and I want to throw a pie at her," Mark said, "for being such a tattletale when we were kids."

"Being one? She still is," Matt said. "She told Mom today that I wasn't planning to come home for Christmas. I get to throw a pie at Megan, too."

"That's not really how the game—"

"You're all getting a pie from me," Mom yelled, cutting Cassie off and wagging her finger around the table. "How many does this game come with? Because I can think of a half dozen reasons each of my kids should be hit with them."

"I just need one," Dad said. "I've got good aim, and the target's front and center and plenty big to see."

"You take that back, Tom, or you can sleep on the air

mattress with Matt." Mom pushed back from the table and stood. She began tromping toward the other end.

"Can spouses play, too?" Laura asked.

"After me," Megan said.

"And me," Mark added.

"I think you're all forgetting who's in charge," Mom shouted. "Who made the pies you think you're going to eat?"

"I think they've all lost their minds." Matt stood and whispered to Cassie, who appeared completely taken aback by his family as her head moved side to side, trying to follow the ping-ponging conversations. Megan and Mark were arguing about something, and Mom was descending on Dad, the wrath of God written on her face.

"Did I warn you about my family?" Matt asked.

"Not nearly enough." Cassie bit her lip and looked concerned over the chaos her simple suggestion had created. What she didn't realize was that it would have started sooner or later anyway. It wasn't a Kramer holiday without someone getting in a fight.

"I suppose you'd like to throw the first pie in my face?" Matt asked.

"You have no idea." The same annoyed expression he'd received from her shortly after their arrival yesterday reappeared.

"Deserved," Matt said. "I'll give you a free throw."

The sound of a baby crying interrupted the bickering.

"Shh." Mom held her hand up for silence.

"It's Catelyn." Laura put her napkin on the table. "Oh, well. I almost made it through dinner."

"I'll get her," Cassie offered, seemingly eager for an excuse to leave the table. She started walking toward the hall. "I remember those 'haven't had a hot meal in months' days."

"Thanks." Laura smiled warmly.

"I'll bring back the game," Matt offered as he got up and followed Cassie from the room. She took the stairs two at a time, then disappeared into Mark's room at the top. A few seconds later Matt caught up and found her sitting on the edge of the bed, cooing at the baby in her arms.

"You look good with those," he said as he entered the room. He sat beside her on the end of the bed.

"Yes, well—" Her eyes darkened with sorrow. "I wanted to have four babies. Devon and I had it all planned out. One every three years, two boys and two girls."

"There's still time for that." It bothered Matt that this was something he couldn't fix for her or give to her.

"Not as much as there used to be. I'll be thirty-two soon."

A joke was on the tip of his tongue, but he held it back. This wasn't something to joke about. Cassie was a wonderful mother and ought to have a houseful of kids. It wasn't fair that she couldn't. Then again, he'd learned in the last year that much of life wasn't fair. It just seemed especially wrong when the unfairness happened to someone as great as she was. Someone he cared about a lot.

"Where's that game at?" Matt slapped his thighs and stood.

"In your room. I'll show you." Still holding Catelyn, she stood and followed him to his old bedroom. "In there." She nodded her head toward the duffle on the chair.

"May I?" Matt asked, before he opened it to look.

"Go ahead."

He found the game quickly, seeing nothing more personal than the oversized t-shirt she slept in at the top of the bag, but it was enough to have him remembering that morning in September when he'd fixed her stairs and she'd made him breakfast. The bacon and pancakes had been good, but the real feast had been seeing her standing on the stairs in just that shirt with her hair tousled and a still-sleepy expression on her face. It had felt like a drink of water after being in the desert a long time, and he'd drunk it in greedily until she'd scolded him and reminded him how wrong that was. It was still wrong now, and he felt even thirstier.

Matt turned around to find Cassie softly humming and bouncing as she walked the baby around the room. Instead of taking the game downstairs, he paused, watching her and yearning for all kinds of things he had no business to be thinking of. *What if Cassie was my wife and that was our baby?* Those thoughts were dangerous territory. She'd be on the next plane home if she had any idea of them. He wondered what she was thinking, what she thought of his family and being here. Matt looked around the room that had been his for all of his growing up years and tried to see it through her eyes.

"Just a few trophies in here." Cassie followed his gaze to the shelves above his bed.

"A few," Matt said. "Our high school basketball team was pretty good."

"Because you were their all-star player?" She'd leaned closer and was reading the plaques.

"Maybe." He shrugged. "Funny how stuff like that just doesn't matter when you're grown up."

"It mattered to you for a while." She faced him. "Or basketball did and does at least; I see you played in college, too." She was staring at a picture of the team beneath his OSU pennant.

"I played," Matt said, "and quickly realized that being a small town big shot didn't mean anything outside of Newport. By mid-semester my freshman year, I realized that my dream of playing in the NBA was just that, a dream."

"You still made the sport your career." Cassie had moved onto his desk, where his mom had created a shrine of his brief and intense career with the Trail Blazers.

"Yes and no," Matt said. He picked up a photo of him with the team a couple of years ago. Since he'd left his position with the Trail Blazers, he'd found his enthusiasm for the game just wasn't there. He supposed it could be because, as his mom said, he worked for the enemy now, but really, Matt thought and hoped it had more to do with realizing that being a dad was much more fun and rewarding than any sport.

"Thank you, Cassie. I'll take her now." Laura entered the room, her arms outstretched.

"Thanks for letting me hold her." Cassie passed Catelyn to Laura. "She's adorable."

"Except at three o'clock in the morning," Laura said.

"I remember those days, too," Cassie said wistfully. Matt imagined that she would find a baby adorable any time of day or night if she was given the opportunity to be a mother once more.

Laura took Catelyn and left the room.

"Ready to teach this game to my crazy family?" Matt asked.

"Yep." Cassie squared her shoulders, and her usual look of resolve returned. He knew how wearying that look could be and the toll it took to keep pressing forward day after day when sometimes you just wanted to stay in bed and not have to face life.

"How about later when things are getting out of hand with the pie throwing—because you know they will—we go outside and have a little one-on-one basketball? You've humbled me enough times, running circles around me on the soccer field. I think a little payback in is order."

"You're on." Cassie sounded almost chipper as she took the game from him and bounded down the stairs.

"What, is basketball your game, too?" It'd be a little embarrassing if she trounced him at that as well as soccer.

"Maybe," she threw over her shoulder, leaving Matt to spend the evening wondering, and thinking about Cassie a lot more than he should.

Twenty-Six

Matt pulled his high school letterman jacket from the front closet. "You can borrow this one." Before Cassie could protest, he lifted it over her head and placed it around her shoulders.

She slumped forward, as if the coat was flattening her. "This weighs a ton. How am I supposed to shoot hoops wearing this."

"You're not." Matt flashed her a purposely diabolical grin. "The better for me to win, my dear." When she'd shoved her arms through the sleeves, he stepped closer and began snapping up the front.

"I'm not five," Cassie complained.

"I know." Standing this close to her, he definitely knew. He brushed a section of her long hair out of the way, over her shoulder, and the aroma of whatever perfume or lotion she wore made its way to his brain, numbing all common sense. He moved a bit closer and kept snapping, and she let him.

"There. Now you'll be warm." He'd fastened all but the top snap, wanting her to be able to breathe, though he hardly could right now. It was just the two of them, alone in the dark foyer of the house. The dishes had been done, the boys had been tucked into bed, and even his parents and siblings had said goodnight and gone to their rooms. It was the most alone he and Cassie had been since the night they'd cleaned his apartment. That had turned into a pretty good night, and basketball promised to be even more fun. He supposed they should go outside and start their game.

"Ready?" he asked.

"Yes."

Their eyes met, and for a brief second, he imagined that her *yes* didn't refer to playing a game but was a response to the desire he'd been battling since he'd arrived at her apartment Wednesday morning. *Yes. You may kiss me, Matt.* If their circumstances ever changed, if they were ever in a position where kissing her wouldn't be ten kinds of wrong, he intended to do it properly and ask her first, just as he'd asked to be her friend. He wasn't being a very good one right now, standing so close, alone in the dark, her lips mere inches from his.

"Let's go." His voice was hoarse, and he cleared it as he reached past her for the doorknob.

"Don't you need a jacket, too?"

Probably not. He felt about to burst into flames any second, but he grabbed a sweatshirt from the closet anyway.

Once outside, he led her around the garage to the pad on the side of the house. "The caveat here is that if you overshoot too much, you're chasing the ball to the beach," he warned. "Shoot carefully unless you like sand in your shoes."

"Love it." Cassie stood hunched over, legs spread, her hands out to receive the ball. "Ladies first, right?"

"Wrong." Matt shot from the far corner of the pad, a full nineteen feet, nine inches. He knew because his dad had measured exactly before they'd poured the court years ago. He'd wanted his growing son to have a good place from which to practice three-pointers. The ball swished through the net, a feat made not only impressive by the distance, but by the fact that the garage light closest to the hoop was out.

"Why don't we play pig," he suggested, not wanting to show off or be too aggressive with her. "Or, if you're worried you'll lose too quickly, we can make it horse."

"More like elephant." Cassie collected the ball and crossed the cement to take his spot. She dribbled a couple of times and feigned shooting. "Just trying to remember how this is done." With that, she released the ball. Its arc was nearly as perfect as Matt's, and with just a little rim, sank into the net. "My turn to shoot, or do you want to play a real one-on-one?"

"Yeah. I want to play." Matt grabbed the ball and dribbled near the hoop. Cassie was there in a second, hands held high as she bounced around in front of him, trying to block his throw. He ducked around and tossed it almost effortlessly into the basket. "Two for me. We play to eleven."

"Two all." She shot and scored after only one bounce and before he'd made it over to the side. "You're gonna have to be faster, old man."

Matt laughed. "All right. That's it. No mercy for you." He worried she just might outrun him on the court as she had on the soccer field.

"I don't want mercy," Cassie said. "I want to play."

"You got it." He was sure the hungry look in her eyes matched his own. He snatched the ball on the rebound and went immediately for a lay-up. She jumped and knocked it away at the last second.

"Did you just use your head? This isn't soccer." He claimed the ball again.

"It was interference only. Not on purpose." Cassie rubbed the right side of her head, near her ear.

"Are you okay?" Matt stopped in front of her.

"I will be when I beat you." She stole the ball right out of his hands and tossed it backward. It bounced off the backboard but managed to make it into the net anyway.

"Cheater." Matt scored a lay-up and then another, using his size and strength to keep her away. She might be able to outrun him, but he still had some advantages.

Cassie shrugged out of the jacket and tossed it at him, just as he sank another basket.

"Hey!" He caught the jacket as she caught the ball and shot it, making two more points.

They forgot about playing only to eleven, and the next twenty or so minutes was a heart-pounding, perspiring, rule-breaking game of trying anything and everything to outmaneuver each other. At last, when Matt had scored three three-pointers in a row, Cassie raised her hand, waving it back and forth slowly.

"White flag. You win." She leaned over, panting, her breath visible in the cold air. Matt tossed the ball through the hoop one more time, then came over to her.

"Good game." He held out his hand, and she shook it. "You don't play like a girl. I like that. Wish you'd been my sister instead of Megan."

"Thanks." Cassie straightened and started to pull away, but he didn't let her.

"Thank *you*," he said. "I wasn't looking forward to coming home, to this weekend, but you've made it great."

"You're welcome." She ceased trying to pull away from him. "Even though your family is a little nuts, this has been really fun for me, too. Noah is in heaven with all these kids. I wish he had some cousins on my side or that Devon's sister didn't live so far away."

"I wish—" What he wished didn't bear saying and would hurt her terribly. "Come on. Let's go sit on the sea wall and cool off." Reluctantly, he released her hand, then turned toward the beach. She stepped up beside him, and they walked through the backyard, out to the low wall separating the patio and narrow strip of grass from the beach. Matt sat down, and Cassie hopped up on the wall beside him. Ahead of them, the surf crashed onto the shore, soothing and exhilarating at the same time.

"I used to come out here a lot when I was growing up," Matt said. "It was my place to calm down when one of my siblings upset me, my place to brood when our team lost or when the girl I asked to prom said no."

"She didn't." Cassie turned to him, and in the moonlight, he could barely make out her appalled yet sympathetic expression.

"Did," Matt confirmed, "but it was my fault really. She had a boyfriend already, and I hadn't done my homework to find out. I just knew she was a pretty girl in my chem class, and I wanted to take her out."

"What about you?" he asked. "Who took you to your senior prom?" He had no doubt she'd gone. Girls as kind and as pretty as Cassie always got asked, and he was sure she'd been both, even back then.

"Devon took me." Her voice was wistful.

"You two knew each other in high school?" Somehow, for all the conversations they'd had, Matt hadn't known this.

"Knew each other, went steady, were practically engaged when we graduated."

"Wow. That's some serious history." Maybe he understood her devotion a little more. "Was he your first boyfriend?"

"He was my first and last everything." Cassie's feet kicked slowly against the stone wall. "We called each other just about every day the whole time I was away at school, and I came home every chance I could to see him. We got married as soon as I had my undergrad and Devon had graduated from the police academy. We were on our way to this wonderful life, or so we believed."

The catch in her voice was too much. Matt couldn't not offer comfort. It would be wrong. Friends were supposed to be there for each other, a shoulder to cry or lean on, and he and Cassie were friends, weren't they? Without examining his motives any further, Matt scooted closer to her on the wall. He put his arm around her and pulled her close. After a slight hesitation, she came, leaning into him.

"I'd tell you I'm sorry about all you've had to go through, about the life you wanted and haven't been able to have, but that's lame and inadequate."

"You don't have to say anything," she said. So he didn't, just continued to hold her close to his side, his arm around her doing as much or more for his solace as it possibly was for her. The air was cool and heavy, the fog that would engulf them come morning already making its way to shore. Matt could barely make out the surf rolling and receding on the beach, its sound contributing to this perfect moment with Cassie.

"You know," she said after a few minutes, breaking their silence, which had become almost magical. "I'm kind of jealous of you."

"Why?" He turned his head and leaned forward to better see her expression. "Other than my amazing free throw abilities, that is."

She laughed. "That is something. You're good. I can see why you earned all those trophies."

"You were good, too," Matt said. "Was basketball your sport?" Several times now Cassie had mentioned being on teams and competing, but she'd never said what, exactly, those teams had been.

"Nope. Not basketball. Not soccer."

"If I guess, will you tell me?" His arm was getting tired, so Matt let it slide from hers, bracing it on the wall near her hip.

"Sure. But you'd probably sooner guess Rumpelstiltskin's name."

"I love a good challenge, and the gauntlet has been thrown."

Cassie gasped. "How did—" She pressed her lips together, but Matt had already realized she'd given him a clue.

"Ah ha." He gazed at her speculatively. "Really?"

She looked away and didn't say anything.

"It would certainly explain you being fast on your feet all the time."

"Motherhood explains that," she said flippantly, but he saw through her attempt at appearing nonchalant.

"Were you, by chance, a member of a fencing team?"

She sighed. "I made that way too easy for you."

"You did," Matt agreed, chuckling. "I don't think I ever would have guessed, except for your faux pas. So how did you get into that sport? I didn't even know people still did things like that."

"Most people don't, but my dad was a fencer, and since I was his only child, it fell to me to carry on the tradition."

"Is Noah going to carry on this same tradition?" Matt realized there may have been more to the choice of the Three Musketeer costumes than he'd thought.

"Only if he wants to," Cassie said. "Once you get over the nerdiness of it, fencing is pretty fun."

"And killer good training for a lot of other sports. too," Matt guessed. "No wonder you run circles around me. Remind me never to duel with you."

"All right." She let out an overly dramatic sigh. "Guess I'll just have to get over being jealous instead of getting out my rapier."

He tucked away the part about being jealous, the second time she'd used that word, to be addressed in a minute. For now he was still stuck on the sword fighting. Instead of thinking it was nerdy, he was fascinated. "You have a rapier—a real one?"

"A few," she said. "Most were my dad's. They're at my mom's house."

"Knowing this, I am not sure how you were able to give the boys those horrible, floppy foam swords on Halloween. I mean, come on."

She winced. "I know. But they're too little for real swords yet."

The *yet* excited him. "Promise me you'll let Austin and Asher in on the fun when you start teaching Noah?"

"If they want to, and you approve." She looked at him sideways, and Matt realized again how close they were, sitting side-by-side, his arm around her, but more than the physical closeness, it was their friendship warming him. He still wanted to kiss her. He still thought she was gorgeous and tempting, and he wished they could take their relationship to the next level, but what they had right now, the way they'd been there for each other the past few months was nothing short of awesome and inspiring and miraculous. Cassie was his best friend, in a way Jenna hadn't been for a long time the past years of their marriage. He had only himself to blame for that, and he did—he forever would—but being someone else's friend, being there for Cassie, to make her life and Noah's a little better, was somehow cathartic. Maybe this was his chance to do better, without any other motive or reward than having her as a friend also.

"Why are you jealous of me?" He pulled his gaze from her lips out to the dark sea.

"A dozen reasons," she admitted. "Both of your parents are alive. You have siblings, so your children have cousins. You have *two* children. I'd love for Noah to have a brother."

"So my mid-thirties athletic physique has nothing to do with it?"

She tapped a finger to her lips. "Nope."

"Man." He hunched forward, pretending hurt. "In that case, the best I can offer is to share my nutty family. They're all yours whenever you want them. Now that my mom is fairly certain you don't really tattoo people for a living, I think you'll be welcome to stay anytime."

"I don't know if I'll be able to come again." She sounded sad. "I shouldn't be away from Devon."

"I know, but I'm glad you came this time."

"Me, too. It's going to be a memory Noah never forgets."

"What about you?" Matt nudged her shoulder.

"I'll always remember this weekend, too," Cassie said. "Especially tonight."

Twenty-Seven

Matt's parents' shop resembled their house, as far as the signage went at least. "Kramer's Crabbing and Fishing" hung over the entrance to the humble little building near the pier, and tacked along the wall inside were a dozen other signs and slogans. Cassie wondered if any had ever driven a potential customer away.

We'd love to see you naked, but state code requires shirt and shoes and *Prices subject to change according to customer's attitude* seemed like they might be a bit of a turn off for some people. *I can only please one person. Today is not your day. And tomorrow isn't looking good either,* didn't exactly seem friendly, but the young man wearing overalls and working behind the counter had a ready smile and cheerful greeting for them.

"Good to see you again, Matt. Taking a boat out today?"

"We're going with my dad," he said. "Cassie's never been crabbing before."

Cassie's never been on a boat in the ocean before. She'd worry about the crabs later. For now she was just hoping not to be seasick.

"Cassie, this is Cole, Dad's right-hand man," Matt said. "Cole, this is my friend Cassie, a tattoo artist from California."

"Really?" Cole's eyes lit up. "Savage. I've been wanting to get something on my other arm. Something feng shui to balance with this one. Maybe you have some suggestions?" He pushed up the sleeve over his left arm, revealing sculpted biceps and a tattoo of a compass.

Cassie shot Matt a you-are-so-dead look as she scrambled for fake tattoo advice. "Well—have you ever considered getting . . . a treasure chest, like one that might belong to a pirate? I wouldn't put a skull or crossbones anywhere on it, though. Too common and stereotypical."

"Yeah?" Cole nodded as if absorbing some sage wisdom.

"The thing about a treasure chest," Cassie continued, "is that it could have a lot of different meanings. I'd have the lid slightly open but without revealing what might be within. That way no one really knows for sure unless you tell them. Your 'treasure' could be any number of things. The compass"—she pointed to the bulging circle on his arm—"is what you use to find your treasure."

"I like it." Cole slapped his hand on the counter. "I may have to take a trip to California to have you do it personally."

"That could be painful." Matt winked at Cassie when Cole wasn't looking.

"Tell you what," Cassie said, ignoring the wink. "Why don't I do one on Matt first, and you can check it out the next time he's home. If you like what you see, we can talk then."

"That's lit. You're on."

"And we have to be off," Matt said, rescuing Cassie from further tattoo talk. "Just sign this waiver, and we're good to go." He reached behind the counter and pulled the top form off a stack.

"What rights am I waiving away here?" Cassie took the pen Cole offered.

"Oh, you know, just the basics." Matt leaned against the counter.

"You won't sue us if you drown and that sort of thing," Cole added.

Cassie rolled her eyes. "It would seem that I can't sue you if I've drowned already."

"Yeah. Probably not," Cole agreed.

"But in case you're prone to haunting people from the grave, we have you sign anyway." Matt's casual attitude and grin were less than reassuring. She loved the beach and the ocean, but that was when she was firmly on shore. Going out onto it was entirely different.

"Just you two and your dad going out?" Cole asked.

"And the boys and you, of course." Matt flexed his arm and shook his head. "These middle-aged muscles may need help pulling in those pots. Or at least keeping our kids from going overboard. That reminds me. Cassie, you'll need to sign a waiver for Noah as well." Matt handed her a second form. This one she had a harder time putting her signature on. It was foolish enough to endanger herself, but to put Noah in harm's way as well . . .

"I was just teasing. No one's going overboard. Everything's going to be fine." Matt placed his hand over hers on the counter, and their eyes met briefly. She knew hers were filled with apprehension, but Matt's reflected confidence.

"I won't let anything happen to you or Noah," he promised. "We're going to have a great time."

Cassie swallowed back her worries and forced a smile. "We're going to have a great time."

"I'm having a great time!" Cassie shouted some two hours later over the noise of the wind and ocean spray as she and Matt and Cole pulled on the rope to haul the basket filled with crabs onto the back of the boat.

It landed with a thud, and Austin, Asher, and Noah crowded around eagerly as Cole reached in to pull out the first crab.

"Who remembers what kind this is?" He held it up, pincers faced away from him.

"A Dungeness," Austin said, almost pronouncing it correctly.

"Good," Cole said. "Boy or girl?"

"Girl," Noah said. "The triangle on its tummy is shorter and fatter."

"Right again." Cole grinned. "I'm gonna tell Tom to hire you three next summer. Would you like that? Working on a boat all day, catching crabs and fish?"

"Yes," the boys chorused. Cole handed the female crab to Matt, and Matt beckoned Noah closer. "Want to throw it back?"

Noah nodded and stepped up closer to the creature. Cassie pulled out her phone to take a picture.

"Can I wear your gloves?" Noah asked Matt.

"Sure." Matt set the crab on the floor of the boat where it began an escape attempt that Asher and Austin promptly put an end to, dancing around it as they were. Matt pulled off a glove and knelt down in front of Noah, then patiently helped him fit it over his smaller fingers as best he could.

When both of Noah's hands were safely covered, Matt retrieved the scuttling crab and stood behind Noah so they could both hold and toss it into the sea.

Cassie snapped a picture just as they let go. The expression on Noah's face was priceless. His ear-to-ear grin showed clearly that he was having the time of his life. Matt seemed pretty happy, too, as he high fived Noah. Cassie's heart melted at the scene, so perfect in every way, except that it should have been Devon teaching Noah how to catch crabs, Devon who carefully fastened his life jacket earlier, Devon who taught him to fly a kite, attended Dads and Donuts at the school, held his hand for kindergarten shots, coached his soccer team. All things she—and now Matt— were doing in Devon's place. *You're missing it. You're missing everything, Devon.*

Today, just now, she felt grateful that Noah wasn't missing out on this experience, that he was right there with Austin and Asher, with Matt to guide him.

"Look, seals!" Asher exclaimed. He leaned over the side as he pointed to the animals lounging on a nearby buoy.

"Sea lions," Matt's dad corrected. He started the boat up and cruised slowly toward the buoy so they could have a closer look.

Cassie snapped more pictures, a few of the sea lions, but most of the three boys lined up against the side of the boat, pointing and laughing, rapt attention and adventure written on each of their faces. Three matching, hand-knit, wool hats, courtesy of Matt's mother, topped their heads, making them look like they all belonged together, like brothers. Her heart ached. How was it possible to feel so happy and sad at the same time?

"Pretty great out here, isn't it?" Matt asked as he came to stand beside her at the rail.

"It's wonderful," she agreed. "I can't believe you grew up doing this. Talk about an amazing life and a fantastic summer job."

"I think I need it again." He flexed his arm and frowned. "I was a lot more buff as a teen. Pulling crab pots all day had its advantages."

"You have other, better things going for you now," Cassie said, careful to steer clear of any compliments regarding his physical appearance. She found Matt plenty attractive, but she was trying to avoid focusing on that and felt pretty sure he wasn't vying for her attention that way either. "You've got parenting muscle now. You're a great dad to Austin and Asher and a really great substitute dad to Noah."

"I'm happy to do it," Matt said. "Thanks for letting me and for coming this weekend."

"Thank you for inviting us," Cassie said sincerely, her heartbeat escalating suddenly as he moved closer and looked down at her. "This will be a memory Noah and I will always cherish." There she was, sad and happy all at once again, only now she understood why. This moment was happy, one of those perfect moments in time, like her wedding day when she'd stood up through the sunroof on the Golden Gate Bridge. She felt so alive out here with the wind in her hair, the fresh ocean breezes, and a sea of blue surrounding them, but she'd learned that these moments, those thrilling bursts of happiness, couldn't last. Hers and Noah's had been far and few between, and this one, this amazing, precious weekend, was slipping away all too suddenly, like literal sand in an hourglass.

And she didn't want it to end.

Twenty-Eight

Matt stood at the stove, stirring the caramel that was to go over the quadruple batch of popcorn he'd just popped. "For some families, watching the *Wizard of Oz* or *It's a Wonderful Life* is traditional on Thanksgiving weekend. Here, we get out the lightsabers. It's all about *Star Wars*—old school *Star Wars*, that is," Matt added, looking sternly down his nose in an attempt to convey just how steeped in this culture his family was. "None of that punk kid racing around and having attitude."

"Or flirting with that senator much older than him," Cassie added, tsk, tsking as she bounced Catelyn on her lap. "Old school is fine by me."

"We always start with *A New Hope*," Matt said, noting again how natural, how great, Cassie looked holding a baby. "Then *Empire Strikes Back* is on Saturday and *Return of the Jedi* with brunch Sunday morning before everyone has to start packing up and going home."

"What about the new movie?" Cassie asked. "Was it true enough to the originals for the Kramer clan?"

"I think so," Matt said, "but I'll have to check with my mom. She's the boss of this whole thing. And you don't want to mess with her where movies are concerned, especially *Star Wars*."

"Good to know." A mischievous twinkle came to Cassie's eye.

"I'm serious," Matt warned. "You don't believe me?"

"Oh, I do," Cassie assured him. She tucked Catelyn in the crook of her arm, then placed her free hand over her heart as if preparing to recite the Pledge of Allegiance. "It is duly noted that messing with your mom's movie plans would be very unwise and likely cause me to be excluded from future invitations to visit."

"Just remember that," Matt said, still attempting a stern look while his insides were spinning at Cassie's casual remark, which suggested she would be open to coming home with him again, that the thing they had between them, whatever it was, would continue. That possibility brought an infusion of happiness. "Any chance you could help me with this in a minute?" He'd poured the caramel by himself before, but it *was* easier with another person to scrape the pot with a spatula and help spread the caramel evenly, not to mention it was another excuse to be near Cassie.

"Give me a second," she said. "I'll put Catelyn in her pack and play."

Matt nodded, and Cassie left the kitchen to relocate her charge. Mark and Laura were having a great weekend, too, with Cassie volunteering to watch their baby every other minute. This afternoon they'd gone into town to do some Christmas shopping, leaving Catelyn in Cassie's care. Matt was pretty sure that Cassie was enjoying babysitting at least as much as his brother and sister-in-law were enjoying getting out.

Cassie returned to the kitchen and stepped up beside him at the stove. "All right. What do I do?"

"Use the spatula there." He nodded to one in the crock beside the stove. "Try to get the caramel to cover all the popcorn evenly. Ready?"

She nodded, and he picked up the pot and started pouring. Cassie crowded in close, stretching beneath his arm so she could reach to scrape the pot.

Matt took the opportunity to breathe in the scent of her hair. Coconut. Come to think of it, she did always seem to have a bit of a tropical aroma about her. When the silk strands brushed against his chin, it was all he could do not to nuzzle or drop the pot and run his hands through her hair.

"Is that good?" Cassie asked, bringing his mind back to the task at hand.

"Great," he murmured, thinking of their proximity and not the caramel.

Cassie stepped back, then held the spatula out to him. "This looks good enough to lick."

"Ladies first." Matt set the pot on the back burner to cool, which is just what he needed to do.

Cassie's tongue darted out to test the caramel. "Mmm. It's cool enough to eat already." She took a longer lick, then held the spatula out to Matt again. "For a guy whose specialty is PB&J, this is pretty good stuff."

"Old family secret." Matt licked the spatula, and though it was the best thing he'd ever tasted, he imagined that Cassie's lips would be even sweeter. *Especially right now.* His eyes zeroed in on those lips, plump and pink and slightly sticky. *Just one taste.* He leaned a little closer.

Catelyn's cries pierced the air.

"Uh oh. Better go." Cassie handed him the spatula and hurried from the room. Matt watched her leave, then released a long, ragged breath. *That was close.* He braced his hands on either side of the counter and leaned forward, head down while he tried to wrestle his raging desire back in control.

"Just friends, huh?" Megan entered the kitchen through the sliding glass door. "You look at all your friends like that, Matty? Like you want to eat them for dinner?"

"Stay out of it, Meg." He meant to tease her back, but there was no humor in his tone, because nothing about his and Cassie's situation was at all amusing.

Cassie secured the last bobby pin in her hair and studied her reflection in the mirror, wondering if Matt's family was going to think she was crazy or what, but she couldn't contain her grin at the giant buns swirled on either side of her head.

She'd had the idea when Matt had told her of his family's thing for *Star Wars.* After all, she had the hair for it—her long, brown, oft-neglected mop ought to be good for something once in a while—and she had dressed as Princess Leia for a Halloween party several years ago. Too bad she hadn't brought a costume, though maybe that would have been overkill. Walking out to the family room in these babies—she touched the sides of her head gingerly—was going to require enough bravery.

Mustering her courage, Cassie opened the bathroom door, stepped into the hall, and descended the stairs. With what she hoped was her usual, nonchalant stride, she walked into the family room, her eyes zeroing in on Matt and the vacant seat beside him on the sofa. She hadn't taken two steps into the room when his mom shrieked out a hoot of laughter.

"Look! Look at Cassie."

Anyone who hadn't been looking her way before swung their gaze toward her, and Cassie felt her blush begin. "I just thought, you know, since you're all so into the movie . . ." She shrugged.

Matt laughed out loud, then stood and began clapping. His brother and sister followed, bursts of laughter included, and his mom still hadn't stopped exclaiming over her.

"Oh, my gosh. Those are the best Princess Leia buns I've ever seen. You could be her double. Come here."

Cassie obeyed, pausing long enough to high five Matt as she made her way over to his mom.

"You darling girl." Maureen reached up, patting the sides of Cassie's head. "I'll be. I never—" She wiped a tear from the corner of her eye. "If that don't beat all. Where's my phone? I've got to take a picture and post this on Facebook."

"I don't know about Facebook," Cassie said. "This was just a joke for you guys."

"Oh no, dear. Everyone's got to see this. You've started a new tradition. The rest of you"—she leaned around Cassie to stare at her children—"had better follow Cassie's example. I expect to see you also appropriately attired for this occasion next year. This young lady has just taken this holiday weekend up a notch. Now where's my phone?"

Cassie looked over her shoulder. "Sorry," she mouthed to Matt and his brother. Then, "Save me," to Matt as his mother poked her hand into the side of her Lazy Boy and continued mumbling about her darn phone.

"I finally got it altogether, and now I don't know where I put it," Maureen muttered. "It's got to be here somewhere."

Matt walked over, slung his arm around Cassie's shoulder, and steered her away from his mom. "No sharing pictures today. These buns are mine, and mine alone." He bumped his hip into Cassie's.

Mark chuckled at his brother's joke. Cassie rolled her eyes while feeling an inkling of discomfort at such personal teasing. It sounded like something Devon would have said, but Matt wasn't Devon.

"Oh, I've found it." Maureen waved her phone in the air. "Just one quick picture?"

"*No*, Mom." Matt led Cassie to their seats on the couch, front and center before the large screen.

"Careful, you'll mess up my hairdo." Cassie wriggled out from under his arm, worried he might try to keep it draped over her shoulder during the movie.

Seemingly undeterred, Matt leaned close to whisper in her ear. "What, no appreciation for risking my mother's wrath to bravely rescue you? I seem to recall that Luke received a kiss for his efforts."

Cassie turned her face to Matt's, so close that their lips were only a couple inches apart. His eyes sparkled with mischief, and a reckless smile upturned one corner of his mouth. He smelled fresh and clean, like the Oregon coast, and he looked even better. Against her will—or maybe with it—her eyes were drawn to his lips, and the desire she'd banished successfully at every turn threatened to burst to the surface. It would be so easy to kiss him. *And so wrong.*

Instead she looked up at the ceiling, shook her head, and twisted her mouth in a look of annoyance while fighting to hide her real feelings. "Have you forgotten the part where Leia turned out to be Luke's sister? How gross was that kiss then?"

Mark chuckled. "Smooth move, bro." He left the couch to start the movie.

"Just one picture." A flash momentarily blinded Cassie, and she looked up to see Maureen standing over them, beaming. "You'll have to teach us how to do those buns, Cassie." She patted the sides of her hair, as if imagining such an updo.

Cassie looked sideways at Matt. "Some rescue," she muttered good-naturedly.

Matt shrugged. "What can you expect? The reward wasn't there."

But plenty of tension was, hovering just beneath their banter, light but loaded with meaning, and stretched taught between them, seated so close on the couch, their arms and legs touching.

The opening theme blared from the ceiling speakers, making her jump, and Cassie could only feel grateful for the interruption to her thoughts and churning emotions.

"Turn it down," Laura pled. "You'll wake the baby."

Did Matt really just ask me to kiss him? Did he actually think that I might? Cassie licked her lips that felt suddenly dry. Now that Matt had suggested it, however jokingly, she couldn't seem to think of anything else. *What would it be like?* Desire that felt all too much like teenage hormones played havoc with her traitorous body while her mind fought off the more pressing problem, the yearning she felt to make Matt's life better, to heal his heart, to love him as he deserved to be loved. He was such a great guy, and he'd done so much for her and Noah. *He deserves a kiss.*

I can't. Cassie kept her eyes glued to the screen, reading the prologue as it scrolled and trying her best to ignore Matt's proximity. Mark rejoined them on the couch, squishing her and Matt together even more. It was cozy—too cozy. His leg pressed against hers. His hand was practically in her lap.

Cassie wished she could gauge Matt's reaction to what she hoped was a discreet but firm rejection. She'd let things get out of hand this weekend, but it wasn't too late to get back on track. She and Matt hadn't crossed any lines that couldn't be put back into place.

I haven't been unfaithful to Devon. But she felt like she had. These past weeks, her heart had been turning to someone other than him, and this weekend—magical as it had been—threatened to pull her completely from Devon's side. She couldn't let that happen.

As she watched Leia hide from the storm troopers, Cassie told herself over and over that she needed to keep her distance from Matt. He was like a brother, a good friend, but he could never be anything more.

Wanting him to be more had to stop.

Twenty-Nine

Cassie stepped out of the tub, one towel wrapped around her middle and another piled on her head to dry her mop of soaking hair. Though she'd taken the Leia buns out before going to bed last night, the damage had already been done. She'd woken this morning to a head full of kinked, knotted hair that could only be tamed with an overabundance of conditioner. She had hurried to shower, hoping the others weren't up yet, but voices, one in particular sounding frustrated and raised, carried through the vent on the bathroom floor. Cassie sat on the toilet seat and leaned forward to better dry her hair and to see if she could hear what it was that had upset Matt.

"I'm not fifteen, Mom. If I felt like I needed your advice, I'd ask for it."

"You're also not a very fast learner," his mom shot back. "The last time we gave you advice you didn't take, you lived to regret it. You still are, in fact."

"Thanks for the reminder," Matt said sourly. "I know I screwed up before. Okay. I was a lousy husband and father—I'm paying for that, believe me—but I'm learning to be a better dad. I'm trying, really, and it's in large part because of Cassie's parenting example. I've learned so much from her."

"We can see that you have, son," Matt's dad's voice was softer, kinder, and more patient than Maureen's had been. "We're so pleased and proud of all that you've done. You've picked your life up admirably. You're a better person for all you've gone through."

"Thanks," Matt said, sounding anything but grateful.

"Cassie is a lovely young woman," Matt's mom began.

But . . . Cassie knew she should leave the bathroom and go somewhere else in the house where she couldn't overhear their argument, but there was no way she could leave now, not when this conversation concerned her.

"But?" Matt asked, echoing her thoughts.

"She's got a ring on her finger," Maureen said. "She's married; she has a living, breathing husband."

They don't like me because I'm married. Cassie certainly couldn't blame them, and she felt almost relieved that was the issue. *Something I can't change and don't feel the least bad about.*

"I don't think you can qualify her husband's condition as living," Matt said. "Devon hasn't been awake for six years."

"Still," Maureen said. "He is *alive,* and Cassie is his wife."

"I know that."

Cassie thought she heard Matt's weary sigh and imagined him running his fingers through his hair in exasperation, or was he standing with his hands shoved in his pockets like he did when he wasn't sure what to do with them?

"Cassie and I are just friends," Matt said. "We help each other fill in the gaps for the boys."

"For now," Maureen said, "but you're not too far from filling in the gaps for each other as well. Last night you practically asked her to kiss you."

He did *ask me to kiss him.* Cassie set the towel on the counter and reached for her brush.

"We were just joking around," Matt said. "Besides, you heard her. She turned me down flat. Cassie is the most dedicated wife and mother I know. She's incredibly faithful to her husband."

"Then why are you encouraging her not to be?" his dad asked, voice still kind.

Matt didn't answer, not that Cassie could hear at least. She dropped to the floor, kneeling on the bathmat and leaned closer to the vent.

"Cassie may have turned you down this time," Maureen said, "but she didn't want to. Look at this picture I took. Is this the face of a woman who doesn't want to be kissed?"

What picture? Did she post it? Panicked, Cassie glanced up at the counter before remembering she'd left her phone on the nightstand in Matt's bedroom.

"I've rarely seen such yearning," his mom continued. "It breaks the heart, really. If you think being alone for ten months has been rough, imagine how Cassie must feel, having been alone all these years."

"She feels fine," Matt said. "She's coped with the hand life's dealt her amazingly well. Until she told me, I had no idea that her husband was anything less than ordinary. She coaches soccer, works at the school, and makes this tooth fairy money for Noah. She knows what to do about head lice, cooks healthy dinners, and even made the all boys Halloween costumes. She's completely capable and on top of things."

If you only knew. But Matt did know. They'd talked at length about their situations. He'd seen her cry. *He knows that deep down I struggle.*

"Being capable doesn't mean that someone isn't lonely or wanting more," Maureen said.

"Well of course she wants more." Matt's voice raised. "She wants her husband to wake up. I want Jenna to come back. We don't always get what we want, so we do the best with what we're given."

"You're missing a critical difference," Tom said. "Jenna is never going to come back, but Cassie's husband might. Who knows? Stranger things have happened, and he's hung on this long."

Cassie dropped her brush on the rug and sat back, leaning against the tub as she hugged her knees tight to her chest that was suddenly throbbing. Words she'd tried hard to forget pushed their way to the surface. *Devon lingers because your heart calls to him.*

Matt's father continued. "And if he does wake up, where does that leave you?"

"Exactly where I was before," Matt muttered, sounding angry. "Alone."

"Unless you've become too close to Cassie," his mom said, her voice strangely emotional. "Then you're worse off, and so is she. Think about what that would do to her and Noah. What if she had to choose between her husband and you?"

If you would release him, he would go and find peace at last.

"What about Austin and Asher?" Maureen asked. "They adore her already, but she's not their mother."

"She's so good for them." Matt sounded almost pleading.

It's time to allow what should have happened six years ago to happen now. It's time to let go. Cassie's throat felt swollen. She rested her forehead on her arms as tears threatened.

"I know, son," Tom said. "We see how wonderful Cassie is, too. We were thrilled for you until we realized her situation. Now we're fearful for you both. We don't want to see you and the boys get hurt, and we don't want you to hurt someone else. Matt, that's not who we raised you to be or who you are. You're better than that."

Search your heart . . . tell him he is free to move on, and then you *can move on.*

She couldn't. It wasn't that simple. Cassie threw the towel over the vent and got to her feet. She'd heard enough of both the conversation downstairs and the remembered one in her head. She dressed quickly, fighting tears as she pulled on her jeans and thrust her arms through the sleeves of a thick sweater. She braided her hair in record time, then tidied the bathroom.

A quick peek in the hall showed all the other doors still closed, so she crept silently back to Matt's room, where she wrote a hasty note, jammed a hat on her head, and grabbed her shoes.

Downstairs she could still hear muted voices coming from Matt's parents' room, so she walked on tiptoe across the kitchen and out the back door. She closed the door softly then, put on her sneakers and a jacket she'd grabbed from the hooks by the door.

The sounds of the surf reached her as Cassie crossed the yard and exited the gate. She followed the sandy path down to the beach. Once there, she slowed her steps and inhaled slowly, filling her lungs with the moist ocean air. The beach was only faintly lit and mostly shrouded in fog, but several residents were up already, walking along the shoreline, perhaps anxious to work off the weekend's excess of food. If only that was all she needed to work off or work out, but the problems weighing her down were far greater than an extra pound or two.

Every point Matt's parents had made was right—spot on to the realities of her situation, a situation she'd allowed Matt to become entangled in, too. His parents hadn't said it aloud, at least not during the part of the conversation she'd overheard, but Cassie realized how grossly she had taken advantage of Matt and his kindness. Sure, he might have been the one who first officially suggested that they be friends, but it was really her fault that had happened. That night at the hospital cafeteria, she'd been so distraught after her meeting with Pearl. *I just wanted someone to talk to*, she rationalized, but deep down inside she'd known what she was doing when she sat at his booth and told Matt about Devon. She'd seen how kind he'd been when Noah got hurt, and she'd hoped for his compassion again that night. She'd needed someone, and he'd come through in even more ways than she'd imagined.

Cassie stopped walking and faced the ocean, closing her eyes as she remembered the moment Matt first reached across the table and took her hand, how much that meant, how good it had felt, how she never wanted to let go. In a way, she hadn't. She'd encouraged and enjoyed their friendship to the point that he'd invited her and Noah to come home for Thanksgiving, a rite usually reserved for a couple getting serious about a relationship—something they absolutely could not do.

The tears she'd been fighting all morning finally broke free, sliding down her cheeks one after the other. Cassie zipped up the jacket all the way and pulled the hood up to hide her face as much as possible from anyone she might pass. Then she started walking along the beach in the opposite direction she and Matt had taken the boys the previous day.

What a mess she'd made. What was she supposed to do now? Clearly, she couldn't continue to see Matt as she had been, even under the guise of activities for the boys, but it would break Noah's heart not to see Matt and his boys anymore. Cassie worried about Asher and Austin, too. *Especially Austin.* She couldn't just walk away from him. He was simply too fragile to handle that. If she did, it might be years before he recovered and could feel like he could trust again. Ending things completely was out of the question.

There was no going back to how life was before she'd met Matt and his sons, but there could also be no continuing on as they had been. The next time he asked, she worried she *might* kiss him. *What kind of a wife kisses another man?* She felt wretched even thinking about it and wished more than anything that she could be at Devon's side tonight and beg his forgiveness.

Maybe I can.

Cassie wiped at her tears and tried to think the possibility through. She could rent a car and return home tonight. Noah would pitch a fit, of course. He was having the time of his life. She had been, too, until this morning.

If she made him leave today so she could see Devon tonight, Noah might blame Devon and resent him. She'd glimpsed that resentment a time or two already and had been trying not to use Devon or allow his condition to become an issue. She didn't want Noah to hate his dad before he even knew him.

I could let Noah stay the weekend. She wondered what Matt would think of that. He and the boys could come home on Sunday as they'd planned. She wondered if she could survive in her apartment alone for a night without Noah, but if it came down to his happiness or hers, she'd figure out a way to be alone. A couple of days away from Matt might help her decide how to best go forward from here. She'd go see Devon tonight and tomorrow. Maybe explaining the situation to him would help her know what to do.

Feeling slightly better for having a plan, Cassie turned to head back the direction she'd come and saw a distant figure sprinting toward her. It was Matt. Instead of walking faster to meet him, as she would have the day before, she slowed her steps, then stopped altogether, prolonging the time until he would reach her. *What am I going to say?* She'd hoped for another half hour to work through how to best tell him she needed to leave.

I should never have come. I'm sorry for leading you on. We can't let this get any more serious. Perhaps that was too direct.

I've really enjoyed meeting your family, but this trip wasn't a good idea. He'd want to know why.

I happened to overhear your conversation with your parents this morning. Slightly far from the truth.

I lay on the bathroom floor this morning and eavesdropped on your private conversation. A good possibility for making him lose interest quickly. Maybe she should go for complete honesty, displaying all her flaws.

Your mom was spot on. I totally wanted to kiss you last night. But he might take that as an invitation to kiss her now, right here on the beach at sunrise. Cassie ran her tongue over her top teeth. Had she brushed that morning?

What am I thinking? She brought her hands to her eyes and covered them, as if to block out the image of her and Matt that her mind had so easily conjured.

This was bad. *Really* bad. What was she supposed to do? Matt had almost reached her. She had to tell him something.

Thirty

"Hey." Matt stopped a few feet away from Cassie and bent over, breathing hard. Not playing basketball with the guys might have been a good move for being a better parent, but it had definitely left him out of shape. He needed to start working out on his lunch hour or something.

"Hey, yourself," she said, digging the toe of her sneaker into the sand.

Matt stayed bent over another several seconds, waiting to make sure he wasn't going to heave. *Pathetic.* He remembered Cassie running up and down the soccer field as if it were nothing. Maybe he should sign the boys up for basketball and offer to coach.

"Having a nice walk?" he finally managed to ask. "I would have gone with you." He straightened and experienced a few seconds of vertigo before he began to feel right again.

She shrugged. "I needed to do some thinking."

"And I just interrupted." He gave her what he hoped was a look of chagrin.

"Pretty much." She smiled, softening the reprimand.

If only his mother could communicate so nicely. "Want me to leave?" Matt asked. "I probably have it in me to run another ten feet. I could give you that much space at least."

Cassie shook her head. "No. I'm glad you're here, actually. We need to talk."

Uh oh. "Need to talk" was never good. How many times had he heard that in his life, including this morning from his parents? But this was Cassie. They talked all the time, and it was great. There was no one he'd rather talk with.

"What's up?" He turned and stepped in beside her, shoving his hands in his pockets as they began walking back toward the house.

"My life, my spirits," she said, "since I met you." She smiled at him sideways. Matt felt his own spirits soar with her compliment.

"But my life is also up in the air; I'm suspended, waiting indefinitely for something to change."

"Waiting for Devon to wake up." *Or to die.* He was despicable for thinking it, for wanting to be with Cassie as more than a friend. His parents were right. Who did he think he was, weaseling his way into her life as he had?

She took a deep breath, then exhaled quickly and stopped walking. "Yes. I'm waiting for my husband to wake up." She faced Matt, her eyes searching his in a way that pled for understanding. "I shouldn't have come this weekend. I'm not being fair to you or to Austin and Asher and Noah. I can't have feelings for you. It's wrong. *I'm* wrong. Together we would be wrong. I need to go home. Right now. I'll rent a car, and if it's okay with you, you can bring Noah home on Sunday when you return. I'm sorry."

"Whoa." Matt pulled his hands from his pockets and held them up, palms out as if to stop her from both leaving and telling him anything else. He didn't want to hear it. He didn't want her to leave. He didn't want to do what he knew was the right thing.

"I agree we have a bit of a problem—a challenging situation," he quickly amended. *I'm falling madly in love with you. You're married, which makes me like, super creep or something.*

"An *impossible* situation," Cassie amended. "Matt, this isn't going to get any easier. Last night—" She stopped abruptly, pressing her lips together as if to keep from saying what she'd been about to.

Matt thought of the picture his mom had on her phone. Was there any way she was right? Had Cassie wanted to kiss him? If so, she wasn't saying.

"When you teased me last night, it was the way a couple would tease. We're *not* a couple. We can't be." Her voice broke on the last words, and it was all Matt could do not to take her in his arms.

"I know that," he said quietly. "We're friends." *Without benefits.* He was a jerk for suggesting, even teasing, about that changing. "I crossed a line. I'm really sorry, but you don't have to go home. I'll knock it off. I promise. It's being around Mark that brings out the worst in me. He's such a pain. Even so, I'll be better."

"I like you fine the way you are." Her voice was heavy with meaning and such sorrow that he imagined what the admission had cost her. Her next words were laced with guilt. "I like you too much, Matt. This is all my fault."

"Hardly." He held his hands out again, palms up this time. "That's not true at all Cassie. It takes two to, you know, *want* to tango. I'm the jerk who suggested it, but I won't anymore. I promise. I won't even sit on the same sofa as you tonight when we watch *The Empire Strikes Back*. If you cry when they freeze Han Solo, well too bad. You're going to have to get a hug from my mom 'cause I am off limits, *Mrs. Webb.*"

She looked away and dug the toe of her shoe in the sand again. "I don't know. It's Saturday, and I really should be with Devon."

You should be where you want to be, or where Noah wants to be, at least. "Don't hate me," Matt prefaced the thought he was about to share, "but will Devon even know if you're there?"

She shot him the hurt look he'd expected.

"Hear me out—please."

She nodded, looked at the ground, and continued to bury the top of her shoe.

"For six years you've spent your weekends in town, your Fridays at Devon's bedside. That is good and admirable, and there's nothing wrong with spending the next six years being just as faithful. But—" He paused, praying for the right way to say this, to make it about her and not him at all. "It's time for you to start living life, too."

"I do live—"

"A better, fuller life," he qualified.

"By being with you, I suppose." She folded her arms across her chest and thrust her weight onto one hip in a classic Cassie stance he'd come to love.

"No. This has nothing to do with me. If we never saw each other again after today, I'd still hope you'd take this advice. I'm talking about you taking a Friday night out for yourself with some girlfriends."

"I don't have any girlfriends."

Matt nodded. "Exactly, but wouldn't it be nice if you did?"

She shrugged in response. "My old friends are married,

too, and I don't want to hang out with them and hear them complain about their husbands or talk about their sex lives. I don't need any more painful reminders of what I don't have."

She had a good point, but so did he. "Forget the girlfriends then—for now. What if Noah plays pee wee football in a few years and the games are on Friday nights?"

"Then I'll switch my date night with Devon to Saturdays," Cassie said.

"That's fine, too, but what about taking a week to go on vacation with Noah, to take him to Disneyland or Legoland or wherever he wants to go? You know you want to, and you could, but you're afraid of going without Devon."

"Because he should be there with us, too," Cassie cried, kicking her foot and sending the sand on her shoe flying. "Because I don't want to do anything that will make him miss any more than he's already missing!" She clamped a hand over her mouth as her eyes widened, then filled with tears of discovery.

Well, good then. At least he'd done one thing right this weekend. "I understand how you feel. That first day the boys and I played soccer and then went to ice cream with you and Noah, I realized what I'd been doing—or not doing. What had been missing, aside from Jenna, from our lives. Having any sort of fun without her had seemed wrong, and so we weren't. We were living life, but we weren't *living*." He managed to catch Cassie's gaze and hold it for a second, long enough to see that she knew exactly what he was getting at.

"I'm not saying you're as bad as me," Matt continued, "because you're not. You're a great mom, and Noah's had a good life so far. But you're holding back from living fully. You know it now. Noah's going to know it soon if he doesn't already. Think about what is best for him—a better apartment, being able to have friends over and go to their houses, a mom who makes decisions based not on his dad in a coma, but on the two of you."

"Devon's not in a coma."

"Right. Sorry." Matt held his breath, worried he'd way overstepped his bounds and said too much.

Instead of yelling at him, Cassie's shoulders drooped, and her hands dropped to her sides. "I feel so guilty already. Every second of every day, especially lately."

"Then I'll back off," Matt promised, hating that he had to but caring enough for her that he would. "This isn't about me," he reiterated. "It's about you, about putting Noah's needs and your needs first, still caring for Devon but living life for those who are able to live it best right now—you and Noah."

Cassie gave a slight nod of acknowledgement, though she wouldn't look up at him.

"Obviously I don't know your husband," Matt said, "but from everything you've told me, Devon is a great guy. I have to believe he'd give you the same advice. He'd want you and Noah to be as happy as you can. That's what people who love each other do. They put the happiness of those they love above their own needs." *What I should have done.*

Jenna, for as much as he'd loved her—and he really had—hadn't experienced a whole lot of that phenomenon. Not for the first time, Matt wondered if he'd been more attentive or concerned if they might have realized something was wrong with her. Maybe Jenna had suspected something and not told him. Perhaps she'd been having headaches. He didn't know and never would because he hadn't been home enough *to* notice. Basketball season had meant weeks on the road, away from his wife and children who ought to have mattered the most.

They did now, and while it was too late for him to make things right with Jenna, Matt vowed again, for at least the hundredth time, that he'd be a good dad, that he would get his junk together and get fatherhood right. Now he added a new item to his list of self-improvements: Be a good friend, a true friend. It was time to put Cassie's needs above his own.

"How about a compromise," he suggested.

She finally looked at him, and he felt relieved to see only curiosity in her gaze.

"Let's leave first thing tomorrow," Matt said. "We'll skip the movie and brunch. I'll drive you home but keep Noah with me once we get there. He can hang out with the boys and me. You can go visit Devon and stay as long as you'd like."

"I don't know—"

"It's that or we all leave together today," Matt said. "I'm not even sure where we could rent a car on a holiday weekend, and even if we could, I'm not sending you off to drive nine hours yourself. You want me to go round up the boys and get them ready?"

"No." Cassie sighed. "You know that whole five minute warning thing I do with Noah when it's time to go home?"

"Yeah." Matt had noted and made use of that parenting tip. It worked, eliminating some of the boys' meltdowns, or at least the ones they were prone to in public.

"I do it because he doesn't deal well with sudden change. If I were to tell him we're leaving this morning when he's expecting to spend another day and a half here, you can imagine the reaction I'd get."

Matt could, though he'd yet to see that kind of behavior from Noah, probably because Cassie was purposeful in her parenting.

"Can we leave at six tomorrow morning?" she asked.

"Earlier if you'd like," he said, hopeful that he'd persuaded her to stay out the day. "You're the boss."

"Your family won't be upset that you're leaving early?"

"Nah." Matt waved a hand dismissively. "They're sick of me already. It's Austin and Asher they really like to see, and I already let my mom talk me into coming back for Christmas." Yesterday, when he'd had reason to hope that Cassie and Noah might accompany them again. "She can't complain too much." If anything, his mom would be on board with this plan to get Cassie home to see her husband, but he wasn't about to mention that.

"What about you? You won't mind leaving a half day early and missing the ending of the trilogy?"

Matt felt relieved at the hint of teasing in her voice. "After so many years, we all have the thing memorized. Let's see—third film. Luke and company help Han escape Jabba's hut."

"I think he's actually called Jabba *the* Hutt," Cassie corrected.

"Whatever." They started walking toward the house again. "Nothing much happens in that movie anyway. Luke confronts Vader. The emperor gets toasted. Leia frees Han, and he wakes up after being frozen in Kryptonite."

Cassie laughed. "Now you're really mixing up your movies."

"They all live happily ever after. That's all that matters." Matt thought of the scene when Han awoke and Leia was there to kiss him. He had a sudden vision of Cassie, her arms around Devon in much the same way, supporting him, there for him when he awoke from his long slumber. *It could happen.*

If he was any kind of friend, he'd wish and pray it did. Cassie wasn't his to want. This time the reminder sank in.

Not because of his parents' warnings, but because he knew his attempts to get closer to Cassie only hurt her. He had to back off. He would, but for now, another day here with her felt like an incredible gift.

"Tomorrow morning then," she said, agreeing far easier than he'd believed she would. "I really have enjoyed myself. Your family is fun, and Oregon is beautiful. It's the first time I've been anywhere in forever."

"I hope it isn't the last trip you take in forever." Matt tried not to think of how much he would love to travel other places with her. For starters, he'd been hoping the five of them could explore California next summer. There were a lot of places he wanted to take the boys—and *boys* now included Noah—and of course, he always imagined Cassie seated beside him on their adventures. But then his thoughts had been getting ahead of him.

"Not forever," Cassie promised but didn't say more than that.

Matt didn't push her. They continued down the shoreline, his hands back in his pockets, restricted, like he was, from reaching toward Cassie more than he already had.

Thirty-One

Cassie sat cross-legged on the end of Devon's bed, facing him. "I'm pretty sure Noah had the best time of his life. You should have seen him on the beach and on the boat, picking up crabs, searching the tide pools for starfish . . ." She pictured Matt running up and down the beach with Noah, teaching him to fly a kite. Matt, kneeling in front of Noah, helping him to put on gloves so he could throw the crab back. Matt, just this morning, carrying a sleeping Noah out to the truck. Each memory tugged at her heart and strengthened the depth of her growing feelings.

"The thing is, Devon—" Cassie picked at a fuzz on his blanket. "I had a great time, too." The euphoric feelings she'd experienced when standing alone with Matt in the dark foyer while he put his letterman jacket around her, resurfaced easily, as did the desire she'd felt when making caramel corn with him in the kitchen and sitting beside him during the movie. Though the time she'd cherish most from this weekend was Thanksgiving night when they'd sat on the sea wall talking, and Matt had put his arm around her, not in a particularly romantic sort of way, but as an I'm-here-for-you gesture. It would be so easy to get used to the comfort he offered. She was getting used to it already, given that she was here with Devon but thinking about Matt.

"I'm not being fair to you, Dev," she admitted. "I've been spending all this time with Matt, and I like it. I like *him*. I'm lonely—and human, but I want to be with *you*. I want *our* lives to be great. I want *your* arms around me again." She ran her finger over the back of Devon's hand, motionless on the blanket.

"So—" She breathed in deeply, then exhaled as a promise left her lips. "I'm going to stop spending time with Matt. I'm going to put everything I have into *us* again. I'll write another letter, try again to get you in a clinical trial. We're going to figure this out, Devon, and get you home."

How many times had she said as much to him before? Always she'd meant it, and she wanted to mean it now as well, but the same faith and hope that had carried her through the past six years seemed to be wavering. *I believe in miracles,* she told herself as she bid Devon goodbye and headed to her mom's. This whole thing with Matt was just a test. Once she passed it, Devon would wake up, and their life together would start again.

"You just wouldn't have believed it, Cassie. The shows at night, the endless buffets of food, miles of sandy beaches, water so blue." Cassie's mom spread her arms wide, as if that somehow encompassed all that was marvelous about her cruise.

"So it was a good Thanksgiving?" Cassie took an apple from the basket on the counter and bit into it. As soon as they'd arrived back in town, she'd gone directly to see Devon, and now her stomach was protesting the absence of dinner.

"The best Thanksgiving," her mom exclaimed. She filled two glasses with water and handed one to Cassie. "I may just have to cruise every year. Tell me, how was your holiday?"

Near perfect. "Not quite as exciting as yours," Cassie said. "No dolphins or coral for us, though the sea lions and crabs were pretty impressive. I think Noah would have stayed in Oregon forever."

"I'm so glad you both went," Mom said. "I was worried when I left, though I suppose I needn't have been. I should have known Matt wouldn't leave you to spend the holiday alone. He cares about you, you know."

"I know." Cassie took another bite of apple. There was no point in disputing the fact any longer, nor could she deny that she cared about him as well, but what she'd come over here to get her mom to understand was that she and Matt couldn't keep seeing each other in any capacity.

"Matt is a great guy, and if circumstances were different . . ." Cassie couldn't believe she'd just said that. The only circumstance that would allow her and Matt to be together would be Devon's death, and she did *not* want that.

"If they were different," her mom prodded.

"Then I might be interested in pursuing a relationship with him," Cassie admitted, "but I'm not free to do that, so spending time with him isn't a good idea."

"It's been more than a good idea," Mom said. "You two have been wonderful for each other and your boys."

Cassie couldn't argue with that. "It can't continue, or wonderful might turn to terrible. I can't trust myself around him. Being near Matt is too tempting." She bit into the apple again, considering, as she hadn't before, Eve's choice. *Stay in the garden with Adam or be exiled to Earth but have children and experience joy, sorrow, and eventual death.* Not exactly a clear-cut decision. Staying in the garden would have certainly been the simpler of the two, but not the most rewarding. Somehow Eve had known that and taken the risk.

Mom sighed heavily, then shook her head and muttered, "Still not ready."

"What?"

"Never mind." Mom waved a hand in dismissal. "So what now?" she asked. "You and Matt are just going to part ways and that's that?"

Cassie shrugged. "I'm still figuring it out. I have our boys to consider. Noah needs Matt, and I can't abandon Austin and Asher."

"Well, I'm glad of that at least." Mom pulled up a stool and sat beside Cassie at the counter. "How was Devon tonight?" she asked, surprising Cassie with the abrupt change of subject.

"Fine. The same," she amended. Devon hadn't been fine for a long time.

"Have you ever thought—" Mom paused, reached out, and took Cassie's hand between her older, softer ones. "Have you ever thought that maybe it's time to forgive him—and yourself?"

"Forgive him?" Cassie's brow furrowed. "What could I possibly be mad at Devon for? Getting shot? That's ridiculous."

Her mom nodded slowly. "It would be, but that's not what I was referring to. However, forgiving yourself and realizing it isn't your fault he's in that hospital bed would be a good start."

"You aren't making any sense," Cassie said, more worried than defensive. Had something happened to her mom on the cruise? Maybe she'd spent too much time in the sun, or maybe she had tried some of the activities intended for people much younger.

Mom leaned close to Cassie, as if there was someone else in the room who shouldn't hear what she was about to say. "You need to forgive Devon for not wanting to try other ways to have a child, for feeling that pursuing help from a fertility specialist wasn't what he wanted to do."

"I—I have." The sudden hurt her mom's words roused took Cassie off guard, a reminder of how Devon had broken her heart with that decision and how they'd been at odds with each other over it. "We had Noah. We can have other children, too. So how Devon felt about getting help to get pregnant doesn't really matter anymore."

"Doesn't it?" Mom asked. "It mattered the day he was shot. I know because Devon came to see me on his lunch hour. He didn't know what to do. He knew your desire to have children was eating you up inside, but he felt like it was going to devour your marriage and the only chance of saving it was to let that dream go altogether."

And follow other dreams. Suddenly some of his actions in the weeks before he'd been shot made more sense. "Why didn't you ever tell me he came to see you?" Cassie set the half-eaten apple on the counter, her appetite gone.

"It didn't matter until now," her mom said.

"It doesn't matter now," Cassie insisted. "We were angry with each other, but we would have gotten over it." She gave a half-laugh. "I was already pregnant then and just didn't know."

"Yes. You got Noah but lost Devon." Mom summarized the thought that had plagued Cassie all these years. "You were angry at Devon, you wanted a child . . ."

I got my wish. She'd wished and prayed and pled for a baby, promising God any number of things if he would answer her prayer, but she'd never intended to lose her husband. She hadn't promised him away, had she? She'd wanted Devon to change his mind, to feel the same as she did, but she hadn't wanted him to not feel anything anymore.

Cassie pulled away from her mom and wrapped her arms around her middle, as if to hold back the painful, conflicted emotion let loose.

"Forgive him," her mom urged.

"I did. I do," Cassie insisted. "I never meant for him to get hurt." He'd offered to take that extra shift. She hadn't insisted on it. *But you* were *angry,* an inner voice accused. *You'd fought about money just the night before.* "I didn't want to lose Devon in order to have a baby. That wasn't what I wanted. You believe me, right?"

"Of course I do." Mom placed a hand on Cassie's arm. "This didn't happen because of anything you did or didn't do. *You* didn't hurt Devon. At least not at first."

"What's that supposed to mean?" Cassie asked, pulling away.

"It means that you might be hurting him now, keeping him here when he doesn't want to be here any longer."

"You sound like—"

"Like who, dear?" her mom asked.

"Never mind." Cassie didn't want to think about Pearl or what she'd said right now.

"Let me ask you this," Mom said. "If the tables were turned and you were the one lying in that hospital bed, what would you want?"

"To be with my family, of course," Cassie said.

"If you couldn't? If your body was broken enough that it

could never be restored to who you were? Would you want to stay as you are, as Devon is now?"

Cassie's shoulders slumped forward, and she closed her eyes. "No." She wondered how they'd gone from talking about her staying away from Matt to this.

"If you truly forgive Devon and love him as much as I think you do, then you'll give him the choice," Mom said.

"There is no choice," Cassie said. "What am I supposed to do or say? 'Devon, if you'd like your feeding tube today, stare straight ahead without looking at anything. If you don't want it in, do the same thing.'"

Mom leaned back on her stool, disappointment written clearly in the wrinkles on her forehead and her downturned lips. "I'm not talking about anything with his feeding tube. I'm talking about an honest conversation, during which you forgive him—and yourself—and tell Devon that you will let him go, if that's what he wants."

It was so close to what Pearl had told her that Cassie felt tears building behind her eyes again, but this time she wasn't angry. Her mother had spoken out of love and nothing else. There was no ulterior motive.

"I don't know if I can," Cassie admitted. "And now, with my feelings for Matt—It doesn't seem right to tell Devon anything other than I want him to be well and come home."

"Then tell him that," her mother urged, "and in that same sentence, tell him it's all right if he *doesn't* come home. Tell him that you love him and always will, no matter what."

"I do love him." Cassie wiped at her eye before a tear could escape from the corner. "I'm just really afraid."

Thirty-Two

Matt placed a steaming plate of spaghetti and meatballs in front of Cassie, then slid a bowl of salad beside her plate and a glass of milk beside that. "Your dinner, complete with the dairy, grain, vegetable, and meat food groups." He dropped into the chair beside her and inclined his head toward the kitchen. "And a pile of dishes in the sink to show for such nutrition."

"It looks delicious," Cassie said. "You've come a long way from peanut butter and jelly in just a few short months." It was on the tip of her tongue to offer to wash the dishes, but she knew he'd join her, and washing dishes together was just one of many activities she now deemed off limits. She shouldn't be here eating dinner at his place, but she'd had to pick up Noah, and Matt deserved some sort of explanation for what she was about to do.

"How was visiting Devon?" he asked.

"Okay," Cassie said. It certainly hadn't been her best

visit, more like a confessional. "I told him about our weekend, about sitting too close to you on the couch, letting you put your arm around me when we were outside on the wall, and feeling incredibly attracted to you when we were playing basketball."

"Time out." Matt made a *T* with his hands. "You find me attractive? This is news to me."

"Not all the time." Cassie made a face at him, then instantly regretted it. Here they were, teasing and flirting again when that was the last thing she wanted to do.

"Basically I just had to tell my husband that I've been on the path to being an unfaithful wife."

"I wouldn't. *We* wouldn't—"

"We already were," Cassie said, cutting Matt off. "Sleeping together isn't the only way to be unfaithful. Tonight, when I was sitting on Devon's bed talking to him, I was thinking about *you.*"

Instead of the lighthearted comeback she'd expected, Matt was silent.

"I don't blame you," Cassie said. "Or even myself, necessarily. It's just one of those things that happened, and it can't."

"We're not something that *just happened.*" Matt sounded exasperated. "Our meeting was, I don't know, providential. You're a miracle who came into our lives, and I like to think I might have been a little of the same to you."

"You are—were," Cassie said, "but now it has to stop. Don't you see, Matt? There's nowhere for us to go from here but into trouble. Your parents were right."

He looked up sharply. "You heard that?"

"Overheard your conversation with them, yes." Cassie omitted telling him that she'd knelt on the bathroom floor and pressed her ear to the vent.

"I've ruined everything by bringing you to Oregon." Elbow on the table, Matt leaned forward, bracing his head in his hand. "We should have just stayed here for Thanksgiving."

"You didn't ruin anything." Against her better judgment, Cassie reached out to him, placing her hand on Matt's arm. "The trip may have hastened our arrival at this inevitable crossroads, but it certainly didn't cause it. I'm glad that we went."

At this, Matt looked up at her with what seemed a glimmer of hope in his expression. Cassie exchanged a wistful smile with him.

"It's a memory I'll always treasure. I thank you for that."

"What about Noah?" Matt asked, sounding pained and causing Cassie to wonder if his mind was filtering through the same images as hers—Noah shooting hoops with Matt and the boys, Noah's face, sticky with the caramel corn Matt had made, Noah nestled between Austin and Asher as Matt tucked them in.

"Noah needs you," Cassie said. "You've been like a father to him."

"Anything I've done is little compared to what you've done to help Austin and Asher."

"I want to keep helping them," Cassie said. "I still want to watch them after school on nights you work late, and I'd love for Noah to spend Saturday mornings at your place while I work on getting licensed to start using my degree."

"At least I've convinced you to pursue the career you dreamed of," Matt said.

Cassie withdrew her hand from his arm, where it had lingered too long, and felt a pang of sorrow, thinking that would be their last touch. He'd never kissed her and had only held her hand in a gesture of comfort or to pull her into a room that night they'd cleaned his apartment, but dozens of times, they'd accidentally touched when doing dishes, playing board games with the boys, and getting in and out of his truck. She'd craved that slight contact and having Matt close. She was going to miss it, miss him—his companionship, friendship, and so much more.

She looked down at her dinner and felt bad for not eating it but knew she couldn't. She could barely swallow right now, for the lump that had formed in her throat. *Don't you dare cry,* she told herself. *At least not now, not here.*

But when she chanced a look at Matt as he rose quickly from the table, it was to find that he was fighting his own similar battle, and losing.

Thirty-Three

Mark fell onto the sofa beside Matt. "Why so glum, bro? Santa didn't bring you what you wanted for Christmas?" He nodded at the tree and the piles of discarded boxes and wrapping paper beneath.

"Not exactly." Matt knew he needed to shake his somber mood. He didn't want to ruin the holiday for everyone, especially Austin and Asher, who appeared, for the most part, to be doing all right today.

"If I had a time machine, I'd give it to you so you could be with Jenna again," Mark said, sounding surprisingly sincere. "I wish I could."

"Thanks," Matt said, knowing this was as close as they would get to being able to discuss any of what he'd gone through the past year. Mark was pretty consistent at being good for a laugh, but he'd never been one for dealing with serious issues.

"I don't think I'd choose to go back, though." This wasn't a reflection on Jenna or their marriage, but more on himself and what he'd learned from losing her. "A year ago I was a self-centered jackass."

"Who says you still aren't?" Mark nudged him.

"Only around you and to you." Matt managed a smile. "But not around my boys any more. I love them, really love them. They're everything."

"You wouldn't want to go back and feel that same way about your wife?" Mark asked.

"Of course I would," Matt said. For months now he'd wished for one more night with her, one more hour, a few minutes even, to say he was sorry, to try to express the depth of love he had felt for her, though he'd been lousy at showing it. "But if going back in time meant that I'd go back to being the old me, I wouldn't want that."

"Ah." Mark nodded his head, understanding. "Well, good thing my gift didn't materialize then. Anything else I can get you? Maybe a long-legged, brown-haired, brown-eyed girl from California?"

"You better not have been checking out Cassie's legs when she was here." Matt glared at Mark.

"Not as much as you were—and everything else about her." Mark raised his eyebrows knowingly. "For once, Meg was right. There was a bit of a ravenous wolf aura about you over Thanksgiving."

"You try going without basic needs or affection for almost a year and see how well you fare."

"Imagining such a fate is bad enough," Mark conceded. "I am sorry that things with Cassie aren't going anywhere."

"Oh, they've gone," Matt said. "In reverse. It's like I lived through the death of a spouse and then a divorce less than a year later."

"Can't be divorced if you weren't ever married." Mark kicked his feet up on the coffee table and leaned his head back on the couch.

"It sure feels like it," Matt said. "Like neither of us wanted it, but it happened anyway."

"At least you're not dealing with a custody battle or alimony," Mark said.

"We share our kids very well," Matt said. "In fact, it's all about them. Cassie still watches the boys after school. Noah comes over to my place to play on Saturdays, but she never walks him to the door, never stays to chat for a minute. I'm lucky if I get a wave as she drives away."

"I'm sorry if we scared her off at Thanksgiving. I know I harassed her a bit, but she seemed pretty able to hold her own. I mean, pie in the face and all."

"You didn't scare her off," Matt said. "I did. I started treating her like she wasn't married, like we might become more than friends, and that was it. We were done."

"Before you even started," Mark said.

Matt nodded, but he knew that wasn't entirely truthful. He'd developed plenty of feelings for Cassie in the few months of their friendship, and that morning on the beach, she'd led him to believe that she felt something for him, too. It would have been perfect, everything on his Christmas list and more, if they could just be together.

Life wasn't fair. Not six and a half years ago, not last January, not now.

Cassie stared at her phone on the counter as she wrestled with the idea of calling Matt, much as she'd agonized over a similar phone call to a practical stranger last

September. It had been Matt who'd ended up calling her then, saving her from having to take the first step, reaching out to him. With his phone call, it had been so easy, almost natural, to suggest that their boys play together. Everything had snowballed from there until a crash and burn seemed almost inevitable. And so she'd pulled out before someone got seriously hurt or she made a terrible decision.

Cassie felt grateful for the willpower she'd managed to marshal to keep her distance from Matt the last month. Every day the separation seemed it would kill her. He was one of her first thoughts in the morning and her last at night, like Devon used to be.

She was starting to fear that the adage "Absence makes the heart grow fonder," was not only true but might be her undoing as well. Instead of her feelings for Matt fading into the background as she'd hoped they would, they only seemed to be growing stronger. Life had not returned to the way it was before she met him. Now, along with missing Devon, she had to suffer through each day missing Matt while knowing they could be together if only she'd choose it.

I can't. I won't. This misery is punishment for allowing my thoughts to stray in the first place.

For the week, at least, Matt and his boys were away. She was safe from herself a few more days. So what would one phone call hurt? It was Christmas, after all, and Matt was her friend. She *should* call him today.

This decided at last, Cassie picked up her phone and called, before she could talk herself out of it. She couldn't remember a lonelier Christmas. She needed to hear Matt's voice.

But his voicemail would have to do since he didn't answer. Instead of hanging up like a coward, she left a simple, brief message.

"Hi, Matt. It's Cassie. Sorry I missed you. I'll bet your family is at the theater seeing the next *Star Wars* movie or something. I just wanted to tell you Merry Christmas. I hope your day was wonderful and that Austin and Asher are having a good time. Noah misses them and you."

I miss you. She didn't dare say it and disconnected the call instead, then set the phone down and stared across the room.

"I miss you," she whispered, "and I love you. I shouldn't, but I do."

Thirty-Four

The evening news droned in the background as Cassie folded a week's worth of laundry, stacking the clean piles precariously on the arms and back of the loveseat. She knew she ought to go to bed soon—Noah would be up early as usual tomorrow—but her mind was still too preoccupied with tonight's visit with Devon for her to sleep.

The visit hadn't been anything out of the ordinary. If anything, it felt like the hundreds of other Friday nights she'd spent with him over the past six years, nearly six and a half. Another half of a year had passed without him. He'd missed another Christmas, he hadn't been awake to kiss her at midnight on New Year's Eve. In a couple of weeks, he wasn't going to be at home to spend Valentine's together. In years past, she'd always hoped for those things, but tonight the lonely reality of her life and existence seemed to be staring her in the face. *Nothing has changed. Nothing is going* to change. *I'm going to be alone forever. Even worse, Noah is never going to know his father.*

A pile of Noah's shirts fell off the arm of the couch into an unfolded heap on the floor. With a weary sigh, Cassie leaned forward, collected the clothing, and began refolding. It was a good simile of her life. Wash, dry, fold, repeat. She'd been doing the same things over and over again. While there had been definite moments of joy—all centered around Noah—life wasn't going the direction she wanted it to. She didn't see how it ever could unless something changed.

An image of Devon's strange visitor last September came to mind. Pearl, she'd said her name was. She'd imparted words as if they were priceless pearls of wisdom, and Cassie had ignored them. It had taken some work to do so, particularly during those months she and Matt had grown close and again after her mother had given her practically the same advice, but always Cassie came back to the same conclusion. *I can't tell Devon to go. I can't give up on him.* For better or worse, forever meant just that.

"And so I fold laundry alone on Friday nights." With another sigh, Cassie left the piles to be put away tomorrow and headed to the bathroom. She'd just put toothpaste on her toothbrush when her phone vibrated on the kitchen table.

Her gaze flew to the picture of Devon taped to the corner of the mirror. She'd just been thinking of him, but she'd also been allowing herself to succumb to the bleak possibility that he was never going to wake up. *If I lose hope, does Devon lose, too?* She'd been feeling as if she couldn't do this any longer. *Is that when the miracle will happen?*

No one but the care center would be calling her at 10:30 on a Friday night, and only then if there was some change with Devon. Toothbrush still in hand, she ran to the kitchen and grabbed her phone. Matt's number flashed on the screen.

"No." He hadn't called her for the past two months, not since she'd asked him not to. Why now? Cassie sank into a chair, dropping both the phone and toothbrush, burying her head in her hands, and hurting deeply for those few seconds of hope.

Just one little miracle. I just need Devon to wake up. It wasn't so much to ask, was it? She'd grown up learning about a God who could help man to part the sea and a Savior who raised people from the dead. So why couldn't Devon return to her? She'd had faith that he would for so long, but it didn't seem to matter. Her prayers weren't being answered.

The phone ceased ringing, replaced by the sound of her frustration unleashed in a violent fit of sobbing.

Why God, why? In this moment, those things that had sustained her so long were failing completely. She couldn't think of all those who were less fortunate than her. *Why do they have to be less fortunate, too? Why can't we all have our loved ones whole and with us? Why can't Noah and I have Devon?* All she could think of was sleeping alone for the rest of her life, never having a baby girl of her own, Noah growing up and leaving her by herself.

Tears wet her shirt sleeves, and her nose ran. Cassie's chest heaved with convulsions as she poured out her grief and loneliness. *It isn't fair. I'm so tired of it.* She loved Noah; she was grateful to be his mom, but it wasn't enough. This life she had wasn't enough. It wasn't a life, not the one she wanted, anyway.

Her phone chimed, letting her know there was a message. Cassie felt like throwing it across the room or calling Matt back and yelling at him. What did he mean by calling her at 10:30 on a Friday night? How could he not realize what that would do to her? He wasn't supposed to call anyway. They weren't doing that whole friendship thing anymore. It was too hard, too painful, made her feel too much like she did right now, that she was missing out on what she wanted most desperately in her life.

Someone to love me.

It was like a pathetic, sappy song from the radio from one of those soft rock stations she never let herself listen to because the songs always made her sad. Avoiding them wasn't enough. Everything made her sad lately. Every day her loneliness intensified.

Anger was better. Cassie grasped onto this, directing her frustration at Matt since he'd breached etiquette to call her. She wiped her nose on the back of her already-wet sleeve, then picked up her phone and played the message back. She'd listen and then she'd call him back and let him know what a train wreck his simple little call had set off.

"Hi, Cassie. Sorry to bother you. I was hoping you were still up. I have a favor to ask—"

Of course. She wondered what it was this time. Head lice again? Maybe he needed her to babysit so he could take some other woman out on a date.

"I know we said we weren't going to see each other anymore or do things that felt like a family. I understand and respect that, so I shouldn't even ask."

Yeah. You shouldn't.

"But I'm hoping you'll make an exception."

Cassie blew out a puff of air, sending the hair closest to her face askew.

"It would be for one day only. Tomorrow, actually."

Thanks for the notice. Matt's message was digging him deeper.

"I've got a full day planned for the boys and me, but I

don't think it's going to be enough. Asher will be all right. He's handled it better all along, but Austin is struggling. I've read it in his expressions the past few days. I'm worried, Cassie."

Me, too. The past week or so she'd noticed that Austin didn't seem to be himself. Was he reverting back to the way he'd been when Matt and the boys first moved here? *Is it because the five of us don't spend time together like we used to?*

"I'm not going to lie, it promises to be a hard day for me, too. I'm going to do my best to be patient with Austin, but we aren't starting out good already. I'm a wreck, and he's on the bubble at least."

Matt hadn't been what she'd term a wreck since well before Thanksgiving. What had happened to change that? Cassie pressed the phone closer to her ear, feeling like she must have missed some vital piece of information.

"I have one more picture to take down tomorrow, and I need a really good, new memory to replace it, so even though I shouldn't, I'm asking—will you and Noah spend the day with us tomorrow and help us get through the first anniversary of Jenna's death? Please? I need you, Cassie." There was a break in Matt's voice, his solid tone wavering with his admission. "So do the boys. Please help us make tomorrow about more than losing their mother."

The message ended. Cassie sat unmoving, phone still clutched in her hand as fresh tears coursed down her face. *The anniversary of Jenna's death. How could I have forgotten?* Because she'd been selfish, indulging in a pity party, thinking only of her own woes and completely disregarding Matt's.

Her earlier angry thoughts dissolved in guilt. She was a terrible, awful friend. Her inability to control her emotions and thoughts had hurt Matt, when that was the last thing he needed. It was hurting his children, too.

I can't spend a whole day with him. I have to. The two warring thoughts competed in her mind even as she sent him a text.

"What time and where? Noah and I will be there."

"Thank you! Pick you up at 8. Dress warm."

His response was almost immediate, and Cassie pictured him sitting in his pristine bedroom, alone in that monstrous bed, surrounded by too many fluffy pillows and evidence of what he considered his failure.

Dress warm didn't tell her much; it was the end of January, so they needed to dress warm regardless of where they went, but she didn't want to start a long conversation now. She'd just wait and be surprised.

"K. You're welcome. Night."

"Goodnight, Cassie."

She set her phone down, closed her eyes, and lay her head over her crossed arms again. *Good* wasn't exactly what she'd call her evening. Tomorrow, on the other hand...

How easily she'd justified going, but since she'd made that decision, she intended to be all in. Instead of a terrible day, she wanted it to be the best Matt and the boys had since moving to California. It would be great for Noah, too. He was going to be so excited when he woke up and found out. It was tempting to wake him and tell him now, but then neither of them would sleep.

Cassie found she didn't mind her lack of sleepiness as much as she had a half hour ago. Instead of lying awake missing Devon, she'd be anticipating tomorrow and an entire day with Matt and their boys. Regardless of what he had planned, she really couldn't think of anything she'd rather be doing than spending the day with the five of them together.

Thirty-Five

Matt walked around to the passenger side of his truck, opened the door, and waited as Cassie and Noah descended the stairs from their apartment. "Good morning."

"It is, isn't it," Cassie said pleasantly, leaning her head back to take in the clear sky. She wore a pink sweater and matching knit hat, much like the one she'd worn in Oregon but different because he'd given her this one for Christmas. Matt had noticed she had a hat in almost every color except pink. It looked good on her. He kept the observation to himself, not wanting to start off on the wrong foot. That she'd agreed to spending the day with him was no small miracle, and he didn't intend to squander it.

He closed the door behind her, helped an overly excited Noah into the backseat, then climbed into his own.

"Have you had breakfast?" he asked, holding a box of Krispy Kreme donuts out to Cassie. "I picked them up in

Roseville on my way home from work yesterday, but I popped them into the microwave this morning so they're warm."

Noah reached over the seat eagerly. "You always have donuts."

"Not always." Matt shook his head. "Or I'd start to look like a donut. Today is special."

"No, it's not," Austin said.

"Is, too," Asher said.

"It *is* because we're together." Matt gave each of the boys a look, then started the truck. "Who wants to guess where we're going first?"

"First?" Cassie asked. "We're going more than one place?" She took a donut from the box.

"Yeah—if that's okay." He glanced at her sideways as he backed out of her gravel drive and onto the highway. "Is there something else you need to do today? A time you have to be home by?" He really hoped not.

"Nope. I'm all yours—today." She looked out her window, but not before Matt caught her look of chagrin.

"Great," he said, ignoring her comment that he was sure was a mistake. Nothing had changed or could change between them. He saw the day for what it was—a mercy date—and he was okay with that, grateful.

The clock on the dash said 8:05. *Five and twenty-six minutes.* He wasn't sure why he was mentally counting down the time. He didn't want to think about what had happened at 1:31 p.m. a year ago, but he couldn't seem to help it.

He headed toward Sacramento, the boys chatting happily in the back seat. Matt flipped on the radio, thinking that some music might ease the awkwardness that had settled between him and Cassie, but the DJs or fate must have had something against him this morning. Every station he flipped to played a song—from Jason Mraz's "I Won't Give Up" to Christina Perri's "A Thousand Years"—that seemed loaded with meaning he didn't want to think about and certainly didn't want Cassie thinking of.

"So." Cassie reached forward and switched off the radio, saving him the task. "Where *are* we going?"

"Today is all about the sights, sounds, and tastes of California. We're going to experience a few of the things this golden state has to offer."

"Starting with—"

"I can't just *tell* you," Matt said. "Guessing is half the fun." He hoped it wasn't actually and that the places they were going to would be quite a bit of fun, for the boys at least. When the boys were having a good time, he and Cassie usually were as well. "Our first stop is in Sacramento to a place that makes some serious candy. I've passed it on my way to and from interviews a few times."

"I know where we're going." Cassie smiled. "How about you, boys? Do you know what candy is made in Sacramento?"

All three shook their heads.

"I'm not telling then. You'll just have to wait." Cassie shared a conspiratorial grin with Matt. "Good choice. They'll love it."

The drive passed quickly after that with the boys shouting guesses from the back seat, and Noah exclaiming over everything they saw as they came into Sacramento. Again, Matt was reminded of how little Noah and Cassie traveled. They lived so close to so many things, yet she stayed cloistered in their little community. Matt had seen what she could be like when set free of those restrictions, and he hoped to see that same woman today, the one with a quick sense of humor who'd given him a run for his money in one-on-one basketball.

He needn't have worried. She reappeared again as soon as they pulled into the parking lot of the Jelly Belly factory. Cassie was the first one with her door open, bounding toward the building to get them a spot in the line already forming outside. Matt and the boys joined her, and for the next hour, the paper-hat-topped entourage sampled, giggled, and shopped their way through the factory tour and store. They posed for a picture altogether at the end, then Matt lugged about ten pounds of Jelly Bellies to the truck.

"You're taking at least half of these home," he threatened as he exaggerated heaving the sack into the back seat.

Cassie laughed. "I don't think so. That donut this morning did damage enough."

"Don't worry," Matt said. "You're going to walk it off." He popped a movie in the overhead DVD player for the boys, then headed for their next destination.

"*Where* will I be walking all this sugar off?" Cassie tucked her feet sideways beneath her and leaned against the door, facing him.

It was a look Matt loved, as if she felt completely comfortable and planned to stay a while. "You know the rules. Guessing—"

"Only," Cassie finished. "In that case, I'm going to nap a while and see where we are when I wake up."

"Haven't been sleeping well?" Matt asked, concerned, remembering that had been a problem when they'd first met. One of the many, unfortunate, things they had in common.

"Not particularly," Cassie said. "You?"

He gave a false laugh. "Hardly. But don't worry. I'm plenty awake enough to drive. You nap."

"Thanks, Matt." Her voice and smile overflowed with gratitude, reminding him just how much he'd missed not only being with Cassie but doing things for her. She curled up and went to sleep while he navigated the traffic for the next hour and a half until they were nearing Sausalito.

Noon, the clock on the dashboard read as the boys' movie ended. Austin appeared to be doing better than he had been this morning. *Nothing like a friend and an overdose of candy to cheer a boy up.*

Matt followed the GPS directions to the parking lot where they'd catch the ferry. He'd never been to this part of the state before and had enjoyed the drive, but the ride across the bay promised to be even better. He parked the car and looked over at Cassie, still sleeping soundly. It seemed she'd slept poorly more than a few nights lately. He hated to wake her, but the boys were clamoring to get out.

"Cassie." He touched her shoulder. "We're here."

He unbuckled her seatbelt, and she stretched, slow and languid. Matt looked away, but the damage had already been done as he imagined waking up with her each morning and watching her. *Then persuading her to stay in bed a little longer.* If she'd read his thoughts, no doubt his head would have been against the dashboard.

"Where are—" The words died in her throat as Cassie turned in her seat to look at their surroundings. "Oh, Matt." One hand went to her chest as she looked at him, her eyes brimming with tears.

"I didn't know San Francisco was off limits. I should have asked. We don't have to go."

"I *love* San Francisco." She flung herself at him and threw her arms around his neck, then buried her face there and cried.

Matt froze, then awkwardly patted her back while trying to send a reassuring look to the trio in the back seat, who'd ceased their chatter and were watching the scene with rapt interest.

After only a few seconds, Cassie pulled away, wiped at her eyes, and smiled. "I do love the city, and I haven't been here in so long. I haven't had the courage to come."

"Ever taken Noah?" Matt asked.

She shook her head. "I should have." She turned to him. "This city is special, to me, to your dad, and hopefully after today, to Matt and Austin and Asher as well." Her smile widened. "Come on! Let's go." She slid her feet into her shoes and was out of the truck before Matt could come around to open her door.

With the three boys between them all holding hands, they walked to the ferry terminal, and Matt purchased their tickets. They boarded a few minutes later, and Matt soon found himself watching Cassie instead of the bay; the emotions filtering across her face were so many and so intense. He wanted to ask why San Francisco was so special. Maybe by the day's end, she'd tell him. Maybe he didn't want to know.

Her hands clasped in front of her and absolute joy filled her face at the first view of the Golden Gate. "Isn't it beautiful?" she said.

It was, but Cassie's beauty still held his attention. The closest he'd seen her to this happy was in Oregon out on his Dad's boat. She'd seemed to come to life that day. Here was that girl again, laughing and talking almost non-stop, telling stories about the city, pointing out Alcatraz and then Treasure Island to the fascinated boys.

All too soon, the ride ended, leaving them in San Francisco but far from the more touristy part of town Matt desired.

"It's a pretty far walk to the cable car and Pier 39," Cassie said. "I'm up for it, but I don't think our boys will make it."

"I didn't realize how far it would be," Matt said, staring at the number one on the building. He should have known. Thirty-nine wasn't exactly close to one. "We'll take a taxi," he said, noting how many had driven by. He hailed one quickly, and ten minutes later they were at the pier and headed toward the restaurant Cassie recommended.

The wind outside was chilly, but the chowder in sourdough bowls both filled and warmed them. From there they watched a juggling show, rode the two-story carousel, and let the boys all crank pennies through a smashed penny machine.

"Look, Mom. Sea lions!" Noah pulled away from Cassie's grasp and ran for a closer look at the animals sunning themselves on the floating dock. "They have them here, too, not just in Oregon."

"They have *more* than Oregon." Asher pointed at each, counting aloud and getting lost somewhere in the twenties.

Matt stood at the rail beside Cassie and nudged her shoulder. "You really need to take your kid out more often."

"I know." She sighed. "I owe you for showing me that, for reminding me again. Noah's best days are always with you."

"I wasn't talking about Noah," Matt said. "I was talking about you, about that girl inside, buried beneath all of life's burdens. You know, the one who likes to come out and play and is really good at it."

"I'm glad she's still in there," Cassie said. "Sometimes I'm afraid she's gone for good."

"I won't let her disappear entirely," Matt vowed, then instantly wondered if Cassie would take that wrong. She didn't.

"Promise?" she asked.

"I'll even shake on it." He held his hand out, knowing he

was really pushing things now. *To hold her hand for just a few seconds.*

Cassie looked down at his hand, then lifted her gaze to his and leaned in quickly and kissed his cheek. "That's how a promise is made between you and me."

Matt gripped the weathered rail as his senses reeled. "Cassie?"

"Nothing has changed," she hurried to tell him, "but you need to know that I care about you, so much, and we *are* more than something that just happened. We were meant to be friends, to help each other."

She looked away then, and Matt glanced down at his watch for something to distract his mind from her nearness. 1:31 pm. He squeezed his eyes shut, remembering how the front of the van had been crushed from the head on collision. But he was able to stop himself there, keeping memories of Jenna at the hospital at bay.

Instead he thought of Cassie and the sweet kiss she'd given him at just the moment he'd been dreading. Did she realize what time it was? He doubted it. She wasn't wearing a watch and hadn't had her phone out to take pictures for a while. Matt swallowed with difficulty and glanced around, feeling the need for a drink of something a lot stronger than water. It wasn't because he was overwhelmed with grief as he'd worried he would be at 1:31 p.m. and beyond.

He missed Jenna. He'd loved her. Part of him always would. But another part of him loved Cassie, and knowing she also had feelings for him but was too loyal to her husband to ever act on those feelings was killing him.

"Know what you need?" Cassie asked, looking up at him with an impish smile.

You. He didn't say it. He'd behave himself and be as good as she was if it did kill him.

"Chocolate," Cassie said. "The best chocolate you've ever tasted."

"Ghirardelli." Matt lifted his face and breathed in deeply, as if he could smell it already. That had been on his short list of must do's today.

"Come on, boys," Cassie called to Noah, Asher, and Austin. "It's time for ice cream sundaes."

At Ghirardelli Square they shared a booth and three sundaes—none of which they were able to finish—then waited in line and rode the cable car. Cassie seemed to know everything about the city and proved to be a great tour guide even while wearing the parental safety hat and making sure none of the boys leapt off the moving car.

When she suggested they get off for more sightseeing Matt agreed, then found himself as fascinated as the boys as he stood looking up at the Dragon Gate marking the entrance to Chinatown.

"Did you know this is the oldest Chinatown in North America?" Cassie asked as she led them down a street crowded with as many tourists as Chinese.

"Even older than the one in New York?" Matt asked.

"Since the 1840s," Cassie said, "one of the few things I remember from my high school California history class."

"Lead on, oh qualified guide," Matt said. "These are my state tax dollars at work right here."

The boys wanted fortune cookies, so Matt picked up a bag as they were leaving one of the shops.

"Pearl?" Cassie said behind him.

"You want to get one?" Matt pulled out a ten and handed it to the cashier. It didn't surprise him that Chinatown had one of those stands like they did in Hawaii and quite a few of the cities he'd visited. "I bet the boys would love to see the oyster opened."

Cassie shook her head. "Not *a* pearl. Pearl—a person. Back in a minute. Watch the boys."

She ran from the store, leaving Matt more than a little confused and with six hands to pry from the candy, lighters, fans, hats, and other tempting items for sale near the register.

"Cookies," he said, holding the bag above the boys and luring them out the door with it. By the time they made it outside, Cassie was returning, walking down the street toward them, her lips pursed and expression serious.

"Stand against the wall, and you can each have a cookie." Matt pointed to the large window framing the shop they'd just left. The boys lined up, and he doled out a cookie to each so he'd have a minute to figure out what was up with Cassie. "Austin, read your brother's fortune to him."

"Did you find what or who you were looking for?" Matt asked when Cassie reached them.

She shook her head. "I'm not even sure it was her. I mean, look at this place. There are probably quite a few women here who could fit her description." She leaned around him to peer up and down the street once more.

"I'm sorry," Matt said. "Was she an old friend? Someone you could look up when you get home?" He wasn't quite sure why Cassie seemed so agitated.

"No." Cassie's hands went to her hips, and she let out an exasperated sigh. "I don't *know* Pearl. She's that nurse, or whatever she was, who was in Devon's room at the care center all those months ago, the night I ate dinner with you at the hospital cafeteria."

"Ah." Matt nodded, though he still didn't understand. "And you wanted to catch her just now to tell her off?"

"No." Cassie frowned at him. "I'm not carrying a grudge or anything. I just want to know who she is and what she was doing here, watching us and nodding and smiling. What was that all about?"

Cassie turned a slow circle, craning her neck to see over the crowd. Her face seemed flushed with anger or possibly a fever, either of which caused him concern.

Matt stopped her on her second revolution. He placed his palm against Cassie's forehead. "You feel the right temperature, but you seem a bit overheated." *Overwhelmed? Something.* "Let's get you a cold water bottle."

"I'm fine," Cassie insisted. "Just confused. I swear it was her."

"Maybe it was." Matt shrugged.

"Dad, can you read this to me?" Asher waved the slip of paper from his cookie in Matt's face.

"Sure." Anything to distract Cassie from wigging out, but she'd left the sidewalk and was walking dangerously close to the slow-moving traffic on the narrow street, attempting to get a good look at the passengers in each vehicle.

"Cassie!" Matt stepped off the curb and grabbed her arm, snatching her out of the path of a passing Moped. "Don't make this day about the anniversary of *your* death, okay?" His eyes searched hers, and he watched as the clouded over look was replaced with a return to realization.

"Noah—"

"Is right there, and he's fine." Holding her hand, Matt led her over to the boys.

"Will you read my fortune now?" Asher asked.

Matt opened it with his free hand, revealing the slip of paper, and read, "Change can hurt, but it leads a path to something better."

"Like moving here," Austin said, surprising him.

"Exactly," Matt said.

Austin and Noah held their papers out to him as well.

"The words are too big," Austin complained.

"No problem." Assured that Cassie was returning to

herself now, Matt let go of her hand and crouched in front of the boys. He took Austin's fortune and unfolded it. "Serious trouble will pass you by." Matt laughed. "I have my doubts about that one."

"What does it mean?" Austin asked.

"That you won't get into any trouble." Cassie ruffled the top of Austin's head, the same way she did Noah's frequently. "At least for today."

"Does that mean I can do whatever I want, and I won't get punished?"

"No," Matt said, putting an end to the glint of hopeful scheming that had appeared in Austin's eyes.

"Read mine now," Noah said.

Cassie took his paper. "Your dearest wish will come true."

"No fair. Yours is better," Austin said.

"Any wish?" Noah asked, looking up at Cassie and then Matt.

"Maybe," Cassie said, "but I wouldn't put too much faith in these fortunes. Mostly, people make their own fortunes by working hard for what they want."

"I want to get back to our car in time for the next activity," Matt said as he noted the time on his phone. 4:09. A year ago, he was flying home.

"There's another activity?" Cassie sounded genuinely surprised. "You have something else planned?"

Matt gestured to the boys to come away from the window. "You did agree to spending the day with us, so of course I had to pack as much as possible into twenty-four hours—or about sixteen, anyway. I'll try to have you and Noah home by midnight." He kept his tone light and hoped she wouldn't be upset. Tonight's activity was what he'd had planned first but then realized the whole day would be tough if he didn't fill it with distractions in the form of new experiences and memories.

"By twelve would be good," Cassie said, "because at midnight, Noah turns into a pumpkin and I turn into a serving girl with really messy hair."

"Mo-om." Noah tugged on her hand.

"A pumpkin. Good one." Asher laughed.

Cassie laughed with him, and Matt felt vast relief that whatever weirdness had just happened with her seemed to have passed.

"This way," she said, taking Noah's hand. "We'll catch the California Street car and end up a few blocks from the ferry."

On the ride back across the bay, all three boys fell asleep. Matt could have dozed, too, but he didn't want to miss even one minute of this day with Cassie.

"Fortune cookie?" he asked, holding the bag out to her. She reached inside, pulled one out, then broke it in half.

"You already know the answer to the question lingering inside your head." She leaned forward, chin in her hand, as she thought. "Nope. I have no clue where you're taking us next." She looked up at Matt. "Your turn."

He pulled a cookie out, broke it open, and extracted the paper. "Try? No! Do or do not. There is no try." He frowned then read the paper to himself once more. "What a total *Star Wars* rip off. Yoda says that."

"Maybe he has Chinese ancestry," Cassie suggested. "One more." She held out her hand, and he placed a cookie in it.

"Now these three remain. Faith, hope, and love. The greatest of these is love." She refolded the little paper. "That one's not exactly a fortune."

"Isn't it?" Matt arched his brow. Cassie had faith and

hope in her life, and he wanted to give her love. *The greatest of these is love.* Was his love for her stronger or more important than her faith and hope that Devon would get well?

Matt cracked open another cookie. "It is now, and in this world, that we must live." *That's more like it.* He ought to save these for his mom. Maybe he could get her to replace some of her harsher sayings with thoughts like these to inspire.

Cassie grabbed two more cookies from the bag and opened each. "The greatest risk is not taking one." She unfolded the second paper. "You cannot love life until you live the life you love."

"Good stuff," Matt said, liking these fortunes more and more.

"Finish the bag," Cassie said, sounding irritated.

"Of course." Matt still hadn't eaten his last cookie, but he broke open the last three, letting the pieces fall into the bag while he kept out the slips of paper.

"Joys are often the shadows cast by sorrow."

"That one's pretty good," Cassie conceded.

"And true." Wasn't this day, which had been pretty awesome, a shadow of the sorrow of the past year? He opened the next paper.

"Accept your past without regrets. Handle your present with confidence. Face your future without fear."

Cassie pointed at him. "Now there's a perfect fortune for you."

"Right back at you." Matt handed her the last paper after reading it to himself.

"Welcome the change coming into your life," she read.

He looked at her and shrugged. "Just silly nonsense, right?"

"Right." Cassie leaned forward and dropped the slips of paper into the bag, then stared out at the Golden Gate, leaving Matt to wonder if it was the past, present, future, or the possibility of change that swirled most in her mind.

He checked his watch again. 5:16. A year ago, his plane had landed, and he'd called the hospital to check on Jenna's condition, the phone call that had changed his life.

I'm sorry, Jenna, so sorry I wasn't there that day and so many others.

Matt adjusted Austin's legs so they weren't falling off the seat, then pulled Asher onto his lap and held him close. Instead of feeling overwhelmed by his children as he had those first several months after Jenna's death, he felt overwhelmed with love *for* them. He pressed a kiss to the top of Asher's head.

"You're doing it."

Matt looked up to find Cassie watching him, her expression tender.

"You're leaving regrets from your past behind, handling your present with confidence, and facing your future without fear."

"I still have fears," Matt said, thinking of the one that concerned him the most—a future that didn't include Cassie and Noah.

Thirty-Six

Cassie studied the three boys seated—or at least, *with* seats—between her and Matt. Currently those chairs were going unused as Noah, Austin, and Asher were on their feet again, jumping up and down, waving the giant foam hands Matt had purchased for them, and shouting at the top of their lungs.

Apparently napping on the ferry and the pizza they'd eaten for dinner really reenergized them. Or maybe it was just the sport and the excitement of being in the big arena. Whatever the case, Cassie was sure this was a night Noah would never forget. Their seats weren't quite courtside but were a few rows up—still an excellent view of the Kings' bench and all the players running up and down the court.

Her gaze left the boys and traveled to Matt, and she was surprised to find him watching her instead of the game.

"Are you having a good time?" He pointed at his watch. "Do we need to go?"

She shook her head. No way she was about to spoil the boys' fun. "I'm having a great time."

"Mom, look!" Noah grabbed her arm. "We're on TV."

Cassie raised her head, following his outstretched hand to the jumbotron, then gasped at the larger than life picture of the five of them. She turned to Matt and found him grinning.

"We're looking pretty good for as long a day as it's been."

"Speak for yourself." She resisted the urge to touch her windblown, hat-smashed hair.

"In the crowd tonight, we welcome former NBA commentator Matthew Kramer and his family." The announcer had recognized Matt but obviously mistaken Cassie for his wife. There was nothing to do but smile awkwardly and glance at the screen once more to see if the camera had moved onto some other unsuspecting person in the crowd.

"You do make a lovely family."

That voice. On the screen, Cassie saw the speaker, a petite Asian woman, seated two rows behind them. *Pearl!* Cassie turned in her seat to confront the woman but saw only the knees of the same row of fans—four men who had to be brothers, or at least related to one another—who had been alternately seated and standing there all night. Cassie jumped to her feet then up on her chair, attempting to peer between them to the row behind. *No Pearl.* Cassie looked to the jumbotron again, but the picture was on someone else.

She stepped off her seat and then sat down on the hard plastic and gripped the arms of her chair. *I am not losing my mind. I'm not.* But that was twice today that she thought she'd seen the woman from the care center. *Why?*

Matt faced Cassie at the doorway to her apartment after helping her put Noah in bed. "Thank you for today."

"I wish it wasn't over," Cassie said. "I mean, I'm glad it is for you and that you made it through such a hard day, but—"

"It wasn't hard," Matt said. "I'm sorry it's over, too."

She didn't know what to say to that, to say next. If they were a normal couple in a relationship that was progressing, they'd probably be easing closer to one another, each wondering what the other would think of a goodnight kiss, but there was nothing normal about her relationship with Matt, and a kiss was out of the question. She'd already crossed the line today, kissing him on the cheek as she had. But he'd needed it. Cassie wasn't sure how she'd known, but she'd had an impression she couldn't ignore, and that moment had been all about Matt and making him feel good about himself and life.

"So. " Her weary sigh seemed to say it all. She was tired of being alone, of the guilt, of not being able to have the life she wanted. "I'll plan to pick Asher up from preschool on Tuesday as usual," Cassie said when the silence had lengthened to awkward proportions.

"I appreciate that." Matt took a slight step back. "The boys always look forward to coming to your place or your mom's. They like being with you."

"Noah loves being with you, too," Cassie said. It was a gross understatement. She was pretty sure that, given the opportunity, Noah would choose to move in with Matt and his boys over living with her.

"Cassie, is there any way—"

"No." She held up a hand, palm out, praying he wouldn't ask her to see him again or to resume the friendship they'd had last fall. Today had proven just how easy it would be to pick up where they'd left off and to move swiftly from there. "I can't, Matt. It's too hard. I'm married. Devon is my husband. Anything more than helping each other out with our boys is wrong." Thinking about how much she'd enjoyed the day with Matt while Devon lay in his bed at the care center brought a fresh dose of remorse. "Good night." She reached behind her for the doorknob.

"Night, Cassie. Thank you again." The sorrow in Matt's voice almost broke her. He took another step back so he was outside her apartment, then turned to go.

"Matt, wait." *Stupid. What am I doing?* She held her conscience off a few seconds longer and stepped into his arms, wrapping hers around him in a hug. He returned the gesture at once, enfolding her, one hand on her back, the other at her waist, and leaning forward so that his face was close to hers.

They said nothing, just held each other. It felt so good, Cassie never wanted to let go. She feared she wouldn't be able to. It had been so long since she'd felt this kind of comfort and support. Hugs from her mom were great, but being held by a man who was her friend and understood and cared was completely different. *Completely better.*

She soaked in his warmth and breathed in the scent that was only Matt and which she now associated with Oregon. His hand moved slowly up and down her back, and Cassie thought she might melt from the simple touch. She was lonely, and he was, too. She loved him. Maybe he even felt the same about her, and if he did, she might break his heart, and it had already been broken with Jenna's death.

Cassie pulled away and stepped back, shaking her head

and wiping tears simultaneously. "I'm sorry." She shut the door without looking at his face, knowing she couldn't bear to see his sorrow. Feeling hers was too much already. She turned the lock, then slid down the wall to the floor with her knees to her chest, her face in her hands, and wept.

Thirty-Seven

Cassie's fingers drummed nervously on the folder in her lap as she waited for Dr. Hammond. She'd been to UC Davis before during the first months after Devon was shot and then again the following year. Dr. Hammond had been kind, though not particularly encouraging. She was here to ask again today if he would once again plead her case before the insurance company responsible for Devon's medical care. In addition to his help, she was also seeking the professional recommendation of a Dr. Kyle at UCSF.

Their recommendations were just the beginning. She wasn't going to back down this time. Devon was going to have an MRI. He was going to start taking Amantadine and Zolpidem if she had to give them to him herself. She also wanted him to be considered for a clinical trial of deep brain stimulation. She had the data from the last trial, and while the results weren't miraculous—no one progressed from PVS back to fully functioning that fast, if at all—they were promising. *Part of Devon is better than no Devon.*

"Mrs. Webb, it's good to see you again." Dr. Hammond held his hand out as he entered the office.

Cassie shook it. "I wish I could say the same," she said with a grim smile, "but I am grateful to you for taking time out of your busy schedule to meet with me."

"What can I help you with?" Dr. Hammond asked, not denying that his schedule was full and she'd taken him away from it. He continued around the desk and seated himself in the leather chair behind it.

"I don't know if you remember my husband." Cassie took Devon's file from her lap and placed it on the desk.

Dr. Hammond placed his finger on top of the folder but didn't open it. "Sacramento PD, shot in the head, near the base of his skull with the bullet traveling upward, while on duty. Substantial brain trauma with Diffuse axonal injury, resulting in a coma that lasted seven weeks then transitioned to a vegetative state. What was it, four or five years ago now?" If he'd hoped to impress her rattling off the facts so coldly, like Devon was some piece of paper with bullet points, he failed.

"Six years, seven months, and three days," Cassie corrected him. "Devon is still in a care center in Auburn, still in a persistent vegetative state."

"No change at all?"

"Not outwardly," Cassie said, "but it's impossible to be definitive since he's never had another MRI since the initial incident and his stay in the hospital."

"And you would like me to write a letter to your insurance company, arguing that they pay for one." Dr. Hammond frowned as he leaned back in his chair.

"Yes." Cassie forged ahead. "I am also here to request

that you write a letter of recommendation for Devon to be a candidate in an upcoming clinical trial for deep brain stimulation. In addition, I would like Devon to start taking both Amantadine and Zolpidem, which have each been found to—"

"I know what both drugs have done for PVS patients, Mrs. Webb. That is my field of expertise, as evidenced by your continued requests for my opinion."

Continued? She hadn't seen him for five years. Cassie bit her tongue and clenched her hands in her lap instead of snatching the folder and marching out of there like she wanted to.

"Yes," she said with forced politeness. "You are the expert. Your opinion carries weight with both insurance companies and other medical institutions, and I would greatly appreciate your help. I want my husband back, and my son needs his father. The state and our insurance carrier care little about either."

"You realize that even if Devon were to be allowed as a candidate for this trial, your chances of getting your husband back as you knew him and of your son having a father who can throw him a baseball or take him on a campout are virtually nonexistent."

"I understand," Cassie said. She did now. She'd spent the past two months trying to make up for the previous five when her heart hadn't been in the right place and, emotionally at least, she had been less than faithful to Devon. With renewed purpose she'd poured over the latest data and research, spoken with families of other PVS patients, gathered statistics, and come up with a treatment plan. She'd also come back to reality, which after so long in denial, had been extremely difficult.

Her dream of Devon ever joining her again for date

night at Ikeda's or anywhere else was gone. He'd never live in their apartment again because he'd likely be wheelchair bound for life. He wouldn't be the man he'd once been, but there was still a chance that he would be someone, a part of the person she'd loved.

"Four of the eight patients from the last trial are now able to communicate verbally." *A real conversation with Devon would be such a gift.* "And that possibility as well as the improvements that a small portion of patients taking both Amantadine and Zolpidem have seen are reason enough to try."

"Not to an insurance company which has to be fiscally responsible and accountable to all its customers," Dr. Hammond argued. "It's fifty thousand dollars just to have the device implanted. By the time you add on a year of therapy, you've spent a million or more."

"But in a clinical trial—"

"It's all free." Dr. Hammond leaned forward, elbows on the desk, fingertips touching. "Because patients most likely to respond to the treatment are selected. I know the trial you're referring to, Mrs. Webb. The clinicians are looking for patients who have been unresponsive for six months, not six years. In addition to that qualification, you'd need to have had a series of MRI's tracking your husband's progress, or lack thereof, since his accident."

"So you aren't going to help me," Cassie said, grateful for the moment that her feelings of anger were winning out over tears.

"I am trying to help you," Dr. Hammond insisted, "by telling you the truth. You lost your husband six and a half years ago just as surely as his partner's wife lost her husband. You see, I do remember you *and* your husband. My best advice to you is to move on with your life. Quit hoping for the impossible and wasting years waiting for it."

"I'm not." Cassie stood and grabbed the folder. "So long as my husband is breathing, I'll never stop hoping. *Nothing* is impossible. Miracles happen every day, and there's no reason Devon can't be one of them. Good day, Dr. Hammond."

"Rough week?" Lynn asked as she peeked in on Cassie.

Cassie beckoned her to enter Devon's room. "I struck out at UC Davis. Dr. Hammond refused to write a letter recommending an MRI or that Devon be a patient for the trial."

"Are you sure?" Lynn asked.

"Very." Cassie moved Devon's fingers carefully, one by one, wondering if the exercises were as futile as her appointment had been. Would he really never use his hands again, never talk to her again, never even look at her again? Sometimes she thought she'd take that. She'd settle for just one more chance to look into his eyes and have him look back. To have him know that she was here and that she still loved him.

"Hmm." Lynn came to the side of the bed where Cassie could see her. "That is interesting, especially in light of the information I have right here."

Cassie looked up to see a smile playing at the corners of Lynn's mouth as she opened a chart and withdrew a printout. "Orders for Devon Webb to be transferred to the hospital for his upcoming MRI. Oh, and he's had a couple of promising meds added to his list."

"Are you serious?" Cassie reached for the paper as Lynn handed it to her.

"I'd never joke about this," Lynn said. "I hope this is the miracle you've been searching for."

"It is." Cassie clutched the paper to her heart. "It has to be."

Thirty-Eight

Cassie hung up the phone, then placed her head face down on the table. Could nothing ever go her way? Devon's scheduled MRI had at first been approved three weeks ago and then, just hours before it was to be done today, denied. Somehow his paperwork had been allowed to slip through the cracks, the not-so-nice lady at the insurance agency had explained, but unfortunately, they could not authorize a patient of his status to have unnecessary tests.

He's not dead, Cassie had wanted to scream at her but had instead hung up the phone before she said something that would make things worse. *Could they get any worse?*

Her phone rang again, and Cassie let it go to voicemail without picking up. Only when the chime sounded, letting her know there was a message, did she listen.

"Hi, Cassie, this is Lynn. Just wanted to let you know that we need to take Devon over to the hospital soon. I've got some paperwork I need you to sign before his MRI, if you still want him to have one. You just have to sign for financial responsibility, and they'll do it. They tried to call and cancel, but I told them to hold the spot, that it had just been changed to independent uninsured. You'll need to give them a credit card today as well."

Cassie jumped up, grabbed her keys, and practically flew down the stairs to her car. Since when did Devon's insurance not have to approve? She wasn't sure exactly what loophole Lynn had found to get around that glitch, but she wasn't going to miss this opportunity when it wasn't likely to come again. Of course she'd take financial responsibility. She'd max out her credit card or do whatever she needed to for Devon to have this test.

To have a chance.

"Tell me what you see." Dr. Hammond stepped aside so that Cassie could see the two images clipped in front of the light boxes on the wall in his office.

"Isn't that your job?" Cassie asked with a nervous laugh. "I don't know one part of the brain from another." Not entirely true. She'd actually learned quite a bit about the brain since Devon's injury.

"Do the images look the same or different?" Dr. Hammond asked quietly.

Cassie stepped closer, straining her eyes as they moved carefully over each picture, searching for some difference, any minute change that would offer hope, but the two scans appeared identical, lacking significant color and showing clearly the lack of brain activity. "They're the same," she said finally, waiting for the inevitable, "I told you so."

Dr. Hammond said nothing. He only switched off the

light boxes, removed the images, and placed them on his desk. "I'd show you a scan of what we'd hoped to see, but I'm guessing you're familiar enough with that already."

"Yes. Unfortunately."

"How is the new drug regimen going?"

"It isn't." Cassie looked down as she admitted that failure, too. How hopeful she'd been at the first few doses of the drugs, particularly the Zolpidem, which had shown miraculous results in waking PVS patients, some who'd been in that state longer than Devon.

"I'm sorry," Dr. Hammond said, sounding genuinely so. "When you left my office last time, your conviction that your husband could and should be helped was so strong that I allowed myself to be swayed against my medical knowledge and understanding. I'm sorry if it's given you false hope."

"You needn't be," Cassie said, finding it strange she almost seemed to be comforting him. She summoned an appreciative smile, though she was finding precious little to feel grateful for at the moment. "I've always had hope. I suppose that's what comes of having experience with miracles. Devon and I were told we wouldn't be able to have children of our own, on our own, and then we had our son without any help at all. We had one miracle, so of course I expected another. I thank you for helping us try."

"What now?" Dr. Hammond asked as she turned to go.

Cassie drew in a deep breath and clutched at the thin, worn slip of paper in her pocket. "Now I do my best to build a life I can love without Devon." There. She'd said it, even if she didn't quite believe it yet. She had to, and she'd start by taking his car out of storage and selling it to pay for the MRI.

"Good luck to you, Mrs. Webb." Dr. Hammond walked her through the waiting room to the door.

"Thank you," Cassie said, knowing she was going to need it.

I can do this. Do or do not, there is no try. Remembering Matt's disgruntled expression as he'd read that fortune gave her a boost of courage. She pulled the door to Dr. Hammond's office closed behind her and stepped out into the sunshine.

"I may need some help from the force today, Yoda."

Thirty-Nine

Cassie removed the padlock from the storage unit, grabbed the handle, and heaved the door upward. It creaked and groaned but rolled to the top, revealing the large, cloth-draped shape within.

For a long moment, she stood staring at it, hands on hips as she summoned courage. *It's just a car. Why is this so hard?* She stepped forward and began gathering the fabric and pulling it over the top of the still-shiny black finish. How she'd hated this car when she first saw it. Who wanted to drive a black car? And the Audi's price tag had delayed her grad school plans for a whole semester. *What a fight we had.* Cassie actually smiled at the memory. It was easier to remember the making up afterward now.

She took the keys from her pocket, unlocked the door, and climbed in the driver's seat. She'd never driven the Audi except to move it here when she'd decided to put it in storage. She'd wanted Devon to find his beloved car just as it was before.

He'll never drive again. There was no point leaving it in storage forever, and as much as she didn't care for her beat up Nissan, she preferred that over the Audi.

Closing her eyes, she leaned her head back against the seat and drifted into the past. It wasn't hard. The car still smelled like Devon, of aftershave and ammo. Beneath the seat she knew she'd find the box he locked his gun in on those few occasions he went somewhere that he couldn't carry it. A wrapper from his last piece of candy lay in the cup holder. She'd even left his favorite retro '80s CD, cued to his favorite song, in the player. She used to tease him about his music choices and tell him he'd been born in the wrong decade. What would he think of this last one that he'd missed over half of?

Tilting her head back, Cassie looked up at the sunroof, remembering those magical moments driving across the Golden Gate. *Best day of my life.* She'd had a few days since that competed for that spot. Only a few when there should have been more.

There will be.

"You cannot love life until you live the life you love," she repeated. Matt had mailed her the slip of paper a few days after their trip to San Francisco. Of all the fortunes they'd read together, he'd chosen to send this one and had written a long letter encouraging her to follow her dreams for her career and to do everything possible with and for Noah. *Legoland is calling,* he'd said at the end of his letter.

Maybe it was. Maybe there would be enough money left over from selling the Audi. She understood Matt's message and appreciated that he'd accepted what had to be. She couldn't have him, couldn't have love in her life like she used to, but there was still plenty about life *to* love. She just had to go after those things and make them happen.

She'd gone after the most important, pulling out all the stops for Devon. That hadn't gone as she'd hoped it would, but at least now she knew, and she could move on with a life that was best for her and Noah without the same belief that Devon would ever return to them. Adjusting her expectations and hope was going to take some getting used to and some time, but this was a start.

She turned the key in the ignition, and the engine roared to life. *Thank you*, she thought, grateful for that small miracle. She backed out of the unit, then locked it and returned to the car. She opened the sunroof, letting in the warm spring air, and as she pulled onto the highway Devon's favorite song blared from the speakers. *Don't you forget about me.*

"I won't," Cassie promised.

Forty

A few minutes before nine, Cassie left Devon's room for the night, leaving the door partly open behind her. She knew the staff checked on him regularly. Between rounds if there was any change in his monitor, it would trigger an alarm at the nurses' station, but she always felt better leaving the door open, just in case. For so long she'd imagined him waking, then calling out to her in a panic. If that happened when she wasn't here, she at least wanted to make sure someone else would hear him.

Now that she was trying to face the reality that he was never going to wake, never going to call out to her in a panic or any other way, she still left his door open. It felt like he was less alone that way.

"He would be less alone if you would allow him to go, to join the others who have gone before him."

Pearl. Cassie's head snapped up and she looked around sharply, certain she'd just heard the woman, as certain as she was that Pearl was real and had appeared to her on more than one occasion.

Appeared? As if she's some angel or fairy or something. Maybe she was. A chill worked its way up Cassie's spine, and she hugged her arms to herself, trying to ward off the strange sensation.

Where are you? Show yourself. Instead of continuing toward the exit, Cassie backtracked to peer around the corner to the next hall of rooms. *No one.* She waited for the voice again, but it didn't come. As with both the incident in Chinatown and at the Kings' game, Pearl had simply vanished.

Maybe I am *losing my mind.* Imagining voices and seeing people definitely wasn't good. Cassie retraced her steps and made her way toward the front desk. She passed Devon's room again and glanced in to find nothing changed. *No Pearl there.*

She wasn't usually given to superstition, but that day last fall, it had felt almost as if Pearl was some sort of mystic, what with all her talk of letting Devon move on. *So why have I wanted to see her again?* Why had she chased a woman down the street in Chinatown and later that night stared down the people seated behind them at the Kings' game?

Cassie supposed it was to prove that Pearl really did exist, that she hadn't imagined the entire incident. But what if she had? What if she'd fallen asleep, as she sometimes did, in Devon's room and had dreamed the entire exchange? Except that she hadn't imagined running into Matt and his boys at the hospital cafeteria just a few minutes later. *Something* had prompted her to abandon her usual schedule that night and leave Devon's room early. It didn't make sense.

"On the contrary, I've hardly known a situation or two people who make more sense together."

Cassie paused mid step and stared at the petite woman standing just inside the lobby.

"Hello, Cassandra. So good to see you again," Pearl said. Today she wore a pair of navy slacks and a rose-colored blouse. A delicate pearl bracelet adorned her wrist, and the same antique pearl comb was tucked into the side of her hair, holding back a simple chignon. Aside from the lack of scrubs, she looked exactly as Cassie remembered her from that night so many months ago.

"Who are you?" Cassie demanded instead of returning Pearl's pleasant greeting. "Not a nurse like you pretended to be."

"Not a nurse," Pearl said with a gentle smile, "though I don't recall ever stating that I was."

"You were wearing scrubs," Cassie pointed out.

"Yes." Pearl nodded. "Sometimes a certain uniform or outfit is required for a particular job. For instance, if we were in the 1800s, do you think I'd be wearing these pants?"

The 1800s? Cassie didn't bother trying to figure out what Pearl meant. The woman made no sense, unless—"Are you a patient here?" Why hadn't she thought of that before? Sierra wasn't a mental facility, but many of the residents *were* old, and she'd met a few with varying degrees of dementia. Maybe Pearl was like that but was also here for some type of physical therapy or after-surgery care. Maybe she'd been here last fall as well, and she'd wandered from her room, though that didn't explain the altered visiting hours sign or the security guard.

"Sometimes it's best not to try too hard to figure things out," Pearl advised, as if she sensed the direction of Cassie's thoughts. "I am not a patient here or a nurse; however, I am here to help you, this time at your request. You wanted to see me again, did you not?"

Cassie could only nod mutely.

"Well, here I am, and I *am* real. Long ago I learned the

importance of making that known. Not doing so caused a rather significant problem for a young woman once." Pearl's face was at first troubled then serene again. "It all worked out for her in the end. It always does, no matter what the difficulties." She smiled brightly. "Even in your case, Cassandra." Pearl gestured to the sofa. "Come. Sit with me a minute, and perhaps I can clear a few things up. I see that you're troubled."

Numbly, Cassie followed her and sat beside Pearl on the couch farthest from the door and nearest the large fireplace, which she'd never seen in use once during the entire time Devon had lived here.

"Now then." Pearl angled herself toward Cassie. "Was there something you wished to ask me?"

The confusion, hurt, and anger Cassie had been harboring for months tumbled out in a flurry of questions. "What you said about my husband when you came before— why did you say that? Why did you tell me to give up on him? What right did you have to say such a horrible thing? Why were you in his room that night? How come no one else here knew about you?"

"My," Pearl exclaimed, that same serene smile on her face. "Such a lot of questions. Let's focus on the one that matters, shall we?" She continued without waiting for a response. "I did not tell you to give up on Devon. You are confusing giving up and letting go. They are not the same thing."

"They feel the same," Cassie said, irritated at Pearl's easy dismissal of her other questions. "They are the same, especially if what you say is true, if *I'm* what is holding Devon here on Earth, if without my faith in him, he'll die."

"Death is not what most believe it to be," Pearl said. "It is but the beginning of another, more glorious life. Letting your husband go on, as he should, is not the same as giving up on him, leaving him to suffer here alone." She paused, brow furrowed and lips pressed together in contemplation. "Think of it this way. When you sent your son to kindergarten last September, it was the beginning of a new stage of life for him, and that required some definite letting go on your part, did it not?"

"Yes, but—"

"You let him go off to that big, scary school alone, as you're not in the classroom or at recess or lunch with him each day."

"At the beginning of the year I ate lunch with him," Cassie said, "until he asked me not to." She should have felt surprised or even threatened that Pearl knew of Noah and the stress it had been sending him to kindergarten, but instead it seemed almost natural that she should know, as if they were old family friends or something.

"Noah asked you not to eat lunch with him, so you let him go a bit more, gave him more independence and freedom, even though it hurt."

Cassie nodded. Yeah, it had hurt when Noah had asked her to let him eat with the kids in his class instead of her.

"But you weren't giving up on him as a person, as your son," Pearl continued. "You still loved him. You missed him when the two of you weren't together, but in no way was that *giving up* on Noah."

"That's an entirely different situation." Cassie folded her arms, as if to prove the strength of her point. "Kindergarten is not life and death."

"Of course it's not," Pearl said kindly. "But it's similar enough that you understand what I'm saying. "All that I suggested, then and now, is that you give Devon a *choice* to stay here on Earth in his present state or continue on to Heaven."

"If he isn't conscious of anything, I don't see how offering him a choice will do any good." Cassie frowned.

"There are many levels of consciousness," Pearl said. "Simply because his MRI did not reveal activity in his brain does not mean it isn't there." She leaned back, appraising Cassie. "I'm surprised at you, Cassandra. So easily swayed by those test results when you've had the faith and belief all these years that Devon was listening and could hear you."

"How did you—" Cassie decided she didn't want to know how Pearl was aware of Devon's MRI. Too much of what she said made sense, and Cassie hated hearing it. "I wasn't easily swayed," she said. "I've just been trying to face the reality that he isn't going to come back to us."

"If you can face that, then you can give Devon a choice because you love him." Pearl gave Cassie's knee a kindly pat, then stood. "I wouldn't keep either man waiting too long," she advised.

"Either?" Cassie also stood, looking down on Pearl by a few inches, though she felt the opposite, if anything. Pearl's stature might be petite, but her words and her gentle way of persuasion felt overpowering.

"Many of us do not have the opportunity that you've had," Pearl said, "to be loved completely and thoroughly by a man, to have him give you his name, claim you as his, care for you, protect you, and love you and only you. That is what Devon did, and you were fortunate to have those blessings and now memories. Cherish them, Cassandra." Pearl's eyes grew misty, and her gaze seemed to turn inward and faraway at the same time.

Recalling her own love?

After several long, silent seconds, Pearl inhaled deeply, seeming to come back to the present. "It is not only time for Devon to move on, but it is time for you to move on as well.

Always cherish the old, but make room for the new. Live the life you will love and fill it with love." Pearl reached out, taking one of Cassie's hands in hers. "You are among the most extraordinary and fortunate of women, one of those rare few who has the opportunity to be loved completely once *more*, an experience that will be made sweeter yet from the losses you've suffered. Just imagine"—Pearl stretched out her free hand as her entire face lit—"happiness to equal or excel the sorrow you've known."

A year ago, Cassie would have said she couldn't imagine that if it didn't include Devon, but she'd glimpsed that potential for second chances, a second love in her life, last fall, though to hope for such a thing still felt so very wrong.

"Don't delay your future any longer, Cassandra. Don't keep him waiting forever. He's suffered a great loss, too, and needs you as much as you and Noah need him."

Cassie tugged her hand free from Pearl's and wrapped her arms around herself, wishing she had Matt's comforting arms there instead. "When did this conversation become about Matt?"

"I don't recall mentioning anyone's name." Pearl's voice was chipper, and she tilted her head slightly, a knowing look in her eyes.

A retort died on Cassie's lips as she realized that Pearl was right. She hadn't used a name, but who else could she have been talking about besides Matt?

"You know what you need to do, Cassandra, and the sooner the better. All three of you are suffering for your delay."

"That isn't fair," Cassie said. She didn't need to feel guilt about Matt now, too. She'd hoped that talking to Pearl again would make her feel better, that the woman would have some explanations and maybe apologies, but somehow

Cassie was the one feeling the need to apologize. If anything, she felt worse.

"Look," Pearl said, staring past Cassie at the large clock on the opposite wall. "You still have thirty minutes left until visiting hours are over, time to say what needs to be said to Devon."

"That clock must be wrong." Cassie dug her cell phone out of her purse and glanced at the time. *8:30 p.m. Impossible.* "It was 8:57 just a few minutes ago when I left Devon's room."

Pearl shrugged. "I'm only telling you what the clock says. Thirty precious minutes granted to you. I would suggest you use them wisely. It is not often any of us are given more time."

"Yes. Of course." Feeling as if some spell had been cast or she was in a trance, Cassie turned away. *I know what time it was.* Instead of clarifying her previous visit, Pearl had only confused things even more. Cassie paused at the edge of the carpet before she entered the hall. She looked back at Pearl, wanting to feel a sense of closure after this second encounter. "You don't work here, and you aren't a patient. Will I see you here again?"

"I'm working right now, and no, you won't see me here again." Pearl's smile turned wistful. "My job demands that I travel frequently. Occasionally I am able to linger a while, as I did this past summer, spending several delightful weeks in Hawaii, but even that came to an end. It is rare that I am able to keep in touch with those I have helped."

"I'm sorry," Cassie said, though she didn't quite know why. It wasn't as if she and Pearl were even true acquaintances, let alone friends.

"Don't be," Pearl said. "I have many joys. Many sacrifices, too, as we all do. There is no love or happiness in this life without their counterparts of loneliness and sorrow. You have had your fill of those. Go now and start the path that will lead you the opposite direction."

Words from a wise old woman. It would have all made perfect sense were Cassie the heroine of a fairytale, but in this modern world, kind, wise old women did not often appear to offer advice, wanted or not.

"Thank you." It seemed the right thing to say. Cassie met Pearl's eyes and for the briefest second thought she glimpsed a sorrow that matched her own.

"Be strong," Pearl said. "The road to happiness is not always easy at first." With that parting advice, she turned away and walked the short distance to the sliding glass doors. They parted for her, and she stepped through. The glass closed once more, and though Cassie continued to look, she could no longer see Pearl's shadow in the light on the other side.

Gone from your sight, but not gone entirely. Just as Devon will be—if you will but free him. He will no longer be of this world, but your memories together will always be with you. It was Pearl's voice once more, just as Cassie had heard it in the hall outside of Devon's room. She glanced at her phone, expecting her thirty minutes to be nearer to twenty-five now, but 8:30 still flashed up at her. *Thirty minutes more. Don't waste it. You know what to do.*

Tranquility settled over her. In the past, she'd never felt like this, either when coming to or leaving from visiting Devon. *Everything is going to be all right.* With purposeful strides, she returned to Devon's room. She entered and closed the door behind her, then drew the curtain around the bed for twenty-nine minutes alone with her husband.

Forty-One

"Another story, please, Daddy." Asher dropped the oversized book at just the wrong angle on Matt's lap.

Matt's teeth clenched to avoid the word that came to mind, but he didn't curb his temper entirely. "Be careful, Asher!"

Asher cowered beneath his angry glare. "Sorry." He started to slide from the couch and only the deepest reserves of Matt's long-spent patience pulled him back.

"I know you didn't mean it." Matt put his arm around Asher, reminding himself that he'd best be careful or his son wouldn't want to spend this time with him. Still, he was five now. He needed to understand that a man could be hurt. What was it that Jenna used to tell the boys when they were climbing all over him? *Be careful with Daddy, or you'll never get a sister.*

Austin had always claimed that was fine by him, he didn't want a sister, to which Jenna would roll her eyes. Whenever they visited their friends with the six-month-old daughter, Austin was always first to want to hold the baby.

"Maybe *I* want one," Jenna would say. "Too many boys around here."

It was at that point that Matt usually said, "Oh, yeah?" then pulled her into the fray. Later at night, after the boys were in bed, he and Jenna would practice getting the boys that sister.

Wrong place for your thoughts to go. Matt imagined the emotions in his brain going berserk, just like in one of the boys' favorite movies that portrayed the feelings inside a person as little people themselves. No doubt a large red warning button had just been pushed, again, and there was all sorts of scrambling in his head.

He's done it again. Thoughts in the danger zone. Don't let him cry in front of his kids. It's gonna be a long night.

It was already a long night, longer than usual it seemed. Matt glanced at his watch and was shocked to see it was only 8:30. Hadn't it been 8:30 a half hour ago? They'd already read six books.

"Daddy?" Asher's little hand touched Matt's arm. His voice was penitent but still questioning.

"One more story," Matt agreed. He adjusted the book on his lap, remembering that his mother had read to him from it when he was little. He quickly found what used to be his favorite in the Richard Scarry volume, a story about a pig who could never keep track of his hat and had an extraordinary amount of accidents. In no time at all, Asher was giggling, so much so that Austin even left the game he was playing on the iPad and came over to see what was so funny.

They finished the pig story and read two more, and when Matt finally closed the book, both Austin and Asher were nearly asleep on him. Taking one in each arm, he carried them up the stairs to his old bedroom. He tucked the boys in and kissed them goodnight, only then realizing they probably hadn't brushed their teeth.

Oh well. At least they were all eating better now that they were home and his mom was doing the cooking. He'd have to remember to watch her and get some recipes before they went back to California.

With his parents out for the night and the house to himself now, Matt went through their room and out to the balcony. He sat on their faded two-seater swing and tried not to think of all the times he and Jenna had enjoyed sitting out here—the stolen kisses they'd shared in this spot when they were dating, the time she'd held his hand to her tummy and he'd first felt Austin kick, or the hours they'd sat out here together, swinging and soothing the boys when they had ear infections.

Great memories. He was glad he had them.

The sound of the waves crashing onto the shore soothed the pain into something bearable and bittersweet. Remembering was still painful, but it was also possible now without falling completely apart.

Matt breathed in the fresh, cool, salty air, and his head cleared. The panic inside was over, at least temporarily. Tonight he could think of Jenna and remember the good between them. Coming home for a month had been the right decision. He hoped leaving the boys here for an additional month was also the right thing to do. Returning to his lonely apartment in Auburn was going to be rough, but he'd use the time away from them to work hard, to set things up for the upcoming season, to remember what being a workaholic was like, and then school would start again. Asher would go this year, too. There would be less daycare, less complications. *Less Cassie.* That was going to be tough, too.

Matt pulled his phone from his pocket and went to his messages. He put the phone on speaker and played hers for what might have been the hundredth time. When he came to the last part of the recording, he closed his eyes and imagined that she was here, sitting right beside him.

"I love you, Matt. I shouldn't, but I do."

He felt the same for her but couldn't act on those feelings. It was ironic. He'd had every opportunity to show how Jenna how much he cared, and he hadn't. How the tables were turned now. Maybe this was exactly what was supposed to happen to him, his own personal purgatory where he realized too late what he'd missed and then was tempted with what he most wanted and couldn't have. *Serves me right.*

That Cassie had found something about him loveable gave him at least a glimmer of hope. Perhaps someday . . .

His mom wanted *someday* to come this summer and had a string of dates arranged for him during the month he'd be home. He supposed he deserved her meddling as well, the way he'd brought Cassie home like that, getting not only his hopes up, but his parents' as well. Now his mom was going full out, acting on the cue he'd unwittingly given her that he was ready to date again.

It hadn't been dating with Cassie, or at least it hadn't felt like it. There'd been nothing hard about getting to know her, becoming friends, and falling in love. It had seemed the most natural thing in the world, as if they were destined to be together.

If only.

He played her message again, her admission of love like a balm to his soul. He shouldn't love Cassie either, but he did, and it seemed there was nothing he could do about it.

Forty-Two

Cognizant of the passing time on her phone, Cassie held Devon's hand, still waiting for the right words to come some twenty minutes after she'd returned to his room. Pearl had convinced her it would be so simple to tell Devon he could go, so easy to convince him that she and Noah would be all right without him, but when it came down to it, she found she couldn't do it. Devon was still here, and she wanted him to stay.

"Dev, this is such a mess. Nothing has gone like we planned." She thought back to their wedding night, how they'd sat facing one another on the seat in the bay window, their bare feet touching as they talked for hours while looking out across the bay as the moon traveled over the Golden Gate. Life had been so full of promise then.

Devon was going to make detective in record time—five years, he'd predicted—and then they could start looking at jobs in other cities. Cassie was going to get her master's, become a licensed therapist, and start a practice for troubled adolescents. Her job would be a bit more flexible with her own office and hours of her choosing. About a year into her business, they'd start a family.

"We have to have a boy first," Devon had said.

Cassie pushed on his foot. "A girl would be better. They're more responsible. She'd be a better example to a younger brother."

"You mean she'd torture him." Devon pushed back, so hard that Cassie nearly lost her balance and fell.

"I know what I'm talking about," he continued. "I've spent a life under my sister's thumb."

"All right," Cassie conceded. "Maybe we'll get twins first, one of each."

"Careful what you wish for," Devon had said.

Oh, that she had been. Tears of regret clouded Cassie's eyes. What had happened to Devon wasn't her fault. She knew that, but still.

If only our last conversation had been better.

Forgive him and yourself, her mom had said. *Of course.* Mothers were always right, and this time was no exception. Cassie knew what she needed to say and do.

She moved Devon's arm, then climbed onto the bed beside him, lying on her side facing him, her head on his chest. The staff would not be okay with this, but she needed to feel close to Devon, just for tonight. She needed him to feel close to her, to feel the depth of her apology, even if his mind couldn't understand it.

The steady rhythm of his heartbeat played in her ear, giving her courage. Some part of Devon was alive. Some part of him had to be able to comprehend her regret and sorrow and to forgive her.

"I wished—" Cassie took a deep breath. "—that you

would stop spending money on things that didn't matter." Her voice was little more than a whisper, though she had been plenty loud when she'd said it to the door Devon closed when he went to work that morning.

"I was so angry when you left without talking to me after our fight the night before. I couldn't believe you'd booked a houseboat on Shasta without consulting me, that you'd spent all that money when you wouldn't spend it on trying to make a baby." He'd used some of the money she needed to set up her practice, money she'd felt should only be used for that purpose or a baby, but never a vacation.

"It felt like you didn't care that I'd graduated. It felt like you didn't believe in me. It was almost as if my inability to give you a son had made me incapable of anything else. You were treating me different, Dev."

Cassie took his hand in hers again and twined their fingers together, the way they used to hold hands when they walked up and down the pier in San Francisco.

"Every day of my life since you were hurt, I've wished I said something else to you that morning. I wish I'd let the money go and realized you were just trying to cope, too, that maybe you thought a week on the lake was just what we needed." She'd give a lot for a week like that now. "But I didn't say something else. I let anger and pride and hurt rule me, and instead of telling you I loved you when you walked out that door, I made a stupid wish." That came true.

"I'm sorry, Devon, so sorry. I'd take the words back if I could. I'd take *you* back." Her tears wet his shirt as Cassie lay beside him, holding on, feeling his heart. She paused. Was it her imagination, or was Devon's heart rate increasing? She lifted her head slightly to glance at his monitor. The steady blip, blip, blip continued, yet the needle had moved, creating a zigzag of mini peaks over the last several seconds.

Was it because she was lying beside him? Slowly Cassie loosened their hands, then sat up and turned around on the bed so she was still seated beside him.

"For all this time you've been here, my second wish hasn't overridden my first. You're not spending any money, and you're not with us either. I'd take a whole lot of debt over what we've got now. I imagine you would, too." She watched the monitor carefully, but the lines were back to their usual pattern.

"So I want to ask your forgiveness, for my anger, for not trying harder to understand your point of view as well." It was a fault that her mom had pointed out several times throughout Cassie's life. She tended to be so focused on the future and goals and plans that sometimes she forgot to live in the present or take notice of others and what was happening around her. Seven years ago, she'd been doing that in her marriage, trying to compensate for the loss of achieving her goal of motherhood on her timetable by throwing all of her energy into getting licensed and opening her own therapy practice. Because the sooner she did that, the sooner she'd have clients, and the sooner she and Devon would have had the money they needed to pursue being parents.

She could see that clearly now, almost as if she were looking at a movie of her old self, making mistake after mistake in pursuit of a worthy goal. What she and Devon had each forgotten was that they had been a team in that goal and that their original dream had been to spend their lives together.

There was so much to be sorry for. Why did hindsight always have to be so painfully clear?

She placed Devon's hand between her two. "We're not together now. Noah doesn't know his father, and Pearl says that you're only here in this bed still because of me." Cassie's eyes began watering again. "So I need you to know—" She pressed her lips together and looked up at the ceiling. "That it's all right if you want to go. Noah and I will be okay. We've been okay. Of course it would be better if you were with us, but if that's not possible, if this is as with us as you can be"— Cassie swept a hand across the bed—"then you should go. Be in a better place."

She released Devon's hand and brought both of hers up to cover her face. *I did it.* Tears pooled in the corners of her eyes, then spilled over. Had she done the right thing? Had what she said even mattered? She had an uncanny feeling that tonight it did.

The heart monitor gave an unfamiliar bleep, and Cassie's eyes flew open. A peak, taller than the previous ones she'd seen earlier, marked the screen.

"Devon?" She looked down at him and found him looking back.

"Devon," she breathed his name this time, hardly daring to believe that his eyes were not only open—unusual at this time of night—but seemed to be focused directly on her. They didn't track her movements as she adjusted her position on the bed to lean closer to him, but neither did they seem to be looking past her or unseeing as they usually were. She held his hand again.

"Some part of you understands. I know it." She continued to whisper, terrified she'd break whatever spell they were under. "I love you, Devon, and I want you to get better. I want you home with us, being my husband and Noah's father. But—" Her voice broke. "If you can't come home, then you need to leave this place because more than I want you with us, I want you to be happy—and free."

At her last word, Devon's eyes slid closed. Panicked,

Cassie looked to the monitor, but his heartbeat remained steady. She hadn't killed him. Her relief felt short-lived. She'd meant what she said. She didn't want Devon trapped in his body in this bed another six years, even another six months, if there was a better option.

"I love you," she said once more. "Always. No matter what. Forever."

Cassie kissed him, then cried some more.

Forty-Three

Cassie's phone rang just as she was fitting the key in the lock of her apartment. On the way home, she'd called her mom and asked her to keep Noah overnight—something she never did—but she'd felt worried enough that her head pounded, she was genuinely sick to her stomach, and just needed to be alone.

Before she even took the phone from her purse, she knew. When the lit screen flashed Sierra Care, Cassie simply sank to floor, sitting on the top step with her knees hunched close to her chest as she answered.

"Hello."

"Cassie, I'm so sorry. Devon's heart—" Lynn stopped mid-sentence, and Cassie imagined her struggling to convey this news about a patient she'd cared for for nearly seven years.

"What?" Cassie asked, feeling oddly numb. She needed

to hear Lynn say it even though she knew the truth already. "What happened?"

"It was his heart, Cassie. He's gone."

"I'll be right there," Cassie managed before she disconnected the call. She sat another minute, head in her hands, beneath the motion detector light Matt had installed last year. Lynn hadn't said that Devon was dead. *Just gone. To a better place.* Like Pearl had said he would be. *What have I done?* Cassie felt her own heart rate climb. There was no sense of relief as she'd half-expected, but a note of finality that rang through her mind. Devon was gone. He'd left them. He was never coming home. She and Noah were really on their own.

Always. No matter what. Forever.

"Devon's heart rate started experiencing some unusual fluctuations about an hour ago," the on-call doctor explained.

When I was here. Cassie shifted uncomfortably on the sofa, the same one she'd sat on with Pearl just a few hours earlier.

"Shortly after you left, his alarm went off," Lynn added. She and Doctor Lewis had been waiting in the lobby when Cassie arrived, ready to intercept her and prepare her before she saw Devon. It was Sierra Care protocol; she'd seen this same scenario numerous times before with other patients' families. *But never me,* she'd always thought confidently. *That will never be me.* Devon was going to get well and come home.

"In a matter of seconds, his heart escalated to over four hundred beats per minute," Lynn explained. "I was the first nurse to respond to his alarm, and it was almost like—like his heart was trying to burst right out of his chest."

"You'd signed a DNR," Dr. Lewis reminded Cassie gently. "As such, no measures were taken to restart your husband's heart."

"I understand." With the wadded up tissue in her hand, Cassie dabbed at a tear leaking down the side of her face.

"I have to believe that was the right call in this circumstance," Dr. Lewis continued. "Patients can sometimes be brought back from cardiac arrest, but in Devon's already weakened condition, it was not likely, and any attempts to revive him would have been extreme. I wouldn't wish those on my loved one."

"Thank you," Cassie said, truly appreciative of his words. She was grateful that Devon's chest hadn't been cracked open and shocks administered. He'd been through enough already and for so long. "May I see him?"

"Of course." Lynn stood. "I'll walk with you."

Cassie nodded, grateful for Lynn's support. She'd been more than a nurse all these years. She'd been a friend as well. Dr. Lewis bade them goodbye, and Cassie walked the hallways to Devon's room for the last time.

"Would you like me to come in with you?" Lynn asked when they reached his door.

"I'll be all right, thanks." Cassie entered the room and closed the door behind her. Devon looked the same as he always did, lying still in his bed, but the room *felt* different. The monitor was blank, and there was no rise and fall of the blanket above his chest.

Fear clutched her own chest. *He's really gone.* She grasped at something to be thankful for, to steady herself so she wouldn't fall to pieces. *I'm glad it was quick.* She prayed it hadn't been painful. She hadn't wanted Devon to suffer and could never have made the choice to have his feeding tube taken out.

As she moved closer to the bed, the differences became more apparent. Devon's eyelids sometimes twitched when he slept, but now they were perfectly still. His color was poor. She touched his hand and found it cold. The room felt empty, devoid of the life it had sheltered for nearly seven years.

Behind her, the door opened, and she turned to find her mom standing there.

"Oh, sweetheart." Her mom stepped forward and opened her arms. Cassie rushed into them.

"He's gone, Mom. Devon's gone."

"I know." She hugged Cassie tightly. "I knew as soon as you asked me to keep Noah overnight."

Cassie pulled back. "Is he here?"

Mom shook her head. "I asked a friend to stay with him." She gathered Cassie close again.

Cassie soaked up the comfort of her embrace, grateful that her mom had known to come. When she'd called her earlier, Devon had been fine, but mother's intuition must have been at work.

When she felt able to breathe again, Cassie stepped from her mom's arms and wiped her eyes. She looked over at Devon's bed, at his lifeless body one last time. This wasn't how she wanted to remember him or how she wanted Noah to either. She made the decision that he wouldn't see his father this way.

The reality of funeral arrangements and insurance documents and a cemetery plot suddenly loomed before her. Why hadn't she planned any of this earlier, or at least thought about it?

I didn't think it would come to this. But it had, and the

closure or peace she'd heard others speak of was nowhere to be found. Instead she only felt as the room did. Empty.

Forty-Four

Cassie smiled grimly and shook the hand of yet another police officer.

"Your husband was a fine man. I enjoyed working with him."

"Thank you." She kept her responses short and as sincere as possible. Based on the attendees and their expressions of condolence today, Devon had been a department favorite. Why then, she wondered, had none of these people come to see him in the previous years? At the least, it left her questioning their sincerity, though she did feel grateful so many had come to honor him at last.

When she was starting to feel she couldn't endure another greeting, it was time for her to take her seat and the funeral to start. She made her way alone to the front row, already filled with her mom and Noah, and Devon's sister and her husband.

It was a brief, simple service. Devon would have approved, Cassie thought as she stared at his casket and the spray of flowers covering it. He wasn't one for long meetings, and this one was necessarily short, Annie being the only speaker from the family, giving his life sketch. In a haze of numbness, Cassie listened to the words but didn't really absorb them. No matter, she'd already asked for a copy for Noah to read when he was older.

Her mom prompted her when it was time to rise and leave the building. They followed Devon's casket outside and were ushered into a black limo. The drive through the city was punctuated by those paying respect to Devon. This tribute meant more to her. These were people who hadn't worked with him, hadn't known him but recognized his loss and sacrifice.

"Look at all those fire trucks, Mom." Noah pointed at a half-dozen clustered together.

Cassie swallowed the lump in her throat. "Good people," she managed, "showing us they care."

Noah turned from the window, looked up at her, and clasped her hand. "Don't cry, Mom. Dad's happier now. We'll be all right, too."

"I know." After all, she'd promised Devon they would.

"Police, family, and Sacramento residents paid their respects today as a procession honoring Officer Devon Webb made its way from the funeral home to the Auburn Cemetery."

Matt grabbed the remote off the arm of the couch and turned the television volume up.

"Officers, paramedics, and firefighters lined the motorcade route, saluting the vehicle carrying fallen Officer Webb as it passed by." The camera panned from the police escort to the sides of the street, lined with public service vehicles and the uniformed men and women beside them.

Matt leaned forward. "About time he got some recognition."

"Webb, who sustained a bullet wound to the head during a domestic violence call nearly seven years earlier, leaves behind a wife and six-year-old son." The camera left the motorcade and zoomed in on Noah and Cassie exiting the car behind the hearse at the cemetery. Matt felt a tug at his heart as he watched Noah with his arm around Cassie, as if he was trying to be a man and support his mom.

"Webb had been residing at a care facility in Auburn. Up next—"

Matt turned off the TV. *Up next.* Just like that the world moved on. Less than one minute of airtime honoring Devon Webb's life and sacrifice and only a two-second mention of the family he left behind. If only moving on was so easy.

Give her some time, Janet had said when Matt asked about Cassie. He intended to do just that, though he'd wanted more than anything to be by her side at the cemetery today. Instead, he'd lingered a safe distance away, offering silent support but not wanting to upset her with his presence. If she'd wanted him there, she would have asked, but she hadn't, and that was okay. Sometimes friends just needed some space, too. He'd give her as much as she wanted, at least until the end of summer, another two months away. By then it would be the beginning of another school year and a few other things, he hoped.

Forty-Five

Cassie ran her finger down the soccer schedule, then stopped at the team listed next to theirs on today's date. "We're playing the Rhinos."

Noah snorted, then burst into a fit of giggles as he placed his hand on his forehead, one finger pointing out. "Do you think they'll have horns?" He began charging around the living room.

"Doubtful," Cassie said. "Especially since that could puncture the ball during a head shot." Noah continued his Rhino imitation, and she wondered how they'd ever survived in their smaller apartment for so many years. Their new living room was three times as big, and Noah regularly ran laps around it, scantily furnished as it still was. Maybe it was his way of making up for all those years crammed into a bedroom with her.

She scanned the next page of the city soccer packet for

the name of the Rhinos' coach. A few of the parents who'd coached last year had returned this season, and it was always good if she remembered their names ahead of time.

Her hand stilled, her fingernail resting just below Kramer, Matthew listed next to the Rhinos. Pleasant anticipation mixed furiously with a sudden attack of anxiety. How was she supposed to coach with Matt there? She hadn't seen him since the end of May, hadn't spoken to him since the beginning of June, when he'd facilitated a call from Oregon between his boys and Noah.

During that call she'd learned—inadvertently through Austin—that Matt was dating again. And while she'd been happy for him, she'd had to work hard to suppress her true feelings of jealousy and sadness.

She'd hoped he might call once or twice since then, but she probably shouldn't have been surprised that he hadn't, not when she'd so clearly told him that they couldn't continue their friendship. More than a few times she'd thought about calling him, but what was she supposed to say?

Hi, Matt. It's Cassie. My husband died, so . . . So she hadn't called. Still, it felt like yesterday that they'd gone to San Francisco and about a week since the holiday they'd enjoyed at his home in Oregon.

We could start where we left off. Maybe. If he wasn't involved with someone else. And if she could handle it.

Sure, she was single now, but that didn't mean she could just move on. The relief everyone seemed to expect her to feel at Devon's death simply hadn't come. Instead, she'd spent the summer feeling overwhelmed first with funeral arrangements and insurance policies, then it was going through his belongings, deciding what to save and what to get rid of as she and Noah prepared to move.

When Devon's uniforms no longer hung in the closet, and she'd boxed up those few things of his she'd decided to save, the finality of his death had sunk in, hitting her so hard that she'd sent Noah to stay with her mom for the week and had hardly gotten out of bed for five days.

If she'd thought selling Devon's car was difficult, it was nothing compared to leaving the apartment that had been their only home. When the last of their belongings were moved out and she'd returned, alone, to clean, she'd sat on the top step outside and cried for nearly a full hour.

She'd known it was time to move on, to focus on what would be best for Noah, but leaving the only home she'd ever known as a married woman felt like ripping a piece of her heart out. Along with the void in her life left by the absence of visits to the care center, she'd lost the place she felt safest at and all the comfort and familiarity that old apartment offered.

Noah, at least, seemed happier here. She would be, too, someday, when the numbness she'd embraced wore off.

Someday she might be ready for a relationship with Matt, too, but she wasn't sure that day was here. Everything still felt too new and raw, and she had to put herself back together again first.

"Let's *go*, Mom." Noah tugged on her hand, reminding Cassie of the time and the game that awaited. Matthew Kramer as the opposing coach or not, she had to go. She couldn't let Noah down. Just as when Devon had first been injured, it was Noah keeping her afloat. So long as she had him to focus on and care for, she'd be fine.

As for Matt—Six months ago she'd loved him, and he'd had feelings for her. Had that changed? *Is there a chance it hasn't?*

"Be right there." Cassie tugged free of Noah's grasp and

hurried to her room. She opened the top dresser drawer, dug around for a second, then pulled out a small box.

She stared at the ring on her finger a long minute, then slid it from its place for the first time in ten years.

"Look, Dad," Austin said. "There's Noah's car." Matt looked up from the collection of items he'd haphazardly thrown together in his coach's bag to spot the Nissan pulling into a parking stall.

Cassie. Just seeing her name on the list when he'd signed up to coach had been enough to send him into a pleasant déjà vu of last fall. He couldn't wait to get out on the field with her again, even if they were only coaching today. Just seeing her as she stepped from her car was enough to get his adrenaline pumping.

She got out and walked around to the trunk. Matt started over, enjoying the opportunity to watch her when she was unaware. Her long hair was pulled back in a braid, and he recognized the hat on her head from last year. She wore Bermuda shorts and a red shirt, and the combination somehow reminded him of the day they'd spent crabbing on his dad's boat, one of the best days they'd spent together. She closed the trunk and straightened just as he reached her.

"Hi, Matt!" Noah exclaimed, running up and giving him a big hug. Matt crouched down, hugging Noah in return and realizing just how much he'd missed him. A year ago he'd barely been able to handle his own boys, and now, in addition to loving them, he yearned for the opportunity to be Noah's father as well.

"Are Austin and Asher here?" Noah asked, pulling back at last.

"Right over there." Matt inclined his head toward the field.

"Thanks." Noah ran off to greet the boys, and Matt stood once more and found himself dangerously close to Cassie.

If only she'd run up and give me a hug, too. He was tempted to give her one regardless, but Janet's admonition to give Cassie some time rang through his mind. *It hasn't even been three months.* Three months out from Jenna's death, he'd been a train wreck. That Cassie was here, business as usual, coaching soccer, was seriously impressive.

"Can I help with that?" He reached out, taking her bag, though he knew she was more than capable of carrying it. Some months earlier, she'd pointed out to him that she still toted Noah around on occasion, and he weighed far more than a couple bags of groceries or, in this case, her soccer stuff. It didn't matter. He wanted to help anyway. He'd missed that.

"Thanks." Her hand fell away quickly, but not before he noted the absence of her wedding ring.

Tread carefully. "It's good to see you, Cassie."

"You, too." Her smile was tentative and fleeting, her demeanor far more subdued than he remembered. The death of a spouse could do that to a person.

"Mat-ty." From the opposite end of the parking lot, Ellen, one of his mother's matchmaking attempts, hurried toward him, waving as she came. He groaned inwardly.

She hobbled toward them, still adjusting a sandal or something. "Oh, Matty. Wait for me."

Cassie arched a brow at this greeting, as if to say, "Really?"

"Old friend from home," he explained.

"Whatever you say, *Matty.*" Cassie flipped her braid

over her shoulder, took her bag from him, and walked toward the field, crossing paths with Ellen on her way.

Cassie's hurt, he realized, wanting to run after her and explain, even as his spirits soared at the possibility that she still had feelings for him.

"The little boys are just so darling," Ellen exclaimed as she reached him a few seconds later. "I'm so glad you invited me for the weekend."

Her voice was loud enough that Matt was sure Cassie'd heard, and it was all he could do not to run up to her and tell her it wasn't what she was thinking. He hadn't invited Ellen down for the weekend. She'd come on her own, and he didn't want her here, didn't have any interest in seeing her again. Two dates the month he was in Oregon had been more than enough.

I'm not ready to date again. He'd told his meddling mother. He wasn't interested in getting to know other women. He wasn't searching for someone to replace Jenna.

But he did want the woman who'd become his best friend last year back in his life. And when he got her back, this time he wasn't going to let her go.

Forty-Six

Cassie buckled Noah into the booster seat in the back of her mom's Subaru. "Thanks for picking us up, Mom." She closed Noah's door and let herself into the front passenger seat. "My car should be fixed by tomorrow."

"For how long?" Mom asked as they pulled out of the school parking lot.

"I know." Cassie sighed as she leaned back against the headrest. "I need to get a new car."

"It would be a valid use of some of Devon's insurance money. He would want you to be safe and happy."

Cassie swallowed, not liking the hint of the lecture she knew was coming. "I'm trying, Mom. I really am, but if I use that money it's like—"

"What?" her mom prodded. She looked over at Cassie as they came to the stop sign in front of the crosswalk. "Like acknowledging that Devon is really gone? That he's not coming back?"

"Yeah." Cassie's voice was soft. She didn't want to have this conversation right now. It wasn't one they should have in front of Noah. She glanced behind her and saw that he was busy leafing through the book order that had been sent home.

"I'd tell you that kind of thinking is silly, but it isn't," Mom said, surprising her. "I felt the same way when your father died. Why do you think it took me years to finally go on a cruise? To get a new furnace? To give the rest of his clothes to Goodwill?"

"Oh, Mom." Cassie placed her hand over her mom's on the steering wheel. "I didn't realize."

"I know, dear." Her mom smiled kindly. "You were still a newlywed when it happened, and later you had your own tragedy to deal with."

"But still." Cassie grimaced. "I'm so selfish. I'm sorry I gave you a bad time about the cruise last year. I'm glad you went."

"Me, too. And I wouldn't say that you're selfish." Her mom returned her attention to the road and pulled forward. "You're afraid of what's next, of letting go of the past."

"I let Devon go, didn't I?" Cassie said defensively.

"Have you?"

"I forgave him like you told me to. I told him he could leave us, that we'd be all right." They would be, though she was struggling to find purpose in her life. Being Noah's mom and setting up her practice should have been enough, so why wasn't it?

"Telling Devon he could go was only part of the equation. You have to *really* let him go. And—" Her mom inclined her head toward the back seat. "You don't have the luxury of another seven years to figure out how to do that."

Cassie said nothing to this. It wasn't like her mom to be

quite so direct in her advice, and Cassie wasn't one for arguing, not when Mom had done so much for her. *Not when she's right,* she imagined Pearl saying. It really was too bad Pearl had never met her mother. Cassie had a feeling that they would have been good friends. They would have understood each other. Perhaps Pearl was even a widow herself or had experienced the tragedy of lost love.

"The leaves are changing quickly," Mom noted. "We need to get our autumn hike in before it's too late and they're gone."

"Can I come, Grandma?" Noah asked.

"Of course. You're our best leaf collector, and I need some new ones."

"Thanks." Noah gripped their seat backs and leaned forward between them. "Are we going right now?"

"Where *are* we going?" They'd missed the turn off for her apartment, and Cassie hadn't even noticed.

"A quick errand," her mom said vaguely.

"You sure you couldn't drop us off at home first?" Cassie asked. "It's been a long day." She always felt tired lately. *A sign of depression,* the therapist in her warned. Cassie dismissed the self-diagnosis and chalked up her lethargy to her inability to sleep. She missed having Noah in the same room.

Mom glanced over at her. "You don't look like you've had a long day. You look very pretty."

"Thanks." Cassie said, suddenly wary. "What is this errand? Am I supposed to look nice right now?"

"It never hurts." Her mother smiled, then turned onto Bancroft Road. The only thing Cassie could think of that was up this way was the park. Sure enough, her mom pulled the Subaru into the lot closest to the ball fields and right next to a shiny Chevy Silverado.

"That's Matt's truck. Austin and Asher are here! Look, Mom." Noah was already unbuckling his seatbelt.

"Whoa there, kiddo." Cassie's mom reached back to stop him from leaving the car. "Austin and Asher aren't here right now. Just their dad."

"Oh."

Cassie turned in her seat to see Noah's face fall, then brighten almost instantly. "That's okay. I still want to see Matt."

"Not right now." Her mom kept a hold of Noah's arm while sending Cassie a pointed look. "He and your mom are going to talk for a bit. You and I are going to go to the store and pick out some good Halloween candy."

"We already got some last week," Noah said.

"I ate it all," she admitted with a wry smile. "This time you'll have to hide it better."

"Oh, Mom," Cassie said, half-amused and half-exasperated with her. "You know it's hopeless to buy candy a month before Halloween and expect it to last at your house. What do you mean Matt and I are going to talk? He's dating someone else. Whose idea was this?"

"His, and he's not dating anyone." Mom hit the unlock button for the door. "Don't keep him waiting, and don't worry about being too long. Noah and I will pick up something for dinner, too. I'll make sure he does his reading."

Noah groaned and flopped himself against the backseat. "No fair."

"Be good for Grandma," Cassie admonished, her mind elsewhere. She gripped the door handle but didn't pull. Her heart was already thudding in her chest. *Why does he want to talk to me?* She stared at her mom, trying to read her expression for clues. "Did you tell him—"

"Last summer," Janet said matter-of-factly.

"Oh." *And Matt never called me? He never sent a note or said anything when I saw him last week.*

"I suggested to him that you might need a little space and time to process. If that was the wrong thing to say, I'm sorry." Mom gave Cassie's hand a gentle squeeze.

"No. That was the right thing. That was good," Cassie assured her.

"But you've had nearly three months now," Mom continued, "and a few years before that to prepare. You can't live in the past forever, sweetheart. You've got to take a step forward."

"A step? You think that's what this is?"

Her mom shrugged. "Only you can make that decision."

And Matt. Cassie felt equally parts terrified of and grateful for her mother's meddling. She turned in her seat and touched her finger to Noah's downturned nose. "How about if I talk to Matt about a play date with Austin and Asher? We can make it a late night and get pizza, and I'll let you guys build a giant fort in the front room."

"Okay," Noah said, still sounding a little forlorn.

"Be good for Grandma," Cassie said. "She doesn't like Tootsie Pops. If you buy those, they'll stay safe."

"Chocolate bars are better," her mother grumbled with good humor.

Cassie opened the door and got out. A quick peek inside Matt's truck confirmed it was empty, so she walked to the edge of the field and waited. The sound of her mom's car faded as she drove away, leaving Cassie feeling alone and vulnerable. The field was empty—no soccer games on Friday evenings—and the sun was already starting to sink behind the trees on the west side. She pulled her hat down lower on her head and crossed her arms to ward off the chill.

All right, Matt. Where are you?

As if he'd been waiting for her to summon him, Matt stepped from the shadow of the trees on the other side of the field. For a long minute, neither moved but stood staring at one another.

Joys are often the shadows cast by sorrow. Was this, was Matt, her joy? She'd had a fleeting hope of that last week, but then it had appeared she was too late. *And if I was wrong?*

A step forward. A few steps, a short talk. Such simple acts, but she felt their weight on her heart with an innate knowledge that those actions somehow held the ability to alter the course of her life. While memories of last autumn beckoned her toward Matt, she honestly didn't know if she had the courage to go to him, to truly leave the past and Devon behind and risk opening her heart to another future.

As if he also knew of and understood her hesitation, Matt hadn't moved either but waited across the field. He wasn't going to force her to this. He was waiting. *For me. For us.*

I want to see Matt. Noah's voice in her head finally urged Cassie forward. Her mom was right; she didn't have another seven years to grieve. Noah needed her now. He needed her at her best, and Matt had seemed to bring that out. With her arms still wrapped in front of her, Cassie started toward him, her heartbeat quickening with each step that brought them closer.

He looked much as he had on that fall day a year ago, fitted jeans, untucked denim shirt, hair a bit unruly on top, though she could tell it was recently cut. As they drew closer, she noted the five o'clock shadow along his jawline and the almost somber look in his hazel eyes.

Her heart lurched a little. "Is everything all right?" she asked when they were just a few feet away.

"I hope so," he said, his eyes lightening a little. His mouth curved up as his gaze met Cassie's. "Better, anyway, now that you're here. I wasn't sure you'd agree to come."

"I didn't agree to anything," Cassie said. "My mom tricked me, literally dumped me on the side of the road."

A full-fledged grin appeared. "I love your mom."

"Me, too," Cassie said. "*Usually.*" But she couldn't help returning his smile. "So everything with your boys is okay? Asher and Austin are good?"

"They're great. What a difference a year and some good parenting tips has made." Matt shoved his hands in his pockets. "I owe you."

"Only an explanation why I'm here." Cassie glanced around, as if expecting the answer to appear.

"Walk with me?" Matt asked, half-turning toward the tree line. She nodded and fell into step beside him.

"How was your summer?" he asked.

"Hard." She frowned and looked up at him sharply. "But you already know that. My mom said she told you."

Hands still in his pockets, Matt nodded. "I'm sorry. Really. I want you to believe that, Cassie. I know what it feels like to bury your spouse and then try to go on living. I wouldn't wish what we've each gone through on anyone, especially not on someone as good and kind as you."

"I know you understand, more than anyone else." Even more than her mom. She'd raised her children by the time Dad died. Or maybe that made it harder? Cassie hadn't considered that before. She couldn't imagine what she would have done without Noah to care for, to fill her life with purpose and happiness.

"Do you mind if I ask what happened?" Matt asked. "Was Devon still at the same care center?"

"I don't mind." Just as their conversations had been the

previous year, Cassie found herself wanting to tell Matt everything. Talking to him was cathartic rather than painful. She knew there would be no judgment or platitudes, only understanding and genuine empathy. "Devon was still at the care center. Pearl came back, too."

"Pearl?" Matt's brow drew together quizzically. "The woman who wouldn't let you visit with Devon the first night you and I really talked, at the cafeteria in the hospital? The same woman you thought you saw in Chinatown?"

Cassie nodded. She looked at the ground, the toe of her boot playing with the dry twigs scattered beneath the trees. If California didn't get some rain soon, the state was really going to be in trouble.

Much like you, she imagined Pearl saying. *You have gone so long without a drink, and your well is almost dry. It is time to let love in your life once more, to replenish the bucket you so freely give from.*

"Last fall Pearl told me that it was time to let Devon go. She said he'd been waiting for me to set him free, and until I did, he was lingering in a state somewhere between Heaven and Earth when really, he wanted to be free, to move on."

"That's pretty heavy stuff from a stranger," Matt said.

"I know, right?" Cassie lifted her face and met his gaze. "I was angry. And hurt and upset. I thought it was the cruelest thing anyone could say and that Pearl was just a lazy nurse who didn't want to do her job."

"And you talked to her again this summer because?" Matt's face scrunched in a perplexed look.

"Last fall she also told me that I could be happy again, that if I would just open my heart to new possibilities, Noah and I would have much love and joy." Cassie shrugged. "Then I went to the hospital cafeteria, and you were there. We became friends." With feelings for each other that ran much deeper than that.

"That's even more providential than that woman who gave me the team roster with your phone number on it," Matt said.

Cassie felt the hairs at the back of her neck stand up, and she rubbed her arms against the sudden onset of goosebumps that had nothing to do with the chill autumn air. "What are you talking about? What woman?"

"Right after you left the game, the day that Austin pushed Noah, this Asian lady gave me a paper with your number on it. She suggested that you might appreciate a follow-up call to see how Noah was doing. I stuck the paper in my jeans and forgot about it for a day or two until I was doing laundry. That's when I got it out and called you."

Cassie leaned against the nearest tree for support because both her insides and her knees suddenly felt a little weak. "An Asian lady? Who would that have been, and why would she have my number? We didn't have any Asian kids on our team."

"Beats me," Matt said. "Whoever she was, I'm grateful."

Cassie couldn't let it go, couldn't shake the feeling that something extraordinary had happened all those months ago, and they'd missed it. *Or nearly so.* "Was this woman old or young?"

"Older definitely, but a graceful old—still very pretty. She didn't look like she belonged at a soccer game. I'm not good at recalling this kind of thing, but she looked out-of-place enough that day that I actually remember what she was wearing." Matt stared past Cassie a moment, the lines on his forehead creasing into what she recognized as a look of concentration. "She had on a silk blouse—white, I think. And her hair was done up kind of fancy with this pearl thing in it."

Cassie felt the color drain from her face. "Are you sure?"

"Pretty sure. What's wrong?" Matt stepped closer, reached out as if he wanted to touch her, then let his hand drop to his side.

"Nothing is wrong," Cassie said after a minute. "It's just that the woman at the soccer game and Pearl at the care center sound like they could be the same person."

"Your Pearl wore a silk blouse and pearls in her hair, and she was Asian?"

"Yes, yes, and yes," Cassie said. "Though the first time I met her she was in scrubs." She searched Matt's eyes. "What do you think this means?"

He shook his head. "I don't know. You have a fairy godmother?"

"That might not be far off." Cassie bit her lip as she tried to think of a plausible explanation for the coincidence.

"So Devon was still at the care center and Pearl came back, too?" Matt redirected their conversation back to its starting point.

"Yes," Cassie said. That in itself had been strange. "She was in the lobby as I was leaving the care center the night Devon died. We talked. She told me I had the courage to do what must be done, what he was waiting for."

Matt didn't say anything to this, just watched her intently, a look of deepest concern reflected in the depths of his eyes.

"So I did. Instead of going home after that, even though I'd just visited Devon, I went back to his room. I told him it was okay if he wanted to go, that Noah and I would be all right without him."

Matt let out a slow breath as he ran his fingers through his hair. "I don't know if I could have done that with Jenna. I can't imagine—"

"Don't try to," Cassie said. "It was terrible. I didn't pull any plugs or touch any machines, but it felt like I killed Devon just the same. I lay next to him and told him I loved him enough to let him go and that he should go—and then, a while later, he did."

Matt took her hands in his. "You're made of stronger stuff than most of us."

"So everyone tells me." She pressed her lips together to keep overflowing emotion in check. "I'm kind of tired of that program, you know? I'd like to not have to be strong for a change."

"Yeah." He hesitated a second, then pulled her into an embrace. "I know." Cassie closed her eyes as she pressed her cheek against his shirt. Matt's arms came around her, warm, solid, protective, comforting. She wrapped her arms around his waist and linked her hands behind him.

"It's okay now," he said. "You made it through the worst of it. Take it from someone who's eighteen months on the other side; it gets better. Not great, necessarily, but better."

But I want great. What she wanted—after years of rising in the morning with the hope that today was the day Devon would return to her and going to sleep each night with his picture beside her and that same prayer on her lips—was to know how she was supposed to go on now.

How was she supposed to pack up the photos, give all his things away, and seal off that part of her heart forever? How was she supposed to live without the hope that had sustained her for so long?

Hope is right in front of you. You must only open your eyes and your heart. It is capable of loving again. Pearl's voice, but now Cassie was imagining conversations they'd never had. Perhaps this was the beginning of the breakdown she'd feared.

Gradually Matt released her, and she stepped back,

leaning into the tree for support once more, though she'd vastly preferred the comfort of his arms and could have stayed there a lot longer.

"Thanks," she said. "That was a much-needed hug."

"I offer free hugs anytime you need one. Just ask." His lips curved in a half-smile. "And thanks for not pushing me away on that one, since you *didn't* ask."

"Not in words maybe, but you get mind-reading credit for it." Cassie felt a sudden longing to touch his face with tender reassurance but didn't because she thought that'd be crossing a line.

"In that case, I'm going to test my mind-reading powers a bit more." Matt searched her eyes a moment, took a deep breath, as if mustering courage, then leaned forward, one arm braced on the tree behind her. Beneath her sweater, Cassie's heart raced. Sure they'd been this close a second ago when they hugged, but this felt—different.

"I have a proposal that might benefit both our boys." Matt attempted a straight face and business-like tone—and failed miserably on both counts—as he spoke the words she'd once used on him.

"Oh?" Some of her nerves calmed in the face of his less-than-serious announcement. Amusement tinged her words. "You want to get the boys together to play soccer?"

"Getting together was definitely what I had in mind, but the boys and soccer, not so much." He leaned in, his face even closer to hers.

Her nerves and frantic heartbeat were back. "I'm afraid you're going to have to be more specific."

"How's this?" Matt asked. "I would like to kiss you, Mrs. Webb. In fact, I would like to kiss you so long and so well that you forget about being Mrs. Webb and go back to just being Cassie. Single, available to be loved Cassie." He backed up the slightest bit. "Direct enough?"

She nodded, swallowed, licked her lips. He watched all three as a sort of wolfish grin made its way across his face.

She placed a hand on the front of his shirt, not sure if she wanted to push him away or pull him closer after such an honest declaration. "I'm terrified, Matt."

"I know." His words were gentle. Gone was the teasing, self-assured Matt of a moment before. "You think I'm not?"

"I haven't been kissed for over seven years."

"And who gave you your last kiss?"

"Devon, of course." She frowned at his ridiculous question. Who else did he think she'd been kissing then?

"And who gave you your very first kiss ever?" Matt persisted.

"Devon."

"And you think *you're* terrified? Do you see what I've got to live up to? He was your first love, your *only* love, your first and last kiss. He lived and died a hero. His pedestal is, I don't know, this tall." Matt raised a hand high above his head.

Cassie heard the plea in his words, read the insecurity in his eyes, and found that was exactly what she needed to get over her own fears. *I love Matt, and that's okay now. It's good. It's great.* Not only was she *in love,* but she wanted to give him her love, to make his life better, whole again, and she held that power in her hands.

"Just kiss me already, Matt," she ordered in a throaty sort of voice, meant to be more seductive than frightened, though she wasn't sure.

His eyes widened in brief surprise, then he tilted his head and leaned in. Her eyes barely had time to close before his lips brushed hers, as tentative and gentle as his words had been. *Vulnerable.* They both were. He'd been in love before, too, and he'd lost and suffered. Now she wanted him to win, to have every desire of his heart.

Cassie wrapped her hand around the loose cloth of his shirt and pulled him closer, then parted her mouth slightly to kiss him back. He moaned and deepened their kiss to something far beyond tentative. His lips meant to claim her, and they were. She clung to him as she felt herself falling farther and farther into a glorious abyss of happiness. Every one of her senses reeled; every nerve ending seemed alive. Her heart soared. It felt like waking up after so many years of a self-induced slumber.

Just like I felt.

Cassie froze then stiffened. Her eyes flew open, and she stared into Matt's startled ones for a split second before she leaned away from him.

"I'm that bad, huh?" He tried to joke, but she could tell he was hurt.

"No. It isn't you. It's just—" She'd heard Devon's voice, as loud and clear as if he was standing right beside her. *Impossible.*

It's okay, Cass. This is the way it's supposed to be. You and Matt are supposed to be together.

Tears filled her eyes. Seven long years had passed since she'd heard that voice, and hearing it now brought a tidal wave of memories, good and bad.

Be happy, Cass. I'm going to be all right without you. I want you to be free and happy, too.

"Cassie?" Matt's voice was panicked. He gripped each of her arms, as if afraid she might faint any second.

"I can't—" She was talking to Devon, not Matt. *How dare you use my words on me,* her mind shouted at Devon. *At no one.* For as much as she would have sworn he was standing next to her a second ago, she knew the instant that he was gone. *For good.*

A few leaves rustled in the tree above, then floated

gently down to Earth. Cassie watched their descent and felt herself falling, not in the abyss of happiness she'd felt a minute before but in a swirl of despair. Devon had been here, and now he wasn't and he wouldn't ever be again. Her head fell forward, and the tears spilled over.

Matt gathered her close in another hug. "It's all right Cassie. We don't have to do this. We can be friends. I shouldn't have kissed you."

Courage, Cassie. Sometimes love requires courage. Pearl's voice again.

Maybe I really am going mad. This made her cry harder, thinking of Noah without any parent to care for him. Matt held her tightly for long minutes while she wept. Why did she have to be falling apart now, all these weeks later?

Slowly, when her tears had stopped at last, Matt released her. His hands came up to cradle her face. "I love you, Cassie. If I can only love you as a friend, I'll take that. Just please don't shut me out completely."

"Oh, Matt. I wanted to say it first. I wanted to make you so happy."

"You do. You did say it first." He pulled back, giving her a mischievous smile that spoke of some secret she wasn't in on.

"I did?" She used the back of her hand to wipe her eyes and tried to recall when that might have been. Sure, she'd thought about loving him and fought it for a lot of months, but she'd never said the words out loud, had she?

"On my voicemail, Christmas Eve. You said, 'I love you, Matt. I shouldn't, but I do.' Then you gave this sad little sigh."

Cassie gasped. "I thought I'd hung up." *Devon was still alive then.* The guilt she'd felt for all those months stole over her once more, scattering what remained of the pleasant feelings to the remote corners of her heart.

Matt must have sensed it because he took her hand in his and held it close to his own heart. "I know you didn't mean for me to hear it, and I know you didn't mean to feel it then either. You did the right thing. You told me to take a hike so you could get back to the business of caring for your husband. But you've also got to know how much hope those three little words gave me. I've played that message over and over again; it's kept me going."

"How could that keep you going when it seemed there was no future for us? When I'd made it clear that *we* could never be?"

"Because." Matt's eyes were tender as they met hers again. He brushed his fingers against her cheek and caught a tear falling there. "If a woman as wonderful as you could find something about me to love, even in the broken state I was in, I had to hope that someday, maybe someone else would feel the same, and I wouldn't be alone forever."

No one else. Me. She didn't want some other woman to be with Matt. *Courage, then.* This time it was her own voice that she heard. Cassie shook her head as a second and third tear fell. "No one else for you, Mr. Kramer. I found you first. And I do love you." She leaned forward and kissed him then, long and slow and even sweeter than their first kiss. *I love you, Matt. You.*

He threaded his fingers through her hair, and she felt his heartbeat quicken beneath the fabric of his shirt. "Cassie." He whispered her name with an awe-filled reverence, then sought her lips again, clinging to her as he hadn't before. She felt his reservations melt away as hers did beneath the heat of their kiss. When her mind was spinning and her heart was soaring, Matt pulled himself away, his own breathing as ragged as hers.

He chuckled. "Apparently, neither of us needs a whole

lot of practice to get back in the game." He pressed his lips to her forehead while she struggled between laughter and tears of joy.

"So what are we going to do about this?" he asked.

"About kissing?" Why did they have to do anything? *Why did we stop?* She leaned her head back and looked up at him, hoping her seductive smile made up for puffy eyes.

"Kissing and other stuff, too." Matt brushed a stray hair from her face, then caught her hat when it nearly fell off. He did his best to pull it down over her hair again, and Cassie could only imagine the mess she must be with runny mascara, tangled hair, and swollen lips. His eyes darkened to serious once more, and his words quieted. "My boys need a mother, you know."

Cassie nodded. She did know. They needed someone who could make dinners consisting of more than peanut butter and jelly. They needed someone who understood the timeliness of the tooth fairy and the magic of Santa. Someone who wouldn't let their underwear turn pink in the wash. Someone who would be there after school with a plate of cookies, a glass of milk, and a listening ear.

"Noah could use a father, too," she said, thinking of all the things Matt could offer him.

"What about you, Cassie? What do you need? What do *you* want?" Matt's look was still serious, searching—and still uncertain.

She made an exasperated face as she looked up at him. "If you have to ask after that last kiss." She slid her arms up his shirt front and over his shoulders. Her fingers tickled the hairs at the base of his neck as she kissed him once more, the way a wife would kiss her husband.

A long minute later, they were both breathless again. Matt leaned his forehead against hers and groaned. "You're making me crazy, Cassie."

"That's what I want," she said, turning her lips up seductively. "To make you crazy every day for the rest of our lives."

"Deal." He reached forward and scooped her into his arms as she gave a yelp of surprise. "Let's go out to ice cream and tell the boys."

Forty-Seven

"You want chocolates, too?" Matt exclaimed. "After all the ice cream we just consumed?" Three heads nodded, and Cassie followed Matt's gaze as it traveled the sticky, napkin-covered table the boys and their triple scoop sundaes left behind.

"Oh, let them get chocolates," Cassie's mom said. "After all, this is a special occasion."

Is it? Cassie hadn't been entirely surprised to find her mom and the boys waiting for them at Samantha's, her mom having been the one who'd dropped her off to talk with Matt in the first place. But Matt hadn't made any announcement, hadn't really told the boys anything yet. And as the minutes had ticked by and they finished their sundaes, Cassie had begun to wonder if she'd misinterpreted Matt's questions at the park.

"A year ago today, the boys and I played our first soccer scrimmage with you, and we came here after." Matt began stacking the empty bowls. "That was the day life started to turn around for us."

"I was the one who invited them," Noah reminded everyone.

"It was because I pushed you that we played at all," Austin said.

"The only pushing from you that I will ever be grateful for." Matt placed a hand on Austin's shoulder.

"Right," Austin said.

"Certainly cause for celebration," Cassie's mom said. "Come on, boys. Let's go get those chocolates." She rose from the table and led the boys, marching across to the candy counter on the other side of the store and leaving Cassie alone with Matt and her senses and emotions that had been on hyper drive since their kiss at the park.

She helped him clear and clean the last of the mess from the table, her insides feeling as if they might melt with every accidental brush of their hands. She waited, admiring his walk and everything else about him, while he returned from throwing their garbage away. He sat once more, closer to her this time, and held his hand out, palm up. With no hesitation, Cassie placed her hand in his even as she felt a goofy grin spreading across her face.

"What?" Matt asked. "Do I have ice cream on my chin or something?"

She shook her head. "I'm just smiling." She couldn't seem to help herself.

Matt tugged on her hand, pulling her closer as he leaned across the corner of the table, then stole a kiss.

"Matt. The boys—"

"Are going to be seeing a lot of this." He kissed her again, and Cassie found she was powerless to resist his charm or lips.

"We've got a lot of lost time to make up for, you know," he said.

She did but still wasn't sure what their status was other than friends with kissing benefits, and that didn't sound completely satisfying to her. She wanted to do more than drive him crazy kissing every day for the rest of their lives. She wanted to make him as happy as possible in every way.

"Look. Look what we got!" Asher squished between Austin and Noah as they returned carrying the largest box of chocolates Cassie had ever seen.

"Mom," Cassie complained. "Do you *want* them to throw up tonight?"

"Wasn't my doing." She held her hands up, rejecting all responsibility. "Some kind of special order."

The boys set the box down with a thud in front of Cassie.

"Open it." Noah hovered by Cassie's shoulder.

Cassie looked to Matt for an explanation, but he was leaning back in his chair, one arm around Austin and the other around Asher. "Opening it sounds like a good idea."

She saw right through his feigned disinterest. Something was definitely up. "Is a snake going to jump out at me?"

Asher giggled as she untied the ribbon and slid it from the box.

"You'd better help me, Noah." She needn't have asked. His little fingers were already prying up the side closest to him. She lifted the other, revealing a parchment with writing printed on it.

Cassie and Noah

"I'm glad we're supposed to share these," Cassie said. "This box must weigh five pounds."

"Two and a half," Matt said.

Noah lifted the paper, revealing rows of perfectly arranged chocolates, each bearing a frosted letter, spelling out a question.

*Will you be a part
of our family?*

"Read it, Mom," Noah urged.

"Maybe you should," Cassie said quietly, her heart alternately pounding and soaring and melting. *Matt asked Noah as well as me.*

Noah started. "Will you be a—"

"Part of our family," Austin and Asher chorused together, their looks of expectation no less intense than Matt's.

"We voted, and we want to keep you both," Asher said.

"That was my wish," Noah said. "My fortune cookie said it would come true." He launched himself at Matt. "I wanted you to be my dad."

Matt circled his arms around all three boys. "Me, too, but we have to see what your mom says about all of this."

Three boys and a husband. A noisy, family-filled home. It almost seemed too good to be true, but it also felt so right.

"Mom?" Noah asked. "Please?"

"Yes," Cassie said, meeting Matt's tender gaze with one of her own. "Of course!" She opened her arms and the boys ran to her, embracing her with sticky fingers. It seemed the most natural thing in the world that she and Matt and their boys should be a family together.

She cried, and they laughed and talked over one another as the couple at the next table looked on curiously.

"My daughter and her son have just been proposed to," Cassie's mom said, dabbing at the corner of her eye with a napkin.

Matt cleared his throat loudly, and the boys dispersed. He held a small jewelry box out to Cassie. "I know this is fast, but we don't have to go fast from here. We can take as long as you'd like or need to start our lives together."

Cassie wanted their family to begin today, right now, but she supposed there were some practicalities that would have to be arranged. A new ring on her finger seemed a good place to start. She took the box and opened it, only to find a familiar diamond staring up at her from a different setting.

"Your mom told me how hard it was for you to take off Devon's ring, so I thought maybe you shouldn't have to. He was part of your life, and he always will be." Matt took the ring from the box. "I had this new band made to fit around your original engagement ring." He separated the rings, showing Cassie the outer circle with five smaller diamonds. "One for each of us," he explained, "starting our life together, built around the life you had before. The diamonds are clustered together on this side, so more can be added later, if you'd like."

More, as in more children, that big family she wanted while she'd still have the reminder of the little one she'd started with. It was perfect in every way, and she adored Matt even more for thinking of it. Cassie held her hand out, and he slipped the joined rings onto her finger.

"It's beautiful," Cassie said. "I love it. I love you. I love *us.*" The boys crowded closer, and Cassie and Matt wrapped their arms around them, linking hands to form a circle that enclosed their children. *Our children. Our family. Our future.*

Outside the sun sank lower, filtering through the window, casting its last shadows of the day.

Forty-Eight

"Cassie, there's someone I'd like you to meet before you leave." Her mom touched her sleeve as the last dance of the evening ended.

"Sure. Be right there." Cassie kissed Matt on the cheek and reluctantly turned away from him. Their reception in his parents' backyard had been everything she could have dreamed of, from the temporary dance floor Matt and Mark had laid, to the twinkling lights his sister and mother had strung between the trees, to the fabulous sunset and the sound of the crashing surf. She hated the night to end.

"I'll come with you." Matt linked his hand through hers, and they followed her mom beneath the lights out to the sea wall.

"I want you to meet the friend who came down with me," Mom said. "She had to work and wasn't able to be at your wedding this morning, but she wanted to wish you well before you leave on your honeymoon."

"That's kind," Cassie said. She'd been relieved when her mother had told her she had someone to make both the trip up and back with.

"Cassie and Matt, I'd like you to meet my friend Pearl." She emerged from the shadows and climbed the stone steps to the backyard. "Pearl, this is my daughter and her new husband."

"How?" Cassie looked from her mother to Pearl, standing at the edge of the Kramer's lawn, with that same serene, mystic expression she'd worn the last time Cassie had seen her.

"Hello, Cassandra, Matthew." Pearl nodded at each. "It's lovely to see you again, to see you *together* finally." Her smile blossomed, taking years off her face.

"I don't believe we've formally met." Matt extended his hand while Cassie continued to gape.

"Not formally," Pearl conceded, "but we spoke at a soccer game last year and later at the care center on Halloween. *Eye candy,*" she added with a smile as she inclined her head, revealing the luster of the pearl comb tucked in the side of her hair.

Matt actually blushed.

"But how—wait. You two *know* each other?" Cassie looked from her mother to Pearl once more.

"For a few years now," Pearl said. "A chance meeting at a Bunco night led to a discussion of Janet's lovely and lonely daughter, whereupon I agreed to help when the time was right."

Cassie's mom jumped in the conversation. "Oh, it was so difficult to be patient. Especially after you met Matt, and I knew."

"Knew what?" Cassie asked, still perplexed as to how Pearl had come to be entwined in all of their lives.

"That he is your love match," Pearl said, "that you were meant to heal each other's hearts and live a lifetime of happiness together, to live the life you love," she added with a knowing smile.

Cassie gripped Matt's hand a little tighter as her senses reeled, just as they had that day two months earlier when they'd stood beneath the tree at the park and first realized the coincidences that had led them to each other. They weren't coincidences at all.

"Remember what I told you at the care center," Pearl said, speaking once more as if she'd gleaned Cassie's very thoughts. "Sometimes it is best not to try too hard to figure everything out."

No kidding because this had to be some sort of magic, like in the fairy tales she read Noah sometimes.

"Love *is* magic," Pearl continued, "and all that you both need to know, you do. Between Heaven and Earth are many connections, most of all in here." She placed a hand over her heart. "That you have glimpsed some of those is a great blessing. That you have love in your life again is Heaven's gift. Cherish it."

"We will," Matt promised.

"We will," Cassie echoed, then stepped forward impulsively and hugged Pearl. "Thank you," she whispered. "For everything. For Matt."

"It has been my pleasure and happiness. Now go and enjoy yours."

Forty-Nine

Austin pushed a button on the low, sloped ceiling above his seat. "What's this do?"

"Blasts kids who play with it," Matt answered as he pried Asher's hands from the iPad. "This has to be stowed until after takeoff."

"But we'll lose our score," Noah said.

Matt worried he might lose his mind. He probably already had, bringing the boys on their honeymoon. In addition to feeling wedding night jitters, he had three children grating on his nerves. But, he reminded himself, this was about more than him and Cassie. It was about the five of them forming a new family, starting a life together.

Her eyes tracked him as he finished settling the boys in the seats across from them then took his own beside Cassie. "Ready for this?"

"For what?" she asked coyly. "I have no idea where we're going."

"Nice try." He leaned his head back against the headrest and stretched his legs out, remembering and enjoying the luxury of flying on a corporate jet. That he'd been able to call on old friendships and favors owed from his former life seemed somehow a fitting start to his new one as did the fact that this flight would be far happier than his last trip on a private jet.

Cassie started running her fingers slowly up and down his arm, not quite tickling, but driving him a bit mad nonetheless. "Not even one tiny little hint?"

He pretended to consider a moment. "Nope, but I did forget the blindfolds, so maybe you or the boys will guess before we get there."

"Hmm." She ceased her soft touch and pinched him instead.

"Hey." Matt grabbed her hand. "I'll have to ask you to behave yourself on the flight, Mrs. Kramer." He loved this side of Cassie that had emerged since their engagement. On top of her usual confidence, she'd added playfulness, attitude, and a hefty dose of flirting.

"Of course," Cassie agreed demurely. "But no promises for later."

"It's not a cruise or a resort on the beach." Cassie sounded a little disappointed that he'd ruled out each of those venues after landing in San Diego. "But you said there will still be dancing and kissing."

"Yuck," Austin said, making a face that Matt caught in the rearview mirror. "That doesn't sound fun, Dad."

"Kissing and dancing are what people do on their honeymoon. You're going to have to deal with it." Matt wasn't too worried about the crew in the back seat being happy this week, but he was starting to worry what Cassie would think of his plan. He'd geared this trip toward the boys, believing that any experience with Cassie was going to be golden, particularly if the boys were happy and in their element. For what he'd paid for this place, they'd better be.

"I know where we're going!" Noah practically jumped from his seat in the back of the rented SUV. "I see it. Up there!"

"Legoland," Cassie finished with him as Matt turned into the drive for the Legoland Hotel. She looked at Matt. "Really? We're going to Legoland?" She leaned over and kissed him. "That's brilliant. You're amazing, you know that?" Twisting in her seat to face the back, she said, "You boys have the best dad on the planet."

The chorus of cheers relieved the stress Matt had been feeling for the past couple of hours. "You're really okay with this? I mean, it doesn't exactly make the list of top honeymoon destinations."

"For me it does." Cassie inclined her head toward Noah, who'd yet to cease bouncing. "I'm better than okay with it." She rolled down her window and leaned out to peer at the giant Lego dragon coming out of the front of the hotel. "This is fantastic."

If Cassie was happy about it, Noah was ecstatic, spouting facts about everything they were going to see and do. It was payoff enough for Matt already, and they hadn't even set foot inside the hotel or park.

The lobby lived up to everything he'd read about, and the boys dived into the Lego building island while Matt and Cassie checked in. When it came time to go up to their room, it took promises that tomorrow morning—bright and early before breakfast—they would return to the lobby to explore and play.

With reluctance, the boys pulled their child-sized suitcases to the elevator, but when it opened, the smiles and exclamations were back.

"What is that, Dad?" Asher pointed to the disco ball hanging from the ceiling.

"You'll see." Matt pulled Cassie into the elevator and his arms. "This is the dancing part." The doors slid shut, the music started, and the ball came to life, spinning colors around them.

The Bee Gees "Stayin' Alive" piped through the speakers, and Matt put on his best disco moves.

"*Da-ad*," Austin said, clearly embarrassed. The other boys giggled, and Cassie laughed so hard she was holding her stomach by the end of the ride.

Enjoying this more and more, Matt led his family to their pirate-themed room—a dream come true for any kid, from the Lego models all over the place to the murals and the furniture designed for kids.

"This is your space, boys." Matt leaned over to pull out a trundle beneath the set of bunks. "There's a treasure hidden somewhere in here, a bin of Legos for you to play with, and every kid channel you can imagine. Get your pajamas on and you can play for fifteen minutes. Then it's lights out because we have a big day tomorrow."

Matt led Cassie through a second doorway into their room. "And here, my winsome wench, be our cabin."

"So I'm a wench now, am I?" Cassie batted her eyelashes as she looked up at him. "Is this some fantasy I was unaware of? Will you be wearing an eye patch tonight as the bed rolls with the swell of the sea?"

"I'm pretty sure an eye patch came with the room, and the bed will definitely be rolling."

Her brows rose at this. "With three little boys ten feet

away? Don't count on it." She fell back on the pirate bedspread, then leaned up on her elbows. "But just because there won't be a tempest doesn't mean we can't enjoy the ocean view."

"I love it when you talk pirate to me." He read between the lines of her teasing, that she was as nervous as he was and wanted to take things slowly. It was one of the reasons he'd decided to include the boys and make the trip more about family than just the two of them.

"The view right now is perfect." He sat beside her on the bed and took her hand in his.

"I know this is an unorthodox kind of honeymoon, but there's a reason for that—on top of wanting to include the boys. I want to keep comparisons to a minimum."

"Good idea." Cassie looked down at their joined hands instead of meeting his eye. "I don't want to think about Devon tonight, or our wedding night. And I don't want you thinking about yours."

He couldn't have agreed more. But he hadn't been certain how to stop that entirely. He'd only ever planned on having one wedding night, and he imagined that Cassie had, too, so to be facing a second one with a different spouse felt more than intimidating. It was probably only natural that their thoughts stray to that other night and person.

It was also likely that they'd end up with at least one little boy in bed with them sometime during the night—probably Asher. That was definitely not a typical marriage bed experience and probably guaranteed to keep thoughts anchored in the present, as in—*We are sleeping with an octopus.*

But until the wild things woke them in the middle of the night or early tomorrow, Matt simply wanted to hold Cassie in his arms and wake to find her still there. When they returned home in a few days there would be time enough to love her so thoroughly and so well that she would hardly be able to think of anyone or anything else outside the two of them.

With these goals in mind, he leaned over Cassie on the bed and got down to honeymoon business. Three intoxicating kisses later, Asher appeared in the doorway.

"What?" Matt growled.

"We need to brush our teeth."

"Always with the teeth." Matt rolled away from Cassie and hung his head, exasperated. "You've got to brush them every night, then half of them will fall out anyway, and you have to get them checked every six months."

"Such a hardship." Cassie slapped his leg as she sat up, then scooted off the bed. "At least your kid has a full set to brush."

"*Our* kid," Matt corrected. "He's half yours now."

"I'm glad." Cassie smiled at Asher. "Go get your toothbrush ready. I'll be right there to help." She turned back to Matt. "No worries. I've got this."

"Really? You'll help with their teeth tonight?" He felt like she'd offered him the moon.

"Every night if you want," Cassie said, "But you have to handle immunizations, stitches, and any broken bones. Oh, and we split barfing duty fifty-fifty. Half the time I'll get up with the vomiting kid, half the time you get up."

"You have so got yourself a deal." *Yep. Typical honeymoon talk right here.* This conversation was oozing with romance.

But she wasn't through yet. "And someday, when it's time for *the talk,* you agree to be an active participant and not sit there like you know nothing."

"What if I do know nothing? It's been a while, so I might've forgotten."

Cassie rolled her eyes. "I'll remind you."

"Often?"

She laughed. "Often. I can already tell who the neediest kid in this household is going to be."

She didn't sound like she minded too much.

Matt held his hand out to strike the deal, but Cassie leaned in and kissed him on the cheek instead. "This is how we make promises, remember?"

"Yeah. I do." Overwhelming gratitude hit him along with the memory of their day in the city last January, a day of fortunes then unfulfilled. It terrified him to think that things might have gone any differently. Matt caught Cassie around the waist, pulling her onto his lap. "I love you."

"I love you, too, Matt." She smiled sweetly. "Now go brush your teeth."

At the end of their second day at Legoland, Matt gave the boys fifty dollars each and turned them loose to shop. He and Cassie shadowed them as best they could around the bricksters' paradise, though Cassie felt like she was doing most of the supervising. Matt was as big a kid as the boys. She was pleased when Noah and Asher decided to pool their money and go together on a train set, but twenty minutes later Austin was still deciding, and she'd followed him over to the Lego City section, adjacent to a literal Lego pink paradise.

Cassie watched as an adorable, pig-tailed little girl and her mother discussed which set they would acquire next—the bake shop or pet store?

No superhero play there. Cassie sighed with longing.

"Find something you like?" Matt came up behind her

and placed his hands on her shoulders, starting one of his back rubs that made her insides puddle.

"As a matter of fact, I did." She turned to face him and noticed a rather large bag on the floor between his legs.

"Train accessories," he explained. "What good is track without a lot of cars and cool things to put on them?"

"Of course."

"So what about you? Have your eye on anything? Just name it, and it's yours."

"Hmm." Cassie placed a hand over her stomach, thinking of Pearl and of the past. *Be careful what you wish for.*

She threw caution to the wind. This was a wish that could only turn out good. "Actually, there is something I'd like." She circled her arms around Matt's waist.

"What's that?" He leaned closer and nuzzled her hair.

Cassie smiled as she watched the mother and daughter make their selection. "I want two, actually—two little girls."

ABOUT MICHELE PAIGE HOLMES

Michele Paige Holmes spent her childhood and youth in Arizona and northern California, often curled up with a good book instead of out enjoying the sunshine. She graduated from Brigham Young University with a degree in elementary education and found it an excellent major with which to indulge her love of children's literature.

Her first novel, *Counting Stars*, won the 2007 Whitney Award for Best Romance. Its companion novel, a romantic suspense titled *All the Stars in Heaven*, was a Whitney Award finalist, as was her first historical romance, *Captive Heart*. *My Lucky Stars* completed the Stars series.

In 2014 Michele launched the Hearthfire Historical Romance line, with the debut title, *Saving Grace*. *Loving Helen* is the companion novel, with a third, *Marrying Christopher* released in July 2015.

When not reading or writing romance, Michele is busy with her full-time job as a wife and mother. She and her husband live in Utah with their five high-maintenance children, and a Shih Tzu that resembles a teddy bear, in a house with a wonderful view of the mountains.

You can find Michele on the web:

MichelePaigeHolmes.com

Facebook: Michele Holmes

Twitter: @MichelePHolmes

Power of the Matchmaker
SERIES

12 Novels by 12 bestselling authors in 12 months

Karey White
Rachael Anderson
Kelly Oram
Heather B. Moore
Julie Wright
Heidi Ashworth
Taylor Dean
Michele Paige Holmes
Janette Rallison
Regina Sirois
Sheralyn Pratt
Jaima Fixsen

November 2015... Power of the Matchmaker
(A prequel novella of the Matchmaker's story)

January 1, 2016

February 1, 2016

March 1, 2016

April 1, 2016

May 1, 2016

June 1, 2016

July 1, 2016

August 1, 2016

September 1, 2016

October 1, 2016

November 1, 2016

December 1, 2016

www.ingramcontent.com/pod-product-compliance
Lightning Source LLC
LaVergne TN
LVHW010146070526
838199LV00062B/4275